By Anne McCaffrey
Published by Ballantine Books

Decision at Doona
Dinosaur Planet
Dinosaur Planet Survivors
The Mystery of Ireta
Get Off the Unicorn
The Lady
Pegasus in Flight
Restoree
The Ship Who Sang
To Ride Pegasus
Nimisha's Ship
Pegasus in Space
Black Horses for the King

THE CRYSTAL SINGER BOOKS
Crystal Singer
Killashandra
Crystal Line

THE DRAGONRIDERS OF PERN
Dragonflight
Dragonquest
The White Dragon
Moreta: Dragonlady of Pern
Nerilka's Story
Dragonsdawn
The Renegades of Pern
All the Weyrs of Pern
The Chronicles of Pern: First Fall
The Dolphins of Pern
Dragonseye
The Masterharper of Pern
The Skies of Pern

A Gift of Dragons
On Dragonwings

By Todd McCaffrey
Dragonsblood

By Anne McCaffrey and Todd McCaffrey
Dragon's Kin
Dragon's Fire
Dragon Harper

DRAGON
HARPER

DRAGON HARPER

ANNE
McCAFFREY

TODD
McCAFFREY

DEL
REY

BALLANTINE BOOKS ✦ NEW YORK

Copyright © 2007 by Anne McCaffrey and Todd J. McCaffrey

Published in the United States by Del Rey Books, an imprint of The Random House Publishing Group, a division of Random House, Inc., New York.

DEL REY is a registered trademark and the Del Rey colophon is a trademark of Random House, Inc.

LIBRARY OF CONGRESS CATALOGING-IN-PUBLICATION DATA

McCaffrey, Anne.
Dragon Harper / Anne McCaffrey & Todd McCaffrey.
p.   cm.
ISBN 978-0-345-48030-9 (acid-free paper)
1. Pern (Imaginary place)—Fiction.   2. Life on other planets—Fiction.
3. Space colonies—Fiction.   4. Dragons—Fiction.
I. McCaffrey, Todd, 1956–   II. Title.
PS3563.A255D73 2007
813'.54—dc22   2007027611

Printed in the United States of America on acid-free paper

www.delreybooks.com

2   4   6   8   9   7   5   3   1

First Edition

To Alec A. Johnson

Son, Brother, Father, Patriot

CONTENTS

DRAMATIS PERSONAE

AT THE HARPER HALL
Murenny, Masterharper of Pern
Biddle, Voicemaster
Caldazon, Instrument Master
Lenner, Masterhealer of Pern
Selora, head cook

Journeymen:
Issak, Tenelin, Gerrin

Apprentices:
Kindan, Nonala, Kelsa, Verilan, Vaxoram

AT FORT HOLD
Bemin, Lord Holder
Sannora, Lady Holder
Semin, Bannor, their sons
Koriana, Fiona, their daughters

AT THE WHERHOLD
Aleesa, Whermaster, queen Aleesk
Mikal, ex-dragonrider
Arella, Aleesa's daughter
Jaythen, wherman

AT BENDEN WEYR

M'tal, Weyrleader of Benden Weyr, bronze dragon Gaminth
Salina, Weyrwoman, queen dragon Breth

AT ISTA WEYR

C'rion, Weyrleader
J'lantir, Wingleader, bronze Lolanth
J'trel, blue rider, Talith

PROLOGUE

Dragon's heart,
Dragon's fire,
Rider true,
Fly higher.

ISTA WEYR,
AFTER LANDING (AL) 495.4

J'lantir's brows were thick, gathered like thunderclouds as he
glowered at his wing riders. He had called them to his quarters
and met them in Lolanth's weyr. The presence of his bronze
dragon, eyes whirling menacingly red, left his wing riders in no
doubt as to his mood.

"A sevenday!" he bellowed. "You've been missing for a whole
sevenday."

He glared at each one in turn, ending with J'trel and his partner, K'nad. J'trel, J'lantir guessed, would say nothing, but K'nad
looked both too nervous and too—amused?

Every rider had bags under his eyes as though he had been
without sleep for the whole sevenday. Young J'lian was leaning

against V'sog, who himself looked only barely able to stand. M'jial and B'zim surreptitiously supported the other two.

L'cal's frown was severe and directed toward the rest of the wing, but beneath his bushy eyebrows, the eldest rider maintained a stoic silence.

Cavorting and carrying on, no doubt, J'lantir thought sourly. Their dragons looked even worse, pale and exhausted. J'lantir had never heard of dragons becoming exhausted because of their riders' antics. He narrowed his eyes as he looked more carefully at K'nad. The man had a tan!

"Where were you all this time?" J'lantir growled. K'nad dropped his head, shaking it slowly. J'lantir pursed his lips sourly and peered along the rest of the line of men that comprised his missing wing. "Where were all of you?"

He scanned the line, looking for someone who might answer.

"We were on an important mission," J'trel said finally. The others looked at him and nodded in relief.

"Very important," K'nad added with a confirming nod.

"So important that I didn't know about it?" J'lantir asked in scathing tones.

K'nad gave him a confused look and was about to answer when J'trel nudged him, shaking his head.

"He said he wouldn't believe us, remember?" J'trel whispered to K'nad in a voice not so quiet that J'lantir didn't hear him.

K'nad drew strength from his partner's words and looked J'lantir in the eye. "You said not to tell until the time was right."

"*I* said?" J'lantir bellowed back, causing K'nad to wilt once more.

"I don't recall saying anything of the sort," J'lantir continued when it was obvious that K'nad had gone back into his shell. "I'll tell you what I think," he said to his riders. "I think you've all gone off someplace and had far too much to drink and can't tell yesterday from today."

Half his riders gave him startled looks as though he'd been reading their minds.

"And so, to sort this out," he continued, "we'll be drilling today."

"Could we do recognition points?" K'nad piped up suddenly. The rest of the wing glanced his way and then murmured in agreement.

J'lantir couldn't believe it. He could never get his wing to drill on recognition points.

"From all around Pern?" J'trel added. "We'd like that."

"You would, would you?" J'lantir said sourly. That was exactly what he'd planned to do with his wing to teach them a lesson. Well, several lessons. Drilling in recognition points was tiring, dull work that dragonriders usually preferred to avoid. He was surprised that his riders were so eager for the work and a little suspicious. But, as he had no other plans sufficiently punitive in mind, he could only assent.

"All around Pern, eh?" he repeated. "Just remember that you asked for it."

"Could we feed the dragons first?" K'nad asked. "They're very hungry."

"Hmmm," J'lantir murmured. The dragons had been fed the day before. Dragons typically ate only once a week. He glanced again at his wing riders and noticed how tired they were. He glared at J'trel, but the blue rider merely shrugged. There was no sense in punishing the dragons for their riders' lapses, J'lantir decided. "Very well, you can feed your dragons and rest for the remainder of today."

His riders gave him astonished and grateful looks.

"Tomorrow," he continued, "before first light, we'll start drilling on recognition points."

J'lantir turned and stalked off, already anticipating a grilling from Weyrleader C'rion—wingleaders were *not* supposed to lose their wings for a sevenday. As it was, he didn't bother to turn back again when one of his riders murmured, "He said he'd be like this."

And another answered, "But it was worth it."

DRAGON
HARPER

CHAPTER I

White robe, high hopes
Hatching Grounds, tight throats
Sands heat, eggs move
Shells crack, hearts prove.

HIGH REACHES WEYR,
AL 495.8

"Put this on," D'vin said to Cristov as they rushed to the Hatching Grounds. The white robe was the traditional garb for candidates, as every child on Pern knew from the Teaching Ballads.

Cristov suddenly realized that his heart was racing, his throat dry. In not much longer than it took D'vin's bronze dragon to go *between*—no more time than it took to cough three times—Cristov went from being a miner recovering from an injury to being a candidate for a Hatching.

This can't be happening, he thought. It should have been Pellar.

Pellar was the mute Harper who had rescued Cristov when his mine had collapsed, had saved Cristov when Tenim had purposely exploded the old firestone mine, and who had had a fire-lizard before Tenim's hunting bird had killed it—and had nearly killed Pellar, as well.

Pellar deserved to be a candidate . . . but Pellar had insisted upon remaining at the newly named Fire Hold to help the young holdless girl, Halla, manage the Shunned of Pern to redeem their honor by mining the firestone of Pern.

"Cristov!" The voice, close by his ear, startled him. "You're here! Excellent!"

Cristov's eyes widened as he recognized Kindan. Turns back, he and Kindan had been enemies. Back then, Cristov had despised watch-whers, just as he'd been taught by his father. Kindan's father had been a wherhandler, a person bonded to the ugly night-loving creatures who were only distant cousins to the great dragons that protected Pern. Infected by his father's attitudes, Cristov had despised Kindan, and they'd fought many times as youngsters. In the end, however, Cristov had realized that it was Kindan who had been right and his father who had been wrong—and Cristov had found himself, at an early age, making a grown man's choice and doing what was right instead of what was expected. He'd even come to regard the ugly watch-whers with respect bordering on awe. And now he greeted Kindan with a huge grin.

Kindan saw the robe clasped in Cristov's hand and his eyebrows rose. He held up his hand and showed Cristov that he, too, had the white robe of a candidate.

"Great, we can go together," he said to Cristov, as he pulled his robe over his head and tied it with the white belt.

"I thought you wanted to be a harper," Cristov said in surprise.

"Harpers can be dragonriders, too," Kindan replied with a big grin.

"You'll be certain to Impress, after your watch-wher," Cristov said. "Probably a bronze, too!"

Kindan shook his head. "I'll just be happy to Impress," he replied. "I'll leave the bronzes to you."

"Cristov, Kindan, hurry!"

They both turned and saw Sonia, the healer's daughter, also dressed in white robes. "Oh, I do hope that egg's a queen!"

Cristov knew that Sonia had been eyeing the funnily marked egg on the Hatching Grounds for some time. Traditionally, though, the queen dragon would carefully push aside any queen eggs, and Jessala's Garirth hadn't done so.

In fact, the egg looked so odd that the Weyr's Healer, Sonia's father S'son, had been asked to examine it to be sure it was whole.

Garirth was so old that her gold hide was a mere pale yellow, and Jessala, her rider, was so pained with age that she rarely moved from her quarters. It was entirely possible that age had caused this egg to have come out wrong somehow. But S'son had declared it fine.

D'vin gestured for them to go forward, saying, "I'll watch from the stands!"

Together the three moved to join the other candidates on the Hatching Grounds.

There were only twenty-three eggs on the Grounds. Cristov had learned that traditionally a queen would lay as few as thirty and as many as forty or more eggs. That Garirth had lain so few was a further indication of her extreme age.

Sonia, who had been examining the other candidates carefully, groaned. "There aren't enough candidates! There are only twenty boys and twenty-two eggs. And there are no other girls, either."

A rush of cold air from dragon wings startled them and they turned to see a smattering of boys and girls rush forward, dressed in white robes.

"Those are Benden colors," Sonia said, pointing to a dragonrider waving in the distance. "B'ralar must have sent for them."

"It's M'tal!" Kindan exclaimed, waving excitedly to the Benden Weyrleader. M'tal waved back and gave him a thumbs-up for good luck.

"What if one of the Benden girls Impresses the queen?" Cristov asked.

"She'll stay here," Sonia said. "But I wouldn't be surprised if she found herself Weyrwoman at the moment of Hatching." She cast a worried look at Garirth, whose head lolled listlessly on the ground beyond them. "I think Garirth and Jessala are only waiting for the hatchlings before they go *between* forever; they're both so tired with age."

The humming noise of the dragons rose louder. Cristov felt the sound in his very bones, reverberating. The noise was so loud it should have been deafening, yet Cristov felt no fear.

"Over here!" Sonia called to the other girls, waving toward the strange egg. They gave her a surprised look before joining her. To herself she muttered, "Whew! I was afraid the queen wouldn't have a decent choice!"

"We're supposed to be over there," Kindan said to Cristov, gesturing to the other boys clustered in the distance.

"I shouldn't be here," Cristov said. "I'm a miner."

Kindan shook his head and told him feelingly, "More than anyone you should be here, Cristov. You earned the right and you were Searched."

Cristov started to explain that D'vin had come for Pellar, not him, but Kindan shushed him. "Look!"

Cristov saw that the eggs were now rocking from side to side. One of them had a crack in it, then another, then a third. Cristov thought like a miner, imagining the blows required to break the shell. But suddenly he squinted, perplexed—the shells were cracking far more than he thought natural. He'd rapped one of the shells himself on the Hatching Grounds, and he'd held an old bit of shell in his hands, so he knew its strength.

And yet now the shells were shattering rapidly, and, strangely, Cristov started to get the feel for which shell would crack next. Something about the dragons' humming. It was as if their humming was helping the hatchlings. As if, Cristov realized suddenly, the dragons' humming resonated with the shells themselves.

The dragons' pitch increased just before one hatchling broke his shell in half and burst forth. Cristov started to take a nervous step backward but found Kindan's hand on his arm.

"They're scared," Kindan said. "They're just little and they're frightened."

Cristov could see that it was true. Even though the brown hatchling towered over Cristov, he could see that it was frightened. It creeled sharply as it searched among the candidates and then— it found its mate. Cristov saw the look of glowing astonishment on the youngster's face, the look of fear breaking into a huge grin as boy and dragon were united in a bond that only death could break.

"You are the most beautiful dragon on all Pern, Finderth," the youngster cried aloud as he grabbed the wobbly brown dragonet in a great hug.

Kindan waved at the boy, calling, "Well done, Jander!" Then he blushed and corrected himself: "I mean, J'der."

But not everything went well. Some of the Benden lads were too frightened and didn't move out of the way of a creeling green. One youth was brutally trampled and tossed aside by the green's awkward stumbling to lie in a bloody heap nearly a dragonlength away.

"Look out!" Kindan called, prodding Cristov as a baby bronze came their way, searching among the candidates for its mate. It tore past them and then stopped, crying piteously.

Cristov remembered what D'vin had said would happen if there was no candidate for a hatchling: *It will go* between *forever.*

"Come on," he said, tugging at Kindan. They couldn't let the bronze hatchling get away. But Kindan was gazing across the Hatching Grounds, saying, "Look, Sonia's egg is hatching!"

Urgently, Cristov sidestepped around Kindan and raced up to the forlorn bronze. He grabbed its tail and yanked. "Back here," he shouted desperately. "We're back here!"

There you are! a voice said suddenly. The dragon's whirling eyes were looking right at him. *I've been looking for you.*

"It's a queen," Kindan shouted over his shoulder, unaware of the drama that was unfolding behind him. "And it looks—yes, Sonia has Impressed the queen. Cristov—" And then Kindan finally turned to look over his shoulder.

The grin on his face slipped as his mind was flooded with memories of Kisk, the green watch-wher he had once shared a bond with. He swallowed hard and squared his shoulders. I gave her up, he reminded himself, wondering if perhaps that rendered him undesirable to the hatchlings.

Briefly Cristov recalled Nuella's brilliant smile as Kindan encouraged her to ride the watch-wher *between* to the cave-in that had trapped her father, brother, and eight other miners. Only blind Nuella could have visualized the image needed to guide the heat-seeing watch-wher safely. So giving Kisk to her had been a good decision, everyone had agreed. And it meant that Kindan wasn't trapped forever in the mines with a watch-wher. He was free to become a harper, maybe even a dragonrider . . . but not this time. He shook himself out of his reverie.

"C'tov?" he asked, using the honorific contraction for the first time. "What's your dragon's name?"

The other lad's eyes shone with a brilliance that Kindan had never seen before.

"My dragon?" Cristov repeated in surprise. He turned to the bronze hatchling in silent communion. "His name is Sereth."

"Congratulations, dragonrider," Kindan said firmly, reaching forward to slap C'tov on the shoulder.

A hideous sound erupted behind them and they all turned. Garirth was upright, her multifaceted eyes whirling in a frantic red. She let out one more despairing wail and then was gone forever, *between*.

Kindan bowed his head. Jessala was no more, or her dragon wouldn't have departed so dramatically. The two had survived long enough to see the hatchlings Impressed. Whether it was the joy or the burden of extreme age that finally overwhelmed the queen's rider did not matter—the Weyrwoman of High Reaches Weyr was dead. When he raised his head again, he turned to Sonia and her young queen dragon. Sonia was now the Weyrwoman.

All the eggs had hatched. There were none left for him.

"Forgive me, C'tov," Kindan said, bowing to his friend, "but I think I'd best get my gear. There will be much harpering tonight, and Master Murenny will want to be informed of the news."

C'tov nodded absently, his attention focused exclusively on the most amazing, marvelous, and brilliant creature beside him.

✦

M'tal sent for Benden's Weyrwoman, Salina, as soon as Garirth went *between*. The events of the evening would have been a trial to anyone, and the new High Reaches Weyrwoman was a young lass. He made his way down the stands into the Hatching Grounds, where he could see B'ralar slumped against a wall. Before he could reach him, however, he saw a lad in white robes running toward the bereft High Reaches Weyrleader, carrying a flask of wine and several glasses precariously in his hands. M'tal recognized Kindan. With a bow and flourish, the lad poured B'ralar a hefty glass of wine.

M'tal nodded approvingly as he headed over to join them; the lad obviously had a good head on his shoulders. It was a pity he hadn't Impressed at this Hatching, M'tal thought, but it was obvious that Kindan was more than suitable—surely it would only be a matter of time before he met the right hatchling.

Kindan smiled when he saw M'tal and brandished a glass in his direction.

"No," M'tal said, waving aside the proffered glass. "It will be a long night, I'm afraid." To B'ralar he said, "I grieve for your loss. May I offer my arm and my aid to you and your Weyr?"

B'ralar forced his eyes to focus long enough to recognize M'tal and then he nodded silently, reaching out a feeble hand to the Benden Weyrleader. "She was everything to me."

A rush of cold air disturbed them and then Salina, newly arrived from Benden, rushed forward and grabbed B'ralar's other hand.

"She was a gracious lady," Salina told him. "Let me escort you to your quarters."

"But—"

M'tal raised a hand to deflect anything that B'ralar might say. "Rest easy tonight." He grinned toward Kindan. "Between harper and weyr, we'll see to High Reaches' comfort."

A fleeting smile crossed B'ralar's lips and then he bowed his head, letting Salina lead him away.

M'tal was busy for the rest of the evening. And every time he had a chance to pause in his consolation of the distraught High Reaches riders, he heard the voice of Kindan singing a soothing song or playing a spritely melody on the pipes. Wine flowed freely and M'tal was not surprised to see the Benden mark on many of the casks that littered the tables, nor was he surprised to learn from a chance remark that Kindan had requested it.

It was very late when the last of the wearied and wined dragon-riders faded off to sleep, the weyrlings all in their quarters, and the community of High Reaches Weyr ready to recover from the loss of its only adult queen dragon.

It was so late that M'tal was quite surprised, as he stifled a yawn, to recognize the sound of Kindan's voice singing a slightly off-color lullaby. M'tal remembered the look on Kindan's face earlier that evening and sought him out.

"There will be other Hatchings," M'tal told him, grabbing the lad's shoulder and shaking it affectionately.

Kindan was too tired not to answer honestly. "I'm an apprentice at the Harper Hall; I doubt I'll see many."

"Weyrs have harpers, too," M'tal reminded him.

"Journeymen, not apprentices, my lord," Kindan said resignedly.

"If you're willing, then," M'tal declared, "when you become a journeyman harper, I'll ask for you at Benden Weyr."

CHAPTER 2

They waited for their hatchlings
Lined up on the sand
They waited for the younglings
To leave hand in hand.

High Reaches Weyr

With his small roll of clothes packed tightly into his carisak, Kindan waited anxiously in the High Reaches Weyr Bowl the next morning while Weyrleader M'tal and D'vin, the bronze rider who had flown for High Reaches in the All-Weyr Games, conversed animatedly nearby.

Kindan knew that they were arguing over which one should bring him back to the Harper Hall. He was hoping that it would be M'tal, because then Kindan could believe that the Benden Weyrleader had remembered and not regretted his promise from the night before. Surely, if M'tal accompanied him, the Weyrleader would mention his intentions to Master Murenny. What would it be like, Kindan wondered, to be a harper for a Weyr? In all his wildest imaginings, he had never hoped for more than to return to a small hold like Camp Natalon or a smaller holding. But a Weyr!

A creeling sound distracted him; it was immediately amplified by the noise of other disturbed hatchlings, and he turned his gaze to the weyrling barracks. He caught flashes of movement and found himself stifling a sigh along with another thought: What would it have been like to wake up in the weyrling quarters?

Kindan frowned and turned his eyes back to the dragonriders. The thought of waking up in the weyrling quarters had scared him and he wanted to distract himself from that. Why would Impressing a dragon scare him?

It seemed that his gaze was felt by M'tal and D'vin, for they turned to look at him.

"I'll take my farewells, Kindan," M'tal said. "I've work to attend to. D'vin will return you to the Harper Hall."

Kindan drew himself up and bowed. "Weyrleader."

M'tal growled and rushed toward Kindan, grabbing him in a great hug. "Don't think you'll get away with that!" he said and held Kindan tightly. For a moment Kindan tensed, then relaxed, realizing in a burst of clarity that M'tal truly appreciated him. Kindan also realized how much he missed the rare hugs that his father, Danil, had given him. M'tal was taller and more lithe than his father but, still . . .

"If you're ready," D'vin said drolly. But there was a twinkle in his eyes.

M'tal stepped back, looked Kindan in the eyes, and raised a hand to point at him. "Don't forget what I said."

Kindan couldn't help keep the surprise out of his voice as he asked, "You meant it?"

"Of course," M'tal said. "A dragonrider lives by his word." He stepped close again and clapped Kindan on the shoulder. "Rather like a harper."

Kindan was so thrilled he could barely nod. M'tal gave him one final measuring look and turned, striding over to his bronze Gaminth.

"Don't take too long!" M'tal called as the bronze dragon leapt into the skies above High Reaches Weyr. Then, in a blink, dragon and rider were gone, *between.*

"Let's go," D'vin said brusquely to Kindan.

"Yes, my lord," Kindan replied, tightening his hold on his sak and following the impatient Wingleader.

It seemed only a moment before they, too, were hovering high over the Weyr. Kindan dared himself to peer down over the dragon's neck, and saw the small dots that were weyrfolk starting their daily chores and the larger dragons, looking smaller than fire-lizards, moving to the Weyr's lake. And then, without warning, Kindan found himself engulfed in an oppressive darkness. His whole body was cold and he could hear nothing, feel nothing but the beating of his heart.

Between. The black nothingness that dragons—and watch-whers—could traverse from one place to another in the time it took to cough three times.

Light burst upon him, assaulting his eyes at the same time that his ears were filled with reassuring sound. Before he could even adjust from the change, Kindan felt himself falling as the bronze dragon dropped down swiftly to the ground below.

A jolt informed him that they had landed.

"I cannot tarry," D'vin said, craning his neck around to peer at Kindan. "Sonia will need help. I will trust you to enlighten the Masterharper."

Kindan nodded hastily, still grappling with D'vin's interesting choice of words.

"Fly well," D'vin said, extending a hand.

Kindan took it and nearly fell as D'vin urged him over the dragon's neck.

"Fly high, my lord," Kindan called back formally. D'vin gaped at him for a moment in surprise at Kindan's eloquence, then shook the expression off his face and gave Kindan a curt nod and a slight wave.

The bronze dragon leapt into the air and was *between* once more before it had climbed a full dragonlength.

It was only when D'vin and his bronze had departed that Kindan took in the morning around him. The sun was above the horizon, but there was still dew on the grass. The noises of Fort were muffled and sleepy, while those of the Harper Hall were—

"Get out of the way!" a voice called to him. Kindan looked up and jumped aside as a group of apprentices barreled past him. They were on their morning run. The voice belonged to Vaxoram, the senior apprentice.

Kindan hadn't liked Vaxoram when they first met and the feeling was mutual. Vaxoram had made it a project to torment Verilan, the youngest apprentice.

Verilan was extraordinarily talented at scribing and researching in the Records. Kindan knew that it was only the boy's young age that held him back from walking the tables and becoming a journeyman. Even the prickly Master Archivist, Resler, had a soft spot for Verilan, and Kindan suspected that Verilan felt the same affection, the two being kindred spirits.

That respect irked Vaxoram even more, as his own handwriting was a point of shame for the entire hall.

When Kindan first found out about the bullying that Vaxoram had condoned or even initiated against Verilan, he took action. He was careful not to be caught, but soon those who were tormenting Verilan found themselves tormented—with extra chores and duties. Kindan had even managed to get Vaxoram caught and given a week's extra duties.

Of course, while the bullies were never certain who was getting them back, trapping them in their traps and arranging for their pranks to be discovered, they suspected Kindan and unleashed their full wrath on him.

For the next three months, Kindan had felt every day that he should just leave the Harper Hall. But he hadn't, because he was certain that if he did, Verilan would be the next to suffer.

Things changed for the worse with the arrival of Nonala, the second girl apprentice in twenty Turns.

The first girl apprentice had been Kelsa, a talented songwriter who had arrived nearly a full Turn before and had quickly become Kindan's second-best friend after Verilan. Kelsa was prickly, blunt, and gawky, but those traits were overshadowed by her honesty and her kindness.

She was also shy, at least initially. So when she first arrived at the Harper Hall, she had been only too willing to accept the suggestion that she sleep with the kitchen staff.

"After all," she had said reasonably to Kindan when he'd questioned her, "it's not like there are other girl harpers."

"I don't know," Kindan said mulishly. "It seems to me if you're an apprentice, you should be in the apprentice dormitory."

"Vaxoram wouldn't like that, I'm sure," Kelsa had replied, grimacing. "And I don't need to upset him any more than I already have."

Kindan had nodded in reluctant agreement. Kelsa's ability to write songs had been met with praise by everyone—except Vaxoram, who had no ability in that area. If Kelsa were any less talented or more arrogant, Kindan might have agreed with the senior apprentice that a girl didn't belong among harpers . . . but her songs were just *too* good.

"What will you do if another girl is apprenticed?" Kindan had asked.

"Well," Kelsa had replied thoughtfully, "that will be different."

Nonala came from Southern Boll, recommended by the harper there for her amazing voice and its range. Nonala was not much older than Verilan, having nearly twelve Turns to his ten.

"There's a new apprentice," Kindan had called to Kelsa as they entered the second class of the day. If there was one thing Kindan was good at, it was knowing what was going on in the Harper Hall.

"Great!" Kelsa replied. Then she took in Kindan's expression and gave him a probing look. "What's so funny?"

"She's a girl," Kindan said, grinning at her. "I imagine it'll get rather cramped in with the cooks."

Kelsa snorted. "She won't be staying with the cooks."

"Really?"

"Really," Kelsa told him. She beckoned for him to come closer as the other apprentices rushed into the classroom.

"Here's what you'll do," she said, then pulled his head close to her mouth. Kindan listened with growing astonishment.

"By the First Egg, no!" he exclaimed when she finished.

Kelsa gave him a knowing look. "Oh, you'll do it."

"And what makes you say so?" Kindan wondered. "Vaxoram will having me chasing down tunnel snakes—"

"You'll do it," Kelsa repeated firmly. "You'll do it because you know it's right." She pushed him toward their classroom. "Don't say anything now, we're late."

"I can't do it all on my own," Kindan complained.

"Of course not." Kelsa's response was in such an agreeable tone that Kindan's further protests faltered in shock. "Get Verilan to help," she added with a grin. When Kindan drew breath for another protest, Kelsa continued, "And I'll help." She glanced toward the kitchen quarters and shivered. "I'll be glad to get out of there—all *they* talk about is cooking!"

By evening everything was ready. With Verilan's help, Kindan and Kelsa had put up a sturdy canvas partition separating the back corner of the large apprentice dormitory from the rest. Inside they placed one of the bunk beds and a chest of drawers.

The older apprentices were at first wary, then irate that they had to change their lifestyle to accommodate girls.

"The cook's quarters were enough for one, why not two?" the senior apprentices had grumbled.

"We're harpers," Kelsa said, throwing her arm around a confused and reluctant Nonala. "We should be with the other apprentices."

"We can't have girls here!" Vaxoram, the senior apprentice, declared when he learned the purpose of the canvas partition.

"I suppose we could get one of the spare journeyman's rooms," Kelsa said judiciously, knowing full well that Vaxoram was hoping to make journeyman soon and had been eyeing the vacant rooms proprietarily.

"Hrrmph!" Vaxoram replied, storming out of the dormitory.

"Where are you going?" Kelsa called after him.

"To talk to the Masters!"

Vaxoram, failing to convince the Masters to provide the girls with separate quarters, had tried to shame and scare them into demanding it on their own—or better, to ask to leave the Harper Hall.

It started with silly pranks, water left on the floor just outside the canvas partition. When Nonala tripped and banged her head in the middle of the night, Kindan moved his bunk close by and kept a wary eye out for further pranksters.

It soon escalated to outright harassment, with the older apprentices actively preventing both girls from attending classes. Kelsa bore up well under the strain—tough and wiry, she merely elbowed or pinched her way past the offenders. But Nonala was a milder sort, and the glares and jeers of the older boys were hard on her.

Kindan had only to hear her sobbing softly in her bed one night to decide that he would no longer tolerate the behavior of the other apprentices. Stealthily he left his bunk in the night, crossed over to hers, and grabbed her hand. Seeing that he'd startled her, he smiled and patted her hand in reassurance. Nonala smiled back, sat up, and hugged him. Kindan held her tightly until he felt her relax, then let her go. Nonala lay back down in her bed, still holding his hand. He remained there until she fell back asleep, then silently returned to his bed. As he did, he caught sight of Kelsa, smiling at him in approval.

The next day, Nonala had shown remarkable skill in defending herself when another prankster tried to trip her, and her would-be assailant found himself sprawled on the ground.

"I've three older brothers," Nonala told the older boy as she looked down on him. "They taught me how to fight."

The older apprentice pulled himself up and looked menacingly down at Nonala, his hands clenched tightly to his sides. Things might have gotten ugly if first Kindan and then Verilan hadn't taken a stand on either side of her.

"Don't you need to be in class, Merol?" Verilan had asked.

"You owe her an apology," Kindan had added, glaring up at the older boy. He and Merol had tangled once already and since then, Merol had shied away from him. The incident had occurred not long after Kindan had first been assigned to the Harper Hall and, oddly, it had involved Merol tripping him, as well. Unfortunately for Merol, it had been just after Kindan's first lesson with the Detallor, the Master who taught both dance and defense. Kindan found himself merely pivoting over the offending foot, catching it with his own, and tugging—with the net result that Kindan remained standing and Merol was sent sprawling. Merol's eyes had flashed angrily, but he had just murmured, "Sorry," and rushed off to his class.

Faced again with an angry Kindan, Merol had muttered "Sorry" again, this time to Nonala, before slinking off.

Since then, no one bothered Nonala. But it was clear to Kindan that Vaxoram, always the ringleader, hadn't changed his attitude one bit.

Now here was the entire apprentice class returning from the morning run up to Fort Hold with Vaxoram in the lead. They couldn't have failed to notice the arrival of D'vin's bronze dragon, so it was obvious that Vaxoram had guided the runners this way on purpose.

"Wow, Kindan, you get to ride dragons a lot!" Verilan called breathlessly as he and Nonala passed, last in the long line. Kindan smiled and, with a shrug, joined them as they trotted back toward the Harper Hall. Seeing him, Kelsa circled back from her position near the front of the group.

"How did it go?" she asked.

"I was a candidate," Kindan replied.

"You were?" Verilan asked, eyes wide. "For a dragon?"

Kindan nodded. The realization that, had things gone differently, he wouldn't be here now but at High Reaches Weyr with a baby dragon all of his own suddenly burst upon him. The other day he had been too busy helping with the tragedy of Weyrwoman Jessala's loss to consider his own situation fully.

"I'm not sorry you didn't Impress," Nonala said slowly. "I would have missed you."

"I would have missed you, too," Kindan confessed. He looked at the backs of the other runners. "Come on, you'd better catch up or you'll get extra chores."

———✦———

Kindan knew that Masterharper Murenny would expect a full report as soon as he returned. With a wave, he parted from his friends as they headed for the apprentice dormitories and made his way up to the Masterharper's quarters. It was only when he was outside that he considered that the Masterharper might still be asleep. His desire to "leave sleeping Masters lie" warred with his conviction that Murenny would want to know as soon as possible.

He had just raised his hand to knock on the door when he heard Master Murenny's voice call through it: "Go to the kitchen, Kindan, and bring up some breakfast."

"Yes, Master," Kindan replied in astonishment. How had the Masterharper known he was outside the door? Kindan could guess that Masterharper Murenny would be expecting his report but even so . . . Kindan had been quiet on his way up the stairs. Somehow, the Masterharper always seemed to know.

Shaking his head ruefully, Kindan rushed back down the stairs and into the kitchen.

"Back from the Weyr?" Selora, the head cook, asked as soon as she saw him. She quickly piled a pitcher of *klah,* several mugs, and a plate of morning rolls onto a tray and thrust it into his arms.

"Thanks, Selora!" Kindan said, grinning at her.

She smiled back. "Get going! You know well enough not to keep harpers waiting for their food."

Moving more slowly to avoid spilling or dropping anything, Kindan hustled back up to the Masterharper's quarters. Overburdened, he balanced on one foot and used the other to knock on the door.

"Put it over there," the Masterharper said, gesturing to a table even as he closed the door behind Kindan. Masterharper Murenny's face was outlined with white stubble and his hair was still sleep-mussed.

Kindan placed the tray down carefully, then immediately opened his mouth to start his report, but Murenny restrained him with an upraised hand.

"Eat," Murenny ordered. He poured two mugs of *klah* and handed one to Kindan. "Drink."

Kindan complied and was surprised to discover how hungry and thirsty he really was. The Masterharper observed him silently throughout their meal with a kindly expression. When at last Kindan had leaned back from the tray, Master Murenny said, "Now, are you ready to report?"

Kindan nodded.

"First let me say that while I'm glad you're here, I would have hoped that perhaps you hadn't returned," Master Murenny said.

Kindan shrugged; Master Murenny wasn't saying anything he hadn't already heard.

"I'm happy to be a harper," Kindan said.

Master Murenny smiled. "You could still be a harper and ride a dragon, you know."

"Only if I finish my training." Kindan had been at the Harper Hall over a Turn and a half. Apprentices normally didn't "walk the tables" to become journeymen until they been at the hall for at least three Turns, and more often, four.

Murenny nodded and motioned for Kindan to continue.

"I was present at the Hatching," Kindan began and leaned back into his chair, getting comfortable. As he got deeper and deeper into the report, he found himself wondering how to set it to song and altered his sentences to be more melodic. In moments, all of Kindan's fears and worries had faded away to be replaced only by the spoken song he was relaying.

"Well done, well done," the Masterharper said when Kindan had finished. He sat briefly, lost in thought. When he looked up again, he murmured, "Well, Jessala has her rest at last. I imagine it won't be long before B'ralar seeks his."

"Why, Master?" Kindan asked, surprised that any dragonrider would consider such an act.

"Sometimes the heart gets so heavy that living is impossible," Murenny told him. "Unless there's something to replace a loss, a person just gives up."

He leaned forward, looking Kindan in the eye. " 'Without hope, there is no future.' "

Kindan had heard that before. "Can't we give him hope?"

Murenny shook his head. "We can only give him choices. Hope is something you find for yourself."

Kindan nodded bleakly. Master Murenny noted his expression and smiled wryly. He leaned back, his eyes drifting to the ceiling. When he spoke again, his words were distant but heartfelt. "I hope you never feel that way."

There was a moment's silence finally broken by the Masterharper, who jumped up out of his chair decisively. "But now there's work to be done, a tray to go back to the kitchen, and you to get to your classes."

"Yes, Master," Kindan agreed, glad to see the end of gloomy musings.

———◆———

But it turned out, as the days rolled into seven, and the sevendays into months, that Kindan found himself lost in gloomy musings.

He was distracted, wondering about Kisk—called Nuelsk, now—the green watch-wher he'd bonded with and then had released into Nuella's care. At the time, his bonding with Kisk had seemed like imprisonment, but from the distance of memory, Kindan found himself remembering how kind the awkward, ugly green watch-wher had been, and how brave she had been at the end, to take Nuella on a never-before-attempted ride *between* to rescue the trapped miners. And he found himself wondering again what it would have been like to Impress a dragon, to have a pair of great, faceted eyes whirling anxiously for his well-being, to ride a dragon, to feed it firestone and watch it breathe flame.

His days were filled with feeling overwhelmed by his classes and his various inadequacies; he had neither Nonala's skill at crafting song, nor the fierce dedication to the dry, dusty Records that made Verilan's eyes bright with excitement. Oh, he could thwart silly pranks from older apprentices and he gave as good as he got, but *that* was hardly a harperly calling, and beyond that, Kindan could think of no talent in which he had a gift.

Except perhaps the drums. Drums on Pern were more than a way to keep a beat; they were the vital lifeblood of news between Holds and Crafts. Only a dragonrider could travel more swiftly than a drum message and, as drum messages were available to all, only the drums carried the full news of Pern.

Kindan took to drumming like he'd taken to the coal caves where he'd grown up. He would listen to the "First Call" of morning and the "Last Call" of night; he loved being the first one to decipher the codes; he loved wagering how long it would take Vaxoram who, like Kindan, seemed particularly good at nothing, to decipher the latest messages; and he loved how the words from distant places gave him the feel of a world-traveler, of someone connected with all the people of Pern.

He was worse at making drums than drumming on them. In fact, he couldn't imagine how he could be worse at making things.

"You'll get the hang of it, just keep trying," Nonala had told him staunchly the day Kindan had mentioned it.

"You will," Verilan had agreed, although Kindan felt that his agreement had been more out of loyalty than conviction. "And you're so good at the codes." Verilan had frowned; the drum codes were simply beyond him. He was built slightly and didn't have the strength to make the big drums rebound with the volume needed to traverse outside of Fort Hold's main valley, and his slow methodical ways made it difficult for him to decipher the multi-beat codes. By the time he'd deciphered the first beat, the second beat had already come and gone, lost forever.

Vaxoram took great pains to taunt Kindan on his failures. Kindan sometimes wondered if Vaxoram didn't gloat over the lackings of others to distract himself from his own weaknesses, but the older apprentice's relentless ways never gave much time to consider the ramifications.

The one thing that Vaxoram was good at was fencing. Finesse, naturally, was not the older apprentice's forte, but his reach, endurance, and sheer brutality usually ensured his victory.

"You've no subtlety," Master Detallor said to him at one of their practice sessions. He motioned to Kindan. "You should learn from this youngster. He seems to understand what I'm saying."

Almost immediately Kindan wished that the Master hadn't singled him out so; Vaxoram chose Kindan as his opponent for the next bout. It started well enough. Kindan got first touch, but then Vaxoram charged forward and—to Kindan's utter astonishment—changed hands mid-strike, feinting with an empty right hand and striking a telling blow with the foil now in his left hand.

"Better," Detallor said as Kindan staggered and grunted in pain. "But fighting left-handed won't win against another left-hander," Detallor warned, grabbing up a foil himself. "Here, let me show you."

And he proceeded to administer a left-handed drubbing to Vaxoram that was so ferocious that Kindan forgot the bruise Vaxoram had made on his own chest.

Still, if it weren't that Kindan wouldn't give up on his dream of being a harper, and a Weyr harper at that, he would have left the Harper Hall to free himself from Vaxoram's incessant prodding.

The autumn weather at Fort Hold was not as bitter as the biting cold Kindan had experienced at Camp Natalon in Crom Hold, but the rains seemed to last longer, the fogs of the morning were thicker and colder—sometimes lasting all day—and the miserable weather matched his miserable mood.

Two months after his return from High Reaches Weyr, Kindan found himself at the tail end of a wet morning run accompanied, as usual, by Verilan and Nonala. Verilan was coughing more than usual, a sure sign that he would be in the infirmary with a nasty cough before the end of the sevenday.

The rain had turned the path beside the road to brown mush, but the packed surface of the road was too hard on their feet so they stuck with the slick and muddy path. A noise from behind them startled them all, with Verilan losing his footing and Kindan plowing into him. Both went down and came up covered in muck and mud. Kelsa took one look at their bedraggled appearance and burst into giggles.

"You two!" she said, still giggling. "You look like you've been out making mud pies."

Nonala said nothing, but she couldn't keep a smile from her lips.

Verilan scowled at them. Kindan, meanwhile, had turned around to spot the source of the noise. It was difficult in the fog and rain. Finally he made out a huge dark shape in the distance.

"A dragon!"

"What will we do?" Nonala moaned. "We're not fit to greet him."

"Well, we can't just turn away," Verilan said, his last word breaking into a cough.

Kindan nodded and started walking toward the dragon, searching for its rider. The others followed reluctantly, Nonala occasionally making small distressed noises to herself.

As they approached, the figure of a tall man carrying a heavy object resolved itself out of the rain.

"Kindan!" the rider exclaimed. It was M'tal, Benden's Weyrleader. "Just who I was looking for—" He stopped as he took in the sight of their mud-covered bodies. His mouth quirked into a grin. "Slipped?"

Kindan grunted and smiled back. "Yes, my lord."

"It's M'tal to you," the Weyrleader replied firmly. He nodded to the three figures huddling behind him. "Who are your friends?"

Kindan turned to introduce them. "This is Nonala, that's Kelsa, and this—" He was interrupted briefly when Verilan erupted into another coughing fit. "—is Verilan."

"You should see the healer, immediately," M'tal said, his voice suddenly full of concern. He moved toward Verilan, then suddenly remembered his burden and thrust it toward Kindan. "Carry this, while I carry him," he instructed.

"No, no, I'm all right," Verilan protested, horrified at the thought of the dragonrider getting covered in mud.

"No, you're not," Nonala told him. M'tal nodded in agreement, grabbing Verilan by the waist and hoisting him off the ground. He carried the boy like a small child.

"You're lighter than a sack of firestone," he assured the horror-stricken young harper. With a smile, M'tal said to Kindan, "And, thanks to your friend, firestone can get as wet as you are now."

Verilan glanced in surprise at Kindan.

Somewhat guiltily, Kindan realized that he hadn't had time since his return to the Harper Hall to fill his friends in on the discovery that there were two types of firestone: the traditional firestone, which exploded on contact with water, and the newly rediscovered firestone, which didn't explode when in contact with water—the firestone that had given the fire-lizards their name.

"Firestone explodes when wet," Verilan declared stubbornly.

"Not anymore," M'tal assured him as they trudged under the arches of the Harper Hall.

"Wow, Kindan!" Verilan called over the dragonrider's shoulder.

"Yes, wow, Kindan, why didn't you tell your friends?" Kelsa repeated sourly, glaring at him. Kindan made a helpless, apologetic gesture, which only earned him a further glare.

"Kindan, you'll need to get your bundle to a hearth," M'tal said, "and I'll need one of you others to guide me to the infirmary."

"A hearth?" Nonala asked, glancing closely at the bundle Kindan was carrying. For the first time, Kindan noticed the bundle in his arms; he'd been more concerned with Verilan. It was heavy, and wrapped well in thick wher-hide. There was some sort of bucket inside the wrapping—he could feel the shape pressing through the fabric.

"They need to be kept warm," M'tal said. "I'm afraid I could only get two for the Harper Hall; the rest are for Lord Holder Bemin."

"Fire-lizard eggs?" Kindan asked, his voice rising, his eyes going wide.

"Not the same as dragon, I know," M'tal called over his shoulder as he followed after Kelsa, "nor even a watch-wher. Master Murenny agreed that one would be for you."

"Thank you!" Kindan shouted as M'tal headed up the stairs. Holding his bundle tighter, he increased his pace as he veered toward the kitchen. Nonala tagged along after him.

"Fire-lizard eggs!" she repeated, her step changing almost to the sort of bounce that Kelsa most often preferred. "I wonder who will get the other one?"

Kindan shook his head. As exciting as the fire-lizard eggs were, his thoughts had already turned back to Verilan. The younger boy was always getting sick, especially in winter. Kindan was particularly alarmed that M'tal had decided to bring him to the infirmary immediately, even before seeing the Masterharper.

"What are you doing here?" Selora demanded as she spied them. "You're all wet and mucked up! Don't you know—" She spied the bundle Kindan had in his arms. "What's that?"

"Fire-lizard eggs," Kindan told her quickly. "I'm sorry, Selora, but Weyrleader M'tal said that they needed to get to the hearth immediately."

"Of course they do," Selora snapped, grabbing the wher-hide bundle out of Kindan's arms and placing it on the stone-covered floor near the hearth. Deftly, she unwrapped it while Kindan bent down beside her and Nonala hovered anxiously nearby.

"You're shivering!" Selora declared as she glanced first at Kindan and then at Nonala. "You need a warm bath, both of you." Her eyes narrowed. "And where are the other two, your accomplices?"

"M'tal took Verilan up to the infirmary," Kindan began.

"The infirmary?" Selora exclaimed. "He's not hurt, is he?"

"He's coughing again," Nonala said in her mother-hen voice. Kindan could never understand how a girl with three older brothers could be so motherly, but that was how Nonala was.

"You, then," Selora snapped to Nonala peremptorily, "up to the baths. Throw the boys out—they've been in too long if they're still there."

Nonala froze, her eyes going to Kindan, and Kindan started to rise, torn between the fire-lizards and protecting his friend from the older apprentices.

The interplay was not lost on Selora. "So, it's that way, is it?" she asked, nodding sagely. Neither Kindan nor Nonala was able to get a half-formed protest spoken out loud as Selora barreled over them. "I'd thought so, but I wasn't certain." She glanced at Kindan. "You follow her up, then, and make sure she's not harassed." As Kindan made to protest, Selora shushed him with a hand, her expression softening. "I've looked after fire-lizard eggs before, you know," she told them. With a wave of her hand, she said, "Now, go! Both of you, and both of you in the baths." Her waved hand turned to a pointed finger as she continued, "And mind you, not the same one, either!"

Nonala and Kindan, both too red with embarrassment to re-spond, hustled mutely out of the room.

"I'll send someone up with more coals," Selora called after them, searching the kitchen for a likely candidate. Not surprisingly, she had no lack of volunteers, all hoping that the fire-lizard eggs would hatch in their presence.

✦

There were still several apprentices up in the dormitory, including Vaxoram.

"Where were you?" he demanded as they entered. "And where are the other two?"

"Infirmary," Kindan replied tersely. "Selora sent us up for baths."

"Are you going to wash her back?" Vaxoram asked, smirking vul-garly. He was rewarded with a scattering of chuckles. "Mind you, she's still a bit young, but so are—"

"Shut up!" Kindan shouted, his eyes narrowed, fists clenched at his side.

"Kindan . . ." Nonala said soothingly at his side, as though en-couraging him to drop it.

"No," Kindan told her firmly. He turned back to Vaxoram, rais-ing his head to stare at the taller boy. "You apologize."

"To her?" Vaxoram demanded, a sneer on his face.

"To both of us," Kindan replied, stepping toward the older ap-prentice. Kindan was shivering, and he realized that not all of it was with rage; some of it was from the cold, wet clothing he wore.

Vaxoram peered down at him consideringly. He shook his head. "I don't think so."

Kindan's temper snapped. In a move that surprised him, he swung his arm swiftly, palm open, and slapped Vaxoram hard on the cheek.

"I challenge you," he declared.

"Kindan, no!" Nonala cried.

But a hot, burning anger had overcome Kindan and her words didn't even register.

"Challenge me? Do you think the Masters will permit it?" Vaxoram snorted. He bore down on Kindan. "No, I'll beat you to a pulp here and now, and you'll not tell anyone, or I'll do it to you *and* your friends."

Some of the other apprentices looked at one another apprehensively.

"Kindan," Nonala pleaded. Kindan heard her worry for him, but he also felt her concern for the long-term repercussions. She knew as well as he did that if he gave in now, Vaxoram would not only torment him more but would also see it as permission to harass both Nonala and Kelsa. He couldn't allow that, no matter what.

"No, you won't," he said. "And if you beat me, I'll still be here and I won't give in."

"Let's see," Vaxoram said, slamming a fist down into Kindan's nose and lips, pulping them.

Kindan felt his teeth rip into his lips and swallowed the hot blood that spewed from the tattered inside of his mouth. It only made him angrier. He swung, but Vaxoram had stepped back, smirking, admiring his handiwork. Then Vaxoram bore in again for another blow to Kindan's jaw, but before he connected, a voice rang out. "Hold!"

Everyone in the room froze as Weyrleader M'tal stormed into the room.

"What is going on here?" the dragonrider demanded, turning from Kindan to Vaxoram, his eyes narrowing as he took in Nonala's distraught, teary-eyed face.

"I challenge Vaxoram," Kindan said, his words slurred with blood and pain. "I call him a coward and a bully and a man who would use his strength to have a woman."

There were gasps from the entire room, including M'tal and

Nonala. Eyes locked onto Kindan. In front of him, Vaxoram's anger was a palpable thing; the older lad's breathing was ragged and outraged.

Kindan had issued the harshest condemnation possible of a man on Pern—that he would use his strength to overpower a woman.

"I demand the right of cold steel," Vaxoram responded through clenched teeth, his eyes tight, beady, and glaring angrily down at Kindan's bloody face.

"You shall have it," Kindan replied, matching the taller lad's glare. He caught the look of surprise in Vaxoram's eyes and, deeper under it, a flash of fear.

"Kindan!" Nonala shouted. "No! He'll kill you."

"Are you certain of this, Kindan?" M'tal asked intently.

"Yes," Kindan said.

"And if you prove your claim?" M'tal asked. In a duel such as this, if Kindan prevailed, he had the right to exact whatever penalty he desired, given the severity of the claim.

Kindan stared up coldly into Vaxoram's eyes and saw the fear grow there. Kindan could have Vaxoram banished from the Harper Hall. Kindan knew that before coming to the Harper Hall, Vaxoram had been the son of a minor holder. If banished, Vaxoram would certainly not be accepted back by his family, particularly under such shame. Banishing Vaxoram would be worse than Shunning him, and Kindan had seen enough of Shunning. His thoughts turned to C'tov and his Shunned father.

"He'll serve me," he said.

"Never!" Vaxoram roared.

"Heard and witnessed," M'tal declared, overriding Vaxoram. He looked at the older apprentice. "And what is your penalty?"

Kindan met Vaxoram's eyes. He could see clearly that the older apprentice intended to kill him. He was pretty sure that if Vaxoram succeeded, he'd be asked to leave the Harper Hall anyway—no one would tolerate a killer in their midst. Something else flickered in Vaxoram's eyes, then he said, "He's to be banished." He gave Kindan a gloating look. "For lying."

"Very well," M'tal said. "I've heard and witnessed both claims." He turned to Vaxoram. "You are to report this to the Masterharper." He glanced at Kindan and Nonala. "Selora told me that she sent you to the baths. Get going now."

Kindan nodded and, numbly, trotted over to the bath rooms. He was inside and peeling off his clothes before he heard the rustle of the curtain and felt Nonala enter beside him.

The bath room was laid out with four large baths in the middle and a row of showers along each wall. When Kindan and the others bathed, by unspoken agreement they turned away from each other as they undressed and got into their baths, respecting each other's privacy. They never spoke until they were safely in their baths, usually covered by bubbles. When they showered, they followed the same rules, keeping their eyes on the wall in front of them and being respectful.

Now, however, Nonala spoke while she was disrobing. "I could have taken care of myself," she told him, her anger barely masking her concern.

He pointed to his mangled lips. "But could you have sung afterward?"

She sloughed off the last of her clothes and hopped into her bath, churning up bubbles with both hands.

"No," she admitted after a moment.

Kindan stepped into his own bath and sank down quickly into the water. The water was only warm, not hot enough to reach the cold that had settled deep into his bones. He heard a happy groan from Nonala and looked over at her.

"It feels so good to stop shivering," she told him.

A moment later, two apprentices called from the outside of the room, "Can we come in? We've got coals."

"Come in," Nonala told them.

They hustled in and placed the coals under the baths, then

scurried out again, one of them calling as he left, "Selora says she'll have others up with hot water in a moment."

"Thank you!" Nonala and Kindan chorused. As the two apprentices hurried away, one whispered to the other in a voice that carried, "Did you see his face?"

"I heard Vaxoram plans to kill him," came the other's reply.

Nonala turned anxiously to look at Kindan, her eyes welling with tears.

"No, he won't," Kindan declared.

"Kindan . . ." Nonala began worriedly, only to be interrupted by another voice from the outside.

"Are you decent?" It was Kelsa.

"Come on in," Nonala called. "You can steal some of my coals, the water's not that warm yet."

"Selora said she'll send someone up with hot water," Kindan added as Kelsa pushed aside the curtains and entered the room.

Shivering worse than Kindan and Nonala had, Kelsa had trouble undoing the fastenings on her clothes. It didn't help that her eyes were locked on Kindan's face.

"Shards, Kindan, you're a mess," she declared as she peeled off her outer clothes, her eyes still locked on his.

"And, uh," Kindan said in embarrassment, "you're not in your bath."

Kelsa glanced down and back up at him. "So?" she asked absently.

"Kelsa!" Nonala growled. "You're embarrassing him!"

"I am?" Kelsa asked in surprise. She looked back to Kindan. "Well, I suppose if you're going to let Vaxoram kill you—"

"I'm not going to die," Kindan declared. Kelsa smiled at his fierceness and rushed over to him, kneeled down beside him, and planted a swift kiss on his cheek before he could even flinch away.

"Of course, you aren't," she agreed, wrapping her arms around his neck and kissing him again. Huskily, she repeated, "Of course you aren't."

Then, without another word, she sprang up, shucked off her undergarments, and settled down into the next bath over.

Nonala glanced back and forth between the two, her look somewhat wistful.

Kelsa caught her look. She turned to Kindan. "Kindan?"

"Yes?" Kindan said, turning to look at Kelsa. He saw that tears spangled her eyes.

"Kindan, I don't want you to die!" Nonala blurted suddenly.

"What Nonala meant to say, Kindan, is that she loves you," Kelsa told him. She nodded slowly. "And so do I."

Kindan didn't know what to say. He liked Nonala, he knew that. In fact, he loved her like a sister. Kelsa was different . . . sometimes he found himself thinking of her in ways that made his throat go tight. And then he realized—"I love you, too," he said, glancing at both of them. He smiled, even though it hurt his lips. "You're the best friends anyone could have."

With a splash, Nonala sprang from her bath grabbing a towel from a nearby hook and quickly tying it around her. She rushed over to Kindan, wrapping two wet arms around his neck and planting a warm kiss on his cheek before hopping back just as quickly into her bath.

"You know your face is really yucky," Kelsa spoke into the silence that followed. "You should try washing that blood off."

"You should see the Masterhealer, too," Nonala added.

"Kindan," Masterharper Murenny called from outside the curtain.

"Sir?" Kindan replied, glancing at the two girls to be sure that they weren't concerned.

"M'tal told me what happened," the Masterharper said. "I'd like to speak with you as soon as possible."

"He should see the Masterhealer first, sir," Nonala spoke up.

"I quite understand," Murenny replied. "In the meantime, I've posted Master Detallor outside."

Master Detallor was the dance and defense master, a short,

wiry man who moved with a limp—except when he was dancing or fighting, and then he moved like liquid fire.

"Thank you," Kelsa called back.

Something about the Masterharper's tone alerted Kindan, who said, "Did you want to talk to me about relinquishing the duel, sir?"

"No," Murenny replied. There was a moment's silence before he continued. "Who will be your second?"

"I will," Kelsa and Nonala said in chorus. They glanced at each other, then Nonala said, "You're taller, maybe you should go first."

"All right," Kelsa said. She turned to Kindan. "If you don't win, I'll kill him," she told him matter-of-factly.

"I'm going to win," Kindan repeated.

"Well," Master Murenny called from outside the bath curtain, "I'll see you after you've seen the Masterhealer."

"Yes, sir," Kindan replied. Murenny's steps echoed to the dormitory door and faded away.

"You'd better hurry up, then," Kelsa ordered him. "You don't want to keep the Masterharper waiting."

As this was obviously true, Kindan made no response.

✦

"The Masterharper says you challenged Vaxoram," Masterhealer Lenner remarked as he carefully dabbed at Kindan's split lip.

Kindan nodded.

"I can't approve of dueling," Lenner said, shaking his head. "You'd think, with these injuries, that you'd not want it."

"I want it," Kindan replied. "He's a bully."

"A bully?"

"He threatened Nonala," Kindan said. The Masterhealer's quick intake of breath was all that Kindan needed to hear.

With one final, gentle dab, Lenner released him. "I've done all I could for now," he told Kindan, handing him a small glass vial. "Use this daily both on the wound and with your food."

"Arnica?" Kindan asked.

"Of course," the Masterhealer replied, his tone approving of Kindan's knowledge of herbs.

Not five minutes later, Kindan stood outside the Masterharper's door. He paused for a moment, then knocked.

"Come," Master Murenny's deep voice carried clearly through the thick door.

Kindan entered the Masterharper's quarters. Murenny smiled at him and gestured to a chair by a small, round table. Weyrleader M'tal was already in another seat. From his position, Kindan guessed that the Masterharper had been pacing—never a good sign.

"There's some herbal tea," Murenny said, gesturing to a pot. "Selora sent it up along with word that the eggs are warm and settled."

Kindan took his seat and gratefully poured himself a cup of the pungent herbal mix. He knew that Selora would have laced it with restoratives and not sent it up so hot that it might inflame his cuts.

The sound of the rain that had been lashing down earlier had dissipated somewhat, but it still could be heard falling softly around the Harper Hall.

The Masterharper took another turn around his dayroom, glanced at M'tal, and settled himself into the third seat, nearly opposite Kindan.

"Kindan—"

"Masterharper, I will not yield the challenge," Kindan interrupted softly but firmly.

"I know," Murenny said, nodding firmly. "I did not intend to ask that of you."

Kindan gave the Masterharper his full attention, setting his cup back carefully in its saucer. Masterharper Murenny looked chagrined, even apologetic as he continued, "I wished, instead, to apologize to you."

"Master?"

Murenny let out a long, heavy sigh. "When Vaxoram arrived

here, he was young and had the most beautiful voice," the Master-harper explained, half closing his eyes in memory. "But it broke wrong and he lost it. I had hoped that he would find some other talent, but none seemed to come to him and it turned him bitter." He met Kindan's eyes frankly. "I made a mistake: I should have released Vaxoram back to his hold Turns. I'd heard enough rumors of his behavior to know that he was a problem and a bad influence on several others, as well." He frowned in thought a moment, his head bowed, then looked up at Kindan once more, determinedly. "In fact, until you arrived, I'd made up my mind to do just that."

"Me?" Kindan couldn't keep the surprise out of his voice.

"When you stood up for Verilan, I thought that perhaps Vaxoram would learn his lesson and mend his ways," the Masterharper confessed. "Even more so when Kelsa and Nonala appeared, especially as his behavior meant that releasing him of his apprenticeship would be seen as prejudiced."

"I'm sorry, Murenny," M'tal interrupted, "but I don't follow that."

"Consider for a moment," Murenny replied, "what would be the effect on your wings if you had female riders." As M'tal made ready to reply, Master Murenny added, "Women riders in your fighting wings."

"Oh," M'tal said after a moment. "That would be awkward, wouldn't it?"

"But I do not believe that talent should be subservient to sex," Murenny said. "Our survival depends upon our children and it always will, but it should not be at the expense of the lives of the women holders and crafters."

M'tal regarded him carefully for a long moment. "You've been thinking about this for a long while," he decided.

"Yes," Murenny agreed. He looked over to Kindan. "Your friend Nuella is an excellent example."

"So are Kelsa and Nonala," Kindan added loyally.

"Indeed," Murenny agreed. "And perhaps even more so as they

will influence many others when they walk the tables and move on to mastery."

Kindan tried for a moment to imagine Kelsa as a masterharper and found the image difficult to merge with the ever-moving, hyperkinetic, graceful, and gawky girl he called his friend. Although, Kindan remarked to himself, if she *wanted* it, nothing and no one could stop her.

"But there are too many hidebound holders and crafters," M'tal objected. "They'll never permit—"

"Given the way that the holders and crafters are so loath to yield apprentices to the Harper Hall, the time might be sooner than you think," Murenny replied. He turned to Kindan. "And women won't be respected as harpers in hold and crafthall if they're not respected in the Harper Hall."

"Then I must fight him," Kindan declared. The Masterharper glanced at him quizzically. "Not just for Kelsa, or Nonala, but for Verilan and other people who bullies hate for their talents."

"Spoken like a true harper," Murenny said approvingly. "But—"

"What, Master?" Kindan asked, his tone verging on a challenge.

"If you lose . . ."

"I won't lose," Kindan declared.

"If you kill him, it won't be much better," M'tal observed.

Murenny nodded, saying in agreement, "That will only open the door for the next bully or retaliation."

"I won't kill him," Kindan said.

"But he means to kill you," M'tal said.

Kindan let out a long, slow sigh and nodded. "I know."

"Vaxoram has demanded the earliest possible date," the Masterharper said.

"I would prefer that also."

Murenny nodded understandingly. "I have set the date for a sevenday after your wounds have healed."

"Thank you."

"He's larger than you, heavier than you, and has the greater reach," M'tal declared. Kindan turned to him and nodded bleakly. "What can I do to help?" the Weyrleader asked.

"Take me to Mikal." Mikal was a legend at the Harper Hall: the ex-dragonrider who had found himself a home in a natural cave in the hills beyond the Harper Hall, the man who could track anyone across bare rock, who used crystals and meditation to effect healing in ways that not even the Masterhealer fully understood. He was a better swordsman than Master Detallor, himself a master of the blade. When Kindan had last seen Mikal, the man had been at Master Aleesa's camp, tending to the sick Whermaster.

"When?" M'tal asked.

"Now," Kindan replied.

"I've set Menengar and Detallor to keep an eye on Vaxoram," Murenny said. "He's been posted to the infirmary."

"What about Verilan?" Kindan asked, concerned.

"He's in the isolation room," the Masterharper replied. "Vaxoram would have to get past the Masterhealer before he could harm him. And there are guards beyond that."

Kindan nodded but his fears were still not quite relieved. "Someone might try to harm Nonala and Kelsa."

For the first time since the interview started, Master Murenny smiled. "*They're* Verilan's guards."

"What about the fire-lizard eggs?" M'tal asked.

"I will send them up to the Hold," Murenny decided. "Most of them will go to Bemin and his folk." He glanced at Kindan. "You should be able to get to a hatching in ample time."

"Better," M'tal suggested, "assign him up there." Kindan started to protest, but M'tal held up a hand. "For now."

"What about Mikal?"

"When he's ready, I'll come for you," M'tal promised.

"Thank you, Weyrleader," Kindan said, feeling honored.

"I feel partly to blame," M'tal said. "If I'd been a bit quicker, I would have heard him myself."

Kindan furrowed his brow in confusion.

"And then he would have fought *me,*" M'tal explained.

"But you're a dragonrider!" Kindan exclaimed, appalled at the thought of Vaxoram striking the Weyrleader with a sword.

"Which would have given me the right of weapons," M'tal said with a grin. He held up his hands in a fighter's style. "I wouldn't have killed him, but he would feel it for the rest of his Turns."

Kindan grinned back at him, imagining the look of horror on Vaxoram's face as he squared off against the older, stronger, taller, and fiercer dragonrider.

CHAPTER 3

Be sparing with your wrath
Take not the angry path
Lest harsh words create harsh deeds
And fill your heart with bitter seeds.

ALEESA'S WHERHOLD

I hear you let your green go to a girl," Master Aleesa said when Kindan and M'tal arrived at the wherhold two days later.

"Yes, Master," Kindan replied.

"I hear she did good," Aleesa added. "Flew *between* just like a proper dragonrider and saved her father."

"Yes," he agreed, "I was there."

Aleesa stared deep into his eyes before nodding. "You did a good thing."

"Thank you."

"And now you're here to take Mikal?"

"Not unless he wants to go," Kindan replied.

Aleesa glanced beyond him to M'tal, then back. "This dragon-rider says you're here to learn how to fight someone."

"Yes," Kindan agreed.

"Over a girl," Aleesa said.

"No," Kindan corrected, shaking his head. "For women harpers."

"Women harpers?" Aleesa repeated, chortling. "Women harpers," she said again, more softly, shaking her head. "What next?"

"I've met many strong women in my time," M'tal remarked.

"Anything is possible," Kindan said, meeting Aleesa's eyes squarely. "When women harpers become respected, all women will be more respected."

Aleesa mulled this over for a silent moment. Finally, she said, her expression hardening, "You be sure you win."

"Yes, Master," Kindan agreed.

"Mikal!" Aleesa called, turning back to the cave the wherhold-ers inhabited. "Your youngster is here!"

"How is Aleesk, Master?" Kindan asked.

"You can see her tonight," Aleesa replied, turning away from him and retreating slowly into the dark cave. "She'll be awake then, as you should well know."

Kindan remembered how the nocturnal behavior of his watch-wher had driven him to distraction. Aleesa's irritability was mostly fatigue, he guessed—although he'd never heard of her being any-thing other than grouchy.

A silver-haired man met her at the entrance and waved to Kindan.

"Aleesk will send word when we're done," Mikal told M'tal as they got within earshot. The ex-dragonrider eyed Kindan critically, then said, "Are you prepared to get hurt?"

"Yes, sir," Kindan replied.

"And you've brought blades?"

Kindan nodded, indicating the long bundle on his back.

"Good," Mikal said. "Start now with fifty push-ups." He walked over to a rock. "I'll watch from here."

"I just want to learn to fight left-handed," Kindan reminded the older man.

"And I want to see you live through it," Mikal told him, gesturing for Kindan to get on the ground. "Start with those push-ups."

"I'll leave him in your hands, Mikal," M'tal called.

Mikal merely grunted in response, not quite meeting the bronze rider's eyes. M'tal nodded and strode quickly out of sight. Kindan knew that M'tal had carefully landed his Gaminth out of Mikal's sight, just as Mikal had steadfastly remained in the wherhold until the last possible moment; even the sight of a dragon was torment to a man who had lost his own.

"Stop thinking and start working," Mikal growled at Kindan. "You've only a sevenday at best."

Kindan got into a prone position, then, putting all his weight on his arms, lifted up and began the push-ups.

By the end of the day, Kindan nearly wished he were dead. He didn't know which exercise proved the greatest torment, although arguably the worst was running with a heavy rock clenched in each of his outstretched arms.

On the second day, Mikal began fencing with him in earnest.

"We'll start right-handed," the ex-dragonrider informed him, tossing a blade to Kindan and sweeping a blade up for himself. He made a quick salute, then took the en garde position.

"But I already know how to fight right-handed," Kindan grumbled.

"Then show me," Mikal said, lunging suddenly. Caught off guard, Kindan was struck on the shoulder.

By evening, Kindan was a mass of scratches and bruises, even though the padded practice leathers had deflected the worst of the blows.

Kindan spent the first part of the next day learning how to bruise tomatoes.

"You've got to have control of your blade," Mikal had told him, showing him how to lunge and twist in such a way that the ripe tomatoes showed only the slightest of scratches on their surface. By midday, Kindan was covered in tomato juice, much to the amusement of the wherholders.

In the evening, Mikal insisted that Kindan sing or play around the warm coal fire that the wherholders kept inside their quarters.

"Murenny's supposed to send us a harper," Mikal remarked that night, eyeing Kindan consideringly. "But while I'm here they don't need it."

Kindan cocked an eyebrow. The ex-dragonrider was well known at the Harper Hall: He had originally settled into a cave in the hills not far from the Hall, where even the Masterhealer was not above seeking him out for his amazing ability to heal others with herbs and crystals. It was only recently that Mikal had moved from the Harper Hall to Aleesa's wherhold.

"They're afraid I'll leave," Mikal added with a bark of a laugh and a shake of his head. He jerked his head toward the others. "Stand up and sing them the Hold song."

Kindan groaned and almost protested but instead stood up, thinking of Nonala's beautiful voice. He put his sore hands to his side, ignored his aching chest as he filled his lungs and began the long, slow song that named all the Holds, major and minor, the Lord and Lady Holders, and their relative locations throughout Pern.

He went to bed late that night and woke up early the next morning, kicked none too gently by Jaythen.

"Arrows today," the irascible wherman told him. "Mikal says you're to hunt with me."

Kindan's protests died on his lips. He forced himself up and nodded in acceptance. In three more days he would be fighting for his life and his friends, and while he couldn't see what hunting had to do with fighting Vaxoram, he trusted that Mikal had a good reason.

By the end of the day, Jaythen and Kindan had scored two wild-hens and a smallbeast. It was not a great haul, but they had lost none of their arrows, Jaythen insisting that Kindan race after every shot.

Again that evening, sorer and more tired than he'd ever felt, Kindan found himself in front of the wherholders, singing songs and teaching ballads. He practically crawled into his bed that night.

"Up!" Mikal barked into his ear early the next morning. When Kindan rolled over, trying to find his energy, Mikal doused him with a bucket of cold water. "Up—now!"

Then Mikal forced a soaked Kindan out into the cold morning air. "Run until you're dry," he ordered.

Kindan obeyed, and when he returned, his clothes fully dry, he was surprised to realize that he felt better than he'd ever felt before.

"Come with me," Mikal ordered then, hiking a carisak to his shoulder and taking off at a brisk pace. They were far beyond the wherhold by the time he stopped—evidently at a spot that suited him specifically, though Kindan could see no distinction between it and any other place—and ordered, "Close your eyes."

Kindan obliged and felt Mikal roughly tie a strip of cloth over his eyes.

"Now fight me," Mikal ordered, thrusting a practice blade into Kindan's right hand.

"Uh . . ." Kindan began uncertainly. A sharp pain struck him on his left chest.

"Parry," Mikal ordered. Kindan blindly twisted his blade and was surprised to feel it connect with another blade. "And again."

Again and again Kindan parried, then thrust, then probed.

"Stop," Mikal ordered after several minutes. "Listen. What do you hear? Smell. Where are the scents?"

Kindan listened carefully. He heard the few noises of mid-autumn, the soft rushing of a stream, the gentle hissing of leaves in the wind. Then he heard it—the faintest of crunches as Mikal moved forward. He parried and connected. He heard Mikal move away, then nothing. He waited tensely for several moments. Then, from his right side he smelled it—the faintest odor of sweat with a hint of smoke. Kindan wheeled and raised his blade. He connected again.

"Better," Mikal told him. "Now, I'll stop being so easy on you."

The pace increased, the time between decreased. The sounds and the telltale smells of an impending attack grew harder to detect—masked, Kindan guessed, by leaves, flowers, or other greenery. Blows landed on him and he whirled around defensively, only to connect with nothing. He started sweating, his breath became ragged, his nerves flared.

"Stop," Mikal ordered. Kindan stopped. "Rest. You can't win when you're winded."

Kindan was about to protest that he couldn't win when he was blind, either, but stopped as he realized that not only could he win, but that he already *had*. He calmed himself, took several deep, steadying breaths, and listened carefully. He heard the merest of noises, smelled the faintest of smells, then he whirled and connected, hard, with Mikal's blade.

"Better," Mikal said, his voice full of approval. "Now, take your blindfold off and fight me left-handed."

By the end of the day, Mikal had Kindan parrying alternate blows with either hand.

"Tomorrow," Mikal told him as they trudged back to the wherhold, "I'll teach you how to go for the eyes."

"I don't want to blind him," Kindan said, aghast.

"But he wants to kill you," Mikal replied. "Think what you're going to do about that."

All through his dinner and singing, Kindan mulled over the ex-dragonrider's words. Even as he crawled into his bed, he thought them over.

Kindan slept fitfully that night.

———✦———

"No one fights well when they're worried about their eyes," Mikal told Kindan as they started their practice the next morning. "And, as you've seen, it's nearly impossible to fight when blinded."

Kindan could only nod, appalled at the thought of blinding

someone. His friend Nuella was blind, and though she coped with it very well, Kindan knew from first-hand experience—walking through the dark, dust-laden mines just after a cave-in—what that meant to her.

He knew that Vaxoram was bigger, heavier, older, and had the greater reach.

"A person's reaction to a thrust to the head is instinctual," Mikal went on. "They will always parry the blow."

In a quick series of exchanges, Mikal demonstrated this on Kindan. Kindan felt sweat and cold fear running down his back—and he *knew* that Mikal would not hit him.

"Now, I want you to attack my head every third strike," Mikal said.

"But I might hit you!" Kindan protested.

Mikal looked around the practice area he'd chosen. "There are no rocks or holes here," he said. "If you get me within a sword's length of the edge, we'll break. Otherwise, I'll be able to take care of myself." He raised his sword, one of the heavy wooden practice blades they'd been working with. "And this is more likely to give me a black eye than a permanent injury." And with that, Mikal thrust forward, sword raised toward Kindan, giving him the choice of fighting or being hit. Kindan fought.

They continued for two hours, breaking only four times. Once, Kindan nearly landed a blow on Mikal's cheek, just below the left eye. Mikal, on the other hand, landed a solid blow on Kindan's right cheek; Kindan knew that it would be black and blue in the morning.

"Good," Mikal said as he lowered his blade after their last bout. "We'll get some water and food. When we start back, we'll use a dummy."

After a quick bite to eat and a gulp of water, Mikal brought Kindan over to a hastily built figure. It was dressed in Mikal's old clothes, a stick forced into the ground with a crosspiece tied to it at shoulder height representing arms. The clothes were filled out with

old straw, so that the overall effect was that of a scarecrow. However, Mikal had rigged ropes to the "hands" so that he could pivot
the scarecrow around the upright pole. The scarecrow's head was a
gourd with two large holes in it where eyes would be. In the holes
Mikal had placed two ripe tomatoes.

He handed Kindan a steel blade and walked back to grab the
ropes behind the scarecrow.

"Now go for the eyes," he ordered. Kindan lunged, but Mikal
pulled the scarecrow around so that Kindan's stroke hit the side of
the gourd. He pulled his blade free and prepared to strike again.

In twenty minutes he scored ten times, none of them on the
eyes.

"We should take a break," Mikal said.

"No," Kindan replied, his sides heaving, "let's continue."

Again he thrust and missed. And again. And then—"Excellent!"
One of the tomatoes was skewered and remained stuck on the end
of Kindan's blade. Kindan looked at it and his triumphant smile
died on his lips as he grew pale and turned away from one-eyed
scarecrow. He pivoted swiftly and moved his blade just enough to
get it out of the way as he heaved his guts.

Some time later, Mikal handed him a flask of water and Kindan
realized that the ex-dragonrider had dropped his ropes and was
kneeling behind him, gently rubbing his shoulders.

"Drink and spit it out—it'll clear out the aftertaste," Mikal told
him softly. Kindan obeyed, his insides still shaking. After a while,
he felt better. "Are you able to stand?"

Kindan nodded and stood up. He was glad to get away from the
stench of his own vomit. As he stood, he caught sight of his blade
once more, with the tomato neatly skewered at the end. It was just
a tomato.

"Kindan," Mikal called softly. Kindan turned to him. "Now you
understand what you're doing, don't you?"

Kindan nodded mutely.

"And you understand what Vaxoram will do?"

"He'll kill me," Kindan answered. "But that's stupid."

A trace of a smile crossed the old man's lips. "So don't let him." He gestured for Kindan to pick up his blade and return to the exercise.

Gingerly, Kindan retrieved the blade, flicked it so that the tomato flew off, and moved toward the dummy. He noticed that it once more had two tomato eyes.

Mikal moved behind the dummy and grabbed the control ropes once more.

"Now," he called, "go for the eyes!"

They practiced for another three hours, by which time Kindan had exhausted Mikal's store of tomatoes.

"Maybe we should stop," the ex-dragonrider suggested.

Kindan shook his head. "No, I've an idea. Let's see if I can score just below the eye."

"Why?"

"I want to convince Vaxoram that I can have his eyes anytime I want," Kindan replied. "If he understands that, perhaps he'll surrender."

"And if he doesn't?"

"Then he'll lose an eye," Kindan replied staunchly, his stomach in a tight knot.

"And if he doesn't stop then?" Mikal persisted.

Kindan heaved a deep sigh. "Then I'll blind him and leave him fighting his own shadows."

Mikal locked eyes with him over the distance and then nodded in acknowledgment of Kindan's conviction. "If he *knows* that you won't stop, he'll surrender." He tugged on the ropes once more. "Very well, let's begin."

Kindan worked for two more hours, fighting with both his natural right and his newly trained left hand.

As the sun set, Mikal called a halt.

"Tomorrow you'll practice with Jaythen, then Aleesa," Mikal told him.

Kindan looked surprised at his mention of the elderly wherhandler.

"She fights dirty," Mikal told him with a wink.

———✦———

Kindan was just as tired that night, but instead of going to bed exhausted, he found himself led to his quarters by Arella, Aleesa's daughter.

"Strip, and lie down there on your stomach," she ordered, pointing to a raised platform. "Put your head in the hole."

All feeble concerns Kindan had over nudity were completely banished by her next words: "Mikal has asked me to give you a massage."

As with all harpers, Kindan had received some training in healing and so, from that, he already had some training in massage and understood its benefits to not only muscle tone and skeletal alignment but also just peace of mind. His nostrils pricked as he recognized the smell of warmed, scented oil.

The head hole was well padded with furs and let Kindan relax completely on his stomach without tilting his head to one side or the other. He let out a deep sigh as he settled in, aware only of the cold air on his back. That was soon relieved by a soft fur bundled over his butt and legs. The sounds of Arella pouring and rubbing oil on her hands alerted Kindan to the start of the massage. She first got his back well covered with the oil, then started on his muscles, massaging shoulders and neck first, and then moving down to the base of his spine. In moments Kindan was lost in the luxurious feeling of having the kinks in his muscles all worked out.

Kindan awoke on his sixth day at the wherhold to the smell of fresh *klah*. He looked up to see Mikal holding a mug nearby.

"Bathe and then join us," the old ex-dragonrider instructed him.

After a quick—and welcome—bath, Kindan dressed carefully, aware of the parts of his body that were still sore. Outside the wherhold he found Master Aleesa, Jaythen, and Mikal waiting for him. Arella hovered nearby.

"What sort of fighter is Vaxoram?" Aleesa asked as he approached.

"Answer her *now*," Mikal barked.

"Don't think!" Jaythen yelled.

"He likes to overwhelm," Kindan shot back.

Mikal nodded. "Good, then what must you do?"

Kindan started to think, but Jaythen barked at him, "Answer!"

"Talk!" Aleesa added.

"Overwhelm!" Kindan shouted in frustration.

"Good," Mikal said. He smiled at Kindan. "You spoke from your gut, which is the best judge of a fighter's character. Why?"

This time they gave him the time to think through his response. "Because fighters fight from their gut," he said at last.

Mikal nodded.

"So this morning we will practice overwhelming," Mikal told him. "The three of us will try to overwhelm you."

Kindan swallowed hard. Three? How could he fight three at once?

"Not with swords, just with glances," Mikal told him. "You must make us look away, all three."

"How do I do that?" Kindan asked despairingly. "You're all older than I am. And bigger."

"So is your opponent," Mikal replied. "He will be expecting to see you afraid, to see you glance away from him, to see you admit your defeat before he ever raises his blade."

"If you keep your eyes on his, meet his willpower, then *he* will be afraid," Jaythen added.

"It is the test of wills that decides the fight," Aleesa said.

"You must make us back down," Mikal said. "Use your mind, your willpower."

"When you get it, when you use your willpower, we'll feel it and back down," Jaythen added.

"Arella will help," Mikal added, nodding toward the younger wherhandler. "She'll be your coach, shouting encouragement from behind you." He paused a moment. Then: "Ready? Begin!"

Arella put her hands soothingly on Kindan's shoulders and told him, "You can do it, Kindan. You can do it."

Mikal darted toward Kindan, his brows furrowed, an angry look on his face. Beside him, Aleesa and Jaythen also rushed forward, their gazes intent, focused, angry.

"Go on, Kindan, you can do it," Arella's voice sounded in his ear, but he didn't notice it, didn't feel her hands. Instead, he locked eyes with Aleesa, then looked away, frightened by the expression on the tough old woman's face. He glanced to Jaythen and saw the fighter's strength and raw power. He turned his gaze almost imploringly to Mikal, but he knew the old dragonrider had far too much strength for him.

He almost broke down, almost backed away, but then he thought of Nonala and Kelsa.

"You can do it, Kindan," Arella's voice sounded in his ear, her hands kneading his shoulders encouragingly.

I will not lose, he swore to himself. He raised his eyes to Jaythen and locked onto him. Jaythen's age and fierceness melted out of Kindan's sight. He felt his own heart leap, his breath coming in slow deep lungfuls, and he remembered his bond with Kisk, his watch-wher. If he could manage her, he could manage this man. His eyes widened, not in fear but in release of power. And then— Jaythen blinked, looked away.

"Go on, Kindan, you can do it!"

Kindan immediately changed his focus to Mikal. He locked eyes on him. *I will win,* he thought to himself. Again he felt the strength within himself, the support and power of Kelsa and Nonala, and he realized that no matter how old, how skilled Mikal was, he would never win against Kindan because Kindan was supported by so many friends. Mikal's eyes widened, then broke off.

"One more, Kindan, and she's just an old hag!" Arella shouted behind him.

When Kindan turned his attention to Aleesa, she had already lost.

"Such power!" she exclaimed, glancing to Mikal. "Did you expect this?"

"Yes," Mikal responded. "He wants to win." He smiled at Kindan. "Now, we're going to up the stakes. We're going to shout at you, try to defeat you with our voices. You have to shout back and defeat us with yours. If you can defeat the three of us, you'll have no trouble overpowering Vaxoram."

"And you won't have me to help this time," Arella added, taking a step away from him.

Kindan nodded and beckoned for them to begin.

It was much harder this time, with the roar of three voices coming at him, but he never doubted the outcome for an instant. First Mikal, then Aleesa, then Jaythen were all subdued, dropping their eyes from Kindan's stare. Kindan's throat was raw and hoarse, but he was exhilarated, feeling he could fly without even a dragon. He had done it!

"Now it is time to rest and reflect," Mikal told him, his own voice raspy from overuse. "Don't say another word today. Make certain that you have everything you need without using your voice."

Kindan nodded. Suddenly Aleesa, Jaythen, and Mikal rushed forward and sandwiched him in a giant hug. When they finally broke up, Aleesa leaned down and hugged him to her. "I am glad you had a watch-wher: you are worthy."

Kindan nodded in thanks, his eyes bright with tears. At the side, Arella stood, smiling at him.

"You fight well," Jaythen said, hugging him in a tight bear hug that reminded Kindan of his dead father, Danil. "You will win."

Mikal hugged him last. "Remember that you have friends here now. You earned them."

Tears rolled down Kindan's cheeks. He stood for a long moment while the others departed. After a while, realizing that he was alone, Kindan sat down on the grass.

His glance dropped to the soil beside him. He saw the blades of grass, the dark, rich soil, small rocks on the surface and finer grains of dirt. He drew a deep, full breath and exhaled slowly. One pebble caught his eye and he reached for it. It was smooth, rounded, and black. He rolled it between his thumb and forefinger, savoring the sense of the smooth and cool stone.

Stone. Kindan remembered his earlier conversations with Mikal about stones, rocks, and crystals. He recalled that Mikal had decided to stay in the wherhold because he liked the stones and crystals to be found in the area. Kindan knew that crystals had healing powers, and could also be used for meditation, to focus thoughts. Perhaps if he could find the right crystal, he could use its steadying influence in his fight with Vaxoram.

Kindan stood up resolutely. The best place to look for crystals would be in Aleesk's cave; he recalled that from his foray Turns earlier to get his green watch-wher egg. He wondered if watch-whers found crystals as soothing as some humans did. He walked back to the wherhold's entrance and searched inside for a glowbasket. He took one small glow-covered rock and headed toward Aleesk's cave.

It was daytime, so he knew the watch-wher would be sleeping. He walked in as quietly as he could, so as not to disturb her slumber. Holding the dim glow close, he turned to the nearest wall and ran his hands slowly over it.

He felt it before he saw it—a small stone half-buried in the wall. It came out of the wall easily and he held it in his hand. It felt special, full of power. Satisfied, he went out of the room, returned the glow to its basket, and left the wherhold, heading toward the nearby stream.

In the stream he bathed his find and carefully chipped out a small piece of quartz crystal from the main mass. It was just big enough to hold, but it seemed to vibrate with power as he pinched it between his thumb and forefinger. This will be me, he thought to himself, small and powerful.

Intrigued now, Kindan scanned the streambed and the banks looking for any other rock or pebble that called to him. He was not surprised to find a nice sliver of yellow citrine, which he cleaned and pocketed. He had learned from Mikal during one of the ex-dragonrider's days at the Harper Hall that citrine helped to keep one cheerful and manifest goals, just as white quartz was good at manifesting power and concentrating intentions. Armed with these, Kindan felt he could not lose.

He walked slowly back to the camp, pausing to touch the bark of a tree, check for the sign of animals, inhale deeply of the scents on the air, feeling more at peace and focused than he had since he'd first arrived at the Harper Hall over a Turn before.

He could do this. He could meet Vaxoram and win. But his good feelings faded as he realized one thing: He could not blind the older apprentice to win, any more than he could kill him. It wasn't that Kindan didn't believe he had the ability now, nor that he wasn't willing to do either deed if there was no other way—it was that he realized that winning by those means would be a hollow victory, would leave Vaxoram so utterly defeated that the older boy would have no chance to redeem his honor.

Kindan had to find another way.

He spent the rest of the day in an uneasy, thoughtful silence.

He returned to the wherhold that evening and was grateful to be offered his meal in silence. Even the youngsters were quiet, their chattering voices stilled. Kindan felt guilty about that for a moment, then caught the eyes of one of the smaller girls and saw that she was regarding him solemnly, sharing his silence in a kind and compassionate way. He smiled at her and she smiled back, her eyes shining brightly. Then, as though that were too loud, she schooled her expression to be serious and brought a finger to her lips. Kindan nodded. He held her eyes for a long while. She looked away first, toward her mother, and Kindan found himself following her gaze, to her mother's eyes. He continued, wordlessly expressing his gratitude to every member of the small hold. When the meal was complete, Arella led him once more to the massage table and, in silence, massaged his muscles until he fell into a deep, dreamless sleep.

✦

"Kindan," Mikal's soft voice roused him slowly into consciousness.

Kindan opened his eyes.

"This is the seventh day," Mikal said, his tone neutral.

"I'm ready."

"You only think you are," Mikal told him. "You have one more thing to do."

Kindan sat up and looked at the ex-dragonrider expectantly.

"You must discover ten things to live for," Mikal told him quietly. Kindan opened his mouth, but Mikal silenced him with an upraised hand. "First, we will eat."

It seemed that the whole of the wherhold had gathered for breakfast. The children, including the solemn girl of the previous night, were bright-eyed and loud in the way of all children. The adults were also animated, and even sometimes coarse in their language. They laughed frequently; Kindan found himself smiling a lot.

When they finished, Mikal led him off to their practice area and indicated that Kindan should sit.

"Well, what have you discovered so far?" Mikal asked.

"To live for?" Kindan repeated, partly to buy time. Mikal nodded. "I want to live for my fire-lizard egg."

Mikal nodded and held up a finger.

"I want to live for Nonala and Kelsa," Kindan said.

"What does that mean?" Mikal asked.

"I want to protect them," Kindan replied.

"Why?" Mikal pressed.

This is getting harder, Kindan thought as he grappled with the question.

"Because they're my friends," he said out loud.

"You could get other friends—that doesn't sound like a reason," Mikal replied dismissively. "Find another."

"Because I love them!" Kindan blurted out, surprised at his words and the heat of his reaction. All his half-formed dreams of kissing Kelsa, of dancing through the night with her, maybe even of partnering with her, vanished as he absorbed that. He loved them both, equally, and neither of them as a mate. Kelsa and Nonala were special to him because he knew they loved and trusted him; he would do nothing to alter that—he loved them too much.

Mikal stared at him for a long, tense moment, then nodded and held up two more fingers. "What else?"

"For M'tal," Kindan said.

"The Weyrleader?" Mikal repeated. "You want to live for the Weyrleader?"

Kindan frowned. "No, I want to go to Benden, become the Weyr harper."

Mikal held up a fourth finger.

And now Kindan faltered, groping for a fifth reason. What if he couldn't find five reasons to live? What did that say about his life, he wondered.

"I want to live for my father and my brothers," he said after a moment. "To honor their memory."

Mikal held up his fifth finger and waved the other clenched fist in the air. Kindan took in a deep breath and let it out slowly.

"I want to live for you," he said. "I want to live so that you'll know that your training helped and that you are needed and—" He faltered, nibbling his lip for a moment before he added, "—loved."

Mikal's eyes glistened as he held up the first finger on his left hand.

"I want to live for all that I can learn," Kindan said. Another finger. "For all that I can give." Another finger. "For all that I have yet to see." Another finger—he was up to nine. "I want to live for me and what I can offer."

Mikal put up his hands, fingers spread wide. "Now, do you know what you have discovered?" the old man asked slowly.

Kindan nodded slowly. "I've discovered my strength."

"How many reasons does Vaxoram have to live?"

Kindan shook his head. "Maybe one."

"That's right," Mikal agreed. "You have at least nine more reasons to live than he does." He stood up slowly, stretching, and gestured for Kindan to lead the way back to the wherhold. "Are you ready to fight now?"

"Yes," Kindan replied.

"And do you know what you'll do?"

"I'll win."

CHAPTER 4

Fight only in direst need
Not for lust or petty greed
Honor those that do give birth
Respect them well for their full worth.

HARPER HALL

It was only as Kindan felt the last of the cold of *between* seep out of his bones as the great bronze dragon, Gaminth, spiraled on down to the landing meadow outside the Harper Hall that he finally realized how he could win the upcoming fight on his own terms. A fierce smile animated his lips and remained there all the way back through the archway and into the courtyard of the Harper Hall.

"Are you ready, Kindan?" Master Murenny asked as he approached.

"Could I have some time to practice?" Kindan asked. The courtyard was full of harpers except for the large center expanse that was reserved for the upcoming duel. He saw no sign of Vaxo-ram but he wasn't looking for him. Winning was no longer an issue in Kindan's mind. All he wanted was to win without bloodshed.

"How long do you need?"

"Ten minutes will be enough," Kindan replied. "And can I get some green tomatoes? Maybe half a dozen?"

"I'll see if Selora can provide them," Murenny replied, his eyes dancing in anticipation. Selora was happy to provide eight green tomatoes.

"What are you going to do?" Kelsa asked as she brought him the tomatoes.

"Practice," Kindan replied enigmatically. He stepped into the vacant center of the courtyard, beckoning for Kelsa to follow him. "Throw up one of the tomatoes whenever you're ready."

"Toward you?"

"No, just close enough to lunge at," Kindan replied, grabbing his blade in his left hand.

"Kindan, you're not left-handed," Kelsa said in surprise.

Kindan smiled and nodded, flicking his blade at her encouragingly. Kelsa swallowed hard, grabbed one tomato, and threw it up into the air. Kindan lunged, flicking his wrist as he did so, and the tomato landed, unharmed on the ground. Kelsa's eyes grew wider, nervously. Kindan gestured for her to try again. Again she threw, again Kindan flicked and again the tomato reached the ground whole.

"Excellent," Kindan said over the growing hubbub of surprised apprentices. He knew that to them it looked as though he had missed twice, but he didn't care. He had seen what he wanted with the tomatoes: on each he had left a thin scar. Now it was time for Vaxoram to be scared.

"Throw up two at once, please," Kindan said, loud enough to carry over the murmurings. The noise fell immediately. Kelsa pleaded with her eyes, but Kindan merely nodded to her. She threw two tomatoes into the air, unable to control their arcs, and they separated. Kindan lunged twice and both tomatoes fell to the ground—neatly cut in half. Around him the crowd gasped.

"And again," Kindan instructed Kelsa. She looked at him with unmasked surprise and grabbed two more tomatoes. Kindan lunged twice more and severed both tomatoes before they hit the ground.

"One more time," Kindan said, his voice carrying clearly in the silent courtyard.

Eagerly Kelsa threw the tomatoes in the air, their courses diverging far more energetically, but it didn't matter: Kindan lunged toward one, recovered, twisted, and lunged toward the second before it hit the ground. Both were severed.

"I'm done my practice, Masterharper Murenny," Kindan called loudly. He pivoted on one foot to view the whole courtyard, seeking out Vaxoram. He spotted him and stopped, gesturing with his other hand for Kelsa to rejoin the crowd.

"Good luck," she called softly to him.

"Vaxoram!" Kindan shouted loudly, his voice echoing off the walls of the Harper Hall. Vaxoram looked up at him, his blade held loosely at his side. "Do you yield?"

"Hah!" Vaxoram shouted back, tromping into the center of the courtyard.

Masterharper Murenny and Master Detallor strode after him.

"Are you determined to do this?" Murenny asked Kindan and Vaxoram in turn. Each nodded, although Kindan noticed that Vaxoram was swallowing nervously, his eyes wide with fear. Kindan locked onto Vaxoram's eyes until the other glanced away. Kindan kept his eyes on Vaxoram's face, meeting his eyes every time the older boy glanced nervously in his direction. Kindan was certain that Vaxoram had seen the tomato demonstration, just as he was equally certain that Vaxoram thought that Kindan had missed the first two tomatoes.

"Very well," Detallor said. "If that's the case, I shall check your blades." Both Kindan and Vaxoram reversed their blades, proferring the hilts to the Defense Master. This was a mere formality, as both blades belonged to the Harper Hall. Still, in all solemnity, Detallor took Vaxoram's first and examined it carefully before flexing it and handing it back. He repeated the same inspection with Kindan's blade and returned it in the same manner.

Kindan was glad to get his blade back in his left hand, and managed not to smile when he saw Detallor's look of surprise—at least the Defense Master had paid attention. Kindan had counted on Vaxoram not to care which hand Kindan fought with.

Detallor stepped back, his own sword at his side.

"Salute each other," Detallor said.

Vaxoram and Kindan raised their blades in the salute, then lowered them again.

"You may begin," Murenny called loudly.

As expected, Vaxoram charged instantly. Kindan, who had been watching him carefully, waited until the last moment and sidestepped, pivoting around to whack Vaxoram hard with the side of his thin blade. He knew that the blow would at best leave a welt but would probably anger Vaxoram more. He was counting on that.

Vaxoram stopped and turned, eyeing Kindan, who waited for him impassively. Vaxoram started forward slowly, advancing in proper fencing style. When he was near enough to lunge at Kindan, he stopped. Kindan eyed him, waiting. Vaxoram's lunge was telegraphed by the flaring of his nostrils. Kindan beat it aside and jabbed in return into Vaxoram's right shoulder. He heard Vaxoram's hiss of pain, but withdrew quickly and stepped back. Vaxoram retreated as well, his expression a mixture of surprise, fear, and anger.

"Do you yield?" Kindan called.

Vaxoram answered him with an angry growl and charged. Kindan parried and thrust again, but his blade slid off Vaxoram's shoulder. Kindan retreated.

"Running away?" Vaxoram sneered.

Kindan said nothing, locking his eyes once more on Vaxoram's. He was ready again for Vaxoram's lunge, parried once more, but this time in his riposte he raised his blade higher and threatened Vaxoram's face. The older apprentice jerked his head aside.

Kindan stepped back, to his right. Vaxoram stood en garde, eyeing Kindan carefully. The older boy's sides were heaving, but Kindan thought it was from fear rather than breathlessness.

"Did you see what I did to those tomatoes?" Kindan asked. He saw a flicker of curiosity in Vaxoram's eyes. "I can split your eyes just like that." He saw a look of horror creep over Vaxoram's face. The large apprentice charged blindly with a loud yell, but Kindan was ready and sidestepped, turning around to keep his blade pointed at Vaxoram.

Vaxoram stopped uncertainly. It was a moment before he turned to face Kindan. In that moment, Kindan knew that the fight was over, that Vaxoram was looking for a way out, an honorable surrender. And Kindan would give it to him.

He rushed toward the larger apprentice. Vaxoram took a step back, then held his ground, his sword in guard position. When Kindan struck, he beat Vaxoram's blade to the side and curved back across Vaxoram's exposed face—just below the right eyeball, leaving a thin, red welt.

Vaxoram bellowed in pain and horror. He charged, but Kindan was ready; he sidestepped once more, but this time held out a foot, tripping Vaxoram. He whirled around and stood over the fallen lad, his point coming to Vaxoram's throat.

"Yield," Kindan called loudly. He flicked his point up toward Vaxoram's other eye, then back down to Vaxoram's throat. "Do you yield?"

Vaxoram licked his lips, his eyes huge, his heart racing, his Adam's apple wobbling, but he voiced no words.

"I won't kill you," Kindan declared, his eyes locked on the other apprentice's. Vaxoram's eyes narrowed in surprise. "If you don't yield, though, I will blind you." Kindan flicked his point up to Vaxoram's left eye. "Think about that," he said very carefully.

"Think about it and yield." He gestured to Vaxoram's sword, still held in the apprentice's hand. "Throw your blade away," he ordered.

With a slight heave, Vaxoram threw his blade away. It landed not far from him.

"Now yield."

Vaxoram didn't move, his whole being clearly conveying defeat.

Kindan backed away and gestured with his blade. "Get on your knees in front of me and yield yourself to me," he said, using the formal words he'd been taught by Detallor, words he'd never thought to hear spoken for real, let alone utter himself.

Slowly, Vaxoram rolled over onto his knees. As he did, one hand lunged toward his blade, but Kindan saw the motion and, with a flick of his own blade, sent the other flying through the air. He flicked his blade back toward Vaxoram once more, this time with the point resting hard on the top of the other's back just over the left lung.

"Say you yield now," he said, his voice rasping in anger. "Say it loud so everyone can hear, or I'll pop your lung."

"I yield," Vaxoram said softly, flopping face down onto the ground.

"Get up," Kindan ordered, nudging him with the point of his blade. "On your knees."

Vaxoram pushed himself to his knees.

"Yield."

"I yield," Vaxoram said more loudly.

"Say it all," Kindan commanded.

"I yield to Kindan, apprentice of the Harper Hall," Vaxoram said, his voice rising loud enough to carry. "I yield his judgment on my body and I acknowledge forfeit to him."

"What forfeit?" Master Murenny's voice called from the crowd.

"He's to serve me," Kindan called back.

"For how long?"

"Until I release him," Kindan replied.

"Vaxoram, do you forfeit?" Murenny called formally.

"I do," Vaxoram replied, tears streaming from his eyes. He looked up at Kindan. "I forfeit. I will serve you until you release me."

Kindan kept his eyes on the older boy who had just agreed to become his personal drudge. And he was surprised to see a sense of relief in Vaxoram's eyes. The bully had found his place in the Harper Hall—at Kindan's side.

◆

"He's not going to sleep with us, is he?" Nonala spoke quietly into Kindan's ear as she and Kelsa congratulated him on his victory.

Kindan glanced over at Vaxoram who was staring steadily ahead, his eyes dull, his bleak expression marred only by the tracks of tears that had cleared paths through the grime that encrusted his face.

"Yes," Kindan declared at once. "There's a spare bunk nearby."

"But—" Nonala cut herself off as she caught Kindan's set look. "Okay."

"Kindan!" Master Murenny's voice cut through the noise of the massed harpers.

"Master?" Kindan called back, glancing toward the sound of the harper's voice.

"Meet me in my quarters."

"Immediately," Kindan replied. He glanced toward Vaxoram. On impulse, he handed his blade to him. "Clean up the blades, then clean yourself up."

Vaxoram took the blade and hefted it consideringly. Kindan could tell that the older lad was wondering what he could do to Kindan armed with two swords against his none. Kindan shook his head just fractionally and Vaxoram nodded in acquiescence—sword or no, Kindan would win, and Kindan knew that Vaxoram could see it in his eyes.

"Yes, sir," Vaxoram said.

"No, call me harper," Kindan ordered. Vaxoram nodded and started off on his chores, ignoring the sympathetic calls from his former cronies.

———◆———

"Come!" Masterharper Murenny called immediately upon Kindan's knock. Kindan entered the room and was not surprised to see that Master Detallor and Weyrleader M'tal were already present.

"You could have killed him," M'tal said with no preamble.

"That would have not been a good idea," Kindan replied.

"Explain," Murenny said, waving his hand to turn the terse word into an invitation.

"If I had killed him, the rest of the apprentices would have decided that perhaps Vaxoram was right, that there should be no girl apprentices because they caused trouble," Kindan said. Murenny nodded in agreement. "And they might also decide someday that I deserved retribution."

"What will you do with him now?" M'tal asked.

"Can he still take classes?" Kindan said, turning to the Masterharper.

"Certainly."

"Then, in his free time he'll serve me," Kindan replied. "I'll have him do any chores Selora needs, help guard the bath, and make sure that the other apprentices behave themselves."

"Do you trust him with the girls?" M'tal asked Murenny.

"Do you?" Murenny asked, turning the question over to Kindan.

Kindan frowned in thought before nodding. "Yes," he said. "I think that he will be trustworthy. In time he'll realize that if he wants a mate, he'll need to seem appealing to women, and that his good behavior is his only chance to do that."

Murenny nodded.

"I think he has seen the error of his ways," Detallor agreed, his face set in a wry smile.

"We shall keep an eye on him, all the same," Murenny said. Kindan noticed the way the Masterharper regarded him and felt that there was something that remained unspoken.

"I had three older brothers," Kindan said. "I won't treat him badly."

"Good," Murenny said. "Let me know if you need any help."

"I won't need it," Kindan told him. The Masterharper raised an eyebrow in curiosity.

Kindan explained, "Vaxoram lost, fair and square. He won't cause trouble now."

"You seem quite certain," M'tal observed.

"He's acknowledged his loss in front of the whole hall," Kindan said.

"But he tried to attack you again!" M'tal protested.

"I'd be worried if he hadn't," Kindan replied. "Now, he knows for certain that I'll beat him, so he won't try."

"You're saying that now that he knows his place, he won't cause any more trouble?" Murenny suggested.

"Yes," Kindan replied.

Murenny pursed his lips, his eyes half-closed in thought. Finally he looked up at Kindan and nodded. "I think you have a good understanding of his character," he said. He wagged a finger warningly at Kindan as he added, "Make sure you don't forget."

"I won't, Master," Kindan said. Taking the Masterharper's nod for a dismissal, he turned to M'tal. "Thank you for helping me."

M'tal snorted. "Do you think you were the only one I was helping?"

Kindan shook his head. "Thank you for helping my friends, and Vaxoram."

M'tal nodded. "You're welcome."

With a final nod, Kindan left the room. Just after he closed the door, he heard Murenny's voice carrying clearly: "Zist will want to know."

Master Zist had been the harper at Kindan's mining home, and the one who had recommended him to the Harper Hall. Since he had been at the Harper Hall, Kindan had learned that Master Zist was respected by all the Masters, this information usually being relayed in the form of a groaning question, "And you are *sure* that Master Zist recommended you, Kindan?"

———◆———

"Verilan's much better," Kelsa filled Kindan in at lunchtime. "He'll be so disappointed that he didn't get to watch the fight." She cast her eyes toward Vaxoram, who sat at the end of their table, eating distractedly. She glanced over to Kindan, her expression making it plain that she wished he hadn't invited Vaxoram to sit with them. Kindan gave her the merest frown in reply and gestured for her to continue with her story.

"He's still coughing a bit," Nonala said, not missing any of their exchange of expressions. Her glance toward Vaxoram was thoughtful, almost pitying. "But Master Lenner says he'll be released later on today."

"What herbals did he get?" Kindan asked, mentally developing his own list of herbals. At the beginning of his second year at the Harper Hall, Kindan had been offered the chance to become a healer and declined, feeling that he wasn't suited for the duties. He'd meant it when he'd said that he didn't want to be a healer, but he also knew that harpers had to know some healing: They were often called upon to assist the local healer or expected to provide remedies when no healer was available.

As Nonala recited the list in a singsong fashion, Kindan could see Kelsa nodding approvingly and only once frowning, as though she would have ordered the words more melodically. Kindan wondered when "Herbs for Colds" would be sung around the Harper Hall.

"That sounds like 'Minor Green Dragon,'" Vaxoram murmured.

"Pardon?" Nonala asked, turning to him in surprise.

"It's a song I learned," Vaxoram said, looking at her uncomfortably. "It talks about different herbs and what they treat. One de-coction is Minor Green Dragon—it's used for minor colds and coughs."

"Could you sing it to me?" Kelsa asked. Vaxoram started to an-swer, then turned to Kindan.

"Later, maybe," Kindan said. "We've got to get to our classes."

"And me?" Vaxoram asked.

"You, too," Kindan told him. "You're to keep to your standard schedule."

Vaxoram nodded, but Kindan could see that he looked trou-bled.

"You still want to be a harper, don't you?" Kindan asked him.

"But I'm not good enough," Vaxoram protested.

"You are if you say you are," Kelsa snapped at him. "But at least you don't have people saying you can't be a harper because you're a girl."

Vaxoram paled. "You could be a harper," he told her. "I was wrong."

"You're not the only one who thinks I shouldn't be a harper," Kelsa snapped back hotly. She gestured to Nonala. "Nor Nonala."

"But you can sing!" Vaxoram said to Nonala, then turned back to Kelsa. "And you can write songs I only dream of!"

"Keep saying that," Kindan told him. "Keep telling them and anyone you meet. Maybe the others will get it."

Vaxoram closed his mouth suddenly, his lips thin. Kindan got up from his place and walked over to Vaxoram. He leaned close by his ear, groping for the right words.

"We can all help each other here," Kindan said at last. Judging by the twitch of Vaxoram's shoulders, he hadn't made his point. He sighed to himself. Maybe the next time he would figure out a bet-ter way to express himself. "Let's get to our classes."

That evening, Vaxoram joined them for dinner. He ate silently.

As they prepared for bed that night, Vaxoram came over to Kindan with an expectant look on his face. Kindan pointed to an empty bunk.

"You're to sleep there," he said. Vaxoram nodded tersely, and Kindan could tell that the older apprentice was still adjusting to his new position. "The four of us—me, Verilan, Kelsa, and Nonala—are from different years; there's no shame in joining us."

"Another outcast," Vaxoram muttered resignedly, going over to his old bunk and retrieving his chest.

"You're still the senior apprentice," Kindan reminded him.

Vaxoram shook his head. "How can I be? I take orders from you."

Kindan had nothing to say to that. As Vaxoram was arranging his bed, Kelsa came over to Kindan. "Does he really have to sleep with us?"

"Yes," Kindan said. "Unless you want me to move."

"No," Kelsa replied hastily, shaking her head in emphasis. "It's just that—"

"He serves me; he needs to be near me," Kindan told her, his face set. "If that's a problem for you, we can move, or you can move."

"You'd better be right," Kelsa snapped. She stomped off, casting angry glances in his direction until she finally climbed into her bunk.

Kindan settled into his bed not much later, then crawled out to turn out the glows.

"I can do that," Vaxoram said from behind him. Kindan started to protest, then stopped himself and nodded. Turning out the glows was, after all, the duty of the senior apprentice.

"Thanks," Kindan said when he'd finished.

"Glows over," Vaxoram called loudly to the rest of the room. Scurrying noises showed that he was obeyed.

Kindan settled into his bunk, reviewing all the amazing events of the day and realizing with a shiver that had things gone differently, he would have been dead.

He drifted slowly off to sleep, considering all the ramifications of his actions and trying to imagine the future. He was startled awake suddenly by the one thing he hadn't counted on: Vaxoram snored.

———◆———

The next issue occurred after their run next morning, as Kelsa and Nonala cast concerned glances between Kindan and the bath room, clearly asking him what he intended to do about the bathing situation. Vaxoram, however, had an answer, rousting out the remaining laggards and handing out large fluffy towels to the four of them. Kindan kept a smile to himself as he reflected that in most ways Vaxoram was still a bully—just *his* bully.

"He's not bathing with us, is he?" Nonala hissed worriedly toward Kindan. Vaxoram stiffened, but he continued on his journey into the bath room with them. Inside, he pulled another set of towels off his shoulder and hung them lengthwise between the front and back rows of baths.

Kindan understood at once.

"An excellent idea," he told the older apprentice. Vaxoram gave him the faintest of grins that vanished before Kindan could reciprocate.

"The girls are getting too old for us not to respect their privacy," Vaxoram said. He glanced at Kindan and Verilan. "And so are you."

"But we like talking when we're in the baths!" Kelsa complained from the far side of the towel partition.

"You can pull them down when everyone's in their bath," Vaxoram replied. "And when you're ready to get out, let us know and we'll look away while you wrap yourself in your towel."

"That's no fun," Nonala protested.

"But he's right," Kelsa said. "We are getting older."

———◆———

Kindan was surprised to see Vaxoram interrupt his last class of the day, Archiving with Master Resler. He thought perhaps that Vaxoram had misunderstood, but instead of approaching him, Vaxoram went directly to the Master and spoke quickly, pointing at Kindan.

"Kindan, you're excused," Resler called. "You're to go up to the Hold—the eggs are hatching." Kindan started to put away his work, as Master Resler was known for his fastidiousness.

"I'll get that," Vaxoram said, rushing to Kindan's side.

"Meet me up there," Kindan replied, scuttling out of the Archive Room.

Outside, in the Harper Hall courtyard, Kindan broke into a slow, steady trot. He and the other apprentices made the kilometer run every morning, so he was used to it, but he paced himself now, so that he'd arrive ready for anything. As he ran, he tried to recall everything that he knew about the clutch of fire-lizard eggs. M'tal had said that the eggs were actually the combination of two finds, that some might hatch before the others but that he was pretty certain that there would not be more than two days between the first and last hatching.

Of the seven eggs, only two were marked for the Harper Hall, his and one other. Kindan had heard that the second was to go to Issak, one of the younger journeyman harpers. Tenelin, the senior journeyman at the Harper Hall, had already had a chance and had failed to Impress his fire-lizard. Kindan had been surprised to hear that, as Tenelin had always struck him as a kind, considerate individual. But sometimes, Kindan reflected with growing unease, that wasn't enough for a fire-lizard. Certainly it wasn't enough on its own to Impress a dragon.

The rising slope slowed him down only a little and soon he was under the great arches of Fort Hold and sprinting into the courtyard proper, heading for the huge doors that opened into Fort's Great Hall.

"The fire-lizard eggs, where are they?" Kindan called to one of the guards as he sped past.

"You'd better hurry," the guard replied, gesturing to the far end of the hall, "they're in the kitchen."

Kindan increased his pace to a full run, his breath now coming in gasps and his sides aching with effort.

Kindan had no sooner entered Fort's huge kitchen, a room nearly three times the size of the Harper Hall's, when Issak's voice called out, "Come on, Kindan, they're hatching! One's already gone *between*."

Unless immediately fed—stuffed senseless, in fact—a fire-lizard would go *between* in search of food on its own, which meant that it would go wild and never be Impressed.

Kindan raced over to the hearth and took in the scene: there were several young men, Issak, and a girl somewhat older than Kindan. At that very instant, the egg nearest her burst open and a beautiful golden queen fire-lizard emerged, creeling with fear and hunger.

"Feed it," Issak shouted, thrusting a bowl of scraps toward the girl.

But the girl did nothing, her eyes only on the gold fire-lizard, wide with both fear and amazement. In that instant, Kindan fell in love.

"Koriana!" An older woman's voice called. Kindan turned to follow the voice and saw an older version of the girl, dressed all in finery—Lady Sannora, Fort's Lady Holder.

Kindan dropped to the girl's side, grabbed the bowl of scraps, and pulled one out of it. He thrust the wet bit of meat into one of the girl's limp hands.

"You must feed her," he said. "Feed her and make her come to you."

Koriana jerked at his words and looked down to the piece of meat in her hand. Kindan put his hand over her forearm and guided it forward to the mouth of the fire-lizard. The little queen saw the meat and pounced, gobbling it down. Kindan grabbed another piece with his free hand and put it in Koriana's hand, drawing it back slightly toward her lap.

"Kindan!" Issak called. "The other eggs, you need to pick one!"

"You said one had gone already," Kindan protested.

"That was mine," one of the Lord Holder's sons declared. He gestured to Kindan. "You should have a chance. After all, you seem to have brought us luck, for Koriana at the very least."

Kindan continued to pass scraps to Koriana, leaning so close that he could smell the fresh scent of her hair, the warmth of her trembling body. Her hair was honey blond and her eyes a brilliant blue. A smattering of freckles showed on her arms and Kindan guessed that she also had some on her face. She was breathing raggedly.

"Calm down, it'll be all right," Kindan told her soothingly. "You're doing fine. Just feed her and have her come to you. You want her in your lap. Then feed her until she falls asleep."

Kindan started to move but Koriana made a terrified sound and grabbed at him.

A figure came from around behind him. It was Vaxoram. He looked over at the rocking eggs and back to Kindan.

"Which one?" he asked Kindan. For a moment all eyes were on Kindan. He pointed to a brownish egg and Vaxoram retrieved it, bringing it and some warm sand close to Kindan, then he retreated silently.

Lady Sannora frowned as she noticed the raw, red scar under Vaxoram's right eye and turned to scrutinize Kindan with a tight expression that Kindan didn't see.

"Keep feeding her," Kindan instructed Koriana, leaning back now a little from the intoxicating closeness of her.

In front of him, the brownish shell rocked hard and cracked. Kindan tensed, grabbed a handful of scraps with his other hand, and held it above the shell. In a moment a head emerged and creeled. Kindan fed it a scrap. The fire-lizard hatchling shook its egg and burst it still further, reaching for the next scrap. Kindan fed it, then pulled his hand back.

"Come on," he called soothingly. "There's plenty here. You can have it all, come on."

The hatchling burst out of its egg and took an awkward step toward Kindan and another scrap of food.

Beside him, Kindan heard Koriana speak in imitation, "Come on, you beauty, have another."

"Come on," Kindan said. He was surprised to see that his fire-lizard was bronze. He'd thought he'd picked a brown. "Oh, you're such a pretty one, aren't you?" he murmured encouragingly. "You're so clever, too! Come on, come a little closer."

"Come on, my beauty, come closer," Koriana cooed. Kindan glanced at her long enough to grin and was rewarded with the most beautiful smile he'd ever seen. It was with an effort that he turned back to his fire-lizard.

It took only a few more minutes to get his fire-lizard perched in his lap, stuffed with scraps. Beside him, Koriana's gold had found her way into *her* lap also and had curled up, fast asleep.

"What do I do now?" Koriana murmured fearfully to Kindan.

"Stroke her," he told her. "Stay with her while she sleeps. Feed her when she wakes up."

He looked down to his own fire-lizard and stroked the bronze beauty softly. Soon the miniature dragon had also curled up comfortably and, with a final shiver of abandon, fallen asleep. He turned back to Koriana, still oblivious to the others. "What are you going to name her?"

Koriana's lips tightened into a frown as she thought. "Koriss," she said finally. "She shall be Koriss." She looked at Kindan and his heart leapt as she smiled and asked, "And yours?"

"Valla." The name seemed right the moment he said it.

Two eggs remained unhatched and unmoving.

"M'tal said that there were two different clutches," Kindan announced when he noted Lord Bemin and his Lady Sannora exchange concerned looks.

"But when will we know that they're hatching?" Lord Bemin asked.

"M'tal said that they should hatch within two days of each other," Kindan replied.

Lord Bemin looked relieved. He glanced at Kindan with his bronze fire-lizard in his lap and then at Koriana with her gold fire-lizard. A frown crossed his face as he noticed how closely the harper was seated to his eldest daughter.

"Could you stay here tonight?" Lady Sannora asked Kindan. "I'll send word to the Hall—"

"I could go," Vaxoram offered.

"Could you?" Lady Sannora asked, her face brightening with relief. Vaxoram glanced at Kindan, asking, "Is that all right?"

"Certainly," Kindan replied. "I'll be back in the morning."

"You'd trust me on my own?" Vaxoram asked with just a hint of surprise in his tone.

Kindan turned his head and probingly locked eyes with Vaxoram for a long moment before nodding.

"Go carefully, the roads can get slick at this time of night," Issak advised. Vaxoram nodded, bowed to Lord Bemin and Lady Sannora, then left swiftly.

"That boy!" Lady Sannora exclaimed to her husband. "Did you see the scar under his eye?"

"He was fighting," Lord Bemin replied, turning his head to eye Kindan thoughtfully. "There was a duel. He lost."

"I don't approve of duels," Lady Sannora pronounced, her face set in a grimace. "What overmuscled cretin picked a fight with him?"

Lord Bemin raised an eyebrow in Kindan's direction.

"I did," Kindan said, meeting the Lord's and Lady's outraged looks steadily, though he felt the heat in his cheeks. "He had threatened to use his strength over a woman," he explained. With a shrug, he added, "Several women, actually."

"Why didn't you kill him?" Bemin's eldest son, Semin, demanded.

"Because, my lord," Kindan replied, "I believe in second chances."

Semin was surprised at Kindan's response.

"And because it would have done more harm than good," Issak chimed in from the other side. He inclined his head toward Kindan. "Master Murenny recounted your thinking to me."

Was there a hint of respect in the journeyman's eyes?

"Well!" Lady Sannora said in surprise.

"Well," Lord Bemin agreed, "we have offered our hospitality for the night; please do not hesitate to ask for anything you need."

"Thank you, my lord," Kindan replied, fully aware of the emphasis the Lord Holder had placed on "the night"—and the implication that Kindan was expected to leave in the morning.

Koriana had listened to the exchange through half-lidded eyes as though drowsing, but Kindan had noticed that she had opened them once or twice with such haste that he wondered if she hadn't been feigning her fatigue. Now she spoke up. "Father, could you have pillows and blankets brought to us?"

"Us?" Lady Sannora repeated in surprise.

"I don't want to disturb Koriss," Koriana said, bending her head toward the fire-lizard sleeping in her lap. "And I might need help if she wakes in the night. I'm sure Issak and"—here Kindan felt her eyes upon him—"Kindan will keep me company."

"Of course," Issak declared instantly, flicking a half-wink toward Kindan. Kindan, wisely, said nothing.

"Very well," Bemin agreed, although he had a hard time veiling an uneasy glance in Kindan's direction. He signaled the hearth drudge to comply with Koriana's request. Once another drudge was dispatched for the requisite sleeping gear, the hearth drudge returned to her task of carefully banking the kitchen's great fire. Issak, Kindan, and Koriana arranged themselves comfortably when the blankets and pillows arrived.

"Good night then," Sannora called from the entranceway as the last of the glows were turned.

"Good night, Mother," Koriana called sleepily over her shoulder and curled her body around her gold fire-lizard. Kindan emulated her in the same direction so that they looked like a large pair of Cs shielding small fire-lizard dots.

"Good night, my lady," Issak said formally.

"Sleep peacefully, my lady," Kindan said.

After a moment the last of the footsteps dwindled into silence and they were left with the crackle of the coal fire, the smell of smoke, warm scraps, and scented pillows. Just before he dozed off, Kindan thought he detected the faintest smell of Koriana's hair.

He woke much later in the middle of the night and turned quickly to see Koriana staring at him.

"She's up, what do I do?" the girl whispered frantically.

"Feed her, soothe her, get her back to sleep," Kindan replied softly, groping for and pushing a bowl of scraps her way. He examined the belly of his bronze fire-lizard carefully but Valla made no motions toward wakefulness.

"Help me," Koriana whispered in despair. Kindan rolled over, carefully rolling Valla into his lap, and turned around to face Koriana. He passed her scraps that she fed her fire-lizard until, finally, the hungry gold's eyes slowly faded in the firelight as she fell back to sleep. Kindan watched Koriana for a moment more. He was surprised when the girl reached out and grabbed his hand, clasping it with hers.

"Thank you," she said.

Kindan nodded. Very carefully, he stretched himself out, still facing her, and rolled over, depositing Valla in the center of a bundle of blankets. Reaching behind him, he pulled another blanket over himself.

Koriana followed suit, but being taller than Kindan, she had trouble getting her blanket to cover her. In moments she was shivering. Kindan raised a finger to his lips to caution her to silence, then reached further over his shoulder and pulled more blanket over himself and on top of her. Koriana smiled gratefully at him and then snuggled closer, so close that their two fire-lizards were almost touching. Koriana leaned forward, her head resting lightly against his. Her knees brushed his. In moments she was asleep.

Kindan did not fall asleep until much later.

◆

"Kindan!" a voice spoke urgently in his ear, rousing him. "Kindan, get up, now! The other eggs are hatching, the Lord and Lady are on their way." It was Vaxoram.

Kindan sat up slowly, remembering his charge, then looked down at Koriana who was still sleeping peacefully, her fire-lizard half-clutched in her hands.

"If they see you like this . . ." Vaxoram said, shaking his head. "You can't think that they'll accept a harper for her!"

"No!" Kindan said, looking at Vaxoram in surprise. "It's not like that." But Kindan wondered to himself, what would it be like to wake up to such a peaceful sight every day?

"Check the eggs," Issak ordered from the other side of the hearth. "And get some distance, muss up those pillows and blankets."

Vaxoram jumped in with a will, ignoring Kindan's protests for quiet.

"You don't want to upset the Lord Holder," Vaxoram told him. Kindan sensed that the older apprentice was talking from some past experience, but he had no time to ask more.

The remaining two eggs were rocking.

"Come quickly, the eggs are hatching!" Issak called, cradling his fire-lizard in the crook of one arm and rushing to the kitchen's entrance.

"What's up?" Koriana asked muzzily as the noise roused her.

"The other eggs are hatching," Kindan told her. "Be sure to feed yours if she wakes."

Koriana nodded, then looked around. She glanced at the pillows and blankets spread about her, then at Kindan, her eyes intent and mouth open, but before she could say anything, her mother, father, and two older brothers strode into the room.

"They're hatching?" Semin asked, glancing toward the hearth.

"Yes," Kindan said.

"Sit down close by and grab some scraps," Issak said, gesturing toward the ground close to the rocking eggs.

"Bannor, come on!" Semin called, gesturing for his younger brother to follow him. "We can't let Koriana be the only one of us with a fire-lizard!"

Bannor laughed as he strode into the room. "No, indeed we can't, little sister."

Koriana waved groggily at him, then angrily as the motion disturbed her queen.

"If you wake her—"

"Perhaps you should go to another room?" Lady Sannora suggested, not quite glancing toward Kindan. It was clear that Lady Sannora was unhappy with the thought that Koriana had spent the night in his presence.

Koriana noticed the glance and smiled back at her mother. "And have a chance to miss my sibs' triumph? Oh, no, Mother, I must be here for every moment!"

Was the girl deliberately trying to goad her mother, Kindan wondered.

"Well," Lady Sannora said consideringly, regrouping her thoughts, "perhaps the harpers would prefer to return to their hall."

"We are at your service, my lady," Issak replied with a carefully choreographed bow that managed to keep his fire-lizard level throughout.

"Keep the lucky one here," Semin said, indicating Kindan. "The others can go."

"We could help," Issak suggested. Vaxoram nodded mutely. Kindan couldn't tell if the older boy was more interested in the spectacle of Impression or in fulfilling his duty to Kindan. Or perhaps he wanted to watch Kindan's growing discomfiture in the presence of both Koriana and her mother.

"I'm hungry," Koriana said. "I'm sure the others are, too."

"Indeed," Lady Sannora agreed drily. She started to say something more but caught herself and instead nodded to the harpers. "Pardon me, I'm forgetting my manners in all the excitement. I'll have someone bring you *klah* and rolls."

"It is a hectic time for all of us," Issak said, nodding politely. "No apologies are necessary, my lady."

Lady Sannora nodded graciously but cast a cold look toward her daughter. Koriana merely smiled back.

Kindan thought that Koriana was playing a dangerous game, goading her mother so. He realized that the tensions between the two were long-standing but felt that somehow his presence had exacerbated them.

But the two remaining eggs were now clearly hatching, so he put his thoughts on hold.

"What should we do?" Bannor asked, looking to Issak, then Kindan, then Koriana in desperation.

"Don't panic," Koriana told him sternly. "Just stuff its face full of scraps and talk soothingly."

"Tell him you love him," Issak added, looking down fondly at the brown still sleeping serenely in the crook of his arm.

"What if it's a green?" Bannor asked worriedly.

"Then tell *her*," Semin answered with a disgusted look, adding snidely, "Though why you would want a green . . ."

Kindan glanced at Bannor, wondering if the younger holder was hoping for a green. Gold and green fire-lizards were female, just like gold and green dragons . . . or watch-whers.

"You can't be certain from the size or color of the egg," Kindan said suddenly. "Nor from past experience," he added as he noticed both older lads looking at him expectantly. "I impressed a green watch-wher, and now I have a bronze fire-lizard."

"Forsk is green," Bannor said, glancing toward the kitchen entrance. "Forsk is bound to Father."

Ah, so it wasn't a question of preferences, Kindan thought to himself. Perhaps it was jealousy. Perhaps Bemin's sons envied their father his bond with the watch-wher. Clearly from the number of his offspring, there was no question of Bemin's virility. The knowledge that Fort's Lord Holder was bonded to a green watch-wher eased some of Kindan's unconscious worries about himself and his prior acquaintance with a watch-wher.

"It's cracking!" Koriana shouted, raising one arm to point at the egg nearest Bannor. "Feed it, feed it!"

"You'd best feed yours," Kindan told her calmly, noting that the noise had disturbed the queen.

"It's a bronze!" Bannor exclaimed. "Oh, you great beauty, you!" He started to feed the creeling fire-lizard scraps from his hand. But before the fire-lizard had stepped more than twice from its shell, Kindan's Valla had woken up and chirped questioningly.

Suddenly Koriss hissed loudly, her voice warbling in a horrible noise and the little newly hatched fire-lizard gave one terrified squawk and went *between*.

"She scared it!" Bannor cried, pointing a finger at the gold. "She scared it away!"

"No, she didn't," Koriana protested hotly, grasping the gold tightly in her hands. "She was scared and she cried out."

"She scared it away," Bannor persisted, his tone both bereaved and outraged. "And now I won't have one."

Semin's egg cracked at that moment and Bannor turned toward it. "Let me have yours, Semin."

Semin saw the look of longing in his younger brother's eyes and was startled, caught between acquiescing and taking the fire-lizard himself. The hatchling squawked hungrily.

"Feed it," Kindan urged.

But Koriss squawked again peremptorily before the little brown had even emerged from its shell and, with a horrified yelp, the little brown went *between*.

"Oh, no! Now look what you've done!" Bannor exclaimed angrily to his brother. "You should have given him to me, you oaf." He turned toward Lady Sannora. "Mother, I want a fire-lizard." He gestured toward Kindan and Issak. "Make them give me theirs."

"It doesn't work that way, Bannor," Koriana told him heatedly. "And how *dare* you say such a thing? Call yourself a Holder's son?"

"Mother!" Bannor complained, turning back to his mother.

"Koriana, really!" Lady Sannora cried, wringing her hands. "Your brother has had a trying time here, at least you could be sympathetic."

But Koriana looked like the last thing she wanted to be was sympathetic.

Issak stirred and asked Kindan, "Have you ever heard of such an occurance before?"

"No," Kindan replied, surprised that the journeyman would ask his opinion.

"Nor have I," Issak said. He turned to Lady Sannora. "My lady, if it pleases you, we will report this sad affair to the Masterharper. Perhaps he has some suggestions that would help in the future."

"Yes, yes," Lady Sannora said hastily as she crossed toward the distraught Bannor. "That sounds like an excellent suggestion."

"But I still don't know what to do with my fire-lizard," Koriana protested, glancing pleadingly at Kindan.

"For the time being, just feed her," Kindan replied. "And oil any patchy skin, just like the watch-wher."

"You're the one who had a watch-wher?" Lady Sannora asked, turning suddenly back toward Kindan. "And you gave her to that blind girl who saved her father?"

"She's not blind, not really," Kindan said. "But that's about the gist of it, yes, my lady."

"You must have been very sad," Koriana said, looking at Kindan with renewed interest.

"Or very stupid," Bannor snapped, glancing sulkily at his mother.

"Perhaps both," Kindan agreed, not letting the Holder's middle child upset him. Koriana rewarded him with an impish grin, quickly hidden from her mother.

"My lady," Issak prompted, "with your leave . . ."

"Oh, do!" Lady Sannora assented, waving her hand and turning her attention solely toward Bannor. "We'll send a messenger if we need anything."

"We could use the drums," Semin suggested.

"We'll send a messenger," Lady Sannora repeated in a tone that brooked no argument.

Issak nodded, again not jostling his fire-lizard. "As you wish."

And with that, he signaled Kindan and Vaxoram to follow him as he led the way out of the kitchen, through Fort's Great Hall, and down toward the Harper Hall.

Kindan had much to think about on the journey.

Nothing was said until they were once more under the arches of the Harper Hall.

"You two go to your classes," Issak instructed. "I'll report to the Masterharper."

"Valla is getting hungry," Kindan said.

Issak nodded in understanding. "By all means feed him whenever he wants," he responded. "We don't need to perpetuate the tragedy of today."

Kindan said nothing but Vaxoram snickered. Issak raised an eyebrow in inquiry of the older apprentice.

"It wasn't us and you know it," Vaxoram replied. "It's that spoiled Bannor and his airs." He glanced toward Kindan. "And don't be too certain his sister is any better."

Kindan bristled.

"It doesn't matter," Issak told him, holding out a placating hand. "You're not a Lord Holder candidate, and Lord Bemin will trade his daughter to his advantage."

"Trade?" Kindan repeated in outrage.

"She'll go willingly, when the time comes," Issak said to cool Kindan's anger.

"It's for the good of the Hold," Vaxoram added, gloating over Kindan's outburst. "You must understand, you're a harper."

"And harpers aren't good enough?" Kindan demanded.

"Not for Lord Holders," Issak agreed with a sad shake of his head. He said to Vaxoram, "Help him to understand."

Vaxoram sighed and nodded, his gleeful mood subsiding. He gave Kindan a look that was almost sympathetic, then told Issak, "I'll tell him while we feed his fire-lizard."

Issak smiled and strode off, calling back with a finger pointed at the fire-lizard, "Don't forget to show him off, as well!"

Guided by Vaxoram, Kindan and Valla entered the kitchen and found Selora bustling about, overseeing several drudges as they prepared the day's meals.

"Kindan's Impressed a bronze," Vaxoram declared as they entered. "Just last night, a real beauty."

Kindan was surprised at the pride in Vaxoram's voice.

"He would," Selora agreed heartily, peering down to the small figure nestled in Kindan's crossed arms. The little fire-lizard yawned and looked up sleepily at Selora. "He'll be hungry in a moment," she declared, kicking a stool nearer to the hearth. "Sit down and I'll get him some scraps."

"A strange thing happened, Selora," Vaxoram continued as Kindan sat down, too lost in concentration on Valla to speak, "Koriana's little fire-lizard—"

"Koriss," Kindan interjected suddenly.

"—Koriss," Vaxoram agreed with a playful smile, "frightened off the two hatchlings that came to her brothers."

"Males, were they?" Selora asked, cocking her head shrewdly.

"Yes," Kindan agreed, his eyes narrowing. "How did you know?"

"She frightened them away on purpose," Selora said. "Didn't want her siblings paired with her mistress's siblings."

"Why?" Kindan asked in confusion.

Selora started to reply but had a coughing fit instead. "You'll find out in time, I've no doubt," she said, a grin spreading across her face. She pushed more scraps toward Kindan. "Be sure to stuff him good, they don't like being moved much in the first sevenday."

Hastily Kindan complied, fearful of losing his beautiful fire-lizard.

"Did you know, Selora," Vaxoram continued conversationally, "when the two fire-lizards were frightened away, Bannor demanded that Issak or Kindan give up theirs?"

"Oh, he would," Selora declared, throwing up her hands in disgust. "Just like his father, that one."

———◆———

The next two sevendays passed in a blur for Kindan, who felt that he spent all his waking hours feeding or oiling Valla, despite all the help he had from Verilan, Kelsa, Nonala and, most of all, Vaxoram.

Somewhere in that time Vaxoram moved from being a brooding, vanquished opponent to being truly dedicated to Kindan. Kindan could never point to the exact moment nor quite understand why, but there it was.

"He's changed," Nonala remarked one evening. Kindan glanced at her and she corrected herself, speaking directly to Vaxoram, "You've changed."

Vaxoram grunted in surprise, then nodded in agreement.

"But why, though?" Kelsa wondered later when she was alone with Kindan, helping him oil Valla's patchy skin. "Why has he changed?"

Kindan thought for a moment. "Master Murenny said that Vaxoram had come to the Harper Hall with a great voice as a child. When it broke wrong, he couldn't find any new talent to replace it. He came from a small hold, Master Murenny said."

"So he was afraid," Kelsa guessed, nodding sagely. "And now he's got something to do, guarding you."

"Maybe," Kindan agreed. Kelsa cocked her head at him questioningly. "Maybe there's more to it. Perhaps because the worst has happened to him, he's realized that he has nothing to be scared of."

"Maybe," Kelsa replied, but she didn't sound convinced. She changed the topic. "What about this girl?"

"What girl?" Kindan asked innocently.

"The holder girl who impressed the gold, Kindan," Kelsa responded tetchily.

"Who told you about her?" Kindan demanded. "Vaxoram?"

Kelsa shook her head. "This is a harper hall, news travels, silly."

"Does everyone know?"

"Yes, everyone," Kelsa replied with a wave of her hand to include the whole Harper Hall. "So what about it? Are the rumors true?"

"I haven't heard the rumors," Kindan returned heatedly, "so I can't say."

"The rumors are that you and she were all sparks together, that her fire-lizard scared any other suitors away, that she pines for you every night, and that her evil mother and father won't let her see you no matter what she says."

Kindan rolled his eyes in disgust. "The trouble with rumors is that they're mostly wrong," he declared.

"Mostly?" Kelsa pounced. "What's right about them, then?"

"Kelsa," Kindan growled warningly.

"Oh, Kindan, come on," she pleaded, making big eyes back at him and looking pitiful. "You can tell *me*."

"There's nothing to tell," Kindan said. "It's true that the other fire-lizards were frightened *between* and it may be that Koriss did it. Koriana was upset and her brother demanded that Issak or I give him our fire-lizards—"

"The brat!" Kelsa interjected.

"And I don't think Lady Sannora likes me very much," Kindan finished lamely.

"She doesn't like harpers, you mean," Kelsa corrected him.

Kindan glanced at her in surprise.

"Rumor has it," Kelsa told him excitedly, "that she fell in love with a harper when she was younger but he spurned her."

"Which harper?" Kindan demanded. He'd never heard such a rumor.

"Isn't it obvious?" Kelsa asked him, shaking her head at his obtuseness. "Why do you think Lord Bemin never visits?"

Kindan thought about that for a moment. "Not . . . Master Murenny?"

Kelsa nodded approvingly. "Right the first time." She patted his arm condescendingly. "You'll make a harper yet."

CHAPTER 5

Harper, treat your words with care
For they may cause joy or despair
Sing your songs of health and love
Of dragons flaming from above.

HARPER HALL,
AL 496.11

It seemed to Kindan at the start of his third year at the Harper Hall that everything went wrong. He blamed it on the food at first. If they hadn't fed him so well, he wouldn't have grown so quickly.

If he hadn't grown so quickly he wouldn't have been moving so awkwardly, nor, come to think of it, having to beg for new clothes so frequently. If he didn't move so awkwardly he wouldn't be knocking over everything in his path. If he hadn't outgrown his clothes so quickly, he wouldn't have found himself in oversized clothes—"with room to grow in, you'll need that"—which exacerbated his awkwardness by making it hard to find the ends of things, like sleeves.

If there was an accident waiting to happen in the Harper Hall it only needed Kindan's presence to complete it. It wasn't his fault that he couldn't see the latest stock of dyes as he blundered through the Archive room overladen with Records. Someone else, it was admitted later, shouldn't have placed them there. But, miraculously, it *was* his fault that he tumbled over them, breaking the dyes all over the newer Records and rendering so many permanently illegible.

"You're to work with the instrument maker, Kindan," Master Resler said. He sighed as he retrieved and classified the last of the legible Records.

———◆———

"Just because you're now taller than me doesn't mean I can't handle you," Caldazon grumbled in warning the moment Kindan presented himself to the small instrument maker.

"You duck your head and don't knock any of the woods that are curing above you," Caldazon continued, pointing to the various lumps of wood hanging down from the cavernous instrument maker's room.

"Of course, Master," Kindan replied, bobbing his head—and accidentally bumping it against a stout beam of wood when he straightened.

Caldazon wheezed a dry laugh. "Maybe the wood'll knock some sense into you."

Kindan certainly hoped so, particularly as the days went by. He worked with the other apprentices and made a passable drum, but he'd been making those Turns before he'd left Camp Natalon to become a harper. He had less luck with pipes—the spacing of his holes made them awkward to play.

"A waste of wood, that," Caldazon grumbled, tossing Kindan's first effort onto the scrapheap. "Luckily it's bamboo; the stuff grows like crazy down Boll way."

Kindan knew that until he could master the making of pipes,

he'd never be allowed to use the precious wood required to make a guitar. Still, he showed a skill at sanding and polishing.

"Those big muscles of yours are good for something," Caldazon opined, assigning all the sanding to Kindan. Kindan didn't grumble—he knew better—but he went to bed with sore shoulders every night for two sevendays.

Even so, he was learning and he knew it. By sanding the work of others, Kindan started to get a feel for the wood and how to work it.

"You're to help make glue and polish today," Caldazon barked at him one morning not long after. As he made to leave, he added, "And be certain you don't confuse the two."

It was as though the Master's words were a prophecy. The light in the room was not the best, even though Kindan had brought in extra glows, and—he could never figure it out—he somehow managed to mix the wrong ingredients into both mixtures.

"This is not glue!" Caldazon swore when he examined the bubbling pot after lunch. He turned to the pot that was supposed to contain finish and found that he couldn't even lift the spoon. "And this! This has hardened! Whatever it is, it's ruined now."

He glared at Kindan, who hung his head.

"I guess I got muddled," Kindan explained. "The light was—"

"It wasn't the light," Caldazon broke in. He pulled the first pot off the heat and gestured to the second pot. "You'll clean this one out first, and mind you don't damage the surface or the pot'll be useless forever. When you're done, you can find someplace to empty *that*"—he jerked his thumb to the other pot—"and clean it out as well." With a final glare, Caldazon stalked off.

"Master?" Kindan called after him, not trusting himself alone with his disasters.

"I need to talk with Harper Murenny," Caldazon replied grumpily. "And maybe take a nap." He glanced again at Kindan and amended, "A *long* nap."

"I could clean it," Vaxoram offered quietly. Kindan was surprised to see him; he must have come straight from his last class and, Kindan guessed, had caught the last of Caldazon's railings.

In the past ten months, the relationship between Vaxoram and Kindan had grown deeper, more complex, yet still no less perplexing to both of them. It was as though the older apprentice was sometimes Kindan's older brother, other times his apprentice. Yet it worked, and Vaxoram was now an accepted member of the "outcasts," as he had once named Kindan and his friends.

"No," Kindan replied, shaking his head. "I made this mess, I should clean it up."

Vaxoram nodded. Kindan hid a grin and turned to his messes.

Cleaning the failed glue out of its pot was easy and, to bolster his spirits, Kindan did that first. It was probably just as well because, try as he might, Kindan could not clean out the hardened polish without chipping Master Caldazon's prized pot. In the end, just short of tears, Kindan returned the two pots to the instrument maker's room only to find it empty; the Master was obviously still ensconced with the Masterharper.

Somewhat relieved, Kindan decided to honor the old adage of "leave sleeping Masters lie" and made his way to his afternoon voice lesson with Master Biddle.

Twenty minutes into his lesson, Master Biddle lowered his baton and looked straight over the heads of the other apprentices to Kindan.

"I'd say, Kindan, that today is not a good day for you to be using your voice," Biddle told him politely.

Red-faced, Kindan could only nod. It was not just a bad day, it was a horrible day, and it was clear that it was going to be the first of many more—for Kindan's voice seemed determined to settle at neither bass nor tenor, but merely to crack indeterminately whenever he tried even the slightest range.

"Perhaps," Biddle suggested kindly, "you'd care to conduct?"

Kindan's eyes widened with excitement. If there was one thing that Kindan truly enjoyed, it was conducting others in the making of music. At Biddle's insistent gestures, Kindan made his way down to the front of the class and, with a nod of thanks, took the baton from the Voice Master.

Perhaps the day would get better.

He had just raised it to start the choir singing when a voice barked out, "Kindan!"

It was Master Caldazon. The color drained out of Kindan's face and he reluctantly turned the baton back over to Master Biddle.

Perhaps the day would get worse.

———✦———

"It's only because you're growing," Nonala consoled him at the evening meal. At thirteen Turns she was still half a head taller than Kindan, but that was far less than the full head's difference between them only a Turn before.

"You'll find your height," Verilan added staunchly. Kindan smiled at him but couldn't help feeling a bit jealous—Verilan was assured a place in the Harper Hall; his skill at copying alone would guarantee it.

"Just try to stay out of trouble," Kelsa added sagely, looking up from the slate on which she was writing.

"Eat, Kelsa," Kindan and Nonala said in unison. The others all shared a private smile as Kelsa gave them a startled look and wistfully pushed her slate away. Kelsa was always writing. The dark-haired girl was another who Kindan was certain would find a place in the Harper Hall, even if the Hall was traditionally a man's world; Kelsa's songs were so original that none could forget them, and she herself had a perfect memory for not only words but notes as well.

Play her a song once and she'd know it forever; start a melody and she'd write a whole new piece from it. It was dangerous to whistle near Kelsa, for she'd often lurch to a sudden stop—to the consternation of all behind her—and start writing.

Kelsa and Pellar had an amazing affinity for each other whenever the mute Harper visited from his Fire Hold; she seemed able to take his merest notions and put them to music. Surprisingly to Kindan, Halla, Pellar's mate, never seemed to mind the way Kelsa and Pellar acted around each other. In fact, she seemed to encourage it, when Kindan would have preferred that she be jealous and keep Pellar away from Kelsa. Despite his recent understanding that he didn't feel that way about Kelsa, Kindan still wanted the hope that if he ever did, he'd stand some chance.

He shook his head self-deprecatingly and, noticing that Kelsa had once again dropped her fork in favor of her stylus, cocked his head at her warningly. Nonala noticed his movement and growled at Kelsa.

"Shards!" Kelsa groaned. "It's only food."

"But you need to eat," Verilan told her. "Not even you can tune on an empty stomach."

"I'm not a workbeast," Kelsa snarled, glancing at Kindan. "I don't need so much food that I blunder about all day."

"Kelsa!" Nonala said in admonishment and the others all looked at Kelsa angrily.

Kindan's face drained of all color; there was no way he could pretend that the remark hadn't hurt.

"Well," Kelsa said in a lame defense of her words, "maybe if you didn't eat so much—"

Kindan rose stormily and loudly pushed his plate across the table in front of Kelsa.

"You eat my portion then," he snarled as he rushed out of the dining hall.

✦

It wouldn't have mattered so much except that Nonala, Kelsa, and Verilan were his only friends at the Harper Hall—except also perhaps Vaxoram, but that relationship was so odd Kindan didn't know quite what to call it.

When he had arrived at the Harper Hall three Turns back, Kin-

dan had joined a group of apprentices who had already been together for half a Turn, some as much as a full Turn, and all his
attempts to fit in with the others had failed. Out of the other forty
apprentices at the time, only Verilan had shown any signs of friend-
liness. Eventually, Kelsa and then Nonala had joined their ranks,
and now striding into the large courtyard in the center of the
Harper Hall, Kindan realized that he had become the leader of the
group. Perhaps it was because he was older, or perhaps it was because of his defeat of Vaxoram, or perhaps it was because he wasn't
as intensely focused as the other three, he couldn't say, but there it
was. Or perhaps—

A noise from above him caused Kindan to look up and raise an
arm—not for protection but as a perch. With a contented cry, the
small bronze fire-lizard alighted on Kindan's arm.

"I haven't got anything for you, Valla," Kindan said as he
reached with his other arm to stroke the fire-lizard's cheek. Valla
chirped in understanding and Kindan's foul mood evaporated.

Perhaps that was the other thing that marked Kindan apart
from the rest of the apprentices, even his own small group of
friends; he was on intimate terms with two Weyrleaders and countless dragonriders.

There had been a time when that would have been enough for
Kindan: To be a harper and to be friendly with the Weyrleaders of
Pern had seemed an impossible goal when he was Turns younger.

Well, Kindan mused, that's what I *thought* I wanted.

Valla, alert to Kindan's feelings, cocked his head and crooned
inquiringly.

"It's all right," Kindan said soothingly, his lips turning up affectionately at the fire-lizard. "I was just woolgathering."

The sound of footsteps behind him indicated the approach of
Vaxoram. Kindan turned and nodded at him and the older apprentice nodded in turn, then Kindan looked forward again feeling
oddly reassured that Vaxoram was nearby.

Valla cocked his head suddenly, peering upward and then, with a happy cry, launched himself into the air above the courtyard, climbing swiftly over the top of the Harper Hall. Craning his neck to follow Valla's flight, Kindan was not surprised to see the dragon burst into view in front of the Harper Hall from *between*.

Kindan raced across the courtyard and under the arches out of the Harper Hall to the clearing beyond.

A bronze dragon was just settling on the ground, his head canted up toward Valla hovering close by.

Kindan paused at the end of the archway, squinting. The dragon rider leapt down from his dragon and reached up to help another smaller person down.

A new apprentice? Kindan mused. He hadn't heard anything about a new apprentice. Nor had he heard any drum messages recently, nor was there any gossip about a new arrival.

"Kindan!" the dragonrider called, gesturing for Kindan to come over, still bundled up in riding gear, his face obscured by a warming scarf.

"M'tal?" Kindan murmured to himself in surprise, trotting over immediately.

"I see that Valla is doing well," the Benden Weyrleader said affably once Kindan got close. M'tal gave Kindan a scrutinizing look and said, "And harpers' food seems to agree with you!"

Kindan smiled and nodded, but his attention was on M'tal's passenger, a young boy who looked to have no more than ten Turns at best. The boy had pale hair and a sickly complexion, but perhaps, Kindan reflected, that was from the cold of *between*.

"This is Conar," M'tal said, resting a hand on the boy's shoulder. "He's the youngest of Lord Ibraton."

Kindan nodded to the youngster quickly, then looked back to M'tal. The dragonrider's tone was disturbing and Kindan noticed that M'tal looked weary.

"Valla," Kindan called, "tell Master Murenny we've got guests."

The little fire-lizard chirped once regretfully toward Gaminth, the bronze dragon, then disappeared *between*.

M'tal shook his head in wonder. "You've trained him *that* well? Master Murenny will know that we're coming?"

Kindan smiled. "Well, he'll know that *something's* up."

Kindan noticed a large bag beside Conar and reached for it. "Let me carry that for you."

Vaxoram grabbed the bag before Kindan could get a hand on it and hefted it up easily. Kindan nodded in thanks.

By the time the three of them arrived in the Harper Hall's courtyard, the area was thronged with curious students.

"M'tal!" Masterharper Murenny called as he spied the Benden Weyrleader. "Good to see you."

"And you," M'tal said. He closed the distance between them and whispered urgently, "I need to talk with you in private."

Murenny nodded, then raised an eyebrow toward Conar.

"He's Ibraton's youngest," M'tal explained. "I'd like him to stay here."

"Of course," Murenny said, as though the request were not at all unusual. He waved to Kindan, asking, "Can you get him settled in?"

The duty of welcoming a new apprentice to the Harper Hall should, by long tradition, have fallen to the newest apprentice, which would have been Kelsa. However, Kindan had noticed that Master Murenny had disregarded that tradition with the last two newcomers, assigning the duty to Kindan instead. Kindan had noticed the change but had not commented on it because, after dealing with the first newcomer, he understood the Masterharper's reasoning: that most apprentices would be affronted and embarrassed to be introduced to the Harper Hall by a girl.

"I'll see right to it," Kindan said, gesturing with his free hand toward the entrance to the Apprentice Dormitory and telling Conar, "We're heading that way."

"And make sure he gets fed!" Murenny called after him.

Kindan nodded in acknowledgment as he veered right to the stairway leading up to the Apprentice Dormitory, Vaxoram trailing steadily behind them. The dormitory was a huge room, split length-ways by a wall and further subdivided by thick curtains hung strategically throughout.

"Usually the apprentices are grouped by Turn," Kindan explained as they walked past several bunk beds. "But as long as the Masters don't mind, we can move around as much as we like."

"I don't know if I'm going to be an apprentice," Conar said, speaking for the first time. His voice was piping and his accent was soft, different from the standard speech of Fort Hold or the muted tones that all harpers learned. It reminded Kindan more of a High Reacher than of M'tal's Benden sound.

Kindan turned and grinned at him. "If you weren't, Master Murenny wouldn't have sent you with me."

"I think Father sent me just to get me out of the way," Conar said with a frown.

"But surely your harper recommended you?"

"Our harper is dead," Conar said. "That's why Father wanted to send me away."

"What?"

Conar nodded. "We heard just this morning, he was away in the southern part of the Hold."

"Was he very old?" Kindan asked. "How'd he die?"

"They say it was the flu," Conar said. "But I had the flu months back—"

"So did I."

"And so did Harper Alagar," Conar said, looking bleak. "Mother didn't want me to go because I'm the youngest, but Father insisted, saying that our bloodline must survive." His lips trembled as he asked, "Do you think they're going to die?"

"No," Kindan said, shaking his head firmly. "No one dies from the flu, they just wish they could."

"But what about Harper Alagar?"

"It might have been something else," Kindan told him, shrugging, and adding with a smile, "I think you might have misjudged your father's intentions, maybe he just wants a good harper in the family!"

"But I'm not good at anything," Conar protested. Then he added reflectively, "Except drawing, perhaps."

"Drawing?"

"Well, doodling, I suppose," Conar corrected himself self-deprecatingly. "Father always complained that I was always drawing on something, but Harper Alagar said that I showed promise."

"Well, if Harper Alagar said so—"

"But harpers don't draw."

"Harpers do many things," Kindan told him. "And sometimes we add new skills." He gestured to one of the cloth partitions and pulled up a corner. "This is where my friends and I sleep," he said, dropping Conar's bag. "We'll leave your stuff here until they decide where to put you."

"Your friends?"

"Verilan, Nonala, and Kelsa," Kindan said, pointing in turn to the bottom bed of the nearest bunk, and then to the bottom and top beds of the farther bunk.

"Who sleeps there?" Conar asked, pointing to the top bed of the nearest bunk.

Kindan smiled and pointed at himself. "But if you wanted to sleep with us, you could bunk with Vaxoram here." Kindan winked at the older harper as he said to Conar, "But he snores."

"My brothers snored," Conar said, eyeing Vaxoram thoughtfully. "Is he your servant?"

"Yes," Vaxoram said quickly.

"He lost a duel," Kindan explained. "And he's an apprentice like the rest of us here."

"A duel?" Conar repeated, his curiosity piqued. He saw the scar under Vaxoram's eye. "What for?"

"He insulted a girl," Kindan said, unwilling to dredge up all the details.

"Nonala and Kelsa sound like girls' names," Conar said, looking questioningly at Kindan.

"They are."

"You sleep with girls?" Conar asked in astonishment.

"Yes," Kindan replied. "We treat each other with respect and don't peek, if that's what you're wondering."

Kindan was surprised to see how Vaxoram accepted this statement. It underlined how much the older apprentice had changed in the past ten months.

Conar blushed and shook his head hastily. "I just—I slept in my own room."

"That must have made cleaning it awfully difficult," Kindan said.

"I never cleaned it, the help did."

"Well here, at the Harper Hall, there is no help," Kindan told him. "We do everything ourselves." He walked over to a cabinet and opened it, pulling out a broom and handing it to Conar who grabbed it awkwardly. "In fact, I made this broom myself. It's my second-best broom."

"Harpers make brooms?" Conar repeated in shock, looking down at the example in his hands.

"Harpers have to know what other people do, and the best way to learn is to do," Kindan told him. "So we make a broom, clean our own quarters, mend our own clothes."

Conar looked at him with eyes wide in surprise. "Was it hard, making a broom?"

Kindan smiled and nodded. "That's why I made two." He pointed to the bristles of the broom. "See how tightly I've woven the string through the bristles?" he asked. "That keeps them from falling out."

"I don't know where we get our brooms," Conar confessed to Kindan. Kindan smiled, delighted to see that the young son of Benden's Lord Holder would consider such an issue; many Lord Holders' sons considered themselves above any work. Kindan smiled also because he'd been told countless times by Kelsa and Nonala that going on about making brooms was, as Kelsa had said, "Boring, Kindan, I don't know why you always blather on about it." Even Verilan, who was often willing to appear interested in Kindan's latest fancies, had trouble feigning interest in broom making.

"Are you hungry?" Kindan asked Conar. "It's lunchtime here."

"It was nearly dinnertime when I left," Conar replied, looking confused.

"That's because Fort Hold is on the other side of the continent and sees the sun six hours later than you do at Benden," Kindan explained. He lengthened his stride, calling over his shoulder, "Hurry up, lunch will be over soon."

But Conar didn't catch up. Turning back to see what was keeping him, Kindan saw that Conar was doubled over, gasping for breath. Kindan raced back to him. "Are you okay?" he asked, bending down to peer at the pale boy.

"Can't keep my breath," Conar said as he gulped for air. "Never could, really, but it's been worse since the flu."

"Shards, I wish you'd've told me."

Conar shook his head. "Didn't want to be a bother."

Kindan nodded, understanding the boy's feelings all too well. "I could carry you."

Conar gave him a look of horror.

"Okay, catch your breath," Kindan said, silently hoping that there would still be something to eat when they got to the Dining Hall.

They were still waiting when Murenny and M'tal appeared, heading back to the landing meadow beyond the Harper Hall.

"Kindan," Murenny called, "just the lad we wanted to see!" He paused as he caught sight of Conar. "You're not trying to race him to death?"

"No, Master," Kindan replied. "I didn't realize Conar had short breath."

"He should see the Masterhealer," Murenny said, gazing thoughtfully at the small boy, then turning his gaze toward M'tal with a questioning look. M'tal nodded in reply. Murenny frowned for a moment before saying to Kindan, "We've got another project for you."

"It doesn't involve the Records, does it?" Kindan asked fearfully.

"I'm afraid it does," M'tal told him, smiling sympathetically at Kindan's apparent discomfort. "But you've done so well—"

"By now," Murenny cut in with a twinkle in his eyes, "I suspect Kindan understands the reward for a job well done."

Conar, who had recovered his breath, looked up curiously at Kindan.

"Another job," Kindan said, his tone just short of a groan.

"Do you want to wait while I explain your fears to Kindan?" Murenny asked the Benden Weyrleader.

M'tal frowned thoughtfully, then nodded.

"And I suppose you haven't eaten yet?" the Masterharper said to Kindan, who nodded. "Well," Murenny said, turning back to the Dining Hall, "why don't we eat and talk there."

Kindan's eyes widened for an instant before he could school his expression. Eating with the Masterharper was certain to be noticed and resented by the older apprentices, but he couldn't see any way to avoid the invitation.

As they walked, Murenny fell in beside Conar, asking the smaller boy, "Did Kindan tell you about his broom?"

Kindan turned bright red, to the accompanying chuckles of the Masterharper and Weyrleader. M'tal clapped him on the shoulder, saying, "You have a right to be proud of your accomplishments."

"It's only a broom," Kindan groaned.

"Dragonriders at Benden make their own harnesses," M'tal told him. Kindan gave him an interested look, so the Weyrleader continued, "Our lives depend on them, we have to trust them."

"Well, my life doesn't depend on a broom," Kindan murmured.

"Best not let Selora hear you say that," Murenny warned him. "Or she'll prove you wrong."

"Selora does the cooking," Kindan explained to Conar.

"She does much more than that," Murenny corrected.

"She keeps this whole Hall running," Vaxoram said in agreement. Murenny smiled in agreement.

As they entered the hall, Kindan noticed that Kelsa stopped mid-sentence when she saw him, with a what-have-you-done-now expression on her face. Kindan smiled and shrugged.

"Can we find some space for the Weyrleader and my guests?" Murenny asked the other Masters politely when they arrived at the large round Masters' table. It was obvious from Resler's expression that he would rather not have Kindan at the table. He slowly rose, but Murenny gestured him to sit back down. "You'll want to hear this, Resler."

Resler's look made it clear that the Master Archivist thought otherwise, but he sat down again anyway.

"I've got classes to prepare for," Master Biddle said, rising and nodding to Kindan and the Weyrleader.

"Oh, I'm sorry," Murenny said to Master Biddle. He gestured to Conar. "This is Conar, the youngest of Lord Ibraton of Benden. Alagar recommended him as an apprentice."

Biddle nodded an acknowledgment to Conar before leaving.

"I'll talk with you later," Murenny called after him, "and fill you in."

The Voicemaster waved a hand in response as he walked out the door toward his classroom.

"Alagar, really?" Resler asked with interest, ignoring the byplay with Master Biddle. He examined Conar curiously. "And what talent led Master Alagar to recommend you to the Harper Hall, young Conar?"

Conar dropped his eyes. "I don't know."

"Well," Resler continued crisply, "I'm sure Alagar will tell us in his own good time."

"I'm afraid not," Murenny said shaking his head. "Master Alagar succumbed to the flu."

Masterhealer Lenner sat back in his chair. "I suppose I should stay as well, then."

"Yes, you should," Murenny agreed. He said to the other Masters, "I'll give the rest of you the news later."

He gestured to M'tal. "For now, though, we are imposing on the Weyrleader's time."

The other Masters hastily rose, nodding respectfully to M'tal. "Weyrleader," they said in chorus before departing with pointed looks at the apprentices and journeymen still seated at the other tables. Immediately, the students finished their conversations, took their last bites of lunch, and rose to bring their trays down to the kitchen.

"I hadn't intended to empty the place," Murenny remarked drolly as he scanned the departing bodies. "But perhaps it's just as well."

"What happened to Alagar?" Lenner asked as the noise of the departures faded away.

"We have no idea," M'tal said. "Ibraton received Alagar's fire-lizard late one night and had just retrieved the note it bore when the fire-lizard screamed and went *between*." Before the others could say anything, he continued, "Neither my Gaminth nor Selina's Breth could contact her."

"What did the note say?" Lenner asked, leaning forward intently.

"One word: flu," M'tal replied. He leaned back in his chair, and closed his eyes wearily. With his eyes still closed, he continued, "Alagar had gone down to one of the smaller holds, no more than three or four families but a holding that Lord Ibraton had deemed 'promising.' Gaminth and I flew over the hold the next day. We saw no one."

"What about the cattle?" Lenner asked.

"I saw a few cattle," M'tal said, leaning forward and opening his eyes again. "Why?"

"Sometimes cattle can spread an illness to people," Lenner said. He gestured to Master Resler, adding, "At least so the Records tell us."

"Would Alagar know that?" M'tal asked attentively.

"I don't know," Lenner replied after a moment's thought.

"I doubt it," Resler said. "He was never much of a healer."

"Benden Hold is without a healer," Lenner remarked, shaking his head. "And I'm afraid that there is no likely replacement soon," he added, glancing at Conar.

"Which is why all harpers are taught some healing," Murenny said, "like poor Alagar."

"And just as healers learn some harpering," Lenner agreed.

Murenny snorted. "They'd have to learn some, just because of their duties." When Conar looked confused, Murenny explained, "They learn tact, at the very least, and something about record-keeping."

"I wish they were taught more," Lenner said, glancing challengingly at Master Resler.

"They have the worst handwriting," Resler complained, casting a meaningful look toward Kindan. "And they keep sloppy Records at best."

The Masterhealer looked ready to argue but shook himself, and gave M'tal an apologetic look. "I'm sorry, you were saying?"

M'tal dismissed the apology with a wave of his fingers. "As I said, I saw no one," M'tal continued. "I didn't land but returned to Lord Ibraton and told him my news." Here M'tal paused and glanced toward Conar consideringly before continuing, "Lord Ibraton told me that Alagar had just recently recommended Conar for a harper but that he had decided against it, particularly given the wishes of Conar's mother."

Kindan and the other harpers were surprised.

"She wanted to keep the boy with her?" Lenner guessed. M'tal nodded.

"And Ibraton was willing to go along with her to avoid discord," Murenny surmised.

"*Now* he feels that the suggestion has merit," M'tal continued.

"Why?" Murenny asked.

"Because this minor hold wasn't the only one of his that had suddenly gone silent," M'tal said. He nodded toward Conar. "So Ibraton now thinks it best to send this one away just in case."

"How many holds went silent?" Lenner inquired.

"Was there a pattern?" Kindan added. Resler shot him a quelling look, reminding Kindan firmly that "apprentices should be seen, not heard."

"Good question," Lenner murmured encouragingly to Kindan.

"I don't know," M'tal said with a grin and a nod to Kindan. He turned to Lenner, saying, "Three other minor holds had gone silent in the last fortnight."

"Three in a fortnight?" Lenner murmured. "And no one has gone to check on them?"

"Alagar was supposed to, according to Ibraton," M'tal replied.

"Didn't we just have the flu come through here not six months back?" Resler asked Lenner. "And doesn't that mean that we're immune?"

"Benden Hold had the flu about eight months back," Conar piped up.

"Did it?" Lenner said. "I recall no report."

"But—oh!" Conar turned bright red. "Master Alagar had asked me to write it up," he confessed miserably.

"No matter," Lenner told him kindly. "I'd had reports from Lemos and Bitra and, of course, we had it here ourselves." He shook his head mournfully. "Several oldsters succumbed."

"And some babies," M'tal added somberly. Lenner shot him an inquiring look, to which the Weyrleader replied, "The flu affected the Weyr, too."

"My Records show that dragonriders are immune from normal

disease," Resler commented, glancing sharply—nearly challeng-ingly—at M'tal.

"Yes, dragonriders are immune," M'tal agreed. "But not all our weyrfolk are." He sat back in his chair and glanced up thoughtfully. "We lost seven babies, including a newborn."

"Out of how many?" Lenner asked quietly.

"Not more than fifty," M'tal replied. "Didn't K'tan send a report?"

"He might have," Lenner replied vaguely. "But I know your Weyr is without a harper and it would usually fall to him to make the report."

M'tal glanced at Kindan suggestively. "The Weyr is willing to wait until there is a suitable candidate."

"Tenelin and Issak are available," Resler suggested, not catch-ing M'tal's look. "Both have quite acceptable writing."

"It's important that the Weyrleader have a good rapport with his harper," Murenny remarked. "And I suspect that while both your recommendations are suitably skilled, they lack a certain—flexibility."

"You and your flexibility," Resler responded sourly. "A harper's job is well known—"

"That is neither here nor there," Murenny cut across him, turn-ing back to M'tal. He looked at Lenner. "Alagar's note said 'flu'—could he be right?"

"To incapacitate so many minor holds," Lenner began, shaking his head doubtfully, "I would expect some more deadly disease."

"I recall," M'tal said, speaking carefully, "a time in my youth when we had a flu that was quite nasty." He grimaced. "My mother and younger sister died from it. But while I was recovering, our Weyr Healer at the time—"

"That would have been Selessekt, I believe," Resler murmured. M'tal nodded and continued.

"—said that there had been a much worse flu when *he* was young; a flu that had killed many." He turned to Lenner, "Do you recall that?"

Lenner shook his head. "My hall is besieged with so many requests every day that it is very hard to research into the past, except when immediate needs drive us." He glanced at the Masterharper. "There are fewer healer apprentices than I'd like."

"I quite agree with you," Murenny responded. "However, as you and I have discussed, finding suitable healer candidates remains a problem."

"Why is that?" M'tal asked.

Lenner made to brush the question aside but Murenny gave him a restraining gesture, and turning to M'tal, said, "Since the end of the Second Pass, we Pernese have been expanding all over our continent.

"Now that we're nearing the next Pass, holders and crafters are eager to expand as much as they can, growing spare crops and setting aside materials in preparation."

M'tal nodded; none of this was news to him.

"So holders and crafters want to keep their best and ablest with them, not caring to lose them to the Harper Hall or even the Healer Hall," Murenny continued. "Particularly the Healer Hall, as training to be a healer takes longer than the training for a harper."

"So there's a dearth of suitable healer candidates," M'tal surmised. "But surely the holders and crafters must realize . . . ?"

"So one would think," Murenny agreed. "However, in practice each holder and craftmaster believes that the needs for new healers should be met out of some hold or craft other than their own."

"Perhaps the Weyrs could help," M'tal suggested and then immediately shook his head ruefully. "I see your problem, just thinking about our weyrfolk. We've barely enough youngsters coming along to meet our needs for new dragonriders and weyrfolk."

"We've managed to survive because we insist on training our harpers in some of the healing arts," Murenny noted. "But if there were any disaster—"

"Thread will be enough of a disaster, and less than twelve Turns away," M'tal said. He glanced down at his hands, his eyes narrowed thoughtfully, then looked up at Murenny. "Have you thought to bring it to the Conclave?"

"I have," Murenny replied. "And I *have*."

M'tal cocked an eyebrow questioningly.

"And the Lord Holders have suggested that I ask the Weyrs or the Crafts," Murenny responded, his tone just short of bitter.

"I could become a healer," a small voice piped up hesitantly. The others turned to Conar in surprise. "But I don't know if I would be very good. My writing is not the best."

"There are some," the Masterhealer replied with a pointed glance at the Master Archivist, "who feel that's a failing among most healers."

"Didn't you say you could draw?" Kindan added, trying to bolster both Conar's credentials and his spirits. When the boy nodded, Kindan turned to Lenner. "Wouldn't drawing be useful for a healer?"

"Well," Lenner temporized, "traditionally there hasn't been much call for it, but that may only be because we haven't had anyone with the ability."

"While this is all very interesting, we are off the issue at hand," Murenny said.

"I think I was responsible," M'tal said spreading his hands in apology. "My question stands, however: Do we know if there ever was such a plague of a flu?"

Lenner shook his head and glanced at the Records Master. "I don't recall any, perhaps Master Resler . . . ?"

Resler sighed. "I can only do so much with the staff I have. I, too, must deal with current demands, many of which have to do with our current expansion." He glanced at Conar thoughtfully. "I have many requests for copies of maps, for example—I suppose they're much like drawing."

M'tal nodded in acceptance of Resler's answer, then said to Murenny, "Could I ask that the Records be searched for any such references?"

"My lord," Resler protested, suddenly all formal, "perhaps you didn't hear me, my staff is already overworked." He shook his head regretfully. "Besides, such a search is highly technical and I doubt my apprentices would be suited—"

"I can think of one apprentice up to the task," M'tal interrupted gently.

"Who?" Resler demanded in surprise.

"Someone who's already demonstrated an ability to ferret through the Records for forgotten tidbits," M'tal said, his eye falling on Kindan.

Kindan sat bolt upright, his face flushed with surprise at the same time as Resler noticed the Weyrleader's glance and exclaimed, "Oh, no! You can't mean *him*!"

CHAPTER 6

Records to keep, Records to learn
Knowledge gained from Turn to Turn
Harper keep the truth alive
Thus will all on Pern survive.

HARPER HALL

And so it was settled, over Resler's objections and to Kindan's surprise, that Kindan would search the Records for any mention of a plague or "super-flu," as the Masterharper dubbed it.

Master Resler was more upset, if possible, than Kindan himself, who was overwhelmed both with the sheer size of the task and its importance—not to mention that he also had all his normal classes and duties.

"And you're not to disturb Verilan, he's got an important job and doesn't need distracting," Resler warned Kindan tetchily.

"Yes, Master," Kindan replied tactfully.

"You understand the importance of this task, don't you?" the Masterharper cautioned Kindan.

"We have to know what to expect and any suggestions to counter it," M'tal told him.

"The flu won't be the same," Lenner said, "but this at least will give us some idea of what to expect and might suggest approaches for remedies."

And now Kindan, at the end of his usual studies, found himself late at night in the Archives Hall surrounded by as many glows as he could acquire and stacks of ancient, musty Records.

At the next table over, Conar blinked and tried to stifle a yawn. He failed and Kindan found himself yawning sympathetically. At the table in front of Kindan, Vaxoram yawned, too.

"You don't have to be here," Kindan said to Conar. "You should go and get some sleep."

"So should you," Conar shot back. In the sevenday since his arrival at the Harper Hall, Conar had proven to be shy and reserved around everyone—except Kindan. Kindan had hopes that Conar would soon thaw around Verilan, too, but Conar's relationship with Nonala and Kelsa was marred by their repeated insistences that "He's *so* cute!"

However, strangely enough, it was probably Vaxoram for whom Conar had the greatest affection. Neither spoke of it, and Kindan didn't understand it; he just sensed that the two felt more comfortable with each other than either did with anyone else.

That was why Conar was here tonight: more to keep Vaxoram company than Kindan. Kindan glanced up at Vaxoram's back. The older apprentice hadn't turned the first page of his Record since they'd sat down over an hour ago. Intrigued, Kindan left his chair and walked around to Vaxoram.

"Find something?" he asked, surprised to startle the older apprentice.

Vaxoram was bent low over the old Record, a glow held just above it, hovering over the very first line.

"No," Vaxoram replied brusquely, almost belligerently.

"You've been reading the same Record for an hour now," Kindan observed.

"It's the light," Vaxoram told him. "It's so dim, it's hard to read with."

"Why don't you get some rest, then?" Kindan asked.

"Because you're here," Vaxoram said.

Kindan cut off his reply as the sound of footsteps could be heard coming up the corridor. Both turned to the entrance expectantly.

"What are you three doing up?" Lenner asked them, carrying a glow basket in one hand.

"Still working," Kindan said, pointing at the stack of Records.

Lenner came in and glanced down at the Record in front of Kindan.

"It's hard to read these old Records in this light," Lenner murmured, bringing his glow closer, "especially at night."

"See?" Vaxoram said triumphantly.

"That's the only free time I have," Kindan said.

"Hmmph," Lenner grunted. "We'll have to see about that." He wagged a finger at the two boys. "In the meantime, go to sleep, I'll get this sorted out in the morning."

"But it's important!" Conar objected.

"Yes," Lenner agreed, "it is. *Very* important, which is why I don't want to leave the job to sleepy eyes."

Reluctantly, with Conar still grumbling, the three apprentices went to the dorm.

But things didn't go as they'd hoped when they got there. Kindan had rolled his glow over so that it provided only the barest bit of light and, as they navigated their way to their beds, Conar stubbed his toe on a bunk and tripped loudly.

"Quiet!" a voice shouted irritably from the darkness.

"Sorry," Conar whispered, hopping around and grabbing his toe in both hands.

"Shut up!" another voice shouted in response.

"What's going on?" a third voice added. "Who's making that noise?"

"The new lad," a voice grumbled from the dark.

"He stubbed his toe," Kindan said in explanation. "We were working in the Archives."

———✦———

Kindan was surprised to be shoved awake the next morning, for he usually woke up at the crack of dawn.

"Kindan! Kindan, get up!" Kelsa shouted in his ear.

"What?" Kindan asked groggily.

"We're going to be late!" Nonala urged him.

"Get Conar," Kindan said as he rose from his bunk. Hastily, he pulled on his morning clothes.

Nearby, Conar was roused by Nonala. "What is it?" Conar asked as he rubbed the sleep out of his eyes.

"It's time to get up," Nonala told him calmly. "We start our day with a morning exercise and a run."

"A run?"

"Yes, every day," Nonala answered, with a stern glance toward Kindan. "I suppose *he's* been letting you sleep in this past seven-day!"

Kindan frowned, worried that Conar with his shortness of breath might have a difficult time completing the run from the Harper Hall up to Fort Hold and back. He opened his mouth to make the comment but Kelsa shushed him.

"Don't talk, just move!" Kelsa urged, dragging Kindan by the arm.

As Kindan got out of his bunk, he realized that the rest of the apprentice dormitory was already empty.

As they stumbled out of the apprentice dormitory into the court-yard, Kindan explained to Conar, "We do exercises every morning. At the end of our exercises, we run up to Fort Hold and back again. After that, we get ready for the start of the day and breakfast."

"We usually eat before we do anything," Conar replied.

Kindan could not help but notice Vaxoram eyeing him as he exited the apprentice dormitory.

"We'll start with stretching exercises," Vaxoram called to the massed apprentices.

Kindan always found the stretching exercises relaxing. He glanced around and noticed that Conar was following along with some difficulty. Kindan recalled how difficult it had been for him at first to learn the stretching exercises. He smiled encouragingly at the young holder boy. Conar caught his grin and smiled in return.

As they started their regular calisthenics, Kindan flashed a look at Kelsa, who grinned back at him. Kelsa and Kindan had often joked that girls did stretching exercises better than boys but boys did calisthenics better than girls. It had become something of a competition between the two of them to see who could outdo the other at their "best" ability.

After the calisthenics, they began their morning run up to the main gates of Fort Hold and back to the Harper Hall. Conar fell out of the run just as they were turning back from Fort Hold.

"He has trouble breathing," called Vaxoram who had fallen out beside him, his own sides heaving from exertion.

"Bend over, Conar, get the blood back in your head," Kindan told the youngster.

"You go on," Conar said between gasps, waving feebly after the formation.

"No, I'll stay with you," Kindan told him. "Harpers stick together."

"I'm not a harper," Conar replied, still slowly recovering his breath. "I doubt I'll ever be."

"Don't say that," Vaxoram told him fiercely. "It's just your first day's run. You'll get used to it."

"Sure you will, Conar," Nonala added in agreement, glancing toward Vaxoram quizzically, surprised that he had been so vehement with the young boy. Kindan looked up and saw that not only Nonala but also Kelsa, and Verilan, had stayed behind.

"You should catch up," Kindan told the others, waving them on.

"Harpers stick together," Kelsa repeated to him, putting her hands on her hips and daring him to contradict her.

Nonala knelt down beside Conar and rubbed his back soothingly.

"I could carry you," Vaxoram offered.

"Are you all right now, Conar?" Kindan asked. "We can start walking back."

"We should run," Conar protested.

"Not your first day," Nonala told him, shaking her head. "Vaxoràm should have allowed for that."

"Why do harpers run, anyway?" Conar asked as he stood up and started to walk slowly back toward the Harper Hall.

"Because they can," Nonala said, grinning.

"To keep in shape," Vaxoram said.

"I think it's because harpers have to be ready for anything," Kindan said thoughtfully. "One minute a harper's strumming on a guitar, the next he's—"

A chittering sound burst from the air abruptly above them. Kindan laughed as he looked up and spotted two fire-lizards cavorting.

"The next minute he's paying respects to the Lord Holder's eldest daughter," Kindan finished, turning around and looking expectantly back toward Fort Hold. He saw a group of people approaching them and his throat tightened.

"It looks like Lord Holder Bemin," Kelsa remarked, straightening up quickly and brushing the dirt off her knees.

"Oh, no," Verilan muttered. "He's going to ask about those Records!"

"What Records?" Nonala asked but Kindan waved a hand peremptorily at the others, commanding silence. The others obeyed, glad to have someone take charge.

The group approaching quickly resolved itself into four: Lord Bemin, his lady, Sannora, their eldest daughter, Koriana, and a toddler whom Lady Sannora scooped up just before they met the harpers. Kindan saw that the toddler was the Lord Holder's youngest and last child, Fiona.

"My lord, good day," Kindan said as they drew near. He bowed low.

"Kindan, good to see you," Koriana called out in surprise. "I see that your Valla and my Koriss have already made their greetings."

"My apologies, my lord," Kindan said obsequiously to the Lord Holder, remembering Kelsa's comments about why the Lord Holder never visited the Harper Hall. The last thing he wanted to do was give the Lord Holder a reason to chide the Masterharper and yet, here they were, halfway up to Fort Hold. "My friends and I stopped to rest during our run."

Bemin regarded Kindan silently for a long moment before replying, "So we saw."

"Father!" Koriana whispered chidingly.

"I'm sorry, my lord, I'm not used to the exercise," Conar said on his own, his words punctuated by another long bout of coughing.

"This is Conar's first day with us," Kindan explained. "His father sent him here from Benden Hold."

"Your father?" Bemin repeated, scrutinizing Conar carefully. "Are you a son of Ibraton?"

"I am, my lord," Conar replied, sketching a shorter bow than Kindan had, as was proper from a Lord Holder's child to a Lord Holder.

"Well, Conar, what skills bring you to the Harper Hall?" Lady Sannora asked kindly, moving her squirming toddler from one hip to the other.

"I'm not certain I have any, my lady," Conar replied, flushing.

"He draws," Kindan declared stolidly in his defense.

"And is drawing valued at the Harper Hall?" Lord Bemin asked, glancing first at Conar and then at Kindan.

"I can't say for certain, my lord," Kindan replied after an agonizingly long silence, "but Master Murenny was pleased enough to take him on."

"But that was because Father asked him," Conar murmured to Kindan.

"Well," Lord Bemin said, "I agree that a Lord Holder's request is good enough for a harper." He cast a sideways glance at Kindan and there was no warmth in his eyes.

"As you say, my lord," Kindan replied nonchalantly. He ignored the curious looks that Nonala and Kelsa sent his way. "We were just returning to the Harper Hall, my lord."

"Well, then, we can walk together, can't we, Father?" Koriana said quickly, closing the distance between her and Kindan. "Father has some questions for Master Murenny and I have some questions for you."

"I'll be pleased to help in any way I can," Kindan said. Bemin shot him a measuring look. "Would it have anything to do with fire-lizards?"

"Yes, it does," Koriana said, looking surprised.

"I would be happy to answer your questions—but later, if that would be acceptable," Kindan told her, trying to hide his pleasure. "My friends and I should be hurrying back; we've got chores to do before the start of the day." He turned to Lord Bemin. "Would you mind if we left you, my lord?"

"I wouldn't want you to get into any trouble," Lord Bemin replied with a wave of his hand. "I'm sure that Koriana will be able to find you later."

"Thank you, my lord," Kindan replied with a half-nod. To the others he said, "We'd best hurry back as quick as we can." He looked at Conar. "Are you all right or would it be better if you escorted the Lord Holder?"

"I'm all right," Conar declared stoutly. "As long as we don't run."

Kindan snorted. "Don't be so sure, just see the way Kelsa's long legs eat up the distance!"

Kindan's warning was prophetic; soon Conar was huffing and puffing to keep up with the longer-legged girl.

"Slow down, Kelsa, or you'll leave Conar behind," Kindan cautioned her.

"I just want to get back in time to do the chores and get a shower, that's all," Kelsa grumbled.

"I hope you like cold water," Nonala muttered.

"Oh, Shards!" Kelsa exclaimed, stamping her foot. "You're right, all the warm water will be gone!"

"You could go ahead and we'll catch up," Kindan said in an echo of his earlier suggestion. Kelsa and Nonala merely glared at him. Kindan glanced at Vaxoram, who, as senior apprentice, was responsible for assigning the apprentices' chores. Then he said, "You'd best run ahead and catch up with the others."

Vaxoram looked torn between his duty and his desire to stick with Conar and the others. In the end, he nodded at Kindan's order and raced away.

As they finally passed under the archway into the courtyard, Kindan saw the last of the apprentices dispersing. Vaxoram was waiting for them.

"Finally," he called. "I've got your assignments."

"Lord Bemin is on his way," Kindan reminded him. "The Masterharper will want to know."

"I'll tell him," Vaxoram said. "You and the others are to replace the glows."

"Now?" Kelsa groaned.

"While the sun is shining, yes," Vaxoram returned tartly.

"But we won't have time to eat!" Verilan objected.

"Or at least get a shower," Kelsa cried.

"I can't play favorites," Vaxoram muttered, his eyes looking troubled. "And I must go tell the Masterharper."

"It's his job, as senior apprentice," Kindan agreed, waving Vaxoram away.

"Shards!" Nonala groaned as Vaxoram ran out of sight. "We'll never get it done."

"Here's what we do," Kindan said. "Kelsa, you get your shower—but hurry. When you're done, grab some rolls and butter from the dining hall."

Kelsa nodded and sped off.

"Nonala, you get the glows out of the east side, and take Conar with you. Verilan, you and I will get the west." Verilan and Nonala nodded in agreement. "Meet back here and we'll take turns setting out the glows while the others shower and get dressed." He grabbed Verilan's arm and started to move off, calling over his shoulder, "And hurry!"

Kindan's plan almost worked. He, Verilan, and Conar had just gotten in the shower when Kindan heard the Masterharper shout, "Kindan!"

With a groan, Kindan jumped out of the shower and hastily pulled on his clothes, rushing out of the dormitory just as the Master-harper shouted once again. "Kin—Oh, there you are!"

"Sorry, Master," Kindan called up to the Masterharper who was peering out of the upstairs window.

"Can you join us?"

"Immediately," Kindan replied, rushing toward the stairs that led up to the Masterharper's quarters. At the door he knocked.

"Come in," the Masterharper called back. Kindan opened the door carefully, not entirely sure of his reception. Murenny beamed at him as he entered, and Kindan hid a sigh of relief.

"I hear that young Conar has a problem with his breath," the Masterharper said.

"Yes, sir," Kindan replied.

"Make sure that he sees Lenner later on today, if you would," the Masterharper said. Kindan nodded. "I should have thought of it yesterday and warned Vaxoram."

Kindan caught sight of Vaxoram standing off to one side of the room, looking chagrined.

"I couldn't imagine that Ibraton would want his youngest dead from overexertion," Lord Bemin remarked. "Let alone on his first run."

Kindan wondered if Fort's Lord Holder was upset that Ibraton hadn't asked him to foster Conar. That was usually what was done with Holders' sons and daughters. Lord Bemin's tone reminded Kindan of someone, and it took him a moment to recall: Tarik,

C'tov's father. Kindan gave himself a quick mental shake. Lord Bemin was not at all like Tarik, who had turned out to be a murderer and was ultimately given the worst punishment ever handed out on Pern, being Shunned by all, including his wife and son. No, Lord Bemin merely sounded like Tarik had when he'd been particularly pompous or patronizing. Kindan glanced at the Masterharper, wondering if Master Murenny felt as nettled by Lord Bemin as Kindan had on occasion by Tarik.

Master Murenny turned to Kindan. "Lord Bemin was wondering what you knew about fire-lizards."

"I can't say that I know all that much about fire-lizards," Kindan replied. "However, I will be glad to share what knowledge I have. And I may be able to find more in the Archives."

Master Murenny blinked at him. "I'm not sure that you will find all that much in the Archives, actually."

"Anything you can discover will help a lot," Koriana added, giving Kindan a smile.

Kindan felt his cheeks grow hot. Vaxoram glowered.

"I was particularly anxious to know when we might expect my queen to rise to mate," Koriana said, her cheeks also glowing.

"Koriana, really!" Fort's Lady Holder scolded.

There was an awkward silence.

"Is there anything else we can help you with, my Lord Holder?" Master Murenny asked to fill the gap.

Lord Bemin turned his attention from scolding his daughter toward the Masterharper of Pern, but his features remained set. It was a moment before he replied.

"We were also wondering if perhaps Koriana here could learn your drum codes," Lord Bemin said. "It would be useful to have another pair of ears at the Hold to listen to the drum conversations."

Kindan wondered whether the Lord Bemin was being deliberately insulting to the harpers or merely did not trust Fort's aging harper. A glance at Masterharper Murenny showed him that the same thoughts had crossed his mind, as well.

"We would be glad of her company," Master Murenny said, smiling at the young holder girl. "When would be convenient for you, Lady Koriana?"

Koriana ducked her head in acknowledgment of the Master's question and replied demurely, "I would like to start as soon as I could."

"Kindan's actually very good with drums," Master Murenny said, nodding toward the young apprentice. "We could perhaps combine the two tasks into one."

Lord Bemin glanced sharply at the Masterharper before turning an inquiring look to his own lady. Lady Sannora locked eyes with him for a moment before nodding in acquiescence.

"Well, I'm glad that's settled," said Master Murenny. He looked politely toward Fort's Lord Holder. "Is there anything else I can help you with?"

"Well, actually," Fort's Lady Holder said, "if there's any way you could help Koriana improve her writing . . ."

"Mother!" Koriana protested.

"Well, dear, you really should work on it some more," Sannora replied.

Koriana's cheeks dimpled in embarrassment. Kindan smiled reassuringly at her.

"Actually, there is one other issue I would like to discuss with you," Lord Bemin said to Murenny.

The Masterharper made a motion for him to continue.

"I was rather curious as to why Lord Ibraton thought to send his youngest son to the Harper Hall."

"I'm not entirely certain myself," Master Murenny replied. "I have not heard from him directly. However, Weyrleader M'tal led me to believe that perhaps Lord Holder Ibraton had hopes that his son, Conar, might one day become a healer."

"I see," Lord Bemin replied. His eyes darted over to his wife, who made no response. The Lord Holder turned his gaze back to Master Murenny. "Well . . ."

Beside him, the Lady Holder cleared her throat loudly. Lord Bemin glanced quickly at her.

"Ah . . . yes," Lord Bemin said suddenly. "And there is one other thing, if you could."

"I am at your service," Master Murenny replied.

"Would it be possible to get a list of those holders and crafters who have bronze fire-lizards?"

"Father!" Koriana shouted in protest.

Lord Bemin held up his hand consolingly, shaking his head at his eldest daughter. "Now dear, we've discussed this already and you know that it makes sense."

"Really, you must at least know what the possibilities are," Lady Bemin added.

Kindan glanced nervously around the room, wishing he were elsewhere.

"I am not sure we have that information either," Masterharper Murenny confessed to the Lord Holder. "However," he said with a glance toward Kindan, "I feel certain that we can add that to our list of inquiries."

Lord Bemin nodded, but the glance that he cast at Kindan was not a happy one.

Master Murenny realized that the conversation was over and stood up. "If there's any other way that I can help you, my Lord Holder, please let me know immediately." He gestured them toward the door.

At the entrance, however, he turned to Koriana and said, "Perhaps you would like to begin your studies today?"

Koriana looked inquiringly between her two parents. Lord and Lady Bemin exchanged looks, and finally Lady Bemin nodded.

"Of course, dear," said Fort's Lady Holder. "When shall we expect you back?"

By now, the toddler, whom Lady Sannora had been shifting from hip to hip, had grown impatient and was starting to make irritated noises.

"I should probably be back in time for lunch," Koriana said, looking at Kindan and Masterharper Murenny for approval.

"Of course," the Master said, "you could always eat with us."

"Oh, no!" Lady Sannora said hastily. "You really must come back and eat with us, Koriana."

Koriana fought successfully to keep a triumphant grin from her face as she nodded in acquiescence to her mother; she had succeeded in maneuvering her parents into letting her stay till lunchtime without them even realizing.

Masterharper Murenny looked back at Vaxoram, who was following the rear of the party. "Vaxoram, would you please lead Lady Koriana down to Master Archivist Resler?"

Vaxoram nodded and gestured for Koriana to precede him.

"Kindan," Murenny said, "please remain here, while I escort the Lord and Lady Holder."

Kindan nodded, somewhat perplexed. He raised his hand in a partial wave toward Koriana but dropped it again quickly as he noticed Fort's Lady Holder glaring at him. Waiting in the room by himself, he walked to the large windows and looked down to see Master Murenny guiding the Lord and Lady Holders through the archway of the Harper Hall.

If things hadn't seemed so odd, Kindan would have thought that this was the best day of his life. However, the undercurrents of the conversation between the Masterharper and the Lord and Lady Holder disturbed Kindan. Did the Holders really not trust their own harper?

Could it be that Lord Holder Bemin did not trust harpers at all?

Kindan's stomach grumbled. Kindan looked around the Masterharper's quarters and noticed the tray of dainties that had been brought up—probably, he guessed, for the Lord and Lady of Fort Hold. They won't miss this, he thought as he helped himself to a dainty. He quickly gulped it down and helped himself to another, listening carefully for the sound of returning footsteps.

They came after Kindan's third dainty. The door opened and Masterharper Murenny stepped inside, glancing over at Kindan as he did so.

"Well, what did you think of that?" Murenny asked Kindan. He glanced at the tray of dainties and smiled. "Ah, I see that you have used your time profitably!"

Kindan felt his cheeks reddening, but could only nod.

"Have another," the Masterharper said.

Gratefully, Kindan obeyed, then glanced nervously at the Masterharper, remembering that he had been asked his opinion and feeling torn between filling his stomach and answering the Master. Murenny smiled and waved him on.

"No, no! Eat first," the Master told him firmly. "It's always important to think on a full stomach." He leaned across and helped himself to a dainty. "I think I shall take my own advice."

Chewing, he reached over to the pitcher of *klah* and poured two cups. He passed one to Kindan courteously and then drank deeply from the other. For several moments they ate together, in a slightly awkward but companionable silence.

"Now," the Masterharper said as he finished the last of his *klah*. "Are you ready to tell me your thoughts?"

Kindan could only shrug.

"Well then, just tell me your impressions."

Kindan thought for a moment, then blurted out, "Does he not trust the Fort harper?"

The Masterharper motioned for him to continue.

"Well . . . ," Kindan said consideringly, "it seemed rather odd that he would ask to have someone else trained in the drum codes."

"Ah, you thought so, too," Murenny said.

"And why would he want to know about bronze fire-lizards?"

"Why do you think, Kindan?" the Masterharper asked softly.

Kindan frowned sourly. He was afraid he knew exactly why. He remembered with a mixture of fondness and anger the Impression of Valla and Koriss nearly half a Turn back.

He remembered the looks of outrage and horror when Koriana's newly hatched Koriss frightened away the two last hatchlings—both males—that her brothers would have Impressed, as though the little queen had not wanted to mate with bronzes owned by her own owner's brothers. Kindan was amazed by the fire-lizard's actions, but not entirely surprised at her reasoning: The intense emotions of fire-lizards mating were shared by their human partners just as dragons shared their mating lust with their riders.

Kindan's own reaction to the beautiful Koriana had been enough to cause him many sleepless nights. Even now he sometimes woke with the smell of her hair or shards of her half-wistful, half-joking smile lingering from his dreams.

"Is Lord Bemin afraid that Koriss might mate with Valla?" Kindan asked anxiously.

"Koriana is of an age to be married," Murenny agreed indirectly. "It would not do for there to be any indiscretions on her part."

"That's not fair!" Kindan shouted. "I fought Vaxoram because it's wrong for a woman to be judged—"

"Kindan," Murenny's voice was so soft it demanded Kindan's instant attention. "Consider her choices."

"She could do anything," Kindan said. "She's good at making beads, she made a harness for Koriss and one for Valla here," he said, pointing to Valla's brilliant bead harness marking him as belonging to an apprentice of the Harper Hall. He'd been thrilled and a little apprehensive when she'd presented the pretty harness to him during their fire-lizard training together—he hoped he would fulfill her expectations of him. Everyone had assumed that Kindan would know all about fire-lizard training, seeing as he'd had a watch-wher.

"Do you think that she would be content, who has known servants and finery, to exist on the income of a simple harper?" Murenny asked him seriously.

Kindan sat in silence, mulling over the question. Finally he asked in despair, "Are you saying that she has no choice?"

Murenny shook his head. "No, not at all. I am merely pointing out that for her some choices will be easier than others."

"Don't her parents want her to be happy?"

"I think they do," Murenny said. "And I think that she would be happiest living the life to which she has grown accustomed."

"A broodmare for Holders?" Kindan snapped, shaking his head and all the while wondering at his outraged words to the Master-harper. He'd never felt so angry and so out of control before.

"A Lady Holder, a symbol of grace, beauty, and kindness," Murenny replied calmly. "Her children would be only a part of her legacy, though possibly the most enduring."

"But there has to be more for a woman!" Kindan protested.

"Perhaps you are mistaken about what you believe a mother should be," Murenny replied. "I think that being a parent is the greatest challenge and greatest joy of all occupations."

"I—" Kindan cut himself off, thinking. Wasn't he something of a big brother to Kelsa and Nonala? And even Verilan. Their well-being meant a lot to him. He could never imagine himself as a father, that prospect was Turns away and more, but perhaps he could see . . .

"It just seems so unfair," Kindan ended lamely.

"I understand," the Masterharper said. Kindan glanced up at him sharply. Was the rumor true? Had the Master once been in love with Sannora?

"Why doesn't Lord Bemin trust harpers?" Kindan asked, feeling emboldened.

Murenny took a deep breath and let it out in a slow sigh. "Let us just say that Lord Bemin wishes he had more control over the Harper Hall and leave it at that."

Kindan nodded, not feeling any more enlightened than he'd been before he asked his question.

"Now," Murenny said, changing the subject, "what I need you to do is keep an eye on young Conar; teach Koriana the drum codes without"—he wagged a finger at Kindan and raised a bushy eyebrow warningly—"upsetting her mother; and help her with her writing."

Kindan nodded. Fortunately, Koriss and Valla were probably still too young for a mating flight; that would certainly qualify as "upsetting her mother." Then a thought struck him, sparked by Master Murenny's mention of writing. "What would make it difficult for people to read in dim light?"

Murenny cocked his head thoughtfully and frowned for a moment before responding, "There are several things that could do that. The person could have poor eyesight—not as bad as your friend Nuella's, obviously, but poor all the same." Kindan nodded in understanding. "Or the person could have difficulty in reading altogether," Murenny continued. He glanced up at Kindan. "Do you know this person well?"

Kindan nodded. Murenny glanced at him for a moment longer, giving Kindan a chance to supply him with a name, but when it was not forthcoming, the Masterharper continued, "One way to check on this is to see if the person has trouble distinguishing between b's and d's or u's and n's, m's and w's. Another way is to see if the person has difficulty with the same word on a different Record.

"Such a difficulty is not uncommon and often indicates a great degree of intelligence and ability," the Masterharper said. "People who have difficulty reading often find it difficult to remember tables of multiplication and addition but find it easy to remember songs, particularly those with catchy tunes, no matter how difficult the words." He pursed his lips as he trolled his memory, then brightened as he recalled, "Some of these people are great songwriters or artists."

"Conar brought some colored pencils with him," Kindan offered suddenly.

"Did he?" Murenny replied. "Perhaps we should encourage him in drawing."

"But I thought harpers were supposed to sing, teach, and write," Kindan protested.

" 'Harpers master many instruments,' " Murenny reminded him with another wagging finger. "We are not above adding more to our cache. Who knows when a drawing might prove vital to the safety of Pern."

Kindan gave the harper a look of incredulity, quickly erased as he recalled to whom he was speaking—if anyone could, the Masterharper would be the one to dictate what was acceptable in a harper.

"But most of all, Kindan," the harper said, returning to the original topic, "you must discover what you can in the Records."

Kindan nodded emphatically in agreement, then frowned. Murenny gestured for him to speak. "What about my classes?"

"I think we can safely excuse you from song and instrument making for the moment," the Masterharper said with a slight grin. Kindan looked crestfallen and Murenny held up a hand. "Not forever, mind you! Sometimes a change is all that's needed for a fresh perspective."

Murenny's words must have provoked some new thought, for the Masterharper frowned for a moment before continuing.

"Indeed, I think I'll ask that you spend time with Healer Lenner as well." Before Kindan could protest, Murenny continued, "I know you've learned a lot from Mikal and I think it wouldn't hurt at your level of experience to learn some more traditional lore."

"I don't want to be a healer," Kindan said.

"And you don't have to be," Murenny replied. "But all harpers know a bit of healing and you already know more than most. It would be foolish not to add to your store, especially as it may aid you in your search of the Records."

"Yes, Master," Kindan agreed, accepting the Masterharper's points. "And what if this flu spreads?"

"That's why your search of the Records is vital," Murenny replied. "We must know what to expect."

CHAPTER 7

When sickness comes to craft and hold
It is the healer, oh so bold
Who spends his hours in endless toil
Working for illness and death to foil.

HARPER HALL

I t's just a lot of useless old Records!" Conar complained, sniffling mightily as he flounced around in the small room designated as their work area. "Honestly, Kindan, I'll fall asleep going over them."

"Don't," Kindan told him. "Master Resler has a quick hand for those he finds slouching."

"He does," Vaxoram agreed, stretching in his chair and bending back to his Record. Kindan noticed that once again, Vaxoram's eyes hadn't moved from the top of the Record. He made it a point every day to surreptitiously check on the older apprentice's work, not having figured out yet what to do with his knowledge of Vaxoram's problem. But that was for later, Kindan reminded himself.

Kindan bent more closely over his Record, ignoring the older boy. Resler had already berated him twice for slackness and Kindan could think of no way to tell the Master that *he* had been working, particularly when half his time had been spent either listening to Conar moan or cajoling the older Vaxoram to work.

"You'll want to take slices from each of the various Hold Records," Verilan had told him when they'd started. Verilan had stayed only long enough to get them properly started before Resler had put him onto the task of recopying the Records that had been so inauspiciously destroyed by Kindan's earlier accident.

The Archive Room was a huge cavern dug into the base of the cliff that overlooked the Harper Hall, crammed full of Records. Glows provided light for the room, although it seemed to Kindan that there were never enough to clear out the darkest shadows. Even as huge as the room was, Kindan had been surprised that the Harper Hall had so many of the Holds' Records.

"Of course we do!" Verilan had snorted in surprise when Kindan had mentioned it. "Harpers usually make copies and send them to us as a matter of course," Verilan had explained, surprised that he even needed to explain the procedure. "Holders rarely keep Records for more than fifty Turns, so they send us those, too," Verilan had continued, adding with a shake of his head, "when they remember." Kindan gave him a quizzical look and Verilan explained in a horrified tone, "Sometimes they actually *destroy* their old Records."

"Why wouldn't they?" Conar had asked sourly, punctuated with another cough. "They're nothing but useless old relics."

"They're *Records*," Verilan had replied, offended to the very depth of his being. "How would anyone know what had happened in previous Turns without them?"

Conar had given Verilan a scornful look and turned away.

Now, a sevenday after they'd been given the assignment, Kindan could partly agree with Verilan—and partly with Conar. The Records were a collection of the most boring things he'd ever read coupled with tantalizing sections that made Kindan wish for more. Why, for example, when the Lord Holder of Igen had first discovered that his wells were running dry, hadn't he started planting hardier, more drought-resistant crops instead of foolishly reducing his acreage and ultimately starving his entire Hold? What had happened that caused the traders to start charging Bitra Hold—and only Bitra Hold—a surtax on all goods delivered?

Neither of those questions had come from a strict reading of the Records but from Kindan's memory and interpolation. He remembered reading about the lowered water levels and then about the reduced plantings; he noticed suddenly that there were entries in the Bitra Hold Records regarding the trader surtax and noticed that there was no mention of them in the Records of Lemos nor Benden.

"Well, how do you know that Lemos and Benden hadn't been paying the tax for Turns already?" Conar objected when Kindan had mentioned his findings. "And why wouldn't the Lord Holder of Igen keep planting his best crops? How could he know that they were in a drought?"

Kindan, torn between astonishment at Conar's obtuseness and his desire to press on with their work—and avoid Resler's complaints—replied noncommittally, turning to a new Record.

Conar set aside the Record he'd been perusing and began noisily to examine the next.

"Huh! Someone left a scribble, here!" Conar exclaimed. "And here! Neither look like proper Records." He turned to Kindan. "I can't see how you expect to find anything from Records when the Harper Hall keeps the works of children."

Kindan's initial angry look dissolved into a frown as he recalled that Conar was going through the old Benden Hold Records. He got up from his workdesk and strode over to Conar's.

"We'll switch off," he said, gesturing for Conar to change seats with him.

Conar rose eagerly, happily seating himself in front of Kindan's much smaller pile. With a frown, he warned, "You'll want to catch up before Master Resler returns."

Kindan nodded in agreement, turning to the Records. Conar was right, the writing of the Records was very poor. He turned back two Records and saw that the writing was far more legible: a fairly large print that Kindan could read easily by the light of the glows surrounding his new desk.

He looked at the top of the page for the author's marks: Harper Bellam, Benden Hold, Second Month, year 389 After Landing.

The next page had no marks. Kindan frowned and turned to the page after it. It had author's marks: Lord Kenex, Benden Hold, AL 390.5.

Lord Kenex? Kindan thought.

"Conar, look at this," he called. Conar jumped up and stood behind Kindan, peering down at the Record.

"Could you imagine a Lord Holder with such poor handwriting?" Kindan asked. He knew already that Conar's writing was not very good, but even it was far better than the scrawling on the page in front of him.

"That *is* odd," Conar agreed. He traced some of the writing with his finger. "It looks like either the person had a bad stylus or they weren't very used to it." He cocked his head to one side. "A child?"

"That doesn't make sense," Vaxoram chimed in from his stack. "That's written on paper, right? That's too expensive to let a child have." There was an awkward silence; Conar had been allowed to use paper for his drawings. Vaxoram noticed it and added, "I mean for writing, of course."

"What does it mean?" Conar asked.

Kindan shrugged. "I'll see what it says," he replied, peering down at the Record.

Conar returned to his own table, but a moment later he let out an exclamation. "There's bad handwriting here, too!"

"What year?" Kindan asked.

"Year?" Conar repeated blankly, then looked down. Once again, he snorted. "There isn't a year."

"What about the Record before?"

Conar gave him a dirty look but turned back to the previous page, scanning the top quickly. "Journeyman Metalar, Bitra Hold, Third Month, year 389 After Landing," he read. He looked up at Kindan and shrugged. "So?"

But Kindan was already moving to the desk that Verilan had abandoned when called away by Master Resler. Piled on the desk were the records from Lemos Hold. Kindan turned quickly until he came to entries from the year 389 After Landing.

"What are you doing?" Conar demanded, craning his neck around to watch Kindan. "Master Resler will know which stack you were working on."

"It's not working," Kindan returned tetchily, "it's researching."

" 'It's makework, best left to unemployed drudges,' " Vaxoram said, quoting Resler's sour opinion.

Kindan ignored him, turning through the Records carefully. Harper Lorkin had good handwriting; his marks were clear and easily read. Kindan scanned the pages—389, 389, 389, 389, 390— what?

Kindan peered down at the entry in surprise. The author's marks read: Harper Lorkin, Lemos Hold, AL 390.5. Frowning he turned back to the previous Record: Harper Lorkin, Lemos Hold, Fourth Month, year 389 After Landing. What had caused the harper to so change his style? And why did he not leave any Records for a whole Turn? Kindan peered down to the contents of the Record itself.

"I write this with great regret: We are a sadly reduced Hold," read the first line. "Fields lie fallow, huts are still empty, or, worse, home to carrion that feed on unburied bones."

Kindan tore his eyes from the Record and sat back, stunned.

"Kindan!" Master Resler's voice called from the entrance.

"What are you doing? You're supposed to be reading the Benden Records!"

"I think I've found the plague," Kindan replied, his voice sounding loud and irreverent to his ears. He gestured to the Records. "I think I know when it started and maybe where."

"You were supposed to be reading the Benden Records," Master Resler repeated angrily, advancing into the Archive Room, grabbing Kindan by the ear and lifting him out of his seat. "Can't you just do what you're told?"

"Sorry, Master," Kindan apologized, ducking out of Resler's grasp and turning to face him, "but I thought I was told to find any Records of a plague."

"In the Benden Records!" Resler growled in response, gesticulating wildly to the stack beside Conar.

"I found it there, too," Kindan said. He gestured over to the Bitra Records. "And in Bitra, too, but the Lemos Records seem the best so far." He turned and snagged the Record from his table. "Listen to this: 'Fields lie fallow, huts are still empty—' "

"That's a Record of a plague?" Resler snorted angrily. "A proper Record would have dates, and times, and—"

"I don't think they had the time," Kindan interrupted as politely as he could. He gestured to the Record in his hand. "I think they were so shorthanded afterward that they could only press on with their lives."

"That's not the way of a harper!" Resler exclaimed. He glanced down angrily at Kindan. "Have you learned nothing since you left your mine?"

Kindan could feel his cheeks burning. "The Records of Benden were kept by the Lord Holder after the plague," he said. "I think that shows that the times were such that—"

"Lord Holders don't keep Records!" Resler chided prissily, his jaw jutting and eyes glaring.

"The Record was marked—"

"Such impudence!" Resler roared. "Go! Get out of my sight!"

"Does that include me?" Conar asked, rising to his feet.

"Yes," Resler replied, "it includes you. It's time for lunch."

Conar left but waited at the entrance for Kindan who was followed, as always, by Vaxoram.

"You aren't much of a harper, you know," he said as he fell in step with Kindan. "You'd think you'd know how to handle a Master by now." He cocked his head at the silent boy. "However do you think you'll manage a Lord Holder?"

"Maybe I won't," Kindan replied sourly, brushing past Conar and racing to catch up with Verilan, whom he spied at the entrance to the Dining Hall.

Catching sight of Kindan's morose look, Verilan asked, "What's wrong?"

"I think I found the plague," Kindan told him, "but Master Resler doesn't believe me."

As if he was listening, Master Resler, who had been following behind them, called out, "Verilan! A word with you, please."

Verilan gave Kindan an apologetic look, then headed back to his Master.

"Something bothers me," Vaxoram said as he finished chewing on a roll. Kindan gave him a questioning look. "Well, perhaps Bitra, Lemos, and Benden were hit by this plague, but what about Benden Weyr? Why didn't the weyrfolk help?"

"That's a good question," Conar said, frowning thoughtfully.

"We'll look at their Records next," Kindan declared.

"What about Master Resler?" Conar asked, glancing in the direction of the irritable Archivist. "It sounds like he never wants you near him or his precious Records again."

"He's not the Masterharper," Vaxoram said, glancing at Kindan to see his reaction.

"But Conar's right," Kindan objected, "I have to learn how to work with him as well as the other Masters."

"Maybe you could—" Vaxoram began, but a faint booming sound silenced him, as it did everyone in the Harper Hall. It was a drum message.

Emergency! Sickness in Keroon. Please help.

"It's spreading," Conar declared in a flat voice. No one contradicted him.

✦

"Kindan!" Koriana called as he exited the dining hall. Kindan stopped and turned back to her, unable to keep a smile off his face. "Did I hear the drums right?"

"Depends upon what you heard," Kelsa snipped from behind her; because she knew about Lord Bemin's ill will toward the Masterharper, Kelsa wasn't sure she liked Koriana's interests in harpers—at the very least, it could mean trouble all around. Koriana's smile faded and she moved out of the young harper's way.

"Emergency. Sickness in Keroon," Koriana said. She screwed up her eyes trying to remember the last. "Please help."

"Yes," Kindan agreed, "that's what it said."

"Is it the same as at Benden?" Koriana asked nervously. "Is it spreading?"

Kindan shook his head. "No one knows," he said. "We only know what we hear with the drums."

"Won't the Weyrs go examine?" Koriana asked.

"Keroon would be beholden to Ista now that Igen's gone," Vaxoram remarked.

"We'll just have to wait and see," Kindan said. He gestured to the others. "We should get back to the Records."

"Records?" Koriana repeated. "What are you looking at them for?"

"Signs of the plague," Conar blurted out. Both Kindan and Vaxoram glared at him, Kindan shaking his head at the young boy's rashness: There was no need to add to the fears already at Fort Hold. "But Master Resler—"

"Kindan!" Masterharper Murenny's voice called down from his second-floor study.

Kindan turned and glanced up. "Yes, Master?"

Master Murenny said nothing, merely beckoning for Kindan to come up to him. Vaxoram and Conar fell in behind. A moment later, so did Koriana.

When Kindan knocked on Murenny's door—and one always knocked on the Masterharper's door, because no one could ever tell when he might be in the middle of something, even if he'd called for you just moments before—he expected the others to leave him alone. However, Conar pressed himself against Kindan's back, Vaxoram drew closer, and Koriana peered around him into the Masterharper's study.

"I see you have some companions," Murenny remarked as he noted the three additional heads. He said apologetically to the others, "My request was only meant for Kindan."

"Please," Koriana said, "if it has anything to do with this illness, I'd like to hear."

"Me, too," Conar added quickly. Vaxoram stood in stalwart silence.

"It may," Murenny said, pursing his lips in consideration. After a moment he nodded. "Very well, you may come in. But remember," he cautioned, looking directly at Koriana, "this is a harper matter."

"Surely it's a Pern matter, Master," Koriana replied demurely.

Murenny smiled in response.

"Harper matters are always Pern matters," Vaxoram remarked.

"Too true!" Murenny agreed with a snort. He focused his attention on Koriana. "My point being, my lady, that it is sometimes better not to spread news that might cause panic without first determining its truth."

"And some remedy," Koriana said in agreement. "That is true of a Holder, too."

"Indeed," Murenny agreed. He turned to Kindan. "Have you made any progress in the Records?"

"Yes," Conar said at once.

"Maybe," Kindan temporized, glancing at Conar quellingly. "We have some indication that there was a major incident that affected Lemos, Bitra, and Benden Holds around Turn 389."

"Mmm," Murenny said his eyes focused on some distant point. "I see what you mean." He glanced back to Kindan. "What do you plan to do now?"

Kindan frowned. "I, uh,—"

"Master Resler thinks we're mussing his Records," Vaxoram interjected. Kindan gave him a fulminating look, but the older apprentice merely shrugged.

"I am not concerned with Master Resler's feelings in this matter," Murenny said firmly. "Although I would caution you not to 'muss' his Records as you may find yourself needing them later."

"I think we can work with him," Kindan said.

"Don't let his concerns stop your work," Murenny instructed. Kindan nodded in understanding. "But you haven't told me what you plan next."

"I want to look at the Benden Weyr Records," Kindan said. "I'll have to ask Master Resler where they are; I looked but couldn't find them."

"I suspect that's because they are at the Weyr itself," Murenny replied.

"What about copies?" Conar protested.

"The duties of a Weyr harper often preclude time to make copies," Murenny replied smoothly. He sent a darting glance to Kindan, his eyes twinkling. "For some reason, Weyr harpers seem less inclined to make copies, possibly because their Records are so extensive."

"But I still need to see those Records," Kindan persisted.

"Yes," Murenny agreed. "Do you suppose your fire-lizard is up to sending a message?"

Kindan's eyes widened at the notion. Slowly he nodded.

✦

"Go to M'tal, Valla, to M'tal at Benden Weyr," Kindan said, concentrating on the image of the dragonrider and his bronze Gaminth. Valla chirped in surprise and preened himself.

"Perhaps he's too young," Koriana suggested anxiously, stroking her own Koriss as the queen peered intently at Valla from her perch on the girl's shoulder.

"We've been training for a while now," Kindan said. He was nervous and he knew it. He and Koriana had practiced sending the two fire-lizards *between* to each other with much success; they had even sent notes to each other. Kindan had kept the first note from her—"Kindan, this is great! Love, Koriana"—because she'd used the word "love" in it. Their other notes had been more succinct, but Kindan still felt that there was a special warmth in Koriana's and he knew that there was a special warmth in his responses.

"Valla, go to M'tal, make sure he gets your message," he said again, concentrating on an image of the Weyrleader carefully removing the message from Valla's harness.

Valla chirped once happily and disappeared, *between*.

"How soon until he comes back?" Conar asked curiously.

"*If* he comes back," Vaxoram murmured darkly. Kindan glared at him; the elder boy returned his gaze impassively, but Kindan could still imagine how Vaxoram would have liked to have his own fire-lizard.

"Come on," Kindan said, jerking his head toward the Archive Room. "Let's get back to work."

They worked until dinner, adding Keroon, Igen, and Telgar to their list.

"It spread fast," Koriana observed as she looked over Vaxoram's shoulder. Going over the Records from Telgar was his responsibility, but Kindan knew that reading was difficult for Vaxoram, so he surreptitiously helped or had Koriana "read over his shoulder."

Now she observed, "Less than a month to get from one Hold to the next."

She had grown more and more pale as the day had progressed and Kindan, Conar, Vaxoram, and she had unearthed more grim records of the plague over a hundred Turns past.

"No mention of a cure," Conar added morosely. "They tried the Minor Green Dragon decoction at Igen, but it didn't work."

"They tried Major Blue Green Dragon decoction at Telgar," Kindan added, setting the Record to one side silently.

"All those deaths," Koriana said softly, as if just to herself. "Where were the dragonriders? Why didn't they help?"

"I don't know," Kindan said, shaking his head. "Perhaps there is just no mention in the Records here."

"How come no one tried Bronze Dragon?" Vaxoram asked. "Or Gold?"

Kindan shook his head condescendingly. "The names are ancient. Some say they came from before Landing and have nothing to do with the dragons of Pern."

"If they're so ancient, why don't we look in the ancient Records?" Koriana asked. "Perhaps there are remedies that have been forgotten."

"I doubt it," Vaxoram replied.

"Most things that work are remembered," Kindan agreed.

"But what if they only work against a plague?" Koriana persisted. "Wouldn't they then be forgotten until someone looks in the ancient Records?"

"Master Resler—," Conar began cautiously.

"*I* can handle him," Koriana declared, turning toward the oldest stacks of Records determinedly. The others glanced at Kindan expectantly. He stood still for a thoughtful moment then shrugged; she probably *could* handle Master Resler.

She pulled out a stack and brought them to an empty table. As she sat herself down, she looked over to Kindan. "I'm sorry if this will slow down your other work," she told him. "But—"

"That's all right," Kindan said. "Vaxoram will keep working."

"But he can't read," Koriana declared, brows furrowed quizzically. "Didn't you know?"

Conar gave a grunt of surprise and Vaxoram turned bright red, looking anxiously at Kindan.

"I meant to talk to you about it," Kindan said slowly. For some time he'd guessed, which is why he'd asked the Masterharper about reading in dim light over a sevenday before. "Some people have trouble with letters. That doesn't mean they're dumb, some of the smartest people have this problem—" he didn't get any further, Vaxoram ran out of the room.

"I'd better go after him," Kindan said after a moment. He glanced consideringly at Koriana, thinking of his duties and his responsibility to avoid making trouble for the Masterharper. "Your parents will be worried about you—"

"I've sent a message to them," Koriana replied peremptorily. "And shouldn't you let Nonala or Kelsa deal with him?"

Kindan slapped his head in surprise. "Nonala and Kelsa! I hadn't thought of them."

Conar looked at him questioningly, his expression making clear that he couldn't see how they could help with Vaxoram.

"They could help us search," Kindan declared excitedly. He glanced toward the doorway and then back to Koriana, a sudden question on his mind. "Where will you sleep?"

"I was hoping to find a place near you," Koriana replied. Across the distance Kindan could see her dimples stand out. He felt a flush of excitement roar through his veins. It was a moment before he recovered his senses. "I'd better go after Vaxoram and see if Nonala and Kelsa will help."

Kindan found Vaxoram standing outside in the courtyard. The night air was chilly and Kindan found himself shivering as he approached the older apprentice. Vaxoram's head was craned up to the brilliant night sky. The Dawn Sisters could just be seen and there, still faint but pulsing menacingly, was the Red Star. In less than a dozen Turns it would approach close enough to send Thread crashing down upon Pern; the only protection was the flaming breath of dragons and the courage of their riders.

"Who else knows?" Vaxoram asked after they shared a long moment of silence.

"No one," Kindan said. "I'd noticed only recently—with the Records—but I wanted to find a way to talk with you about it."

"Why?" Vaxoram asked bitterly. "I'm stupid, I can't read. There's no way I can be a harper."

"You're not stupid," Kindan replied. "Master Murenny says that many people who have this problem are very smart—"

"Murenny knows?" Vaxoram asked accusingly. "I thought you told no one."

"I didn't," Kindan repeated. "I only asked the Masterharper about the symptoms, I didn't mention you."

"He must suspect, then," Vaxoram replied bitterly.

"He could think that it's Conar," Kindan said. "Lots of people with this problem are great artists." Vaxoram cast a sidelong glance at him. "Others are great with lyrics, particularly long ballads."

Vaxoram snorted; he was most skilled with the longer ballads.

"Master Murenny says that people can learn to work around this," Kindan told him. "We can teach you."

"Why would you?" Vaxoram demanded, his voice full of pain. "Why would he?"

"I think he would teach you because anyone with your problem is very smart and he values intelligence," Kindan said slowly. "*I* want to teach you so that you can be a harper and stop hating yourself."

Vaxoram turned to face him, his eyes picking out Kindan's in the darkness. Kindan found no words to say but he could feel Vaxoram's emotions. After a moment, he clapped the older boy on the arm. "Come on, we're going to wake Nonala and Kelsa."

Vaxoram put up a restraining arm. "No," he said, "let's leave them until morning. If we wake them now, they'll just be crabby."

"But Koriana—"

"She's your problem," Vaxoram declared.

"What do you mean?" Kindan asked.

"You know what I mean," Vaxoram replied. "The two of you practically burn the air with your stares."

"But—"

"She likes you, Kindan," Vaxoram told him frankly. "Perhaps more." He smiled. "And it's obvious that you love her, too." His smile faded as he added with a shake of his head, "It's a pity she's the Holder's daughter. It'll never work." Before Kindan could respond, Vaxoram's mouth opened in a great yawn. "If you'll let me," Vaxoram said, "I'm going to bed. I'm no good to you the way I am."

"Sure," Kindan agreed.

"And send Conar up, too," Vaxoram said in a tone that was half-order, half-suggestion. "He'll be useless without some rest."

"But that will just leave me and Koriana," Kindan protested.

Vaxoram nodded, his teeth gleaming in the dim light. "Yes, it will, won't it?"

———— ✦ ————

"I spoke with him," Kindan called as he reentered the Archive room. "He'll be all right."

Conar glanced up at him and nodded, then yawned in exhaustion. Koriana smiled at the younger boy, then surprised herself with a yawn. Sure enough, just as she finished, Kindan yawned himself.

"Conar, you should go to sleep," Kindan ordered.

Conar blinked at him then shrugged and started to tidy his pile of Records.

"Leave them, just get some rest," Kindan added.

As the young boy left, Kindan glanced over at Koriana.

"I'm staying," she declared resolutely.

"You should get some sleep, too," he said.

"So should you," she replied, turning over another ancient Record.

"I will if you do," Kindan declared. "Otherwise, I feel duty-bound to keep you company."

Koriana didn't respond, her attention fixed on the gleaming Record in her hands.

"This is odd," she said. She gestured for Kindan to come over. Kindan approached slowly, his eyelids feeling heavy. "Have you ever seen a Record like this?"

As she turned to hand him the Record, their hands touched briefly. It was as though sparks had flowed between them. Kindan found himself looking not at the Record but at Koriana's brilliant blue eyes. He reached for her other hand, pulling her up out of her seat. Koriana rose and let him take it, her eyes locked on his. Her lips parted and he felt her breath gently on his face. He placed the Record carefully back on the table and drew her toward him. She came willingly, her eyes level with his.

Koriana closed her eyes and their lips met and Kindan wrapped his arms around her shoulders, pulling her into a tight embrace. Then he closed his eyes and felt only the touch of her tongue and the softness of her lips. He heard only her breathing, heard when it altered to a faster pace, felt when her arms squeezed him against her, felt his hands in her hair, her hands in his, the supple warmth of her body against his.

"Oh, Kindan," she cried when they finally broke the kiss. She buried her head against his and he turned and kissed the soft folds of her neck. Her breath coming faster, she pushed him back and looked at him with tear-spangled eyes, "What are we going to do?"

Kindan hugged her tight to him again and she responded willingly. "I don't know," he whispered into her ear. "All I know is that I love you, Koriana."

She pressed herself tightly against him, then pulled back and kissed him gently on the forehead. "I love you, too, always and for ever," she told him fervently. They kissed again, long and slow, savoring the sweetness of each other, hands moving tenderly over each other's body.

Emotions swelled up in Kindan that he'd never had before. Immense tenderness, overwhelming desire, deep passion. They amazed him as much as they frightened him. At long last, his body still quivering with passion, Kindan pulled back from Koriana, who murmured in protest, then nuzzled against him once more.

"We need rest," Kindan said, pulling back and tracing the line of her cheekbones with his hands. Koriana opened her eyes and smiled at him.

"It's too long to walk back to the Hold," she said. "Where shall I sleep?"

"You can sleep with me," Kindan said impulsively.

Koriana lowered her hands to his waist and pulled him tightly against her body. "I like that!" she declared with a devilish look in her eyes.

Kindan turned, holding on to one of her hands, and led her from the Archive Room, glows still unturned.

In the cold night in the courtyard, Koriana draped herself on him for warmth. Kindan had to shush her as they entered the apprentice dormitory; she was giddy with emotion and Kindan was afraid that everyone would hear them, but he finally got her into his bunk and pulled himself in alongside.

"I'll get too hot with these clothes on," Koriana declared, pulling off her trousers. Kindan was scandalized, he'd never been in bed with a woman before, let alone in the apprentice dormitory. But Koriana was right and Kindan found himself pulling off his trousers, also. Koriana nuzzled against him and Kindan thought to kiss her once more, but he spied a gleam in the dark—Vaxoram was looking at him impassively. Kindan froze for a moment, then nodded toward Vaxoram in understanding. Vaxoram held his eyes for a moment longer, then nodded himself and rolled over.

"We must go to sleep, Koriana," Kindan whispered to her.

"If you say so," Koriana replied drowsily, throwing her arm over him. Kindan found himself cuddling her head with one arm, stroking it softly while her breathing grew shallower and shallower as she drifted off to sleep. If anything, Kindan mused as he looked at her sleeping face, she was more beautiful asleep than awake.

——✦——

"Come on, get up!" Vaxoram said urgently in Kindan's ear the next morning. Kindan rolled over away from the noise but found his arm trapped. "Get up, Kindan!" Vaxoram said again, then disappeared.

Kindan opened his eyes and found himself looking at Koriana's sleeping face. His left arm was asleep, trapped under her shoulder.

"Koriana," he called softly. She jerked and then was still. "Koriana, wake up!"

She jerked again and Kindan leaned back to look at her. Her eyes were open and wide with fear.

"We've got to get up before the others wake up," he told her. She nodded in understanding. Kindan looked around for their trousers and found them folded neatly on the end of the bed. He handed Koriana's to her and she took them gratefully, trying to slide the trousers on under the blankets. Kindan motioned her to stop, grabbed his trousers, and quietly left the bed dragging them on. Koriana followed suit, the noise of her exertions masked by Kindan's.

Dressed, Kindan motioned for her to precede him toward the door.

Outside, Koriana giggled with delight as she sprinted forward, dragging Kindan along behind her with a tightly clasped hand. She whirled around to face him and pulled him against her like a dancer. She kissed him fiercely and declared, "I've never felt so alive!"

They kissed again for a long moment. The dark night turned gray and they shivered in the early-morning air.

Koriana pulled away from Kindan, her expression suddenly concerned. "What will we do? Mother will know that I stayed here."

"And Master Murenny will know that you weren't in the journeymen's quarters," Kindan added with a grimace. He thought for a moment, leading Koriana aimlessly across the courtyard. Then inspiration struck. "How about if we say you fell asleep in the Archives?"

"But why didn't you wake me?" Koriana asked, her face a mixture of curiosity and mock-outrage.

"I tried, but I couldn't," Kindan suggested. "You were too tired."

"You'd fallen asleep, too," Koriana retorted. "At your table and you didn't notice that I was still there."

"If that's the case," Kindan said, "then when we woke up we'd be heading to the night hearth for some *klah*."

"Excellent," Koriana agreed. "I could do with some *klah*."

Giddily, they traipsed down the steps to the kitchen only to freeze in fright as they heard footsteps following behind.

"Kindan?" the Masterharper called as he caught sight of him. "Are you—?"

Murenny spotted Koriana and his face went inscrutable, although Kindan wondered if for a moment the Masterharper's eyes weren't twinkling with some diffused delight.

"Lady Koriana, I thought you had returned to your Hold," Murenny said stiffly.

"I—"

"We fell asleep," Kindan finished. "In the Archives."

"I see," Murenny said in a dry voice. He glanced back up the stairs. "And is Vaxoram still there?"

Kindan thought fast before shaking his head. "I think I sent him off to bed and then—"

"I interrupted him," Koriana interjected. "And then we went back to the Records and—"

"Well, fell asleep," Kindan finished, doing his very best to look chagrined.

"And now?" Murenny asked with a slight nod of his head.

"We woke up and thought to get some *klah* before we went back to work," Kindan said.

"And perhaps breakfast?" Murenny suggested, gesturing for

them to continue. He glanced around and asked Koriana, "Where is that marvelous gold fire-lizard of yours?"

Koriana gave him a startled look and was only saved by a triumphant squawk as Koriss appeared at the top of the stairs and flew down to perch on Koriana's shoulder.

"Ow!" Koriana exclaimed, quickly reaching for Koriss and moving her to the crook of her arm. "Your nails are just too sharp, dear."

Koriss looked up at Koriana, faceted eyes whirling red with growing hunger.

"We'd better feed her right now," Murenny said, chuckling. "Then perhaps she could bear a message to your parents?"

Koriana looked skeptical. "She's not yet quite as adept as Kindan's Valla, Masterharper," she temporized, looking down fondly at the small gold. "But I can try."

"Well, I'd hate for you to lose her," Murenny responded. A fire-lizard given poor directions could easily get lost or, worse, lost forever *between*.

"We've been neglecting her training," Kindan said, grimacing.

"Perhaps later in the day, then, or tomorrow," Murenny suggested.

"Oh, no!" Koriana protested. "We've got to keep searching the Records." Kindan understood her concern: while it would only take a moment to send Koriss on her journey, their worry about her safety would completely distract Koriana—and Kindan—until they received news of her arrival.

They entered the darkened kitchen and made their way to the night hearth. Kindan grabbed some tongs, filled a kettle, and hung it over the glowing coals. He then went back toward the kitchen ovens and glanced inside, surprised to see bread already rising.

"What are you—" Selora's voice bellowed from the back room as she raced out, only to stop as she spotted Murenny. "Oh, Masterharper, I didn't see you."

"No problem," Murenny said dismissively. "Kindan, Koriana, and I were just trying to steal an early breakfast."

"The rolls are almost done," Selora informed him. She glanced sharply at Kindan. "With a bit of help," she added, "I could have them glazed with sugar and ready to eat, if a bit hot."

"That sounds marvelous!" Koriana exclaimed.

Kindan nodded and moved to follow Selora. "What do I need to do?" he asked as he headed toward the back room only to find the Masterharper following him.

"Many hands make short work," Murenny called cheerfully, pushing up his sleeves.

"Too many cooks spoil the broth," Selora responded sourly, holding up her hand. "No disrespect, Masterharper, but you've been banned from the kitchens for the duration."

"Duration?" Koriana asked, brows raised.

"Of my life," Murenny confessed unhappily.

"Burnt a sevenday's worth of cooking," Selora added, shaking her head in sad acknowledgment.

"Well, I can help," Koriana offered.

"You'd be better off helping the Masterharper," Selora said, pointing toward the hearth. "He's the only man I know who can burn water."

Reluctantly, Koriana accepted this suggestion and followed the Masterharper back to the hearth. Murenny contented himself with puttering around the large room, turning over the glows.

In the back room, out of earshot, Selora shot Kindan a sharp look and asked pointedly, "And where did he find you two?"

"On the way downstairs," Kindan replied, carefully pouring some confectioner's sugar into a cup of cold water, stirring all the while.

"And where were you before that?" Selora demanded.

"We fell asleep in the Archive Room," Kindan said, hoping to sound convincing.

Selora snorted. "You'd better be a better harper than you are a liar."

Kindan turned bright red.

✦

"Let's eat up in my study," Murenny suggested several minutes later when Selora announced that the rolls were ready and Koriana had the *klah* made. With a wink, he explained to Kindan, "I wouldn't want the other apprentices to feel that I've picked a favorite."

While Kindan examined the awesome possibility that perhaps the Masterharper *had* picked a favorite, he and Selora quickly set out a tray and filled it with a selection of rolls, a pitcher of still-steaming *klah,* and several mugs.

They made their way to Murenny's study and, at his gesture, seated themselves around the breakfast table. Kindan sat facing the window. As he was pouring his mug of *klah,* he spotted Vaxoram exit the apprentice dormitory, looking furtively around the courtyard in the growing dawn.

Masterharper Murenny noticed Kindan's look, got up, and peered out the window himself. With a speculative glance toward Kindan, Murenny leaned out of the window and shouted to Vaxoram, "Why don't you come up and join us?"

A few moments later, Vaxoram knocked on the door and Murenny invited him inside.

"Come in, come in," the Masterharper said, gesturing cheerfully for Vaxoram to join them. He rose and pulled a free chair from his worktable over to the breakfast table, indicating that Vaxoram should sit with them. "I see that Kindan remembered to set a spare mug, so pour yourself some *klah* and grab one of those delicious rolls before they're all gone."

Vaxoram glanced nervously at Kindan before filling his mug and grabbing a roll. Then, deciding that he was safe, the older apprentice carefully began to slowly chew his roll.

Murenny waited in a genial silence until Vaxoram finished his roll and had a sip of *klah* before continuing, "Vaxoram, how well do you know the codes regarding dueling?"

The older apprentice gave the Masterharper a startled look. "I remember all that Master Detallor taught me," he replied defensively.

"I'm sure you do," Murenny agreed. "Do you remember the rules of dishonor?"

Vaxoram flushed and bowed his head. "Yes."

Murenny shook his head. "I don't think you're following me, Vaxoram."

The older apprentice glanced up, first at Kindan, then at Murenny.

"Do you remember the rules for a re-challenge?"

Vaxoram creased his brow in thought, then in slowly dawning surprise. Kindan gasped as he realized what the Masterharper was aiming at and Vaxoram turned his attention to him, consideringly.

"If the victor dishonors the cause of the challenge, the vanquished can demand a rematch," Koriana said slowly. She glanced at Kindan, biting her lower lip nervously.

"Yes," Murenny said, his voice completely serious. He looked long and hard at Vaxoram. "Is there reason for you to demand a rematch?"

"No," Vaxoram declared immediately, his eyes locked with Kindan's. He glanced back to the Masterharper. "No, Masterharper, there is not."

Murenny nodded, then turned steely eyes on Kindan.

"Where were you last night?"

"I was in my bunk," Kindan replied in a small voice. "Koriana was with me."

"By my choice," Koriana declared, reaching out to grab Kindan's hand. Her strong grip felt feeble and distant compared against the huge hole in the pit of Kindan's stomach.

Murenny did not so much as glance toward her, asking Kindan directly, "Did you break your word?"

Kindan's mouth was dry and he swallowed hard, not knowing what to say. More than anything, he wished he were somewhere else, that events were different, that he wasn't pinned under the terrible glare of the Masterharper's wrath.

Murenny's lips tightened in Kindan's silence. "Were you hoping to convince us of a lie?"

"Yes, Master," Kindan answered feebly, feeling totally ashamed.

"Then how can you hope to be a harper?" the Masterharper asked, his voice challenging.

Kindan could only shake his head mutely. "I don't know," he confessed finally. He felt torn between getting up then and there, packing his things and leaving the Harper Hall, or just leaving. He had never felt so dejected.

Murenny turned his attention to Vaxoram.

"Why did you permit this?" Murenny asked. The older apprentice shook his head mutely and Murenny pressed him, "Who woke them in the morning?"

"I did," Vaxoram confessed.

"Why?" Murenny asked him, his face full of curiosity. "Why did you not report this? With Kindan dishonored, your honor would be restored."

"He was not dishonorable," Vaxoram said, meeting the Masterharper's eyes frankly. He glanced to Kindan. "I will not betray you."

Kindan could only nod glumly, too numb to appreciate the depth of Vaxoram's admission.

"Masterharper Murenny," Koriana interjected, "I love Kindan. I would never let him do anything that would cause him dishonor."

"Yet you have," Murenny snapped. He gestured at the hand clasping Kindan's and Koriana dropped it as though stung. "You have dishonored him, your father, me, your Hold, and the Harper Hall." Murenny shifted his gaze to include Kindan. "Both of you."

"I love her," Kindan responded, reaching out to regain Koriana's hand with his own.

"More than your honor?" Murenny asked relentlessly. "More than her honor?" He did not wait for their response before continuing, "What sort of love is it that demands dishonor and lies to even exist?

"How," and his voice filled the room with its strength, "can any of you think for an instant that this stained emotion can last?"

"But I *love* him!" Koriana protested, breaking down into tears and burying her face in her hands.

Murenny shook his head, with a sad expression on his face. "I see only need, not love."

Koriana looked up at him in silent shock and outrage.

"And betrayal," Murenny continued, his voice quiet but firm. Kindan glanced hotly at the Masterharper, furious that he should cause Koriana so much pain, but Murenny met his eyes sternly, as he continued, "Betrayal of your honor, betrayal of your family, betrayal of yourself."

"But Father would never—" Koriana began in protest.

"Not now!" Murenny cut her off. "Now you will never know how he would have behaved had you come to him honestly, with your heart open, and told him your true feelings." He glanced toward Kindan. "Nor will you ever know how I would have responded, how I might have helped you." He shook his head. "The two of you have betrayed each other as surely as if you'd fought a duel to the death."

The horrible silence that fell lasted only for an instant and was shattered as a brilliant splash of gold burst into the room. Koriss entered from *between*, bringing a crisp air into the room and filling it with her loud, raucous cries, her eyes whirling red in anger and confusion. Koriana grabbed for her, missed, grabbed again, cradling the agitated fire-lizard tight against her body. It was a number of minutes before Koriss's red faceted eyes changed to a calmer green and the fire-lizard nuzzled against her partner, chirping concernedly.

Kindan watched the proceedings with a growing sense of unease.

"Koriana," he asked tensely, "does Koriss have an image for you?"

Koriana gave him a puzzled look. Kindan told her, "Close your eyes and concentrate on her."

Koriana did so, her expression still quizzical, but only for a moment as her eyes popped open again and she told them in alarm, "Father's coming and he's got guards with him!"

"Yes," Murenny murmured, glancing at Kindan and Vaxoram, "just as I'd feared."

✦

Under the Masterharper's direction, the four of them met Lord Holder Bemin just outside the archway into the Harper Hall.

"Lord Holder," Murenny called in greeting, bowing low. Bemin regarded him coldly, flanked on either side by two burly guards and trailed by four more, all carrying swords. "We were just about to come to you."

"I see," Bemin said. He gestured curtly to his daughter. "Koriana."

"Father," Koriana replied, ducking her head obediently.

"Your mother was most worried," Bemin said. Kindan thought that that was a lie; it seemed that the Lord Holder was most agitated, which made more sense if he'd ever heard rumors of Murenny's involvement with Sannora.

"I was fine, honestly," Koriana replied. "We were late going through the Records—we think we might have found something vital—"

"If it were so vital, why didn't the Masterharper send us a messenger?" Bemin interjected, a foreboding look on his face. "Why didn't he drum a message?"

As if in answer to his question, the faint sound of distant drums echoed into Fort's valley. Kindan, Vaxoram, Murenny, and Koriana all strained to hear the faint throbbing notes.

"Emergency," Koriana repeated as she deciphered the first

code. She and Kindan locked eyes, much to Bemin's anger. "Emergency," she added, her eyes going wider. "Emergency."

The noise faded and everyone strained for any new notes.

But there were none.

"Three, not four," Vaxoram remarked in relief, only to himself.

"A major Hold emergency," Koriana said, sounding a bit unsure. "Not a minor Hold emergency."

"But from where?" Murenny asked, turning as if for an answer toward the repeater tower lost in the distance.

Bemin glanced nervously at each of them in turn, ending with his daughter.

"What does it mean?" he asked Koriana. Behind him, Kindan noticed that the Fort guards had unconsciously shifted toward each other as if for protection.

"It could be Telgar," Vaxoram suggested.

"Or Igen or Ista," Kindan responded.

"Even if it were two, that wouldn't be a Pern-wide emergency," Bemin protested. "There'd have to be something involving more than half of the major Holds for that."

Murenny nodded but his words were not reassuring. "True, but the illness was in Keroon, so why couldn't it spread to Igen or any of the seaward minor Holds, and then how long would it be before Ista was infected?"

Bemin responded with a sour look. "If that were so, how come we haven't heard anything from the Weyrs?"

"A good question," Murenny replied, rubbing his chin thoughtfully.

"Well, it's neither here nor there," Bemin said after a moment spent fulminating. He glanced toward his daughter. "Koriana, your mother is most anxious for you."

"My duty is here, Father," Koriana replied resolutely.

"Your duty is where I say it is," Bemin replied, his eyes narrowing in anger.

"Yes, my lord," Koriana agreed with a nod of her head. "And you instructed me to be here, searching the Records, learning the drum codes, and how to control my fire-lizard." She paused for just a moment. "So I am here, doing my duty to you and Pern."

"Pern?" Bemin repeated, one brow arched in surprise.

Koriana nodded. "I believe, Father, that anything that we can learn about previous plagues like this will save many lives on Pern," she replied.

"Saving lives is a job for healers," Bemin snapped.

"And Holders," Koriana retorted, her blue eyes flashing.

"Who told you that?" Bemin demanded in surprise.

"You did."

"I never—"

"You said that a Holder is responsible for all the lives in the Hold," Koriana reminded him. The Lord Holder closed his mouth with an audible click, glaring at Masterharper Murenny accusingly.

When Murenny made no reaction, Bemin turned back to his wayward daughter. "That's correct," he told her. "And the holders owe their lord service, even including his own children."

Koriana opened her mouth for another retort, but before she could speak, the air above them suddenly darkened as a large bronze dragon appeared from *between*.

Moments later, Valla plummeted down to Kindan, pulling up just in time to land—hard—on Kindan's shoulder.

"It would seem that Benden has gotten your message," Murenny said, nodding to Kindan.

The Fort Hold guards, having bunched up close to their lord, now sidled discreetly around him so as to put him between them and the bronze dragon that settled in the meadow beyond the Harper Hall, his hide gleaming bright in the full morning sun.

Not a moment after M'tal alighted from Gaminth did the sky darken again. Kindan craned his neck up to see a lithe blue dragon with three riders descend to land beside the Benden Weyr dragon. Kindan spotted the rider's Ista Weyr colors and instantly recognized the rider as J'trel.

"What's Ista doing here?" Bemin asked as the blue dragon landed.

"That would be Talith," Murenny responded. "J'trel is his rider. He's been here to the Healer Hall a number of times with—"

"Ki'da'!" a young boy cried, rushing across the field.

"Druri!" Kindan called back enthusiastically. He waved toward the blue rider and nodded at the woman who trailed along behind. "J'trel, Jalenna!"

When J'trel waved back, Kindan felt that something was wrong; the older rider was usually much more enthusiastic in his greeting. Jalenna, Kindan saw, was carrying a small bundle in a sling. The bundle squirmed awkwardly; it was not usual for Jalenna to bring young Jassi with her. Kindan felt dread and urgency emanating from both adults as they approached.

"Kindan, stand away, please," M'tal called urgently as Druri approached.

Murenny moved to intercept the young man, diverting him from Kindan, Koriana, and Vaxoram.

"Is the plague in Ista?" M'tal said to J'trel.

"Not yet," J'trel replied. "It may be only a matter of days, however." He turned to the Masterharper. "I've come to beg a favor, Murenny."

"What's going on?" Bemin demanded, surprised and nervous at the sudden change in the situation.

"I've come for Kindan," M'tal said. "His Valla requested that he come to Benden." M'tal glanced down at Kindan as he added, "Though I've no idea why."

"We were hoping to examine your Records," Kindan explained with a nod toward M'tal. Bemin's reaction made it clear to everyone that he thought Kindan was being overly familiar with the Benden Weyrleader.

"Of course," M'tal said willingly. "If it weren't for you, our dragons would still be chewing that hot firestone and we'd never know anything about the abilities of watch-whers."

Bemin's expression changed; he glanced at Kindan with a look of appraisal on his face.

"I've come to ask sanctuary for Druri, Jalenna, and Jassi," J'trel said to Murenny.

"I see," Murenny replied noncommittally, still keeping a hand on the restless Druri.

The story of Druri's debility was well known at the Harper Hall, where the dim but kindly lad had been a regular visitor for several Turns, working with the Healers as they strove to retrain a brain tragically damaged in a near-drowning nearly five Turns ago.

The rumors in the apprentice dormitory—always rampant if not always accurate—were that J'trel had been performing aerobatics when Druri and some other boys had been out of Ista Harbor sailing in a small skiff. Their amazement with blue Talith's antics had caused them to neglect their navigation and the skiff hit a reef, the mast fell on Druri, cracking his skull and many precious minutes were lost before he was brought out of the water, drowned and dead. At Jalenna's request, J'trel had taken quick action to revive the boy, but it had been too late to prevent Druri's brain from being severely damaged. Rumors went on, wildly, to assert that J'trel had had a romantic liaison with Jalenna resulting in Jassi. Kindan tended to discount such rumors as everyone knew that blue riders preferred to partner with green riders, and that both riders were usually male.

"We should leave now," M'tal said to Kindan, nodding apologetically to J'trel as he added, "I don't want to risk the chance of Kindan catching the illness."

"There's a risk of the illness from these?" Bemin demanded, waving at the three Ista holders and the blue rider.

"I don't think so," J'trel replied, "or I wouldn't have brought them here."

"But you don't know," Bemin persisted.

"No, Lord Holder," J'trel answered, his voice going stiff.

"I can't permit it," Bemin said. "I can't let my Hold—"

"I make this request of the Healer Hall, not Fort Hold," J'trel interjected.

"All the same," Bemin retorted hotly. "I won't let—"

"Lord Holder, I don't know if you really have a choice," Murenny interrupted in a soft voice.

Bemin shot him an angry look and Murenny contined quickly, "How many ships have docked at Fort Sea Hold since we received the first word of the illness?"

"But—"

"And how many have offloaded fish?" J'trel asked, guessing the train of Murenny's reasoning. "And how many fished off Ista or Keroon? How many set in to one of those Holds or minor Holds or merely put a boat ashore to gather water?"

"But—but—we don't know—" Bemin spluttered.

"You are absolutely correct, my Lord Holder," Murenny agreed with a nod of his head. "We don't know." He frowned. "In fact, with that last drum message we don't know if the emergency was in Igen, Telgar, or even Southern Boll Holds." He glanced toward M'tal. "We need more information."

The Benden Weyrleader nodded in understanding.

"We think the last plague started on the east coast," Kindan said, inserting himself into the conversation despite the knot in his stomach. "That's why I've asked to review the Records at Benden Weyr."

"But what about the Harper Hall Records?" Bemin demanded.

"Fragments, scattered reports, nothing to give us a decent picture of what to expect," Koriana said, meeting her father's angry eyes with her concerned ones. "Let me go with him, Father," she pleaded. "For our Hold, for our people."

"Why do you have to go?" Bemin asked, his tone less belligerent than worried.

"Because I know what to look for," Koriana replied. "And because we need to know as soon as we can." She gestured to Kindan, Vaxoram, and herself. "We three are best at that." She gave

Vaxoram a sympathetic look before she continued, "Vaxoram has a hard time reading, Father. It takes him twice as long as it does me. If I don't go, it will take nearly twice as long to get our answers—and what will happen in the meantime?"

"Your mother—"

"Mother would say, 'Go, do what you must,'" Koriana predicted.

Bemin let out a long fuming sigh and nodded reluctantly. Then he turned to Kindan. "And you, have you been honorable?"

"No, my lord," Kindan admitted. "I have not."

M'tal gave him a startled look, a look which Kindan would have given anything never to have earned.

"We slept in the same bed," Koriana said. "We kissed but nothing more." She reached out toward Kindan as she told her father, "I love him."

Bemin turned furiously toward Murenny. "No," he said hoarsely. "This cannot be. I will not permit it."

Before anyone could respond, another drum message rumbled through the valley.

"Emergency," Kindan and Koriana translated in unison, their eyes locking in a rush of fear and dread. "Emergency. Emergency. Telgar Hold. Send help. Please."

Even before the words had registered, the drums started again.

"Plague in Nabol, please help," Kindan translated, his heart pounding heavily in his chest.

"Plague in Crom," Koriana added, turning to her father pleadingly.

Bemin looked at her for one moment more before nodding decisively. "Go!" he told her. He turned to M'tal and gestured to Kindan, "You will guard her honor?"

"My word as a dragonrider," M'tal responded in leaden tones.

"You have my word, also, Lord Holder," Kindan added in a small voice.

"Your word has no value to me," Bemin responded harshly. He

gestured to Vaxoram. "He'll go with you, too, won't he?" Kindan nodded and Bemin told Vaxoram, "You will sleep in the same room with him; never leave without him."

"My lord," Vaxoram agreed with a stiff bow.

"Go then," Bemin said, waving his hand angrily. He turned to Murenny. "You and I will discuss these other matters now."

"Come on," M'tal said gruffly to Kindan and the others, turning on his heel and speeding his way back to his bronze dragon. He arranged for Koriana to be sandwiched between himself and Vaxoram, with Kindan seated behind the older apprentice.

Gaminth rose into the air with an urgency that seemed almost angry to Kindan, as though the dragon were reflecting the rider's mood. As they went *between,* Kindan reached a hand forward to touch Koriana but dropped it as he remembered his promise.

He felt as doomed as all Pern.

CHAPTER 8

Harper to your word be true
Holder, crafter you also hew
To honesty, integrity, and respect
All others without regard to intellect.

BENDEN WEYR

The cold of *between* remained in Kindan's bones as they burst out into the waning daylight of a Benden Weyr experiencing a midwinter freeze. The crest of the Weyr was snow-covered as were all the mountains in the distance.

The cold of *between* was also in the air they brought with them from the Harper Hall, the moisture frozen out into a rainbow of ice crystals that surrounded Gaminth and his riders until they dropped through it when the bronze dragon dove steeply into the Weyr Bowl.

Gaminth landed deftly, but Kindan was still so numb physically and emotionally that he nearly fell from his perch on the dragon, slamming awkwardly against Vaxoram and managing to stay on the dragon's back only with the help of Vaxoram's steadying hand.

Mortified, he swiftly clambered off the dragon. After he helped Vaxoram down, he stood in to help Koriana only to be elbowed aside by the older harper.

"My job's to serve you, and you're likely to drop her," Vaxoram told him curtly.

Hurt, Kindan stood back and watched enviously as Vaxoram gently caught Koriana in his strong arms and lowered her to the Weyr Bowl.

"Come on, I'll show you the Records room," M'tal called as soon as he hopped down from his dragon. He led a brisk pace up two flights of stone stairs and turned right, leading through the first doorway.

The room was stacked full of Records, with many more stacked awkwardly in dark alcoves. Dim morning light from the Bowl shone in from a window cut in the far side of the room.

"Kindan," M'tal ordered, "come with me and we'll get some *klah* and glows."

Out of breath, Kindan turned immediately and started to follow M'tal only to be stopped by Vaxoram, who said to the Weyrleader, "I am under vow to be with him at all times."

M'tal pursed his lips, then nodded quickly. "Very well, you may come." He glanced toward Koriana. "Will you get started?"

"Of course," Koriana replied, her gaze reaching out to Kindan for a moment before she turned her head quickly away and began to search through the first stack of Records.

"By the Shell of Faranth!" M'tal swore to Kindan as they trotted down the stairs toward the Weyr Bowl. "What ever could you have been thinking of, Kindan?"

"I—"

"And you," M'tal rounded on Vaxoram. "Didn't you duel him for much the same reason?" Before Vaxoram could respond, he continued, "Don't you know you can re-challenge him and win your honor?"

"He did nothing dishonorable," Vaxoram declared hotly. "They were never out of my sight."

Kindan looked at Vaxoram in surprise and then realized that the older harper had spoken the truth.

"Then why—?" Kindan began questioningly only to be cut off by M'tal who spoke with dawning comprehension, "Forsworn, you could not provide witness to Lord Bemin."

"Yes, my lord," Vaxoram agreed, glancing apologetically to Kindan.

"Thanks," Kindan told Vaxoram feelingly.

"What for?" M'tal demanded. "With your honor in question, there's no hope of having you come *here*."

No hope? Kindan thought to himself. He had no chance of being posted to the Weyr? His heart could sink no further; he felt like it had frozen, stuck forever *between*.

They entered the Weyr's large Kitchen Cavern. M'tal pointed peremptorily in one direction and moved in another, toward the hearth. "Kindan, get the glows while Vaxoram and I get a tray of food and a pitcher of *klah*."

A number of dragonriders and weyrfolk looked up excitedly as the Weyrleader strode by, but he waved them back to their work.

A kindly weyrboy piled him up with fresh glows and Kindan moved much more slowly to catch up with the Benden Weyrleader and Vaxoram, who was carrying a tray of food, while M'tal carried a large pitcher of *klah* and several mugs.

The two harpers arrived out of breath outside the Records Room.

"Set up the glows," M'tal instructed Kindan as he gestured to Vaxoram to place the tray on a free table to which he added the *klah* and mugs. He turned his attention to Koriana.

"You'll sleep in our quarters just beyond the stairs if you need to," M'tal told her. "You can use the necessary there, too." He looked at the two boys. "You'll sleep in the weyrling quarters, they're empty now, and you can use the necessary there—that's across the Bowl, so don't wait if you need it."

Vaxoram and Kindan nodded glumly, daunted at the prospect of crossing the Weyr Bowl so late at night, and when they were so tired. M'tal slapped his hands together briskly and stood up. "Very well, is there anything else you need?"

The three youths shook their heads.

"Then I'll get on with my duties," he told them. "I'll be back soon."

Koriana had already pulled several large stacks of Records and arranged them in front of chairs. Silently, she, Kindan, and Vaxoram took their places in front of the stacks.

"Three eighty-nine, right?" Koriana murmured as she turned over a Record.

"And three ninety," Kindan agreed. "The third month."

Koriana shook her head. "The Records I've pulled go back to the first month, just in case."

"That's a lot of reading," Vaxoram grumbled.

"So let's get to work," Kindan replied, nudging him on the arm. Vaxoram gave him a look that, while obedient, reminded Kindan exactly how much "work" reading Records was for the older lad. But before Kindan could respond, Vaxoram bent over his Record, bringing a thin glow as close as he could.

Silence fell and stretched, disturbed only by the occasional rustle of a turned Record, or a disappointed grunt or irritated grumble.

"I thought that Weyr Records would be better than Hold Records," Koriana murmured at one point. "But, except for notes about dragons and flaming, they're not all that much different."

"Here's one about an exploding bag of firestone," Vaxoram said, casting a glance at Kindan. "A weyrling and his rider went *between*. Another rider was badly burnt but survived."

"Sounds like C'tov," Kindan muttered to himself.

"Who?" Koriana asked, glancing up from her reading.

"C'tov," Kindan said, looking back at her and shifting nervously in his chair. "He was the one who found the proper firestone."

"He Impressed a dragon?" Vaxoram asked, giving Kindan a hurt look for not spreading such juicy gossip sooner. "Thanks for sharing."

"I thought everyone knew," Kindan said. "It happened such a long time ago."

Vaxoram grunted and looked back down at his Record. Koriana gave Kindan a sympathetic smile which he returned in full. They held their gaze for a few moments more before, by mutual consent, they turned back to their work and silence descended once more.

The silence stretched on endlessly, became a companionable thing punctuated by the turning of musty Records and the creaks as they moved in their chairs or changed the way they rested their elbows on the table. At some point the silence became seductive, warm and enveloping, begging for rest and sleep.

A noise startled Kindan and he looked up to see Koriana's head resting on the table, her blond hair covering her face. One of her hands had slid off the table, sliding a stack of Records with it. It was their rustling fall that Kindan had heard. He looked over to Vaxoram to find the older apprentice regarding him through sleep-lidded eyes.

"What do we do?" he asked Kindan.

"We can't leave her here," Kindan said. "We've got nothing to put over her to keep her warm." He looked toward the Holder girl and called softly, "Koriana." She made no motion. Louder he called, "Koriana." She stirred, then settled once more. "Koriana!"

"Huh?" Koriana lifted her head blearily, then leaned back in her chair, a chagrined look on her face. "I'm all right, I must have dozed—"

"You should go to sleep," Kindan told her.

"But the Records!" Koriana protested, bending down bleary-eyed in a feeble attempt to read.

"They'll keep until the morning," a voice called from the door. Koriana, Kindan, and Vaxoram whipped their heads around in surprise to see a woman in a nightgown standing in the doorway. She gestured toward Koriana. "I'm Salina. M'tal sent me to bring you to bed."

Kindan rose instantly, and gesturing for Vaxoram to follow suit, bowed respectfully. "Weyrwoman," he said hastily, "I had no idea—"

Salina cut him off with a smile and a shake of her head. "It's far too late in the night for formalities, harper." She gestured again to Koriana. "Come along, dear, you must be exhausted. "It's nearly dawn."

"Dawn?" Koriana repeated in surprise. "It doesn't feel like it, my lady."

"That's because your body is still thinking it's back at Fort Hold where the hour is only midnight," Salina said. "Though that's still late enough for all of you."

As Koriana joined her, Salina told the other two, "Be careful going down the stairs and across the Bowl. It's darkest before the dawn here, with the Bowl still in shadow."

Kindan nodded.

"There are glows laid out in the weyrling quarters," she told them. "Fresh-made beds, too."

"Thank you, my lady," Kindan replied, bowing once more. Salina smiled at him and, clasping Koriana by the hand, led the holder girl off to bed.

Kindan and Vaxoram followed them out of the Records Room and headed down the stairs, moving slowly with the aches from sitting too long in the same position. The air was cold in the Weyr Bowl and, as much as Kindan wanted to see more, he felt too tired to do more than muzzily register the notion.

"Weyrling quarters," Vaxoram murmured to himself as they spotted the faint glow in the distance. "What would it be like to live there?"

Kindan could only shake his head in response.

✦

Kindan woke early, when the weyrling barracks were just receiving the first rays of morning. He was still tired, but the new and different sounds of the Weyr had disturbed his sleep and piqued his curiosity. In the bunk nearest him, he could see the gleam of Vaxoram's eyes, showing that he was also awake.

Valla was nestled up against Kindan's back but rose into the air eagerly when he moved. With an inquisitive chirp, the fire-lizard flew out of the barracks. Off in search of food, Kindan guessed. As if in sympathy with the fire-lizard, Kindan's stomach grumbled.

Across the way, Vaxoram rose from his bunk. They found the necessary and had quick showers, grateful that towels had been laid out for them in the otherwise empty weyrling quarters. They were even more surprised to see that clothes—slightly oversized— were hanging on hangers just below the towels. Kindan, for one, was glad that he wouldn't be wearing the same clothes two days in a row. He was also glad to find some sweetgrass, which he rubbed on as antiperspirant.

Vaxoram, with a smug look, shaved.

They were quick enough, all the same, to exit the weyrling quarters with the sun only just a little further in the sky. As they crossed the Bowl to the Kitchen Cavern, Kindan spotted a strange shadow high up on the west side of the Bowl and turned to the east to determine its source.

"Star Stones," Vaxoram said, following Kindan's gaze. He pointed to a place high on the top of the western wall of the Weyr.

"I'll bet that's where they put the drums, too," Kindan said.

"They'll reverberate loudly in this Bowl," Vaxoram agreed.

Kindan's stomach grumbled again, as if in response to the larger Bowl's emptiness, and the two harpers exchanged amused looks. Kindan lengthened his stride, eager to appease his stomach and get back to work.

They were almost there when Vaxoram spoke again, voicing

something that had been obviously bothering him all across the Weyr Bowl. "What are you going to do?"

"About what?"

"You and Koriana," Vaxoram replied.

"I don't know," Kindan told him.

"But you love her, right?" Vaxoram persisted. Kindan raised an eyebrow at him inquisitively. "I mean, I really think you love her or I would never have—"

Kindan smiled and bumped his fist on Vaxoram's shoulder in recognition. "I never did thank you for that."

"It was my duty," Vaxoram answered stiffly.

"No," Kindan corrected. "It wasn't really." He was silent for a moment. "So why did you do it?"

"I thought you loved her," Vaxoram repeated.

"I do," Kindan said, his heart fluttering. He regarded Vaxoram shrewdly and slowed almost to a stop. "So why did you do it?"

Vaxoram stifled an abrupt response, his face taking on a suffused look.

"Is there somebody you love?" Kindan asked softly, comprehension slowly dawning. "Is that why you did it?"

"That's not why I did it," Vaxoram said tensely.

"But there is someone," Kindan said. He realized that that would explain much of Vaxoram's behavior: He was trying to impress someone.

"It doesn't matter," Vaxoram snapped, abruptly stepping forward. "I'm as good as Shunned."

"No, you're not."

"The best I'll ever be is a bad apprentice," Vaxoram declared despairingly. "I can hardly even read."

"We'll work on that," Kindan promised.

"Why?" Vaxoram demanded. "And how?"

"There are Records in the Harper Hall or the Healer Hall," Kindan replied. "Some of them will describe treatments."

"Why?" Vaxoram persisted, shaking his head mulishly.

"Well, at the very least, so that you can help more with these Records," Kindan replied.

Vaxoram snorted but his expression was wistful, not angry. He clapped Kindan on the shoulder. Startled, Kindan turned to face him.

"Thanks."

Kindan shrugged and they entered the Kitchen Cavern.

Koriana was already there, seated with Salina and M'tal. She waved at them and gestured to two nearby chairs.

"Good morning, Weyrleader, Weyrwoman," Kindan called as he approached. Vaxoram nodded in silent greeting.

"Did you sleep well?" Salina asked. Koriana poured two mugs of *klah* and pushed them across the table to the boys.

"Very well, thank you, my lady," Kindan responded.

"Ready for another day's work?" M'tal inquired.

"Yes, my lord," Kindan told him.

Salina and M'tal exchanged amused glances.

"You have such excellent manners," Salina remarked in response to Kindan's worried look.

"If only our weyrlings had as much," M'tal groaned.

"We've no harper to teach them, you see," Salina explained to Koriana. Kindan dropped his head to hide his shame.

"There are some good journeymen at the Harper Hall," Vaxoram suggested. "And one apprentice I know, Merol, should walk the tables soon."

"Walk the tables?" Koriana repeated.

"When an apprentice makes journeyman or a journeyman makes master, they walk the tables in the Harper Hall," Vaxoram explained.

"They walk around the tables to their new table," Kindan expanded, seeing Koriana's confused look. He grinned at her, sensing that she had an image of harpers jumping up on tables and kicking food and plates everywhere with gay abandon.

"It's a special day," Vaxoram said wistfully. "Every apprentice dreams of the day."

"I'd like to see it," Koriana said, glancing toward Kindan with eager eyes.

"Merol will walk soon," Kindan told her in a tone that said that he didn't expect to walk the tables himself.

Salina and M'tal looked at each other in a way that Kindan couldn't quite fathom; the sort of looks that parents and elderly people exchanged when dealing with younger people.

"Have some rolls," M'tal said, passing a covered basket to Kindan.

After breakfast they began their second day in the Records Room. They broke for lunch disconsolately, all three overwhelmed by the sheer volume of Records. Dinner came and went and still they found nothing.

"Why did she start so far back?" Vaxoram grumbled as they made their way back down the stairs toward the weyrling barracks for the night.

"I didn't want us to miss anything," Koriana replied from the top of the stairs.

"At this rate it'll be a sevenday before we *find* anything," Vaxoram grumbled.

"No," Kindan replied firmly. "Less. We don't have much more time."

"What do you mean?" Koriana called down, alarmed.

"From what we've seen, the illness is spreading from hold to hold in a sevenday," Kindan reminded her. "If we don't find something soon, it may be too late."

"So let's go back," Koriana called, turning back toward the Records Room.

"No," Vaxoram said.

"We're too tired," Kindan agreed. "There's not enough light with just the glows and we might miss something vital."

His response quelled Koriana's protests and they all went off to sleep fitfully.

And so they continued for another two days, growing more anxious, and more weary.

They awoke again early on the fifth day and were back to work before the sun had lifted high enough to light the whole Bowl. Less than an hour later, Kindan turned to a new Record, then suddenly looked up. "That's odd."

The others stopped and looked at him.

"The last Record was for the twenty-fourth day of the third month of 389," Kindan said. He held up the new Record. "This is dated the eleventh of the second month of 408."

"There must be some missing Records," Vaxoram said unconcernedly.

"I don't think so," Koriana replied, turning her head back to the stacks of old Records. "I checked pretty thoroughly." She looked over at Kindan. "What's that last Record say?"

"I read something near there," Vaxoram said. "The illness had come and the dragonriders were helping."

"In this one, there's mention of the Weyrleader ordering the dragonriders to stay in the Weyr," Kindan said, glancing back at the old Record. "That's why I wanted to see what the next Record said."

"They stayed behind?" Koriana asked with a horrified look. "Why would they stay in the Weyr when there were people dying of this illness?"

"I don't know," Kindan replied, scanning the newer entry quickly. With a sigh, he picked up the next Record and the next and then—"Wait!"

Vaxoram and Koriana jumped, startled.

"Right here it says: 'The weyrfolk are not yet recovered from their losses. Thank the First Egg that Thread is not due any time soon or the dragonriders would be reduced to tending their own injuries.'"

"But that's nearly twenty Turns after the illness!" Vaxoram protested, shaking his head violently. "Something else must have happened, something in the lost Records."

"And why weren't the dragonriders affected?" Koriana wondered skeptically.

Kindan shrugged.

"If the Records are incomplete, we won't find anything useful here," Koriana noted sadly.

Nodding absently, Kindan continued to scan the new Records, one after the other. Suddenly he shouted in surprise. "Listen to this: 'It's been five months since my arrival and the Weyr is showing its first signs of elation since the illness nineteen Turns ago. The Hatching and the birth of several new babies has cheered everyone, even those who were sent from the Holds to live in the Weyr. I am now beginning to feel that Benden Weyr might recover.' "

"Recover?" Koriana repeated, shocked at this deeper revelation.

"We've got to tell M'tal," Kindan said, rising from his seat hastily.

"Tell him what?" Vaxoram asked.

"That the Weyrs can't help the Holds fight this illness," Kindan answered. His face drained of all color as the full impact of his words registered. He didn't know if the illness of today was the same or even similar to that described in the Records. But just as he didn't know, he also didn't know if the current illness might be even more virulent than that mentioned in the Records. In less than twelve Turns, Thread would fall again on Pern—and there *had* to be dragonriders ready to fight it. "We can't let the weyrfolk catch it, or the Weyrs won't be able to fight Thread when it comes."

"That's awful!" Koriana protested. "What will the holders do? How will they survive?"

"They can't survive Thread if there are no dragonriders able to fight it," Kindan declared.

"It's not enough to tell M'tal," Vaxoram said heavily. "We must tell all the Weyrs of Pern."

All the Weyrs? Kindan thought bleakly. This sort of decision was properly the work of the Masterharper. But time was of the essence: If any weyrfolk were exposed, they might spread the illness throughout their Weyr. This wasn't the time to talk, to ask permission—this was the time to act. Kindan pursed his lips for a moment, then said, "The drums."

Vaxoram sprang out of his seat and gestured for Kindan to precede him. "Do you know where they are?"

"Up," Kindan said, turning to the stairs just outside the Records Room.

"Kindan!" Koriana called urgently, trailing after them.

"What?"

"Don't get near any weyrfolk or dragonriders," Koriana said. "Remember, the dragonriders are immune, but they could pass it on to the weyrfolk."

"Too late," Kindan replied.

"Any more weyrfolk, then," Koriana corrected. "If we've caught the illness already, we must limit their contact with us."

"Right," Vaxoram agreed, pressing close behind Kindan.

"Tell M'tal!" Kindan called back, increasing his pace up the stairs.

Six floors up, they reached the end of the stairway.

"This way!" Kindan said, pointing left, to the east. Vaxoram trotted after him steadily. Kindan was breathless from the climb but he didn't slow down. The sooner the Weyrs knew, the better. It might already be too late for some.

He spotted a set of stairs set off the corridor and took them up into the brilliant light of midday. He and Vaxoram trotted past the awesome Star Stones, in search of the enclosed space where they knew the Weyr's drum would be stored.

"Help me with this," Kindan said as he came upon the doors. Vaxoram grunted in agreement and grabbed the handle of one of the two double doors and yanked while Kindan yanked on the other.

Quickly they grabbed the huge drum, larger than that up in the Harper Hall drumheights, and rolled it out into the open air. They had no trouble spotting the drum's proper location, for there was a depression in the stone from hundreds of Turns of previous usage. Together they set up the drum and Kindan tapped a quick test.

He looked at Vaxoram. "Are we doing the right thing?"

"Easier to be wrong and apologize than right and see Thread," Vaxoram assured him. Koriana crested the stairs as he finished.

"He's right," Koriana agreed bleakly. "We'll know soon enough if this illness is like the other. If it isn't, the dragonriders will be able to help." She paused, thinking of her father, her family, and her Hold. "But for now, we must protect the dragonriders."

With a final frown, Kindan nodded and balled his fists together. With all his might he tapped out the message as it formed in his mind:

Emergency. Emergency. Emergency. Emergency. Weyrs must not aid Holders. Danger to weyrfolk.

The great booming of the drum echoed in Kindan's ears, limbs, and chest. He could see the vibrations shake Vaxoram's hair, and even set the older apprentice off balance.

As the last of the message died out, Kindan was surprised to see a huge brown dragon appear beside them.

"Stay away!" Kindan shouted. "We might be contagious!"

"I'm K'tan, Weyr Healer," the dragonrider replied. "What do you think you're doing?"

"Spreading the warning," Kindan said. "The Weyrs must be warned."

"Banging a drum won't do that," K'tan replied sourly. Kindan gave him a shocked look. "Think, lad! Who's alive to relay the message?" He gestured toward the distant drums. "We haven't had a message in a fortnight."

Kindan was staggered. No drummers to pass on messages? This flu was *that* bad? Then he remembered the last interrupted message that had come to the Harper Hall. People were dying on Pern, even drummers.

"The Weyrs must be warned!" he cried. "The weyrfolk are in danger."

"The Weyrs have been warned," K'tan assured him, patting the side of his great brown dragon affectionately. "My dragon has told Salina's Breth and Benden's queen dragon has told the rest of the Weyrs. They all know about the danger now."

Kindan sighed in relief.

"The question now is: What can we do?" K'tan asked.

"We can return to the Harper Hall," M'tal announced, emerging from the stairway down to the Weyr.

A movement near K'tan's brown caught Kindan's attention—it was M'tal's bronze Gaminth. The dragon settled carefully near the Star Stones.

"I'm going back with them," M'tal informed K'tan. "Salina knows; she's in our Weyr. She'll stay there in quarantine until we can be certain she's not contagious. Make arrangements to feed her, but let no one come close."

"And if she gets ill?" K'tan asked anxiously.

"She shouldn't," Kindan said, "she's dragonfolk."

"But we don't know yet for certain if that is enough," K'tan replied, his expression grim.

M'tal shook his head. "Do your best for her but don't risk yourself."

K'tan gave him a startled, then rebellious look.

M'tal looked to Kindan, who turned to the Weyr Healer and said, "The Records say it took the Weyr nearly twenty Turns to recover from the last illness—"

"And we can't risk that when we've less than twelve Turns before the Red Star returns," M'tal finished for him.

"The Records spoke only of weyrfolk, not riders," Koriana protested.

"The Records weren't very accurate," M'tal said. He turned

back to K'tan. "The Records Room should also be quarantined. We believe this illness does not affect dragonriders, but we can't be certain."

"How long does it last?" K'tan asked.

"We don't know," Kindan replied. "It seems to incubate in two to three sevendays."

"Then wait a month, at least, to be safe," K'tan said.

M'tal nodded. "I'll see you in a month!"

He gestured for the others to precede him to bronze Gaminth.

"We'll be waiting," K'tan replied, bowing over his dragon's neck.

CHAPTER 9

With yellow and black over hall and hold
Perils and pains do then unfold
Harper, crafter, holder pray
That you may live another day.

HARPER HALL

As Gaminth burst from *between* into the early morning over Fort Hold and the Harper Hall, Kindan leaned out over the dragon's neck to peer down below looking for any signs of life. He saw none. His throat tightened as he turned his attention to Fort Hold's main walls, searching for any sign of guards on the parapets. His grunt of relief was echoed by the others as they all spotted a tiny guard moving purposefully along the walls. But their relief was short-lived.

"Look!" Koriana called as the first hints of morning wind flickered through the valley, blowing on the Hold's tall flagstaff. A small yellow pennant with a black dot fluttered in the breeze.

"Quarantine," Kindan said, his shoulders slumping. The illness was in Fort Hold. He turned his attention to the Harper Hall's flagpole—it, too, had a yellow pennant fluttering from it and, although he couldn't see it, he was sure that it also bore the black dot of quarantine.

A bellow from the meadow greeted them, and as Gaminth circled back toward the Landing Meadow, Kindan spotted a small blue dragon rearing up.

"J'trel is still here," Kindan said.

"I wonder why?" Koriana said, her voice carrying over Vaxoram to Kindan's ears.

"We'll know soon enough," Vaxoram said.

In a moment Gaminth was on the ground. M'tal handed Vaxoram down, who aided him in helping Koriana, then Kindan dismount. Finally M'tal leapt down himself.

They started off toward the Harper Hall but hadn't gone a few steps before J'trel's blue, Talith, bugled warningly at them. Seconds later, they heard J'trel shouting, "Stay there!"

M'tal glanced toward the blue rider who was running out from under the archway of the Harper Hall, carrying something in a carisak cradled against his chest with one hand. With the free hand, J'trel urged them to stand still.

"I'm going to drop the drum out of the sak," J'trel called. "You can use it to communicate."

"Very well," M'tal said. He turned to his dragon. "Gaminth, ask Talith what is going on?"

A moment later M'tal seemed to stagger, then catch himself as Vaxoram rushed to his aid.

"The sickness has reached both the Harper Hall and Fort," M'tal said. As they already knew that, Kindan waited for the other strand. "Three people in the Harper Hall have died."

"Died?" Koriana cried.

"Many more are ill," M'tal continued. "The Masterharper is coughing, which is the first sign."

J'trel stopped a good dragonlength from them, knelt, and gently upended his carisak so that a small drum fell out. He then backed away.

Kindan and the others moved forward. When they reached the drum, Vaxoram gestured to Kindan, saying simply, "You're better."

Kindan picked the drum up and was surprised to see that it was one of his own making, the second he'd ever made. It wasn't perfect but was sturdy and serviceable.

Harper ready, Kindan rapped out with one hand. Then, thinking better of how long he might be drumming, he sat down on the cool, damp ground with his legs crossed and the drum cradled just above the ground so that its sound would carry better.

Do any of you have fever? A message boomed back. Kindan could tell by the other's style that the drummer was Masterharper Murenny himself.

No, Kindan responded, as he relayed to the others, "Master Murenny asks if any of us have fever."

Do any of you have a cough? Murenny asked.

"None of us have been coughing recently, have we?" Kindan asked, turning to glance up at the other three, standing behind him.

"No," M'tal said. "And no one at the Weyr, either."

No, and none at the Weyr, Kindan rapped back.

You are probably free from infection, Murenny responded. Kindan thought that his drumming sounded a bit weaker than before.

"He says we probably don't have the infection," Kindan relayed. He turned to M'tal. "You should go to back to the Weyr."

M'tal bristled. "I don't take orders from a—" he cut himself short and shook his head apologetically. "You're right, I apologize for snapping at you." He gestured toward the Harper Hall. "Ask him what the Weyrs can do."

Kindan beat the message out and waited. Then he frowned and added a longer message, explaining about the dangers to the Weyr.

They can do nothing, Murenny responded after a long silence. *We cannot risk the Weyrs.*

"Master Murenny says for you to do nothing," Kindan said.

"You told him about the Records at Benden," Koriana re-marked.

"Of course."

M'tal pursed his lips, clearly not liking the answer.

"If your riders come into contact with the contagion, there's no way they can avoid bringing it back to the Weyr," Kindan re-minded him.

"I know that," M'tal said with a touch of acerbity in his voice. He looked away, back toward his dragon for a moment and then said, "J'trel suggests that perhaps we could drop food."

"Where would you get the food?" Koriana asked. "It's nearly winter. The livestock may starve because there's no one to tend them."

"I hadn't thought of that," Kindan said, the color draining from his face.

"We hadn't seen anything in the Records," Vaxoram remarked.

"That may be because they all starved," Koriana pointed out.

"We hadn't looked all that far before we went to Benden," Kin-dan reminded them.

"What will happen if we lose the livestock?" M'tal asked Koriana.

"The Weyrs have some herds of their own, don't they?" Kindan asked.

"Yes," M'tal replied. "But they're for feeding dragons and they get replenished by Holder herds at regular intervals. We couldn't grow back all the herds of Pern from those of the Weyrs."

"Then we're doomed," Vaxoram said.

Kindan nodded solemnly. "We can save the Weyrs, maybe save some holders, but they'll just starve later."

"No," M'tal replied firmly. "There has to be another way."

"Some livestock will survive," Koriana declared. "Not everyone will catch this illness and some of those are bound to be in the small herdholds."

"But will enough survive to feed the survivors?" Kindan coun-tered.

"Murenny must have thought of this," M'tal said, glancing toward the Harper Hall. He looked back to Kindan, noting the bronze fire-lizard hovering over him. "You can have your Valla send us messages, have her drop them on the Star Stones."

"I can do that as long as I don't have a fever or cough," Kindan corrected him.

"Then let's hope you don't get one," M'tal replied with a ghost of a smile.

"My Koriss can learn, too," Koriana offered, then her face fell and she glanced over to Kindan. "But Kindan still has to teach me."

"Your father may have something to say about that," M'tal replied. He glanced toward Fort Hold. "And I think I'd best return you to him now."

Kindan understood M'tal's motivation—Koriana might not be a danger to the weyrfolk, but that was not certain, and as she was a Lord Holder's daughter, she would want to be with her family.

Koriana looked torn, clearly wanting to stay with Kindan, yet also worried about her Hold and family. After a moment she nodded glumly. "But can I ask you and Vaxoram to turn your backs for a moment?"

M'tal raised an eyebrow at her questioningly, but she met his gaze steadily. The Weyrleader's eyes softened and he turned away, gesturing for Vaxoram to do the same.

Koriana stared at them for a moment, then turned to Kindan and gestured for him to stand up. He did so reluctantly, worried about the Harper Hall, the deaths, and whatever was happening on Pern.

Koriana closed the gap between them and wrapped her arms around him, burying her head against his shoulder. He felt her body shake with sobs before he heard them from her throat. He hugged her tightly, and then she moved her head and her lips latched onto his and she was kissing him, deeply, passionately, despairingly.

"What about your honor?" Kindan asked as they finally broke apart, staring deeply into each other's eyes.

"What is honor without love?" Koriana replied, raising a hand and brushing it gently against his cheek. "We may never see each other again."

"I know," Kindan replied, the words tearing his heart. "I love you."

"I love you," Koriana said, leaning forward and parting her lips once more. Their kiss this time was less frantic, more sensual and intimate. When at last they finally broke apart it was because their lungs were protesting and their hearts beating too rapidly to survive another moment in such an intense embrace.

"I'll see you again," Kindan declared. "And then we'll get your father to agree."

Koriana smiled, but Kindan could tell that she couldn't quite believe him.

"Until then," she said, stepping back and releasing his hand.

"I'm ready," Koriana declared loudly to M'tal. M'tal looked back then, as did Vaxoram.

"Then let me escort you to the gates," M'tal said, gesturing for her to precede him.

Kindan bent over and picked up his drum. He turned to Vaxoram. The Harper Hall was his home—there was no place he would rather be. "Let's go."

✦

"Masterharper Murenny is ill," Master Archivist Resler said, approaching them just as they exited the archway into the Harper Hall. "You're to go help Master Lenner."

"But Master Murenny drummed to us," Kindan protested.

"And that sapped all his strength," Resler replied testily. "You are to follow my instructions."

Kindan looked questioningly at Resler.

"Who is the senior harper, Master?" Vaxoram asked politely.

"I am," Resler replied, clearly irritated at such impudent questions.

"But—Master Detallor?" Kindan asked, aghast. Detallor was the next senior harper to Murenny, after Master Zist.

"Master Gennel?" Vaxoram asked, naming the third-most senior.

"Master Detallor died this morning," Resler replied, glancing down at the ground to hide his emotions. "Master Gennel is sick in his rooms and can't be moved." It was clear from his tone that Resler felt that Gennel would soon follow Detallor.

"There were three," Kindan said, waiting for the final shard to crack.

"Journeyman Issak died while attending the others," Resler said, grimacing. "No one knew he'd caught the illness, he kept it from Master Lenner." He glanced up at them. "He was a good man, he would have been a good Master." High praise indeed from the crotchety Resler. Apparently Resler thought so, too, for his voice was full of bark as he roared, "Now, go!"

Kindan needed no further urging. Vaxoram stuck at his side, only falling back when they entered the cramped corridor to the Healer Hall.

"I don't know much about healing," Vaxoram confided as they walked in silence.

"We're both going to learn fast," Kindan replied. He was surprised when Vaxoram clasped his right shoulder from behind and clenched it in firm agreement.

———✦———

When they arrived at the Healer Hall they were turned around again.

"What are you doing here?" Lenner demanded, looking up from one of the many crowded beds in his infirmary. "You're supposed to be in the Archives."

"Master Resler sent us here," Kindan told him.

Lenner sighed and straightened, running a weary hand through his hair.

"You won't do as much good here as you will in the Archives," Lenner declared.

"What about Verilan?" Kindan asked.

Lenner pointed off into the distance. "He's in the Harper Hall infirmary."

"So, he's not too sick then," Kindan said hoping to reassure himself.

"He can't be moved," Lenner corrected him, his eyes full of sorrow.

"What about Conar?" Kindan asked, glancing around the beds.

"He's all right," Lenner said. "He's been helping here, no sign of a cough yet, though." He whistled loudly and called, "Conar! Report!"

A small figure scurried toward them. He brightened when he spotted Kindan and Vaxoram. "You're back," he said, his face splitting with a smile. "And you're alive!"

Kindan grinned back and nodded, but he couldn't help noticing the dark circles under the younger boy's eyes. He turned toward Vaxoram, still grinning, expecting the older apprentice to share his happiness but was surprised by the grim look on Vaxoram's face. In an instant he recognized the cause and asked, "Nonala and Kelsa, are they all right?"

"Yes," Lenner replied quickly. "They're helping in the kitchens. We're keeping most everyone quarantined to prevent the spread."

"It didn't work," Conar said quickly, glancing at the Healer apologetically. "In the Records, they said that it didn't work."

"Find out why," Lenner ordered Kindan. "Go look in the earliest Records, see if they have suggestions, ideas from back before Landing." He turned away from them, distracted by another hacking cough in the distance. "Don't come back until you've got an answer," he called gruffly back over his shoulder.

"Come on," Kindan said, turning back to the corridor leading toward the Harper Hall and the Archive Room.

"What about Resler?" Vaxoram asked. "He's senior. And you know how he frets about his Records."

"Are you going to let people die?" Kindan replied, not caring whether Vaxoram followed or not.

"It'll be on your head," Vaxoram's voice carried to his ears a moment later.

"So be it," Kindan replied fiercely.

———✦———

"We'll need glows," Kindan said as they entered the dark confines of the Archive Room, knowing that Master Resler was too busy managing the Hall to come back to his beloved Records.

"There's light now," Vaxoram said, waving at the lighter patches in the room.

Kindan shook his head. "We'll need more light soon," he replied. "And we're working through the night. Get some *klah* too."

He waved dismissively at Vaxoram. Vaxoram's nostrils flared in irritation; then the older harper shook himself and turned on his heel.

Kindan didn't notice his departure, the sounds concealed by the noise of his rooting through the stacks of ancient Records. Some were so old and dusty that he could see them disintegrating right in front of him; brittle documents that cracked and flaked as he moved them. And then there were others, still supple and pliant, nearly as fresh as when they were first drawn. Kindan set them aside at first, assuming that they were new Records misfiled. It was only when he got to the oldest Records, Records drawn on some material that seemed like a strange combination of thin metal and living flesh, silky, soothing to the touch, that Kindan thought to look back at the stack of "new" Records.

"There are no glows," Vaxoram's voice boomed from the far end of the Archive Room. "None to spare, at least. They're all being used in the infirmaries. I set some up to recharge but they're clamoring for them, so they'll take them before I get back."

"We need light!" Kindan shouted. "Find some!"

Vaxoram glared at Kindan's back angrily but the young harper never noticed. With a deep sigh, Vaxoram calmed himself and turned away once more, leaving the Archive Room to follow Kindan's orders.

Kindan pulled the stack of "new" Records over to a table and started to go through them. They were written from just after Crossing. The writing was small, much smaller than he was accustomed to. In the dim light, they were hard to read. He leaned close, his nose almost touching the Record as he read.

"Contents of Shipment #345-B, offloaded from gravsled #5, 3.10.8 at 22:45," the document began. What was a gravsled? Kindan wondered. And the date, was that the third day of the tenth month in the eighth Turn after Landing? And that number, 22:45—what was that?

Kindan turned through several more Records and then he stopped, grunting in surprise as he read the first line of a poem or a song:

"A thousand voices keen at night,
A thousand voices wail,
A thousand voices cry in fright,
A thousand voices fail."

Maybe this will help, Kindan thought to himself, peering down to the next verse:

"You followed them, young healer lass,"

—young healer lass? Kindan wondered to himself. He knew of no healer lass at the Harper Hall or anywhere on Pern. With a sinking feeling he continued to read:

"Till they could not be seen;
A thousand dragons made their loss
A bridge 'tween you and me."

Kindan shook his head, grimacing. This must just be another harper song, nothing important, Kindan thought to himself, recalling the countless drinking songs harpers wrote and sang for the entertainment of holder and crafter alike. He could imagine the tone of the piece, however, dour with minor chords throughout, a proper dirge—that didn't seem right for a drinking song.

The next stanza seemed to confirm his suspicion:

"And in the cold and darkest night,
A single voice is heard,
A single voice both clear and bright,
It says a single word."

A single word? Help? Kindan mused. Could Nonala, whose voice was "clear and bright," somehow sing a word that would help save all of Pern? Maybe she was training to be a healer and hadn't told him. He peered down to the next verse and read:

"That word is what you now must say
To—"

"I've got a torch!" Vaxoram called excitedly, breaking Kindan's concentration.

"A torch?" Kindan cried, turning around and seeing the blazing light that Vaxoram was holding in his hand. "Are you mad? The Records are mostly paper!"

"You said to get light," Vaxoram snapped. He waved the torch. "This is light. It's even brighter than glows."

Kindan had to admit that even from the great distance of the door to his table, the torch's light was having an effect.

"Bring it here, let's see how good it is," Kindan said.

As Vaxoram approached, Kindan could see more and more of the Record. He noticed small marks which he hadn't seen in the dimmer light and saw that they were chord markings. Yes, it was a song—a song written in a minor key, just as he had thought. The tune started playing in his mind and he realized that, sour as it was, it was quite catchy. Whoever had written this song had meant it to be remembered for a long time.

It was important.

"That word is what you now must say,
To open up the door,
In Benden Weyr, to find the way
To all my healing lore."

"What's this—"
"Shh!" Kindan ordered.

"It's all that I can give to you,
To save both Weyr and Hold.
It's little I can offer you,
Who paid with dragon gold."

Yes, the tune was definitely catchy. But, "paid with dragon gold"? Kindan could think of no one who had lost a gold dragon. Could the song refer to Koriana? But they'd been to Benden already, and found nothing. And—

"This is just some nonsense song," Vaxoram declared, shaking his head, grabbing the Record with his free hand and easily reading it in the torch's bright light. "You're wasting your time."

Kindan shook his head. "I don't know, it looks important."

"Only to the person who wrote it," Vaxoram declared. "A waste of paper or whatever this is." He dropped the Record back to the table dismissively. "But the light helps, doesn't it?"

"Yes," Kindan replied absently, picking up the Record and re-reading it closely. "There could be a thousand deaths from this—"

"More," Vaxoram said, peering down at the Record. "You're wasting time, Kindan." He grabbed for the Record again, yanking it out of Kindan's hands.

Before Kindan could react, a drum message boomed out, echoing across the valley from Fort Hold and reverberating in the confines of the Archive Room.

"Master Kilti ill, please help," the message said. Kindan recognized the drummer—Koriana.

Angrily, Kindan dived for the Record to snatch it back. He caught Vaxoram off guard and as the older lad fought to retain possession, he lost hold of the torch.

"No!" Vaxoram cried, diving for the dropped torch and loosing his hold on the Record at the same time.

"The Records!" Kindan yelled, watching in horror as first one, then another Record caught fire. "We've got to get water!"

"We've got to get help!" Vaxoram added.

In an instant, Valla was there, hovering over Kindan's head and chittering shrilly. Then the bronze was gone again, only to be heard loudly in the courtyard beyond.

"Run!" Kindan shouted. "To the well!"

"To the kitchen!" Vaxoram said, and then both burst into action, Vaxoram retrieving the torch, Kindan darting to separate the precious Records. Vaxoram bumped into Kindan in his haste and Kindan tripped, pushing the ancient Record toward the fire. Before he could do anything, the Record was a burst of flame—and a pile of ashes.

"What is it? What is it?" Harried voices could be heard shouting in the courtyard. "It's Kindan's fire-lizard! Something's wrong!"

Then Vaxoram's voice drowned all others as he burst into the courtyard. "Fire! Fire in the Archives!"

The flames rose around Kindan and he found himself being forced backward by the heat of the rising flames, his attempts to salvage Records thwarted. Despairing, he turned to the exit only to be met by Resler.

"What have you done? What have you done?" Resler shouted, striking at Kindan furiously.

"I'm sorry! I'm sorry!" Kindan cried, trying to dodge the enraged Archivist's blows and get into the courtyard. "We'll put it out."

"Step aside, we've got water," a new voice called. It was Vaxoram. He shouldered Resler brusquely aside, handed Kindan a sloshing bucket, and entered the room, throwing his bucket indiscriminately and racing back for more.

"Form a line!" Kindan heard Kelsa shout. "Form a bucket line! Pass them along!"

Kindan threw his bucket on the flames, found another in his hand, then another, then another, and another—

And then, after an eternity, the flames were out. The Archive Room was a mixture of ash, damp Records, and rising smoke.

"It's out," Kindan called hoarsely. His message carried backward through the bucket line to those at the well. "The fire's out."

Behind him, Resler peered in at the mess that had been made of his precious Records, livid with fury.

CHAPTER 10

Dark rewards
Do dark deeds pay;
Harsh words
Do harsh wounds flay.

HARPER HALL

Kindan didn't pause as he cleared the archways of the Harper Hall. He didn't glance back. He didn't cry, although that took an extreme effort of will.

Gone. All his dreams were gone.

Banished. "And never come back!" Resler had shouted, still hoarse with rage.

Doomed. "You're to go to the Hold, help as you may," Resler had said, pointing toward the Harper Hall's arching entrance.

"But Master Lenner—"

"Doesn't need your sort of help," Resler replied. He shook his head furiously. "For almost five hundred Turns we've preserved the

Records and in ten minutes you've destroyed a quarter of them. Never in the history of Pern has there been greater treachery."

Any words of protest died on Kindan's lips. He could not tell if, among the lost Records, there was a remedy for the illness that now affected all of Pern. His mistake could have cost the lives of millions.

"You've got to keep going," Vaxoram said quietly, nudging Kindan in the shoulders. Kindan turned back angrily, but Vaxoram ignored his look, nodding toward the ramp up to Fort Hold. "Keep going."

"How?" Kindan asked in misery.

"One foot after the other, one day after the next," the older apprentice replied. "It will get better."

Kindan stopped, turning to face Vaxoram bitterly, demanding, "How do you know?"

"Because you taught me." The answer was so simple, so sincere, that Kindan could not doubt it. Vaxoram bent his head and added, "That fire was my fault, not yours."

"I could have stopped you," Kindan said.

"Then it was our fault," Vaxoram replied. He nudged Kindan gently, turning him toward Fort Hold. "And that's our destiny."

"To die in Fort Hold?"

"Maybe," Vaxoram answered. "But at least your girlfriend's there."

Kindan said nothing, he could think of no response. But, unconsciously, he picked up his pace. Behind him, Vaxoram's face lit with a brief smile.

✦

"What are you doing here?" the Fort Hold guard demanded suspiciously as he looked out through the speaking port in the great doors. "There's quarantine."

"We were sent by Master Resler, to help Master Kilti," Kindan explained.

"Are you healers?" the guard asked hopefully.

"Harpers," Kindan confessed.

"All that can be spared," Vaxoram added.

The guard nodded, closed the speaking port. A moment later, one of the double doors opened just enough to admit the two of them and closed again. Kindan glanced around, surprised that only one door was used, only to discover that there was only the one guard at the gate.

The guard turned away hastily, coughing, then turned back to them. "Had this cough for a sevenday now," he told them. "One of the younger lads didn't last that long."

"Younger, you say?" Kindan asked, in surprise.

"Not twenty Turns yet," the guard agreed. "And I've nearly forty." He shrugged. "I thought the young ones were sturdier."

"Me too," Vaxoram agreed, glancing warily at the guard and then at Kindan.

"The Lord Holder will be pleased to see you," the guard said, waving them on to the entrance to the Great Hall. "You'll have to go on your own, I'm the only one still here."

"Out of how many?" Kindan asked.

"Twenty," the guard answered quickly. He turned away again to cough, then back to them, adding bleakly, "Seven are already dead."

———✦———

The doors to the Great Hall stood slightly ajar. Before Kindan approached them, Valla darted forward and through, returning a moment later with an encouraging chirp. Vaxoram gave Kindan a quizzical look, gesturing for him to go first.

Inside, Kindan was shocked to see that the floor of the Great Hall was filled with cots. And the cots, crammed so close together that it was difficult to navigate through them, were filled with people.

"Must be hundreds here," Vaxoram remarked as they proceeded toward the great hearth at the top of the Hall.

Kindan gazed at the listless bodies and nodded in bleak agreement. But Fort Hold was home to over ten thousand; where were the rest?

He glanced around, looking for anyone upright in the filled room. It was a moment before he spotted movement, a white-haired, balding man who looked like a scarecrow and—Kindan drew a sharp breath—Koriana. They rose from one bed and went quickly to another.

With a jerk of his head, Kindan caught Vaxoram's attention and they moved toward the two.

"Master Kilti?" Kindan guessed as they approached.

"Kindan," Koriana said, her voice subdued but her eyes still bright when she spotted him. "What are you doing here?"

"I was sent to help," Kindan said. "By Master Resler."

"Resler's an idiot," the white-haired man muttered before turning his attention to the body in the cot below him. He felt the man's forehead, bent forward, grabbed a wrist, and stood up again, shaking his head. "This one's dead," he said sadly. He glanced up to Vaxoram. "Take his body."

Vaxoram paled.

"Where?" Kindan asked, dropping down to the dead man's cot.

"Ask the guard," Kilti replied dismissively. "You stay, your friend goes."

"He's not big enough—" Kindan began in protest.

"You're to clear the cot and find another to fill it," Kilti ordered. He jerked his head toward Koriana. "Next bed," he told her.

Kindan had just a moment to shake his head in apology to Vaxoram.

"It's all right," the older lad said, bending down to pick up the body.

"I'll help," Kindan offered.

"No," Vaxoram replied, going down to his knees. He grabbed the body at the waist and rolled it onto his shoulder. With a grunt he stood up, staggered for a moment, and began to hobble off slowly toward the front door.

Kindan eyed the mess left behind. The sheets were soiled, they'd have to be replaced. He bundled them up and looked for some place to put them.

"Soiled sheets?" Kindan called toward Kilti. The old healer didn't look up.

"Dump them out in the necessary," Koriana called back. "Then drop them in the great tub in the laundry." She made a face. "There should be someone there."

She sounded like she wasn't sure if there still was. Kindan nodded mutely and headed off on his task, partly familiar with the layout of the Hold from the several events he had attended in the past as a harper.

A small girl met him at the laundry. He dropped the dirtied sheets into the great tub and she tamped them down into the boiling water with a long stick.

"Clean sheets?" he asked. She gestured outside. Kindan found long lines of sheets drying in the cold air. He felt for the driest and pulled them off, returning to the Great Hall through the laundry.

"Are you all right?" he asked the girl as he went back.

She shook her head wordlessly, stamping the boiling clothes down into the tub angrily.

How could anyone be all right, Kindan wondered.

Back in the Great Hall he made the bed carefully, then looked around for another patient. At the far end of the Great Hall, he spied Vaxoram and Bemin carrying two small people over their backs. One was a young woman, the other was a young man.

"Over here," Kindan called, gesturing for Vaxoram to put one of them on his cot. To Bemin he said, "I don't see any others free."

"This one!" Kilti called, looking up mournfully from another full cot.

Kindan helped Vaxoram position the fevered young woman on the cot. As they did, the woman broke into a coughing fit, spraying them in an ugly greenish-yellow mist.

"Now you've caught it," Bemin told them, his voice dead. "Just like Semin." He gestured to the young man on his shoulders.

"Your son?" Kindan asked in surprise. He glanced to the fevered woman, now covered in a fine mist of sputum. "And she is?"

"I don't know," Bemin said, shaking his head. "A holder of mine." His face softened as he implored Kindan bleakly, "Do what you can for her, please?"

"Of course, my lord," Kindan replied, covering the woman's body with a sheet and the blanket. He felt her forehead—it was blistering hot. "I should get her some water."

"No time!" Kilti shouted. "Get this corpse out of here!"

Kindan shook his head and started to obey, but Bemin blocked him. "You get the water, you're the smallest," he said to Kindan. "Just hurry back."

Kindan nodded and raced out of the room. He went back in the kitchen and found a large bucket. While it was filling, he had time to check on the laundry girl. She had collapsed beside the tub. He pulled her away hurriedly and felt her forehead—boiling. His throat choked up in sorrow and his eyes were spangled with tears as he hauled her up and lifted her in the crook of his arm, staggering back to the kitchen to grab the bucket in the other.

He staggered back to the Great Hall.

"What about cups?" Kilti croaked. "And who's she?"

"She was boiling the sheets," Kindan explained, anxiously looking around for a spare cot.

"Alerilla," Bemin said. "She's barely turned ten."

"Fever?" Kilti asked, rising unsteadily to his feet and slowly moving toward Kindan and the girl. Behind him, Vaxoram was lifting the dead body off the cot and Koriana was rolling up the soiled sheets.

"Like a fire," Kindan replied.

"Good," Kilti said, much to Kindan's surprise. The healer noticed his look and explained, "Fever's a body's way of fighting."

Kindan gestured helplessly around the room at all the fevered
people lying in cots.

"The worst seems to be the cough," Kilti said. "Fever without
cough seems to survive." He put his hand gently around the under-
side of the girl's jaw and felt. "Glands are swollen, that can be good
or bad."

He nodded toward Kindan. "If she starts coughing in the next
day or two . . ."

Kindan nodded. "How long after that?"

"It varies," Kilti said with a shrug. "Sometimes a day, sometimes
four. Never more than four."

"After four?"

"I don't know," Kilti said. "Some recover, some get worse and
die." The healer shook his head sadly. "I've never seen the like." He
glanced up at Kindan. "Have they found anything in the Records?"

"Hints," Kindan said. "Fragments. The Records just stop and
don't start until months later, usually written by someone else."

"Harper?"

Kindan shook his head. "No."

"They died trying, then," Kilti guessed, his voice a mix of scorn
and praise. He glanced to Kindan once more. "So are they still
looking in the Records?"

"No," Kindan confessed.

"They've stopped?" Kilti barked in surprise. "They can't! That's
our only hope."

"There was a fire," Kindan told him with a sinking feeling in
his gut.

"A fire?" Kilti repeated, aghast. "The Records, how are they?"

"We lost as much as a quarter, no less than a tenth," Kindan
told him.

"A quarter?" Kilti gasped. "What happened? Who started it?"

"I did," Kindan said.

Without warning, the healer took two quick steps and slapped Kindan hard across the face. "Do you know how many you've killed?" Kilti roared at him.

"It was not his fault," Vaxoram called from his position nearby. "I started the fire."

"So they sent you here," Bemin said sourly.

Kindan hung his head in shame.

Kilti started to say something more in his anger, his hand still poised for another blow, but then he shook himself and lowered his hand. "I'm sorry," he said. "That was uncalled for."

"I don't think so," Kindan said. "Millions will die because of me."

"Millions will die," Kilti agreed. "But you don't own all the blame by yourself." He shook his head. "I shouldn't have hit you, it was wrong."

"I deserved it."

"No," Kilti said with a sigh. "No, you didn't. You made a mistake, right?" Kindan nodded. "Mistakes shouldn't be punished, shouldn't be condemned."

"But there's nothing I can do that will make up for it," Kindan protested.

"Yes, there is," Kilti corrected him. "You can live." He gestured to the listless holders in their cots. "You can live and save them."

"We need more spaces," Bemin announced, carefully not looking at Kindan. Kindan glanced briefly toward Koriana, but she was not looking at him.

"At once, my lord," Kindan said, bowing his head.

———✦———

At some point the day turned to night, but Kindan never knew it. At some point he had food, but he didn't taste it; water, but he wasn't thirsty. At some point he found himself lying against a cot; he pushed himself upright, checked the forehead of the occupant, found it cold, and worked with Vaxoram to haul the body away and find a new occupant.

As the night grew darkest and then lightened with the first light of morning, Kindan realized that there were other people amongst the ill, more people than just himself, Kilti, Koriana, and Lord Bemin. But their numbers were few, maybe four or six more.

Death was all around him. Coughing filled the air, masking the moaning and other sounds of pain as the fevered sick slowly lost their battle with death.

The living fought on. Whenever Kindan's energy flagged, Kilti or Vaxoram or, once, Koriana, would seem to appear and give him a brief nod or a ghost smile, and then Kindan would find the strength to go on.

Valla and Koriss were a strong presence throughout. The two fire-lizards seemed to quickly learn how to check on the ill, how to get attention when it was needed. Their company seemed to cheer all but the most fevered.

But by morning, their energy had lagged and Kindan had sternly ordered his bronze fire-lizard to rest. Valla made it plain by his reaction that he felt Kindan should do the same.

"I can't," Kindan explained. He gestured to the cots. "They need me."

He looked around for the others and, in one panicked moment, found himself totally alone. Had the plague taken everyone? Was he the only healthy person in a room full of the desperately ill?

He spotted a slumped body leaning against a cot. It was Vaxoram. Kindan trotted over to him, the closest he could come to a run. He knelt down, felt the other's forehead, and was thrilled to discover that it was neither stone cold nor boiling.

"Vaxoram," Kindan called gently but urgently. "Come on, you've got to get up, you'll get all cramped like this."

Blearily, Vaxoram opened his eyes. "What happened?"

"You fell asleep."

"I'm sorry." The older harper rose unsteadily on his feet.

"You need rest," Kindan told him.

"Can't stop," Vaxoram muttered in response. His eyes grew more focused as he looked at Kindan. "Any more'n you." He looked around the Great Hall. "Where are the others?"

Kindan shook his head. "I'll look in the kitchen," he said. "Are you hungry?"

"No," Vaxoram replied glumly. Kindan understood, it was hard to be hungry in such a depressing place. "I'll check on the patients."

Kindan nodded.

"It'd help if we could know their temperature without touching them," Vaxoram grumbled as he moved off.

Kindan nodded once more and shambled off to the kitchen and the laundry. He paused at the exit, looking back to the bed where they'd put the little girl who'd been stirring the boiling sheets. With relief he saw that she was still there.

There was fresh *klah* in the kitchen and the smell of baking bread, which surprised Kindan as he saw no other signs of activity. In the laundry, he found that someone had stoked the fires under the boiling tub and a few sheets were roiling desultorily. Remembering the little girl, he grabbed the stick and poked the sheets further down into the pot. He went to the laundry line, found the driest sheets, quickly folded them, then brought them back with him to the Great Hall and laid them on one of the huge tables that had been pushed against the wall to make room for the cots.

His thoughts came back to Vaxoram's idea. Could there be some way to measure temperature? Of course! he thought, remembering some remark of Conar's in what seemed an age ago: moodstone.

The thin flaky crystal changed color with temperature. But where to get it? And how to get it to stick to people's foreheads, even when they were sweating?

"Moodstone!" Kindan called to Vaxoram across the hall. "And glue!"

"What?" Vaxoram asked, looking up from the patient he was checking.

"What do you want with moodstone?" another voice, Kilti's, called from the other end of the hall. Kindan was both surprised and relieved to hear the healer's voice; he guessed now that the healer had been off tending the sick in other parts of the Hold.

"We could use moodstone to measure temperature," Kindan replied.

"How'd you get it to stick?"

"Use glue," Kindan replied. "Soft glue, not hard."

"Might work," Kilti agreed. "But we've no time to try," he said, gesturing to all the sick patients laid out around them.

Kindan dropped his head in acknowledgment and despair. Then he raised it again triumphantly. "We've no time, but the dragon-riders do!"

"How would you get a message to them?" Vaxoram asked.

"Valla," Kindan replied, sending a mental summons to the sleeping fire-lizard. The bronze fire-lizard must have been only dozing, for he looked up from his place among a bundle of blankets and chirped inquiringly. In a moment he was hovering in front of Kindan.

Kindan held out his arm so that Valla could land.

"I've got a message for you to take," he said. He looked around and called to Kilti, "Where can I find a stylus and paper?"

"My office," Kilti replied, gesturing vaguely toward the farther of the two Great Hall exits. "Down the circular staircase to the landing, then over to the broad stair and my dispensary. Take some glows, I haven't been there in days."

"Should I bring anything else back?" Kindan asked.

"Anything you think of," Kilti said. "More fellis, although I don't know when we can make more juice. Numbweed, if you see it."

"Numbweed?" Kindan asked in surprise. Numbweed was great in numbing the pain of cuts or bruises but he couldn't imagine how it would be useful for fever.

"Just get it," Kilti barked.

Kindan shrugged and took off, following Kilti's instructions. He could only find one dim glow in the kitchen, so he collected a bunch of others and put them out with the drying linen. The sunlight, even the feeble light of early winter, would recharge them by nightfall.

He took his dim glow and retraced his steps to the large circular stairway. He moved cautiously down it, came to the landing and stopped—was he supposed to turn left or right? He went left and walked for a long while before he decided that he'd gone the wrong way and retraced his steps. The passageway widened and he spotted the broad stairs just before he stepped down on them. Moments later he was in Kilti's office. He found stylus and paper, searched through the cupboards and found some dried fellis leaves—he took the whole drawer and put the stylus and paper on top. He found a bottle of ink, sealed it tightly, and laid it on top of the bundle. Then he looked around and found a jar of numbweed. Still confused as to why Kilti would want it, he grouped it with the other things, took one last look around the dimly lit room, and left.

Back in the Great Hall, Kindan wrote his message carefully in tiny, neat block letters. He didn't want to overburden his tired fire-lizard—Valla had been his constant companion and had slept no more than Kindan—but he also needed to be sure that the message was understood. Satisfied, he put the message in the little holder that was attached to Valla's bead harness.

"Take this to the Star Stones at Benden," Kindan said, staring into Valla's softly whirling faceted eyes. "Drop it at the Star Stones and let the dragons know."

Valla chirped and bobbed his head.

"Come back as soon as you can," Kindan told the fire-lizard affectionately.

Valla chirped once, rubbed his head against Kindan's jaw, jumped up, and vanished *between*.

Just as Kindan had collected himself to go back to his patrolling of the sick, the sounds of a drum reverberated through the Great Hall.

Report, the message said.

"You handle it," Kilti said, looking up from the bedside of a feverish young holder girl.

"Where's a drum?" Kindan asked, glancing around the hall.

"I don't know," Kilti snapped, "figure something out. You're wasting time."

Stung, Kindan glanced around the hall and then went back to the kitchen. He paused long enough to find a covered pot, fill it with water, and throw in the fellis leaves he'd collected, setting the pot to warm near the flames; he knew they'd soon be out of fellis juice.

He went to the laundry, looked around, and then returned to the kitchen. He found the largest pot he could carry and went back through the laundry to the linen line.

He squatted with the pot cradled upended between his legs and rapped out, *Kindan reports.*

There was a long moment before a reply came. *Status?*

Kindan furrowed his brow. What did that mean? Whoever was on the drums wasn't all that good.

Many ill, many dead, Kindan rapped back.

Kilti, Bemin?

Alive, Kindan responded only to pause—he hadn't seen the Lord Holder all morning. So he added, *Healer.*

Holder? Came the question.

Unknown, he replied. *Sender?*

Kelsa, came the reply. Kelsa was the worst on drums, Kindan recalled. The others must all be sick if she was the only drummer.

Masters? Kindan rapped back.

All sick, came the response. *Murenny dead.*

"Dead?" Kindan said aloud and was startled to hear his own voice. Tears streaked down his face. The Masterharper of Pern was dead, what could they do?

Lenner? Kindan rapped out slowly, his heart pounding.

Sick, Kelsa responded. There was a pause. *Help?*

Was that a request or a question, Kindan wondered.

Coming soon, Kindan replied after a moment's deliberation. *Dragonriders.*

Dragonriders must stay away! Kelsa drummed back, her drumming loud in emphasis.

Air drop, Kindan replied.

?? Kelsa responded, using a code Kindan had never heard before. Was she getting sick or just being brilliant in asking for clarification?

Drop supplies by air, Kindan responded. Wait a minute! Why hadn't he thought of that? The dragonriders could drop supplies by air to all the holders. Kindan was elated, a huge grin on his face.

Just as suddenly as his heart soared, it crashed again as Kindan thought: What supplies? Vaguely he recalled a similar conversation with M'tal and Koriana . . . *when* was it?

The question was driven out of his mind as he heard an anguished cry, "Kindan!"

It was Koriana.

"Kindan, help!" she wailed.

Kindan jumped up and rushed back to the Great Hall.

◆

Kindan found Koriana at the entrance.

"Come with me, it's Father," she cried, grabbing his hand and tugging him.

"Hurry back as soon as you can, boy," Kilti croaked from the far end of the Hall.

Koriana led him out of the Hall and up the great stairs. At the top landing, Kindan stopped, suddenly nervous. They were in the Lord Holder's private quarters. The wall-hangings were opulent, the floor carpeted. Kindan had never seen carpeted floor before.

"Come on," Koriana urged, pulling him into a bedroom. It had the largest bed he'd ever seen. Nearby was a crib and in it a small child was crying feebly. It was Fiona.

Kindan rushed to her and picked her up. Her forehead was roasting.

"How long since she's eaten anything?" Kindan asked Koriana. He noticed a pungent smell and wondered when Fiona's clothing had last been checked.

"Over here," Koriana called, ignoring Kindan's question.

Kindan tucked Fiona in the crook of his arm and trotted over to Koriana.

Lord Bemin was kneeling at the side of the bed, crouched over a hand and weeping.

Wordlessly, Kindan pushed Fiona into Koriana's arms and sat down beside the Lord Holder. Gently, he put his hand beside Bemin's, feeling the cold flesh of the hand that he was holding.

He stood up and looked at the still face of Lady Sannora. It was rigid, waxlike. He reached under her jaw and felt beside her throat for a pulse. The skin was cold. There hadn't been a pulse for a very long time, Kindan decided.

"He won't move, he won't listen," Koriana told him anxiously. With a tone bordering on hysteria, she added, "He's the Lord Holder, he's *got* to move!"

Kindan noticed that Koriana's eyes constantly darted away from Sannora's body, as if denying its existence.

He knelt down beside the Lord Holder, fumbling in his mind for the right words. He draped his arms over the Lord Holder's large shoulders and clasped them softly.

"My lord," Kindan said uncertainly. "You must come away, your holders need you." Gently he pulled Bemin away from Sannora's body. Bemin resisted passively, too bereft to struggle.

"Your daughters need you," Kindan continued softly, pulling Bemin farther away from his wife's body. Koriana took his words for a cue and moved up against her father.

"Take Fiona, Father," she said, gently pushing the toddler into his arms. Reluctantly, Bemin cradled his youngest and then with a sob, clenched her tightly against his body and kissed her forehead.

He felt the heat there and looked up in alarm, tears flowing freely, saying to Kindan, "She's so hot!"

"I know, my lord," Kindan replied. "We must get her downstairs to Master Kilti." He gestured toward the door. "Come on, we must hurry."

"You will save her?" Bemin asked, looking down at his daughter and back to Kindan. A fierce light burned in his eyes. "Promise me you will save her?"

"I will do what I can," Kindan said.

"No," Bemin cried, "I need you to *promise* me that you'll save her."

Kindan locked eyes with the taller man for a long moment. This was the man who said that Kindan had besmirched his honor, that his word was meaningless to him. And here, now, in this moment, the Lord Holder of Fort Hold was asking for a promise to do the impossible.

"I will save her, my lord," Kindan promised. "Or die trying."

"Don't you dare die!" Koriana cried fiercely. "Don't you dare!"

"I will save her," Kindan repeated. He gestured to the door. "But we must get down to Master Kilti."

Slowly, in a shambling gait, the Lord Holder of Fort Hold followed the young harper down to the Great Hall.

———— ✦ ————

How they made it to the next day, Kindan could never recall. Only willpower kept him moving; he slept only when he collapsed, ate only when he thought of it, drank only when his throat was parched.

Little Fiona worsened through the night and Kindan was beside her at her merest whimper. He kept a bucket and a cloth and gently dribbled cool water on her forehead, having been forbidden to touch her by Master Kilti.

"Touch her and you'll get it yourself," Kilti had warned with a wheeze.

"I've already touched her," Kindan replied.

"And maybe you caught it, maybe you didn't," Kilti rasped. "Take enough chances, and you'll get it for certain."

Something about the healer's voice alarmed Kindan but he was too tired to dwell on it.

At Kindan's urging, they cleared one cot next to Fiona and Bemin, Koriana, Vaxoram, Kilti, and any others of those still standing took turns catching naps of a half hour, an hour, never more.

Night blurred into day. Kindan carried some dim glows out to the laundry line, brought fresher ones back. He thought once more of the brave little girl who had stirred the boiling pot and looked for her cot when he returned to the Great Hall. It was empty.

"She died awhile back," was all Vaxoram could say when Kindan asked him.

Kindan shook his head sadly and was depressed to realize that he could dredge up no deeper emotion—his tears had all dried up long ago.

He went back to the kitchen to drain the fellis decoction and let it cool, dragging more soiled sheets with him.

He was about to return when Valla appeared in front of him, chittering excitedly.

"What is it?" Kindan asking, surprised at how much the small fire-lizard buoyed his spirits. Valla chirped again and bobbed his head smugly, then gestured to his harness with his forelimbs. There was a message: Moodpaste ready. Will drop in courtyard.

Ready? Moodpaste? Kindan thought muzzily. Oh! They had figured out how to make moodstone into a paste!

Kindan ran out through the Great Hall, ignoring the cries of the others, and went through the front doors, looking for any sign of a delivery, all the while worrying that the dragonriders might come in contact with the contagion.

A dark shadow crossed over him and he glanced up in time to see a bronze dragon fly overhead. He waved and the rider waved back—it was M'tal, he was sure of it. M'tal threw something over

Gaminth's neck and Kindan stood rooted in horrified fear that the object would break and shatter when it hit the flagstones of the courtyard. Instead, a piece of fabric sprang open and slowed the object's fall. Kindan groped for the name, he recalled reading about it a long time ago—a parachute. How simple, how elegant. A piece of cloth tied at its four corners and attached to the bundle.

The bundle drifted down to the courtyard and Kindan raced to retrieve it. The parcel was just bigger than his two fists. As he untied the parachute, his mind suggested that the shape was somehow significant but he ignored the thought, his attention directed at the bundle. Inside was a set of bottles, all carefully cushioned. None were broken.

He stood up and waved to M'tal who was still above. The dragonrider waved back and soared away, blinking *between* back to Benden Weyr. Belatedly, Kindan wondered why he'd sent Valla to Benden and not to the Fort Weyrleader. Probably it was because he and M'tal knew each other, because the Benden Weyrleader trusted him.

Kindan tottered back into the Great Hall, pausing to let his eyes adjust to the dimmer light. He opened one of the bottles and peered at the paste inside. He turned to one of the nearer patients and gently dabbed a bit on her forehead, careful not to let his fingers touch her directly. She moaned in her sleep but made no other motion. In a moment the moodpaste had turned bright yellow, indicating high fever. Kindan moved on, pasting all the foreheads he could before the first bottle was empty.

"What have you got there, boy?" Kilti croaked as he passed near the healer.

"Moodpaste," Kindan replied. "Dab it on a forehead and you'll know if they've got fever." He put some on the forehead of Kilti's patient and stood back. The paste turned from green to blue and Kindan's spirits sank. "I think this one is dead."

Kilti turned back to the patient, searched for signs of life, found none and leaned back with a deep sigh. The old healer closed his eyes for a long moment, dealing with his grief. When he opened his eyes again, he said to Kindan, "What are the colors, then?"

"Green for healthy," Kindan told him. "Red for hot, yellow for feverish, blue for—"

"Dead," Kilti finished. He held out his hand for one of the bottles. "I'll finish up this row, you get the next."

Kindan checked Fiona next: The moodpaste turned an ugly yellow.

"Let me try you," Koriana said. She dipped her finger in the paste and dabbed it on Kindan, who reciprocated with a dab on her forehead. But he knew, even as he touched her, what color the moodpaste would turn: bright red, verging on orange.

"I'll be all right," Koriana declared as she caught Kindan's changing expression. "I've been taking some fellis juice."

"It doesn't help," Kindan told her. "It just makes you feel better."

"I'll be all right," Koriana repeated firmly. She gestured to the sick people in their cots. "I have to be, for them."

"Your mother—" Kindan began worriedly.

"She was never very strong," Koriana assured him. "She had no constitution and she was always weak after Fiona was born." She touched him gently on the forearm and smiled shyly. "Don't worry about me, Kindan, I'll be fine."

"I need some help over here," Vaxoram called. Kindan rushed off and shortly found himself lost once more in a never-ending field of feverish faces, tormented bodies, and cold death.

The days passed on blearily, one into the next. Kindan could no longer imagine what it was like to wake refreshed, to not have the constant fatigue-induced itching under his eyes, to see anyone smile.

Slowly, however, he began to detect some pattern, some noise, like a music of bodies, in all the suffering. He couldn't say when he noticed it and it took him a long time to identify the feeling but something was nagging at him.

His notion crystallized when he asked sourly about Bemin's elder sons. "Where are they? Why are they not helping?" Kindan demanded of Koriana after he and Vaxoram had labored to haul a particularly large holder's body out of the Great Hall.

"Upstairs," Koriana said in a choked voice. "They died before Mother."

"Both of them?" Kindan asked in surprise.

Koriana nodded, turning back to her little sister and gently dripping some water on her forehead. The moodpaste was still bright yellow. Kindan had lost hope for Fiona the day before. Somewhere around the Great Hall was Bemin, tending to one of the many feverish.

Bannor and Semin had been in the prime of youth, some of the healthiest men in all Fort Hold, and yet they had been among the first to fall victim to this plague. Why?

Kindan looked at Fiona. The child should have succumbed two days ago, or at best a day ago and yet she was still hanging on, hot, fevered, unable to eat, yet still clinging to life. Why?

This flu seemed to attack the healthiest, the strongest, harder than it did the older and infirm. It made no sense.

A cough distracted him. It came from one of the helpers. He followed the noise as it continued and his eyes locked on Vaxoram. The older apprentice looked up and nodded his head slightly before returning to the bed where he knelt, rolled a corpse over his shoulders, and staggered once more upright to carry the body out of the Great Hall.

Vaxoram had the flu. Vaxoram was nearly Bannor's age—and just a little older than Koriana. Would he be the next to die?

CHAPTER 11

For fever, take you feverfew
For pains, take you fellis too
For vomiting, keep your stomach free
For flu, let your eating be.

FORT HOLD

In the next several days, Vaxoram's symptoms grew worse. Kindan kept an eye on the older apprentice as best he could, but it was hard to keep track of anyone—they were all constantly rushing from crisis to crisis, death to death. Once Kindan remembered drumming to Kelsa and he knew she responded but he couldn't re-member either his message or what she drummed in response.

They had expanded their rounds from the Great Hall to all the lesser rooms in Fort Hold, collecting the seriously ill, organizing more help. Somehow they managed to keep the fires in the kitchen going, and another small girl was found to stir the huge pot that boiled the dirty sheets.

It was in the middle of the night on the fourth day since they'd brought Fiona into the Hall that Kindan came across Vaxoram, sprawled on the floor beside a cot, a corpse half-burying him.

"Get help!" Kindan ordered Valla and the little bronze disappeared *between*. Kindan couldn't remember how many times he'd now sent the fire-lizard for help; he couldn't imagine life without Valla. He knelt slowly, his joints aching, and rolled the corpse off of Vaxoram. He reached to Vaxoram's throat, feeling for the artery, afraid of what he would discover.

Vaxoram's body was a furnace; he had a pulse, faint but steady.

"Kindan!" Koriana called trailed by the chittering noise of two fire-lizards.

"Over here," Kindan called back. "Vaxoram's ill."

Together they raised him up onto a cot. His skin was on fire, his face waxlike.

"We'll have to move the body," Kindan said, gesturing for Koriana to get the feet while he reached under the corpse's arms. Together they managed to drag the deadweight out to the courtyard before their strength gave out. It was several minutes before Kindan had breath and strength enough to return into the Great Hall, he and Koriana leaning against each other for support.

"Get some fellis and a cloth," Kindan told her. "I'll go look for Master Kilti."

Koriana nodded, not much more than a jerk of her exhausted head, and shambled off to the kitchen while Kindan headed in the other direction, toward the apartments in the rear of the Hold. He spotted Valla flying toward him.

"Where's Kilti, Valla?" Kindan said to the fire-lizard. "Take me there."

The fire-lizard had to loop back several times, Kindan moved so slowly. He found Kilti in a room crowded with cots, lit only by the dimmest of glows. Fuzzy-brained, he made a mental note to set out more glows to charge as soon as he had the chance.

"Vaxoram," Kindan said, jerking his head in the direction of the Great Hall.

"Red or yellow?" Kilti asked, referring to the color of the mood-paste.

"Orange," Kindan replied, dredging up the memory. "He was burning up."

"I'll come as soon as I can," the old healer replied. As he turned back to his patients, his body was wracked by a long, throbbing cough. "Unless we can figure out a way to stop spreading this blasted thing, we'll reinfect everyone."

Kindan nodded dully and staggered back to the Great Hall. There he spotted Bemin and one of the Fort guards.

"Where's Koriana?" Bemin rasped hoarsely.

"Kitchen," Kindan told him. "Vaxoram's ill."

"Giller here and two others are well enough to dig in the rose garden," Bemin said. "How deep?"

"Two meters, one and a half at least," Kindan said. Bemin's words registered and he took a longer look at the Lord Holder. "The ancestor garden?"

Fort Hold had a special garden reserved for the dead ancestors of the Lord Holder. In the past it had been tended under the direction of Lady Sannora and grew the most magnificent roses.

"We've set the roses aside," Giller said hoarsely with a respectful nod toward Bemin. "I figure we can plant them again, after, if your lordship—"

"That would be splendid," Bemin said, straightening up with a hint of his normal lordly manner.

"Use lime to line the grave," Kindan suggested.

"There'd be more than one grave needed," Giller said, eyeing Kindan judiciously.

"One big grave," Kindan corrected. "You've no time for individual ones."

"But Lady Sannora—" Giller began in protest.

"Let all our dead be mingled," Bemin ordered. "It is fitting; we've all suffered together."

Giller drew himself up to his full height, his eyes filled with tears and respect. "As you wish, my lord."

Bemin found the strength to clap Giller firmly on the back and send him on his way. As the man faded from sight, Bemin's shoulders hunched once more and his chin fell. "Let's see your friend."

Koriana was already there beside Vaxoram when they arrived.

"He's very hot," she said, shaking her head as she met Kindan's eyes. "Feverish. I gave him some fellis juice and cooled his head."

Vaxoram rolled over and coughed at that moment, expelling a visible mist of sputum in the air, covering Koriana who leaned back too slowly to avoid it. His eyes opened for a moment and he murmured, "Sorry." He tried to move. "Got to get up."

"Lie down," Kindan ordered. "You're feverish."

"Must help," Vaxoram protested muzzily.

"Just lie still for a moment," Kindan told him. "You can get up when you feel better."

"Alrigh'," Vaxoram muttered. "Tired." His eyes closed again and his head lolled as he drifted into a daze.

"Master Kilti said he'll check on him," Kindan said, rising and extending a helping hand toward Koriana, who took it gratefully. She slid into his embrace for a warm moment, then pushed back, aware of her father glaring at them.

Then, with a determined "No," Koriana wrapped her arms around Kindan once more and hugged him tightly. She gestured with her free hand toward her father and Kindan was surprised a moment later to feel the Lord Holder embrace him and Koriana both.

"We must get back to work," Kindan said shortly. Bemin and Koriana broke the embrace. Kindan turned to see the Lord Holder looking at him uncertainly. Kindan turned away, unsure of himself, and noted that some of the cots were empty.

"We must get more people in here," Kindan said, gesturing toward the cots.

"There's no one else," Bemin said. "We could carry some from the cots upstairs but that's about all."

"No one else?" Kindan asked in surprise. "Where are they, then?"

"Dead," Fort's Lord Holder responded somberly.

A cough distracted them and Kindan turned, nearly swooning as he tried to locate it. Bemin caught his shoulder, steadying him, and felt Kindan's forehead. He looked grave.

"You've got the fever," the Lord Holder said.

"I'm just tired," Kindan argued.

"Get some rest," Bemin ordered, pointing to an empty cot. "You can check on Vaxoram when you wake up."

"No," Kindan muttered, trying to keep the room from spinning away around him, "too much to do."

"Rest, Kindan," a girl's voice urged him. Koriana? Here? Or was it Bemin and he misheard?

The room spun out of control and Kindan remembered no more.

———◆———

The images in his head spun all around and Kindan groaned in hoarse agony. He was fire, burning bright. He couldn't breathe, couldn't swallow, couldn't feel anything but pain. And the images— a parachute falling from the sky, its four straps wrapping around his head, covering his mouth and nose, Vaxoram on the ground, corpses everywhere, Lady Sannora on her bed, then Koriana on the same bed, then . . . darkness.

"Here, drink this," a voice said in the darkness. Kindan felt his head being lifted, felt the room spin more horribly, feebly tried to bat away the coolness touching his lips, choked on a liquid, choked, and choked, and choked . . . darkness.

"Come on, Kindan, another sip," the voice was kindly but not Koriana. Bemin? The Lord Holder was feeding him? Kindan gulped down the liquid as best he could and then his head was lying, peacefully, once more on the cot. He fell asleep.

"Kindan?" The same voice, urgent, called his name. Kindan opened his eyes. The room wasn't spinning. "Kindan, are you awake? Your fever's broken." Lord Bemin sounded near to tears. "You're going to be all right, Kindan, you're going to be all right."

Something hot splashed on his face. Tears? Was the Lord Holder crying for him?

"Kindan, you've got to wake up," Bemin's voice was insistent. Kindan felt Bemin's hand under his neck, lifting him up. "Kindan?"

"Yes?" Kindan said, opening his eyes. He hardly recognized Bemin's face swimming in front of him. The Lord Holder's cheeks were bristly, his eyes sunken, skeletal. Kindan made himself move, felt the pain in every one of his joints but willed the pain away as he sat up. Beside him, Valla stirred and chirruped encouragingly, nuzzling against his chest.

"That tickles, stop," Kindan murmured to the fire-lizard.

"Tickles?" Bemin repeated.

"Valla, on my chest," Kindan explained. He was ravenous, nearly faint with hunger. "I'm hungry."

"Here," Bemin said, extending a cup toward him. "Soup. Drink slowly."

Kindan started to gulp the warm broth down, but Bemin held on to the cup and tilted it away from him so that Kindan wouldn't choke.

When the glass was empty, Kindan looked up at Bemin. "How long?"

"Three days," the Lord Holder told him.

Kindan threw his legs over the side of the cot and forced himself upright. He was wobbly, and Bemin steadied him. He glanced around—slowly. More cots were empty. He gestured to the cots. "Dead?"

Bemin nodded sadly. "Most. Some live." He turned back to Kindan, his eyes despairing.

"What?"

"Kilti is dead," Bemin said.

Kindan gasped.

"You're the healer now," the Lord Holder went on.

Kindan fell back onto the cot. "Me? I can't—"

"You can," a voice murmured beside him. He turned and saw Vaxoram, his face pallid with fever. "You will. Remember—"

"Moment by moment," Kindan completed for him. "Shh, rest, you'll be well soon, too."

As if in answer, Vaxoram's chest was torn by a wracking cough that seemed to never subside. Helpless, Kindan took his eyes off the older harper and looked to the cot beyond—

"Koriana!" Kindan cried, pushing himself to his feet once more and racing around the head of Vaxoram's cot.

"She collapsed yesterday," Bemin said. Kindan looked back at the Lord Holder, guessing his next words. "She was tending you."

Kindan looked wildly around the Great Hall. "Where's Fiona? Where's your youngest?"

Bemin had a momentary look of panic. "By the First Egg, Bemin, where'd you put your child?" The Lord Holder berated himself, pounding on his own chest with his fists, sobbing in dry heaves, "What sort of father are you?"

Kindan spotted a small child in dirty clothes and moved back to the Lord Holder. Gently he grabbed the distraught man's hands and held them, turning Bemin around. "She's there, she's all right."

With a wordless sob, Bemin staggered over to Fiona and grabbed her, cradling her in his arms. "She's alive!"

✦

Fiona was alive and seemed well enough, although in shock and hungry. She returned Bemin's hugs listlessly, but something sparked again in her eyes, some hint of life that had been missing.

"Take her to the kitchen, get her some food," Kindan ordered. "And get some for yourself."

Bemin started off, then turned back to Kindan questioningly.

"I'll be all right," Kindan told him with a weary wave of his hand. He turned to survey the long line of cots, certain that he was Fort Hold's youngest healer ever.

"Step by step," Vaxoram's words rang in his head. Slowly, deliberately, Kindan put Vaxoram's advice into practice as, step by step, he moved from one cot to another, checking temperatures, uttering useless soothing words, and finding the will to heal.

He was aided by Valla, who seemed to approve entirely of his recovery and actions, chirping cheerfully at one patient, crooning softly for another, and keeping pace with his movements. Only once did Kindan catch the fire-lizard eyeing him carefully—when Kindan staggered at the side of the cot occupied by the new little girl who had stirred the boiling pot.

"How do you feel?" Kindan asked her softly.

She squirmed, trying to turn away from him. "My head hurts," she moaned, too exhausted to cry. Kindan nodded and looked around. The fellis juice was all the way back with Vaxoram, it would take forever to get it—

A sudden noise and then the same noise again and Valla dropped the bottle of fellis juice into Kindan's hands.

"Here," Kindan said, unstoppering the bottle and pouring a small amount into the child's mouth, "this will help."

Moments later, she sighed and closed her eyes again. Kindan rose from her cot and turned to Valla. "Thanks."

The fire-lizard chirped softly, landed on Kindan's shoulder just long enough to stroke his head against Kindan's cheek, and then went airborne again, leading the way to the next patient.

Behind him, a patient coughed loud and long. Kindan turned and identified the patient by the thin cloud of sputum that drifted in the air nearby. The coughing spread the disease, Kindan was certain. Whether it spread other ways also, Kindan did not know. But how could he prevent coughing?

His dream surfaced again, the parachute descending over his face. Not a parachute—a mask!

"Valla, can you get a message to M'tal?" Kindan asked, turning to his fire-lizard. He could tell, now that he was alert enough to look closely at the fire-lizard, that Valla was thin and nearly brown with fatigue. But Valla chirped willingly, diving toward a table at the end of the Great Hall near the exit to the kitchens. Kindan followed, brightening when he noticed a chair and a stylus and some scraps of paper. There was the ink bottle he'd used so many days before.

As he seated himself, he saw some crumpled cloth and dried greenish sputum on the table. Perhaps Kilti had lain here before he died. Kindan stared at the spot for a moment, then gently moved the chair over.

He wrote slowly, using more paper than before, but his instructions had to be clear.

"What are you doing?" Bemin's voice interrupted him brashly.

"Sending a note to M'tal," Kindan explained, not looking up. "I think if we get some masks—"

"Masks?" Bemin repeated.

"To cover coughs, prevent the spread—"

"—of the illness," Bemin finished, nodding so firmly that he wobbled little Fiona in his arms. "That could help, yes." He frowned and Kindan looked up at him expectantly. "But it may be too late, we're running out of food."

"Food?" Kindan repeated blankly. "But the Stores, the grain, the dried fruit—"

"Nothing we can get to without healthy men," Bemin replied. "And nothing that sick people can digest."

"Gruel?"

"Takes a cook and water," Bemin said with a grimace. "And coal, we're almost out of that as well."

"There must be something," Kindan said.

Bemin shook his head resignedly. "You may save them only to have them starve."

"I'll think of something," Kindan promised, attaching his note to Valla's harness. "First this." He looked long into his fire-lizard's eyes.

"Are you up for this?" he asked finally. Valla dipped his long neck twice.

"Make sure you eat something and get some rest before you come back," Kindan told his fire-lizard firmly. "I've put that in the note, so don't forget."

Valla made a scolding noise but Kindan would have none of it. "Just come back after you've eaten!"

With a final chirp, the bronze leaped into the air and *between*.

"He'll be all right," Bemin told Kindan in a kindly voice.

"I hope so," Kindan replied fervently. He pushed himself out of the chair and turned to the Lord Holder. "Let's see what we can do."

———✦———

Valla had not returned the next morning and Kindan started to fret. What if he'd sent the tired fire-lizard to his death, lost forever *between*?

The notion got a grip on him early in the morning as he and Bemin hauled away yet another corpse—there were still too few able men to help—and continued to gnaw at him as the day brightened. Finally at noon, Kindan could take it no longer. He went out to the linen line and found his pot. He beat out a quick staccato: *Attention*.

He waited a very long time for a response.

Proceed. The drummer was slow and shaky. Not Kelsa.

Kindan closed his eyes in despair, wondering if he'd ever see the gawky harper again, drew in a slow deep breath and let it out determinedly.

Ask J'trel: Did fire-lizard get to Benden?

The answer took an agonizingly long time to return.

Yes. Return soon. Kindan closed his eyes again, this time in relief. *Status?*

Kilti dead, Kindan drummed back. *Vaxoram ill.*

Bemin?

Alive.

Help?

Kindan closed his eyes again, tight with pain. The Harper Hall was asking for help . . . and he couldn't give it.

Soon. He drummed back in a forlorn promise. *Food scarce.*

Food gone, the Harper Hall drummer responded.

"No!" the word was flung from Kindan's lips and he pushed the drum aside in anger and despair. No food, no help, no hope. He pulled the drum back again.

Lenner? he asked.

Dead, the drummer responded. *All Masters dead.*

"All of them?" Kindan said to himself. He shook his head, feeling helpless, feeling despairing, feeling . . . angry. Anger rose up and burned inside him, hotter than fever. He would not let this happen. The Harper Hall would survive, he swore. Fort Hold would survive.

"My word as harper," Kindan said aloud with a fury and forcefulness that he'd never used before. He could feel energy coursing through his veins.

Help will come, he pounded back fiercely in an instant. *Hold on.*

Soon?

Hold on, Kindan drummed back. But he had no idea how or when help would come, and he knew that it was the same all over Pern. Those not killed by the plague were dying for lack of food, lack of aid.

———✦———

He returned slowly to the Great Hall, stopping to grab a drink of cold *klah* in the kitchen. In the Great Hall, he spotted Bemin in the distance, near Koriana and Vaxoram.

"I heard the drums," Bemin said as Kindan approached. "What did you say?"

Kindan recalled that the Lord Holder had been suspicious of harpers' drums before; times had changed.

"I asked if Valla had arrived at Benden," Kindan told him. "They said yes."

"How would they know?"

"J'trel, the blue rider, is still with them," Kindan explained. "He was there when the plague broke out."

Bemin nodded.

"The Harper Hall is out of food," Kindan continued. "All the Masters are dead."

"All? Even Lenner?"

"All," Kindan replied. "The drummer was young, unsteady, an apprentice, I think." He stopped suddenly as he realized the identity of the drummer. "It was Conar."

"Conar? From Benden Hold?"

Kindan nodded. "He asked for help."

"We've none to give," Bemin said, gesturing to his own sorry Hold.

"I know that," Kindan replied. "But I promised it to them anyway."

"You promised—"

"At the least they have hope," Kindan said. "At the best . . . well . . . we need food, too."

"Where would you find enough food to share with the Harper Hall?" Bemin wondered.

"Enough to share with all Pern," Kindan corrected him, shaking his head. "I don't know, my lord." He glanced up, a hint of a smile on his lips. "I was hoping that perhaps you might have an idea?"

"No," Bemin said, shaking his head. "If I did, I'd share with anyone who asked for it, not that it would do much good."

Kindan cocked his head at the Lord Holder.

"How would we get it to them?" Bemin explained.

"I don't know," Kindan confessed. He leaned down to Vaxoram, felt the heat of his fever before he was even near enough to see the moodpaste, and dabbed the older apprentice's forehead with some water. He was so hot that the water quickly evaporated. In his delirium, Vaxoram shook his head and coughed once more.

"The masks should come soon," Kindan said pointlessly.

———◆———

The day slipped into night and another dozen holders slipped into death.

Someone brought hot *klah* out to them from the kitchen and some food.

"Give it to her," Kindan said, gesturing to Fiona. When Bemin started to protest, Kindan added, "I'm not that hungry and she needs nurturing or she'll not grow strong."

Bemin shook his head ruefully. "Stubborn harper."

"I was taught by your daughter, my lord," Kindan said with lips upturned.

Bemin smiled back at him. "She got it from her mother."

"Oh, no doubt," Kindan agreed diplomatically. He gestured to an empty cot. "You should get some sleep, my lord."

"You've just recovered, you should sleep first," Bemin protested.

"You nursed me back to health," Kindan replied. "As your healer, I demand it." When the Lord Holder looked ready to respond, Kindan added, "Besides, I'll wake you at half-night."

"We could both sleep, there's almost enough standing for a watch," Bemin offered, gesturing to a group of exhausted holders.

"No, they'll need a healer and a leader," Kindan said, surprised to group himself in either category.

"I suppose they will," Bemin agreed wearily, lying down on the cot. In seconds, he was snoring heavily.

Kindan regarded him for a moment, felt the pull of another empty cot and forced himself to his feet again, roaming the dimly lit halls. He saw that the surviving holders had put out more glows, so it was easier to spot the needy.

Several times that night, he cooled foreheads, administered fel-lis juice, renewed dabs of moodpaste, or called the holders over to carry away another lifeless body.

When he was too weary, he returned to Bemin and roused him with difficulty.

"I'll take over," the Lord Holder said as he sat up. "You rest."

"Wake me at dawn, or before, if you need to," Kindan said, lying down on the cot nearest Koriana.

"Don't think to snuggle with her," Bemin said, shaking a finger warningly at him. Kindan looked at him in tired outrage. Bemin's lips lifted as he said, "We can't afford you getting ill again; wait until she's recovered."

Kindan fell asleep with the first grin on his lips in over a fort-night.

———◆———

It was still dark when Kindan awoke. Something had startled him, some noise—there!

It was a gurgling, rasping sound. Kindan had heard it before: It was the sound of death. His eyes popped open. In alarm, he looked over toward Koriana. She slept feverishly, tossing and turning, but her breathing wasn't the labored breathing that had woken him. He looked beyond her. Vaxoram.

Kindan rolled out of his cot and onto his feet, his joints aching, his breathing sore, his head spinning, and dragged himself over to Vaxoram's bed.

The older apprentice's wheezing was unmistakable. Every breath was arduous, every exhalation ending with a wet cough.

"Vaxoram," Kindan called, shaking the older lad. "Wake up."

Vaxoram's eyelids slid up, then down. Kindan shook him harder. "Wake up!"

Vaxoram's eyelids slid open, focused briefly before his body spasmed in a long wracking cough. Kindan covered his face with his hand. For a moment it seemed as though Vaxoram could not draw in a new breath but then, with a hoarse wheezing noise, the apprentice's lungs filled once more.

"I'm dying," Vaxoram declared on this exhalation. His words were faint but clear, and his eyes blazed.

"No, you're not," Kindan lied stoutly. "You'll get better."

"No," Vaxoram said with another labored, hoarse breath. "Dead by morning."

Kindan knew he was right.

"Tell—tell Nonala," Vaxoram whispered hoarsely.

"I will," Kindan promised. "I'll tell her that you love her."

"Wish I were journeyman," Vaxoram wheezed. "Might have a chance then."

Kindan's throat closed in anguish. "You will be," he promised, tears filling his eyes from some newly tapped wellspring.

Vaxoram shook his head. "Gotta walk the tables," he said. "I can't walk the tables."

"You will!" Kindan declared, his voice rising. He stood up, grabbing Vaxoram's hand and pulled the larger apprentice up out of his cot. "Bemin!"

"Kindan, what is it?" the Lord Holder called back, rushing over.

"Help me," Kindan cried, staggering to keep Vaxoram upright. "Help me with him."

"We could carry him," Bemin suggested, his eyes wide with concern.

"No, he has to walk," Kindan snapped. "He has to walk the tables." He spoke to Vaxoram, "You can do it, you can do it now."

He turned to the startled holders. "Pull a table out from the wall."

"Do as he says," Bemin called firmly. The holders obeyed. Bemin turned to Kindan. "He's dying, you know."

"Not until he walks the tables," Kindan declared fiercely. "Then he'll be a journeyman."

Beside him, Bemin grabbed Vaxoram tighter, rising to his full height.

The table seemed forever away. "We're nearly there, Vaxoram," Kindan said encouragingly. "Stay with us, we're nearly there. You're going to walk the tables."

"You're not a Master," Vaxoram slurred slowly.

"Yes, yes, he is," Bemin declared firmly. "My word as Lord Holder, he is." Together, he and Kindan lengthened their stride, supporting Vaxoram.

Finally, they reached the edge of the table.

"See? We're here, Vaxoram, we're here," Kindan said. "You're going to walk the tables now, do you understand?"

"Come on, harper, walk," Bemin added sternly, his face crumpled with emotion.

"I can'," Vaxoram protested.

"You can," Kindan swore. "You will. One step at a time, moment by moment."

And, one step at a time, moment by moment, Vaxoram walked around the Great Hall table, supported by Kindan and the Lord Holder of Fort Hold.

"See, Vaxoram?" Kindan cried as they reached their starting point. "See, you did it! You're a journeyman now. See, Vaxoram?"

"Kindan," Bemin said softly, his voice torn with sorrow. "I think he's dead."

CHAPTER 12

Harper mourn,
Holder cry,
Every Turn
Till tears run dry.

Fort Hold

W e'll take him from here," one of the holders said as Kindan
and Bemin stood in shock and grief, still holding Vaxoram's
dead body between them.

"Let us carry him now," said the other.

"Thank you, Jelir," Bemin said, shifting his grip with the holder.
"Let go, Kindan, you've done all you can for him."

"For him," Kindan agreed, looking at the long line of cots in the
Great Hall. He started back toward Koriana, but his legs buckled
under him and only Bemin's quick movements kept him from
slamming against the floor.

"You should get some rest," Bemin said, guiding him back
toward the cots.

Kindan saw the two holders carrying Vaxoram's body and shook his head.

"No, I should see to him," Kindan protested, trying to alter their course.

"Kindan," Bemin said slowly, looking down at the young harper, "our duty is to the living. How would that serve them?"

"I need to say good-bye," Kindan pleaded.

Bemin started to argue but changed his mind. "Very well, *then* you'll get some rest."

"My watch should start any moment," Kindan argued.

"'Should' isn't what matters," Bemin replied. "I'll wake you when we need you, you sleep until then."

"Only if you sleep the same amount after, Lord Holder," Kindan replied.

"I'm older, I don't need that much sleep," Bemin objected.

"I'm younger, *I* don't need that much sleep," Kindan retorted.

"Let's pay our last respects to your—our"—Bemin corrected himself—"friend."

Supported by Bemin, Kindan followed the slow march of the holders as they bore Vaxoram to the far side of Fort Hold and the great ditch that had once been the Lord Holder's ancestral gardens.

Kindan stifled a gasp as the two holders unceremoniously threw Vaxoram's body into the ground to rest on top of countless other bodies. Jelir staggered from the toss and nearly toppled down into the mass grave himself, but Bemin reached out just in time and caught him.

"You should get some rest, too," Bemin said to the holder.

"I'm sorry, my lord," Jelir apologized. "He was the heaviest we've carried tonight, I won't fall again."

"Get some rest, we'll call you if we need you," Bemin reiterated.

"Night's over, anyway," the other older remarked, nodding toward the lightening east. As if in agreement, Valla sprang from Kindan's shoulder and flew a slow, mournful arc over the grave site.

They had just started back to the Great Hall when the loud noise of a dragon arriving from *between* startled them. Kindan had time only to realize that it was M'tal once again before the rider threw down four large parcels and disappeared once more *between*. The parachutes of the parcels opened and they floated down to the ground.

"Catch them!" Bemin ordered, rushing after the farthest bundle. Kindan staggered after him, as did Jelir and the other holder.

"What are they?" Jelir asked as he caught his parcel. "Food?"

"Masks," Kindan said, snagging his parcel out of the air and opening it excitedly. He took one mask off the top of the bundle—there were easily fifty in his bundle alone, he could tell by the thickness—and wrapped it around his face, tying the straps at the back. "They'll protect against the plague," he shouted, his voice muffled.

"How?" Jelir asked.

"It'll prevent spreading by containing our coughs and protecting us from others' coughs," Bemin said, walking back to Kindan with his bundle and holding out his free hand for one of Kindan's masks.

"Let's get these on everyone immediately," Kindan said.

"Even the sick?" Jelir asked, daunted at the size of the task.

"Especially the sick," Kindan said. "They're the ones who can spread the disease to us."

"But you were sick already," Bemin said. "Doesn't that protect you from reinfection?"

"I don't know," Kindan told him. "Maybe."

"No point in finding out," Jelir said, grabbing a mask from Kindan's pile and fitting it over his nose and mouth hastily.

"But it's no cure," complained the other holder.

"It might be," Kindan said. The others looked at him challengingly. "If the infection can't spread, then there'll be no new patients. Once the others have recovered—"

"Or died," Jelir added despondently.

"—the cycle will be broken," Kindan finished.

"But how long before the last of the infection is gone?" Bemin asked.

"I don't know," Kindan replied. "It seems like it takes a seven-day for the worst of the symptoms to show." He paused in thought. "Some recover in four days, others take longer."

"Anyone who was sick died in a sevenday," Jelir remarked.

"Yes," Kindan agreed. "That might be right."

"Might?" Bemin queried.

"It seems that the healthiest suffer the most from this illness," Kindan said.

"No, Stennel was healthy as a workbeast and he's right here," Jelir said, jerking his head toward the other holder.

"The worst hit were those in their prime," Bemin said in agreement. "Like my sons."

"And Vaxoram," Kindan added. "Those between seventeen and twenty-one Turns or so."

"Maybe younger," Bemin said, turning bleakly toward the Great Hall.

"We're getting nothing done jawing here," Stennel said, stepping out briskly toward the Great Hall, unwrapping his bundle as he walked.

"Let's keep the other two wrapped up until we need them," Kindan said to Bemin and Jelir. The Lord Holder nodded and looked to the other holder for acknowledgment.

Inside the Great Hall, they separated, each one taking a line of cots and a handful of masks. Koriana was the first in Kindan's line. She was sweating freely and tossing in a fevered sleep; Kindan got the mask on her with difficulty and she shook it off before he could tie it. It took him several more minutes to get it back on her.

The next patient was little better, the third was dead. After that, Kindan moved slowly from cot to cot, growing weaker each time. He ran out of masks and began opening a second bundle just as Stennel reached him.

"I'm out," the older man said, reaching for a handful of the new masks.

"How many are in the Hall?" Kindan asked. "There are fifty masks in each bundle."

"There might be that many here," Stennel said, running his gaze over the Hall. "But there's thousands more in the rest of the Hold."

"But the sickest are here, aren't they?"

Bemin joined them then, having run out of his stack of masks.

"Only those we could find," Bemin said sadly. "I can't say how many are still in their quarters . . . and how many are dead."

"We'll have to start moving the dead, or we'll have worse than this plague to deal with," Kindan said. "There are things that feed on dead bodies and spread to the living."

"Bring the living here," Bemin said, "where we can care for them."

"Which is more important?" Stennel asked, glancing toward the far end of the Great Hall and back toward the doors into the courtyard with its surrounding quarters.

"Both," Bemin and Kindan said in unison. They shared a brief grin.

"Here, first," Bemin said after a moment. "But fill the beds again."

"As we empty a bed, find someone to fill it, my lord?" Jelir asked. Bemin nodded.

"Your garden will soon be filled, my lord," Stennel remarked. "Then what?"

"Maybe help will come by then," Bemin said hopefully.

"If it would've come, wouldn't it have come sooner?" Stennel asked hopelessly.

"One day at a time," Kindan said, turning to his cot. "My lord, I shall rest as you demanded."

"Stennel, Jelir, one of you rest, the other come with me," Bemin said.

Kindan checked on Koriana, who had rolled over on her mask in her delirium. He rolled her back to prevent her from suffocating in her own spit.

"Check that they haven't rolled over," Kindan called hoarsely to Bemin as he collapsed onto the nearest cot. Bemin waved in acknowledgment and bent over the nearest cot.

Sometime later Kindan was shaken awake. He rose slowly, exhausted, to see Bemin looking down at him bleary-eyed.

"Rest, my lord," Kindan said, rising with feigned alacrity.

"The masks are all gone," Bemin said. "We've got two hundred in the cots and many more in the rest of the Hold. The dead . . . I don't know if we'll ever be rid of the smell."

"A good cleaning, a good airing, and only memories will remain," Kindan told the Lord Holder cheerfully, but Bemin's eyes were already closed and he was breathing lightly, on the edge of a deep sleep.

Kindan checked first on Koriana, who had once more rolled over with her face in her pillow. Kindan bundled up some pillows and blankets and propped her firmly on her side.

A sound distracted him and he saw Fiona sitting up in a farther bunk looking around anxiously.

"Hi, Fiona," Kindan called, forcing himself to smile at her. Shyly, the blond-haired youngster smiled back. Kindan's heart skipped a beat as he saw the beginnings of the same beauty Koriana possessed. "Are you hungry?"

Silent, Fiona nodded.

"Let's see what we can find in the kitchens, shall we?" Kindan asked, reaching down to pick her up.

"I walk," the toddler replied, hopping off the cot and tottering over to him, holding out her hand. Kindan took it and was surprised to note that it wasn't burning with heat as it had been—just a day ago? He bent down and felt her forehead: cool. Had she recovered?

"I'm hungry," Fiona complained. Kindan stood up, still holding her hand and led her to the kitchen, stopping every so often to check on a patient.

In the kitchen, Kindan was surprised to find four women all working industriously.

"Why it's Miss Fiona!" one of the women exclaimed, clapping her cheeks in surprise. "I'd no hope of seeing you again."

"I'm hungry," Fiona said.

"Well, then," the woman replied brusquely, "we'll have to feed you, won't we?" She turned her gaze on Kindan and bowed her head, "You're the boy that's been healing us."

"I—"

"You mustn't remember me," the woman interrupted. "I was sick as could be two days ago and you came by and wiped my forehead and dripped some fellis in my mouth. Tasted bitter but stopped the pain." The woman nodded to herself. "I'll never forget that, healer."

"He's the healer?" another woman called from back by the ovens. She came out, wiping her hands on her apron before holding one out. "I just want to shake your hand, sir, for all the kindness you've done."

"But—" Kindan said, shaking his head.

"There's them that gave up all hope, until you came," the second woman said. "I was one of them. Then I saw you and—" She stopped to dab her tears out of her eyes.

"—you spoke so kindly and I could see it in your eyes that you wanted me to live. So I said, 'Right, then, I'm going to live. I'm going to live and make that lad some bubbly pies.'" She nodded toward the oven. "There's no fruit, but we've got some sweet buns cooking for you and everyone."

Kindan could only shake his head mutely.

"You've gone and embarrassed him," the first cook said scoldingly, but Kindan knew she was just covering for him.

"Thank you," Kindan managed to say at last.

"How about we take the miss off your hands, then?" the second cook offered. She peered down at Fiona. "Would you like to help Neesa and me in the baking?" Fiona nodded, wide-eyed at the prospect.

The first cook, Neesa, beckoned Kindan in closer. "I've no wish to add to your troubles, but bread's all we can make just now," she told him. "And that for not much longer, certainly not enough to feed the whole Hold, or what's left of it."

"I know," Kindan replied. "The sick won't be able to swallow it, it'll be too hard for them."

"I'd guessed," Neesa replied. "They'll be weak as lambs if they recover."

"When they recover," Kindan corrected. Neesa didn't contradict him. "What about the stores?"

"Too heavy to move without a team of ten at least," Neesa replied. "Even a barrel of fish and that'd be awful eating."

"Better than nothing," the second cook noted.

Neesa made a face, so Kindan asked, "What would be best, then?

"Fruit'd be best, but it's the wrong time of year," Neesa told him. She frowned. "There's many that will recover only to starve from all this."

"If they recover, I won't let them starve," Kindan swore.

Neesa nodded in fierce agreement. "As you say, healer." She smiled bleakly at him. "We won't fail you, that's for sure."

"I'm counting on it," Kindan said, smiling at the older woman, too exhausted to be more than vaguely amused at his commanding tone.

"I'll let you get back to work," Neesa said. "Sallit or Fiona will be out with those rolls soon."

"And *klah*?" Kindan asked hopefully.

Neesa shook her head dolefully. "We've no bark left worth brewing."

"Make a list of what we need, then, and add *klah* to it," Kindan told her.

"Might as well add the fruits of summer," Neesa grumbled, but she turned toward her chopping table, slapping the sides of her apron in search of a pencil.

———◆———

Nothing was better—in fact, with the beds refilled and Vaxoram and Kilti dead, things were clearly worse—but somehow Kindan's spirits lifted. Perhaps it was the warm rolls delivered to those standing by a wide-eyed, solemn Fiona, perhaps it was her shy kiss when Kindan bent down to thank her, or maybe it was the masks keeping the air so much cleaner.

More people were up and about. As he saw them, Kindan was struck again by the uneasy knowledge that the plague killed those in their prime; the survivors were either much older or much younger.

Again and again, Kindan found himself returning to Koriana, checking her temperature, wiping her forehead, changing her soiled sheets, clearing her soiled mask.

"Time to rest," Bemin told him later that evening, handing him another roll. Kindan bit into it but in the course of the day it had hardened and was tough to chew.

"Call me if you've need, my lord," he said, checking once more on Koriana before lying down on the cot beside her.

"Where's Fiona?" Bemin asked, looking nervously around the room.

"Probably asleep in the kitchen," Kindan guessed. "She's been helping the cooks."

A faint smile crossed Bemin's lips. "Her mother liked to help in the kitchens, too."

Kindan drifted off to a fitful sleep.

Bemin woke him up for his shift and settled down into the same cot, too weary to talk.

Kindan checked on Koriana and was not surprised to see that she had clawed off her mask. Gently he pushed it back up over her mouth and nose. He stopped when he noticed that it was covered with a sticky, red substance. He removed it and brought the mask with him while he searched out Stennel who was helping another man carry yet another body to the grave site.

"Have you seen this?" Kindan asked, waving the mask at Stennel. Stennel recoiled and nearly dropped the body.

"Keep back," Stennel cried. "I've seen that on every dead body we've taken since we put the masks on them." He shook his head. "It's like they're coughing up their innards."

Kindan took the mask through the kitchen, rinsed it in the sink in the necessary, and threw it into the boiling pot. He was surprised to see several others there.

"We're reusing them," Neesa told him when he asked back in the kitchen. "You said they'd help."

"To keep the illness from spreading, yes," Kindan said. "To save those too sick to—" he cut himself off abruptly.

"Whose mask was that?" Neesa asked. Her eyes went round as she added fearfully, "Not Lord Bemin's?"

"No," Kindan told her. "Koriana's."

"I'd heard you were sweet on her," Neesa said, shaking her head sadly. "Seems you've time to say good-bye."

Kindan nodded bleakly and hobbled out of the kitchen as fast as his weary legs would carry him back to Koriana. He found her sprawled beside her cot. Gently he lifted her back into it, ignoring her feeble movements.

"Help," Koriana murmured deliriously, sitting up.

"I'm helping you," Kindan said, brushing her lips with a cup of fellis juice. Koriana raised a hand and pushed it away.

"Me help," Koriana said irritably. "No juice."

"It'll help you get better," Kindan said.

"Hurt too much," Koriana replied, her eyes opening painfully. "Too bright," she murmured, closing her eyes again.

Kindan could barely see in the dim light.

" 'M dying," she said, wobbling in the cot. "Get Father."

"No, drink this," Kindan insisted, holding the cup back to her lips. This time her hand connected solidly and knocked the cup out of his.

"Get my father," Koriana said, sounding quite lucid. "Must say good-bye." She coughed, long and hard, and the force of it caused her to double up in pain. When she looked up again, the front of her dress was covered in bloodred sputum. "Don't let him see me like this," she pleaded.

Kindan grabbed the sheets and laid them around her, covering the stain.

"Must say good-bye," she repeated.

Kindan got up and walked around her cot to the next one, where Bemin lay sleeping fitfully.

"My lord," Kindan called softly, shaking Bemin's shoulder. "My lord, your daughter needs to speak with you." Tears started down his face, surprising him—he hadn't thought he had any more.

"What?" Bemin startled out of sleep, eyes not quite focused on Kindan.

"Koriana," Kindan replied, gesturing. "She wants to talk with you."

"She needs rest," Bemin said, laying his head back down on the pillow. "Take care of her."

"Bemin, she's not going to make it," Kindan said, his tears flowing freely now.

The Lord Holder of Fort Hold sat up slowly, took in Kindan's tears, and looked over to Koriana's back. He got up and beckoned for Kindan to follow him as they went around to the other side of Koriana's cot.

"I'm here," Bemin said as he crouched down in front of Koriana. She was bent double again and when she rose, she looked abashed at the new red stain on the sheets.

"Father," she said slowly, her words slurred with pain and mucus, "I'm sorry."

"Sorry for what?"

"I'm sorry I let you down," she replied. Her eyes drifted longingly toward Kindan. "I'm sorry that I couldn't do as you asked."

"Don't worry," Bemin said soothingly. "There's nothing to worry about."

Another cough wracked Koriana and she threw her hands out at the same time that Bemin pulled himself and Kindan back, avoiding the bloodred mist that erupted from her mouth. It seemed to Kindan that the coughing went on forever and that Koriana was coughing her very lungs out. Finally, she let out a hideous, gurgling wheeze and collapsed, bent over double. With a harsh cry, Koriss leaped from the end of the bed and went *between*.

"Koriana?" Kindan asked, crouching back down and examining her chest carefully for signs of breathing. He stayed there for a long time, until he was certain that Koriana was no longer in pain. But he knew he was only fooling himself, delaying the inevitable admission that Koriana was dead—only her death would have caused Koriss to go *between* like that, forever.

At some point, Kindan felt one of Bemin's hands clasp his shoulder tremulously. Long after that, Kindan leaned forward to give Koriana one last kiss, only to have Bemin pull him back.

"To kiss her is to die," the Lord Holder told him, his voice devoid of all emotion. "Even through your mask."

Kindan nodded slowly, wishing at that moment that his heart would stop, it hurt so badly.

"Will you—" Bemin's voice broke. "Will you help me carry her?"

Unable to speak, Kindan nodded and rose, gesturing for the Lord Holder to take her shoulders while he carried her feet.

As they walked slowly out of the Great Hall, Kindan looked on the face of the girl he loved and saw that Koriana was at peace.

◆

Bemin wouldn't sleep that night, nor did Kindan. They spent the hours walking fitfully among the sick, only paying attention when Jelir or one of the other holders called to them.

Sometime, maybe nearer morning, Neesa came out of the kitchen, bringing some old buns and water.

"We're nearing the end of the coal," she said to Bemin. The Lord Holder regarded her blankly for a moment, then looked away.

"And there's only the one pitcher of fellis juice," Neesa said to Kindan. Kindan shrugged in response. Neesa turned away, scuttling back to her kitchen.

Sometime later she returned with Fiona.

"She wants her father," Neesa said, pushing the girl toward Bemin's arms.

Automatically, Bemin reached out and cradled the small child against his chest, one hand supporting her bottom, the other her shoulders. Slowly, Bemin started shaking. Kindan thought for a moment that the Lord Holder was trying to lull his daughter back to sleep, but then realized that the motion was wrong—Bemin was shaking noiselessly with grief. Kindan circled behind him and reached up, soothingly rubbing the older man's shoulders with his hands.

"We can't survive," Bemin murmured over his daughter's head. "We're all going to die."

Neesa gasped in fright and fled.

"No, my lord, we're not," Kindan told him firmly. "We'll survive. This Hold will survive, your daughter will survive."

"How?" Bemin demanded, turning to face Kindan. "How do you know? Your word as a harper?"

"Yes," Kindan said. "My word as a harper." He responded without tone, without hope, only with the certainty that he would not let Fort's Lord Holder, Koriana's father, down. He would find a way to feed them, to save the survivors.

"May as well wish for fruit from the sky," Bemin snapped irritably. "Your word's no good."

Fruit from the sky! Kindan's eyes lit with hope.

"My word, my lord," he repeated. "My word. You shall have your fruit from the sky." He rushed out to the kitchen and beyond to the linen line, searching for his makeshift drum.

CHAPTER 13

Healer with your craft so sure
Sickness we can all endure
Use your skill and healing notions
To save us with your salves and potions.

HARPER HALL

Y ou look so thin, Conar," Kelsa said as she looked up at the young holder boy gently dabbing at her head with a cloth. "Are you sure you've had enough to eat?"

Conar nodded.

"You eat this," he told her, sitting her up and spooning some porridge into her mouth. He had scrounged it from the kitchen, unable to find anything else not moldy.

"But—"

"It's only fair," Conar replied, "you brought me back to health, now it's my turn."

Kelsa saw that it was useless to argue, especially as Conar placed the spoon on her tongue.

"It's awful!" she groaned as she swallowed. Her throat was so raw from coughing that swallowing the porridge felt like swallowing hot coals. Now she knew how dragons must have felt with that old firestone. Conar—dragons sing his praise—had a cup of cool water to her lips in an instant. But the cool water was almost as much torment on her throat as the porridge.

"Another mouthful," Conar said, filling another spoon. Kelsa twisted her head away rebelliously. Conar opened his mouth to utter another encouragement when they heard the sound of drums.

"Kindan?" Kelsa said in wonder. Conar nodded, listening.

"Fruit?" Kelsa muttered as the drum message beat out. "Where can we find fruit?"

"Did he say, 'J'trel?'" Conar asked.

"He did," Kelsa agreed. "Get him, tell him Kindan's message."

"He's busy with Druri and the baby," Conar said. The blue dragonrider had been working tirelessly with Jalenna's children ever since she had succumbed to the plague four days earlier. Before that, it had been only the efforts of Jalenna, J'trel, and Conar that had kept the others alive. Kelsa didn't know how many had died; Conar refused to tell her.

"Go get him, tell him it's important," Kelsa said, ignoring the pain of her tortured throat.

Conar scuttled off, moving more slowly than Kelsa liked. He looked thin, too. She wondered, had he been skimping on his meals?

Conar slowed down once he was out of the makeshift infirmary, stopping to gasp for breath and get rid of the spots that darted before his eyes. He hadn't eaten in days. He was smaller than the rest, he told himself, he could do without for longer.

"J'trel, Kindan sent a message," Conar said as he caught sight of the blue rider.

J'trel looked up at him, his face gaunt and cheeks full of days-old beard.

"He said for you to get fruit," Conar told him.

"Fruit?" J'trel repeated wearily. "Was that all?"

"Fresh fruit," Conar said, remembering the message and wishing he was much better with drums.

"There's no fruit this time of year," J'trel exclaimed, shaking his head angrily.

Conar screwed up his face, trying to remember the exact message. "He said: 'J'trel, fresh fruit, south of Ista.'"

"South of—?" J'trel repeated, dumbfounded. "There's no land south of—" He stopped suddenly, his eyes going wide. He looked outward, beyond the room to the meadow where his blue dragon rested. "Talith . . ."

———◆———

"What is it, J'lantir?" C'rion, Ista's Weyrleader, asked as the bronze rider caught up with him. C'rion had returned from a patrol over the infected Holds and was not happy. He had followed M'tal's suggestion because it made too much sense—if the weyrfolk were as decimated by the plague as the holders, the Weyrs would be incapable of fighting Thread when it came. But that didn't stop C'rion's stomach from knotting every time he flew over empty fields or saw people waving helplessly at him from below.

They did what they could, guiding unwatched herdbeasts to makeshift corrals, dropping the masks that M'tal had mentioned, but it was too little and too late.

C'rion was itching to do something.

"I just had word from J'trel," J'lantir said.

"How is the Harper Hall?"

"He didn't say," J'lantir replied. "He said that the holders need fruit, fresh fruit—"

"It's the middle of winter, there's none to be had," C'rion objected.

"*South of Ista,*" J'lantir finished.

"South?" C'rion repeated his eyes going wide. "The Southern Continent?"

"The seasons would be reversed there, it's summer," J'lantir observed.

"Then there's no hope there, either, the fruit wouldn't be ripe," C'rion objected.

"Do you remember Turns back, before we met young Kindan and the watch-whers, how I once lost my wing for a sevenday?" J'lantir said.

C'rion nodded slowly, uncertain about the sudden change of topic.

"I think I know where they went," J'lantir told him. "If not precisely *when* they went."

"To feed all the holds—"

"We could drop the fruit, if we found the right sort, just as we're dropping those masks," J'lantir cut in quickly.

C'rion mulled the notion over only for an instant before he said briskly, "Do it."

"You approve?"

"I was about to send a flight of dragons out to help, only I had not the slightest notion what we could do," C'rion told him. "*Now*, there's a chance."

J'lantir smiled broadly and turned to go.

"J'lantir," C'rion called after him. The bronze wingleader turned back. "Have your men pile the fruit by Red Butte, we'll handle it from there."

"How much?" J'lantir replied.

"All of it," C'rion said. "I'll let the other Weyrs know." J'lantir's brows rose in surprise. "You're to get enough to feed all Pern."

"For how long?"

"Until we tell you to stop," C'rion replied, waving the bronze rider away. "Now go and get those miscreants."

"I promised I'd work them like wherries," J'lantir said with a smile. He shook his head in admiration, as he added, "And you know, they never told me what they did."

"You still have to see if you're right," C'rion told him.

"Oh, no," J'lantir called back, crossing the Bowl toward his Lolanth and jumping up onto the bronze's neck. "I know I'm right, Talith seemed too smug."

And with that, the bronze dragon and rider leaped into the air above the Bowl. Lolanth stroked his wings once, twice, and was gone *between*.

◆

J'lantir timed his jump carefully, arriving just at the last time he'd seen his wing before they'd disappeared so abruptly after five Turns ago. He'd been off, he recalled, talking with C'rion about something, probably complaining once more about the firestone. He snorted at the memory.

"J'lantir!" J'trel called as Lolanth landed in the Bowl.

"J'trel, get the rest of the wing and meet me at Red Butte immediately," J'lantir ordered briskly.

"But—"

"No time, just do it," J'lantir replied, urging Lolanth airborne once more. In an instant he was *between*, hovering over the strange landmark that had been a rendezvous for hundreds of Turns and, hopefully, would be for hundreds more to come.

The wing arrived almost immediately after he did.

"J'lantir," V'sog called as he dismounted, "when J'trel said to meet you here, I thought he was joking."

"Weren't you meeting with C'rion?" J'lian asked. "I thought I just saw you—"

"You did," J'lantir interjected. He gestured for them to gather 'round. "Now listen up, I've come back in time—"

"Back in time!" V'sog exclaimed in surprise. "But dragons can't—we're not—"

"V'sog, listen up," J'lantir bellowed. "I went back in time and brought you forward in time. You have to go to the Southern Continent, you have to find the best fruit, fruit that sick people can eat, and collect it all."

"How much?" J'trel asked.

"Enough to feed all Pern," J'lantir replied.

"For how long?" V'sog asked, looking at J'lantir anxiously.

"Until I tell you to stop," J'lantir replied. "Bring it here. Bring it to this same spot one hour from now and keep bringing it."

"But—*timing* it?" J'lian said, peering around nervously at the rest of the wing.

"Where will you be?" V'sog asked.

"I'll be coordinating with the rest of the Weyrs," J'lantir said. "We've got to distribute the fruit."

"To whom?" V'sog demanded.

"I can't tell you," J'lantir replied. "When the right time comes, you'll know."

"And until then?" J'trel asked.

"Until then, I know nothing," J'lantir told them. "And you're not to tell me."

"Time paradox," V'sog guessed.

"Exactly," J'lantir agreed. He looked at B'zim and L'cal. "I want you two to take charge."

The two senior riders exchanged glances and then nodded in agreement.

"When you're all done, I'll know nothing," J'lantir told them. "I'll be very angry, but you're to tell me nothing."

"Tell you nothing?" J'lian asked, clearly confused. "Why?"

"Why are we doing all this, anyway?" K'nad demanded.

"Trust me," J'lantir replied, catching each of their eyes in turn, "it's worth it."

"All right," K'nad replied, "if you say so."

"The Southern Continent!" J'lian exclaimed.

"Timing it!" J'trel added.

"Don't get hurt," J'lantir admonished them, then climbed back on his bronze dragon. "I'll see you soon."

And, leaving his wing behind, J'lantir and Lolanth vanished *between*. When he came out of *between* once more, the sun had moved an hour further into the sky and the top of the Butte was covered with nets full of fruit.

"Best fruit we could find," B'zim called as Lolanth settled in the remaining clear spot. The brown rider tossed J'lantir a large red-fruit. The bronze rider caught it deftly and sniffed it; its odor was tantalizing.

"You can eat it, seeds and all," J'trel told him. "Even the rind."

"Excellent!" J'lantir replied. A rustle of noise and wind behind him alerted him and he turned to see C'rion hovering nearby on bronze Nidanth. Surrounding him were the rest of the Weyr, less J'lantir's wing. A moment later the sky darkened as riders from Benden, Fort, and High Reaches arrived.

"Attach parachutes to those and we'll drop them directly," M'tal called as he jumped off bronze Gaminth and strode over to J'lantir.

"Parachutes?" J'lantir asked. He turned to his wing. "Come back in another hour."

"That's timing it tight, J'lantir," B'zim noted.

"We've no time here," J'lantir told him. B'zim nodded and waved to the other wing riders to mount their dragons.

"Where are they going?" M'tal asked, peering after the rising wing.

"Back in time to get more fruit," C'rion told him.

"They're *timing* it?" M'tal asked in horror.

"There's no choice, fruit isn't ripe in Southern this time of year," C'rion replied.

"They'll be all right," J'lantir assured the Benden Weyrleader.

"How do you know?" M'tal asked challengingly.

"Because they're the wing I lost for a sevenday," J'lantir replied with a grin.

M'tal's eyes widened as he recalled the story. "So now we know where they went and who took them."

"Indeed," C'rion agreed. He turned back to the task at hand. "How many parachutes for these nets, do you think?"

M'tal turned his attention to the large cargo nets and gestured for one of his riders to approach him.

"We must hurry," the Benden Weyrleader said. "We don't have time on our side here and now."

He turned to another group of descending dragons, frowning. "What are they doing here," he groaned, "they could be dropping the fellis leaves *now*. Gaminth, tell them to spread out to the Holds and drop the bundles they've got; they don't need parachutes, the leaves will do fine!"

As if hearing his bellow, the four wings of dragons winked *between* to fulfill their mission.

———◆———

"That's the last of the fellis, there," Neesa told Kindan as she handed him a pitcher. "And the rolls are gone, too."

The sun was not yet at midday.

"Thanks," Kindan told her. He left the pitcher on the counter and went out to the linen line again. Perhaps he could figure out a way to get some from the Harper Hall.

He drummed his message quickly, calling for attention. Then he waited. And waited. And waited. There was no response.

"Conar?" Kindan called out softly, thinking of the young holder boy who had never thought himself worth much.

Valla appeared at his shoulder, crooning anxiously and preening against Kindan's neck, but Kindan ignored him, staring down at the dull pot in despair.

Bemin was right. They were all going to die.

A shadow dulled the pot. Then another. Kindan looked around and saw more shadows. He gazed upward and started as a bundle landed with a thump not a meter from him. Incredulously, Kindan reached for the bundle.

Leaves. Only leaves. Was this some—wait! They were *fellis* leaves.

"Neesa!" Kindan cried, scooping up two bundles and racing to the kitchen. "Neesa, I've got more fellis leaves!"

"What? How did you find them?" Neesa asked as Kindan thrust the bundles into her arms.

"They're in the linen area," Kindan told her. "They fell from the sky."

"Fell from the sky," Neesa repeated, looking at Kindan as though he'd lost his mind. Then his meaning registered and she clapped her hands to her mouth, tears leaking from her eyes. "Dragonriders! We're saved!"

"What is this?" Bemin demanded, attracted by Neesa's loud bellowing.

"Fellis," Kindan said, thrusting a leaf at Bemin. "The dragonriders dropped fellis."

For a moment, Bemin had a look of hope on his face. Then it drained away.

"Fellis will only help the dying," he said, and turned back to the Great Hall.

✦

C'rion and M'tal conferred when the first bundles of fruit were ready to drop.

"The Harper Hall?" C'rion asked.

"No, J'trel says there are only a few there," M'tal replied. "Send them to Fort Hold."

"You think your friend is still alive?" C'rion asked.

M'tal shook his head. "I can't say," he said. "But it was his idea, and B'ralar says there are still people moving at Fort Hold, so we owe it to him to try first."

C'rion nodded and gestured to the laden wing. "Fort Hold!" he called. In an instant they were airborne and gone, *between.*

"Let's hope we're not too late," C'rion murmured. Beside him, M'tal nodded glumly, his eyes filled with sorrow.

✦

Kindan did not follow Bemin. Instead, he waited until Neesa had brewed a fresh decoction of fellis juice, then he took the bottle. In the Great Hall, he worked his way around the room, administering a drop here, two drops there, depending upon the amount of fever indicated by the moodpaste.

He had just finished the first line of cots when Bemin and Jelir walked back into the Hall, clearly having borne another body to the grave site.

"It's almost full, my lord," Jelir said. "Overfull, if we don't want scavengers digging among the dead."

"Then leave the bodies here," Bemin replied disconsolately, throwing himself onto a cot and sitting with his head and shoulders hunched over in despair.

"My lord?" Jelir said in surprise. Fort's Lord Holder made no response. Desperately, Jelir looked over to Kindan.

Kindan sighed and straightened his shoulders. He glanced around for Fiona, but she wasn't in sight; he vaguely recalled a toddler sprawled in the kitchen.

He dropped to his knees in front of the Lord Holder.

"You cannot stop now," he said, peering up to meet Bemin's eyes.

"I can't go on," Bemin said. "We've got no food, only fellis." He barked a laugh. "We could all drink it and feel no pain." He raised his head enough to meet Kindan's eyes. "Mix it with the wine and we'll all feel no pain!"

"No," Kindan said. "This is not the time for wine, my lord. Save it for later."

"Later?" Bemin snorted. "When I mourn my wife, my sons, my daughter? Will you drown your sorrows over your lover then? Will the pain ever go away?"

"I don't know," Kindan told him honestly. "I was hoping you would tell me."

Bemin grimaced and shook his head. "I have nothing to tell you, harper." He snorted and said with a lopsided grin, "You've dishonored your word once more, you know."

"My lord?"

"Only fellis fell from the sky," Bemin told him. "You were half right, though, I'll grant you that." He snorted again in faint humor. "You keep half your word, harper."

"I promised you food from the sky, my lord," Kindan told him firmly, his voice rising to carry throughout the Great Hall. "On my word as harper."

"Harper!" Bemin exclaimed, rising from the cot angrily. "I need no harpers, I need healers!"

"Lord Bemin, Lord Bemin, come quick!" Neesa shouted from the far end of the hall.

Bemin's brows creased in pain.

"Fiona?" he called, then raced past Kindan toward the kitchen. Kindan followed an instant later.

But it wasn't Fiona. Neesa raced past her, shouting, "Come quick, you've got to see! You've got to see it!"

They raced out into the linen yard and Neesa pointed into the sky.

"Dragonriders!" she shouted. "Look at them! They've come!"

"More fellis," Bemin guessed sourly. Just then, a dragon swooped low and a great bundle fell from the sky, to be slowed an instant later by many large billowing parachutes.

"They dropped the fellis," Kindan said in wonder, glancing at the slowly falling bundle. He turned and saw that more bundles were falling in the courtyard outside the Great Hall. He saw yet another bundle dropping toward the cotholds outside Fort Hold.

"It's food," Neesa said, rushing toward the first bundle that crashed onto the ground. "It's food! Fruit!" She reached through the netting and pulled out a large fruit. "I've never seen the like!" She took a huge bite and juices dribbled down her chin. "It's fresh!

And it's marvelous." She turned to Bemin. "My lord, you've got to try it!"

Bemin didn't move. His eyes were on Kindan.

Slowly the Lord Holder of Fort Hold, the oldest Hold on Pern, knelt before the youngest harper on Pern.

"You kept your word, harper," Bemin said, bowing low before him.

"Have a fruit, my lord," Kindan said, taking one of the fruits proffered by Neesa. Bemin looked up at him and slowly took the fruit.

"Then we'll get back to work," Kindan added with a grin.

The Lord Holder of Fort Hold rose slowly, redfruit in one hand, took a bite, then another, and smiled back at Kindan.

"Fruit from the sky," Bemin murmured in amazement.

"We've more work to do now, my lord," Kindan said with a re-newed sense of urgency. He gestured to a bundle. "There's many that will need these, they need them now."

Bemin nodded in vigorous agreement, a new light in his eyes—a light of hope.

CHAPTER 14

What is this I see
I cannot believe my eyes
Fresh fruit and new hope
Floating in the skies.

FORT HOLD

While Bemin distributed the fruits first to the standing able-bodied and then sent out patrols to distribute them to the rest of the Hold, Kindan returned to tending the ill in the Great Hall.

As he had half guessed, the arrival of fresh food meant the arrival of more patients, newly freed from the back rooms of the Hold by the roving parties that Bemin had sent out.

Kindan worked tirelessly through the rest of the day and the night. At some point he drifted off, falling asleep half over a cot.

A hand shook him gently awake much later.

"Healer," a woman's voice called. "Healer Kindan, are you all right?"

Kindan stirred and pulled himself upright.

"I'm Merila," the woman said. "I'm sometimes midwife," she explained. "Lord Bemin sent me to help you."

"The illness?" Kindan asked her.

"I was way back in the apartments," Merila said. "The others all died and I was near the same until the men brought me that fruit."

"What do you know about the illness?" Kindan asked, pushing himself to his feet. He wobbled and Merila deftly inserted a hand under his shoulder, helping him up.

"Nothing much," Merila said. "I had it and I got well, others died."

"Those in their prime," Kindan told her.

Merila's brow creased in thought, then she nodded. "That was the way of it," she agreed. "Couldn't see it until now." She looked at him. "Do you know why?"

"Their lungs were coughed up," Kindan said. "From the inside. Like their bodies fought so hard, they coughed up their own lungs."

"People've two lungs, did you try putting them on one side?"

Kindan nodded. "I tried that with"—he found his throat tightening—"with"—he couldn't say her name, it hurt too much—"with the Lord Holder's daughter. It didn't work."

"It was worth trying, all the same," Merila replied judiciously. She gave Kindan a probing glance and looked ready to ask him another question, but changed her mind. "What can I do to help?"

"Have they got everyone from the back rooms?" Kindan asked.

"Not all," Merila replied. "They're just starting."

A group of holders marched by, carrying a woman; they were trailed by a small group of children.

"There's many a mother who'll die of starvation," Merila said, shaking her head. "They gave their food to their children."

"We've got fruit," Kindan said.

"But for how long?" Merila wondered.

"The dragonriders won't let us down," Kindan assured her.

Merila snorted and waved her hand around the Hall. "I don't see any dragonriders here, harper."

"If they catch the plague, they'll infect their weyrfolk," Kindan explained. "The last time a plague like this spread over Pern they did just that and it took nearly twenty Turns for the Weyrs to recover."

"Twenty Turns?" Merila repeated in surprise. "But Thread's coming—"

"Exactly," Kindan said with a firm nod. "If the weyrfolk were to die from this illness, there'd be no support for the Weyrs, and not enough dragonriders fighting Thread."

"And when the illness passes, what then?" Merila asked. "Will they come then?"

"Who can say when the illness has passed?" Kindan asked her.

"That would be you," she told him. Kindan gave her a startled look. "You're the only healer I see here."

"And when you're done there, check the stables," Bemin called to a workgroup as he entered the Great Hall from the courtyard. "If we can hitch up a wagon, we can bring food down below and the ill back up."

"Aye, my lord," Jelir called, gesturing to the group of four men behind him as they turned to head back outside.

Bemin saw Kindan and walked stiffly over to him.

"I can't be here, there's too much work to do in the Hold," the Lord Holder said. "Can you manage on your own?"

"I'll help," Merila declared.

"And Neesa will keep the food going," Bemin added.

"If only we had some *klah*," Merila murmured.

Bemin cocked an eyebrow at her. "I'll bet we can find some bark down in the village."

"That would be great, my lord," Kindan said, thinking wistfully of the brew's restorative powers.

"We'll make it our second priority," Bemin declared. "Right after tending the sick."

Kindan nodded in agreement. Bemin turned but seemed reluctant to leave.

"Go, my lord," Kindan told him with a wave of his hand. "We'll manage."

As the day progressed, Kindan found it harder and harder to "manage." Even with the fruit and the fellis, there were over two hundred patients and only two carers, himself and Merila. Merila watched over his shoulder while he dealt with the first three patients, marveled at the usefulness of the moodpaste, then took off on her own.

Sometime after lunch, Kindan staggered and fell to his knees. Attracted by the motion, Merila rushed to his side.

"Lie down," Merila told him.

"There are more patients," Kindan protested.

"You're no help to them the way you are," she replied, gesturing to an empty cot. "Lie down. Rest."

"Wake me by dinner," Kindan told her, sitting down on the cot. He was asleep before she answered.

"Kindan," Bemin's voice called to him gently. Kindan's nose twitched, some distant memory, some—"I've got *klah.*"

Kindan's eyes snapped open and he looked up at the Lord Holder, who was clutching Fiona with one hand and proffering a mug with the other.

Kindan sat up and took the mug eagerly. It was warm, it was tasty, it was great.

"We didn't find much," Bemin explained, eyeing the mug sadly. "Only enough for a pot or two." He bent down and kissed Fiona on the head to give Kindan a moment to finish his *klah.* "Merila and Neesa have made a playroom out of the laundry room," Bemin said, adding wryly, "I nearly had to pry her away."

Kindan downed the last of his *klah* and looked up at the Lord Holder, smiling. "That's great!" He stretched, ignoring sore muscles, and said, "I haven't felt this awake in . . ."

"A fortnight or so," Bemin finished with a shrug. "I've lost track of time, myself."

"Time," Kindan repeated, his thoughts still muzzy and distracted. The *klah* was marvelous, but not a complete cure for weeks of sleepless toil. What was so important about time? Merila had said it, Kindan thought to himself, something about time.

"I must go to the Harper Hall," Kindan said suddenly.

Bemin gave him a blank look.

"No one could answer the drums," Kindan explained. "They must be even worse off than we are." He tried to stand up but his legs wouldn't move. He looked up at Fort's Lord Holder. "Could you give me a hand up, my lord?"

Bemin drew a ragged breath. "No," he said wearily. "You need to rest."

"But they *need* me there!" Kindan protested, again trying to push himself up. Feebly he grabbed for the edges of the cot he'd knelt by, trying to lever himself off the floor, but his arms were no better than his legs.

Bemin waved a hand at him. "You can't even stand on your own, lad—what help can you be?"

Kindan shook his head. "It's my *duty*," he whispered, eyes too drained to cry.

"Kindan," Merila called from the far end of the Great Hall. "Rialla has passed on."

"Her children," Bemin groaned softly, clutching Fiona tightly against his chest.

"I'll talk to them," Kindan said. Again he raised a hand to Bemin. "Can you help me up?"

With a sigh, Bemin reached down and helped the lad up from the floor. He's nothing but skin and bones, the Lord Holder mused. He found a sick humor in the thought that all of Fort Hold was reliant on the wits of a tall, thin waif of a lad. "Once you're done with them, you'll lie back down and get more rest," he ordered.

"I can't," Kindan replied. "I've got to go to the Harper Hall."

"You can only walk holding on to my arm," Bemin reminded him.

"And no one there can answer the drums," Kindan told him.

"Lad," Bemin began slowly, dreading the question, "what if there is no one to answer to drums?"

"Then we must know," Kindan replied firmly. "We must tell the others, the Weyrleaders—"

Bemin interrupted with a disdainful snort. "The weyrfolk of Pern are safe enough, high up in their lofty homes. But they can't come and till our fields, harvest our grains, tend our sick."

Kindan shifted his weight, leaning more on Bemin as he used his free hand to wipe his face.

"If they can't come, we'll survive," he declared feverishly.

"If we survive here, at this Hold and the Hall, it will be only because of you," Bemin said. He glanced down, seeing the top of Kindan's head. "Survive and you can have anything you ask for."

Surprised, Kindan glanced up at the Lord Holder. "You know what I wanted most on Pern."

A ghost of a smile crossed Bemin's lips. "No man would have been prouder than I to have you call him 'Father.'"

Bolstered by those words, Kindan found the strength to stand on his own and even lengthen his stride.

As he knelt down beside the two youngsters who looked uncomprehendingly at their mother's body, Kindan turned to Merila and said, "Prepare some supplies, we'll be going to the Harper Hall after this." He glanced up at Bemin and said by way of apology, "I can't rest until I know."

Bemin sighed heavily, but dropped a hand on Kindan's shoulder and clenched it. "I'll go with you."

Kindan nodded in gratitude, then turned his attention to Rialla's children. He took a deep, steadying breath before he caught the eyes of Ernin, the youngest, and Erila.

"Your mother didn't want to leave you," he told them softly, reaching out and grabbing their hands. "She was very brave and she fought for days as hard as she could."

"She did?" Ernin asked, looking at the still form of his mother. "She fought the plague?"

"She did," Kindan affirmed. "But she was very weak and it was very strong."

"It beat her?" Ernin asked, his eyes watering. Kindan nodded sadly. Ernin pursed his lips in desperate thought. "Can she play again?"

"No, lad, I'm afraid she can't," Bemin said. "She's gone, like my Lady Sannora."

"She's dead?" Erila asked, shifting her gaze from Kindan up to Bemin.

"She is," Kindan told her softly. "But she asked us to look after you, and we promised her we would." He found it hard to speak and it was a moment before he continued, "Lord Bemin and I, we'll keep care of you."

"But I want to go with Momma!" Ernin wailed.

"That would be the easy way," Bemin told the boy chidingly. "You seem stronger than that. Are you up to the challenge?"

Ernin looked up wide-eyed at the Lord Holder until his sister nudged him, and hissed, "Answer the Lord Holder!"

"Yes, my lord," Ernin told him.

"I *knew* you were!" Bemin replied with a firm nod of his head. "I'll need you two to find your way to the playroom, you'll find it by the noise. There are others there who are ready for the challenge." Bemin gestured to the door. "Off you go!"

As the youngsters scurried away toward the kitchen, Bemin shook his head sadly. He waited until they were out of sight, then signaled to two holders to come and take Rialla's body.

He turned to Kindan, his features set. "Very well, harper, let's go to your Hall."

He drew Kindan to his side and together they walked out of the Fort Hold's Great Hall toward the ramp that led down into the valley below and onto the road that forked to the Harper Hall.

✦

Kindan's first sight of the Harper Hall in nearly three weeks set his heart plunging into despair. The whole place had a disused, abandoned appearance, looking nothing at all like the purposeful bustling center of learning and arts on Pern.

Worse, he could see a huge mound of dirt and a bigger ditch just outside the entrance to the Healer Hall set in the cliffs far to the right of the Harper Hall. A blue dragon was working busily nearby. It took Kindan a moment to see what the dragon was doing, and then his heart nearly stopped. J'trel's blue Talith was gently carrying bodies in his front claws and lowering them into the ditch. He could see where another ditch nearby had already been filled in.

He picked up his pace, startling Bemin.

"Valla, go ahead, tell them we're coming!" Kindan called to his fire-lizard. The little bronze did a quick circle in the sky then sped off, chirping loudly at the blue dragon and then disappearing through the doors of the Healer Hall.

"There's a bundle of fruit over there," Kindan called, veering off the paved road.

"Let the dragon get it," Bemin replied, steering them back. "We can also send down a cart later. First we must see . . ." he let his words trail off, unwilling to complete his sentence.

As they passed near the outside of the Harper Hall, a fresh breeze blew in from the valley, carrying with it the distinct odor of death and decay.

"We'll send a party in as soon as we can," Bemin promised.

"No, we'll do it, our duty as harpers," Kindan replied.

"No, as Lord Holder, I am telling you that Fort will do it," Bemin told him forcefully. In a softer voice he added, "It's my choice and our honor."

"I thought you didn't trust harpers," Kindan snapped back before he thought about what he was saying. He instantly regretted it but Bemin laughed and waved it aside.

"You're right: I *didn't* trust harpers," Bemin agreed. He nodded down to Kindan. "But now that you've produced fruit from the sky, I've had to revise my thinking." He paused for a moment. "Let us clean up the Harper Hall," he repeated. "You shouldn't have to deal with that horror."

"Very well," Kindan said. He cocked his head up to meet Bemin's eyes squarely. "Thank you, Lord Holder."

Bemin started to reply, but halted abruptly as Valla flittered out of the entrance to the Healer Hall, chittering in distress, eyes whirling red.

Together Kindan and Fort's Lord Holder entered.

———◆———

It was a moment before their eyes adjusted to the dim light. During that moment, their nostrils were assailed with the smells of death and dying, and the sick.

Kindan walked through the entrance, turning toward the infirmary.

"Valla," he called softly, "find J'trel."

The rows of beds in the infirmary were full of bodies. Kindan's heart sank.

"Something moved over there," Bemin said, turning to the left, near a window.

Kindan rushed past him.

"Kinda'?" a young voice asked. Kindan saw Druri sitting on the floor, cradling little Jassi between his knees.

"Druri?" Kindan called. The young Istan looked tired, underfed, but no worse.

"Kinda'!" Druri exclaimed, his face breaking into a smile.

"Shh!" Bemin said urgently. "I hear something."

The noise came from the end of the room. It was a rustling. Kindan turned to locate it, but Bemin found the source first.

"Over here," he called softly, standing over a bed. He knelt down and pulled out a hand. "She's still alive," he said after a moment.

It was Kelsa. Her cheeks were so gaunt, she looked like a stick figure.

"I heard the drums," Kelsa said. "Conar, where is he?"

A noise distracted them and a well-built haggard-looking man walked into the room and quickly took in the scene.

"J'trel, rider of blue Talith," the dragonrider said with a quick nod to Bemin.

"You managed all this by yourself?" Bemin asked in surprise and awe.

"No," J'trel said, shaking his head sadly. "A youngster, one of the apprentices, was helping me until yesterday." He jerked his head toward the outside and the dirt mound. "Talith just laid him with the others."

"Conar?" Kindan asked. "The drummer?"

"That was him," J'trel agreed dully. He leaned closer to them and continued in a voice that only they could hear, "He skimped on his food to save the others."

"How many are there?" Kindan asked, so numb with grief that he couldn't imagine feeling worse.

"Five or six in this room, maybe twice that in the next," J'trel said. He glanced sadly around the room. "I was coming in here to take the others out."

"We'll help," Bemin said.

"First, the living," Kindan told them. He leaned over to Kelsa. "It's all right, we're here, we're taking you back to the Hold; we've got food, you'll be fine."

"Kindan, you're alive!" Kelsa sobbed, grabbing his hand fiercely.

"Nonala? Verilan?" Kindan asked her hopefully.

"Over there," Kelsa said, pointing first to the bed beside her and then to the one opposite.

Kindan felt his spirits lift—at least some of his friends were alive.

He heard a noise from Nonala's bed and saw her looking at him entreatingly. He turned to her and grabbed her hand.

"It's all right, help's here," he told her.

Her lips were dry and her throat parched. She beckoned him close enough to whisper, "Vaxoram?"

"Journeyman Vaxoram didn't make it," Kindan told her with a shake of his head, tears filling his eyes.

Nonala closed her eyes and turned away. Then she turned back and opened them again. "Journeyman?"

"He walked the tables," Kindan told her. Her eyes widened. "He said that then maybe he'd be worthy. He said he loved you."

Nonala moaned and turned away again.

"The air is better in the Great Hall," Bemin said, looking at J'trel. "And we've a playroom for the children. Can your Talith carry some of the ill?"

"In shifts, he can carry them all," J'trel declared stoutly.

"Good, let's start now," Bemin replied nodding to the dragon-rider. "We've food and everything except *klah*."

"There'll be some in the stores," Kindan said. "I'll get them." He turned to Kelsa. "We're getting you out of here." He went over to Verilan's bed and repeated the message, but the young archivist was sleeping fitfully.

As Bemin and J'trel started moving the patients out of the infirmary, first moving Druri and Jassi into the fresh air and sunlight, Kindan steeled himself for one more, difficult task.

"Did you bury Master Lenner?" Kindan asked the blue rider.

"Yes," J'trel replied, grimacing. "He caught the flu eight days on, and survived another three."

"He would have made notes," Kindan said hopefully.

"If he did, they weren't on him," J'trel replied. "I checked."

Kindan nodded, relieved of the worst of his fears—that the notes were buried with the Masterhealer.

"What do you need them for?" Bemin asked.

"Lenner would have taken careful notes, they might help us

understand this illness and how long it lasts," Kindan said, heading off to the Master's study. It was in the back, in a room too dark to see much more than shadows. He tried the desk but found nothing. Had Lenner succumbed too quickly to make any notes? Kindan shook his head, recalling how the Masterhealer had talked about the importance of good notes whenever he visited the Archives.

The Archives! Kindan thought to himself. *Verilan!*

Kindan left the study quickly, returning to the infirmary just as Bemin was hauling Verilan on to his back.

"Did he have anything with him, my lord?" Kindan asked as Bemin trudged by.

"A sack full of notes," Bemin said. "But we can always get them later."

Kindan continued back to the infirmary and found the sack. He brought it out into the light and pulled a note out at random—he recognized Lenner's handwriting. The Masterhealer must have guessed his own fate, to stash the Records with Verilan.

Further, Kindan realized, Lenner must have figured out that youngsters were more likely than others to survive the plague. Perhaps Lenner had uncovered other secrets before the illness took him.

"We'll take the first lot," Bemin said, as he climbed up on Talith behind Nonala, Kelsa, and Verilan. "I'll want to alert Jelir and get them settled. Then we'll come back for you and the others."

Kindan nodded, smiling at Druri as the youngster stared raptly at the great blue dragon. At Kindan's voiceless request, Valla approached and entertained both Druri and Jassi with antics and aerobatics while Talith rose into the air and flew the short distance to Fort Hold's great courtyard.

The blue dragon returned soon enough with Stennel and another holder Kindan didn't recognize. Between the three men, they loaded Kindan, his notes, Jassi and Druri in no time.

"I'll be back in a moment," J'trel promised Stennel.

"We'll get started in the meantime," Stennel replied, turning to his fellow and muttering, "Did you hear that? A dragonrider's helping us!"

"If only there were more," the other replied mournfully.

In front of Kindan, J'trel snorted in what seemed to be agreement.

"You know why they can't help," Kindan said to J'trel.

"I do, lad," J'trel replied, calling over his shoulder. "That doesn't mean I don't understand how the holders feel."

Kindan nodded in agreement. The worst plague ever seemed to be ravaging the planet, and all the Weyrs of Pern appeared to be idle. But the Weyrs were duty-bound to fight an even greater menace.

"They'll understand when Thread comes," Kindan reassured the rider.

"If they're still alive," the blue rider replied sourly.

CHAPTER 15

Rider, dragon, tried and true
All life's hope now lives with you
Dragon, rider, work and toil
Save the earth, save the soil.

RED BUTTE

No sign of life at Benden Hold, Valley Hold, Brum, or Bay Head," Wingleader L'tor reported to M'tal. "Something's been eating the fruit at Fork, Keroon, and Plains Holds. We've seen signs of life at Lemos and Bitra Holds."

"Very good," M'tal said with a sigh. "There are probably many small cotholds, but we don't know how to find them."

C'rion, the Istan Weyrleader, had been listening in on the conversation.

"I think I know a way to help," he said. He had his dragon call for J'lantir and the bronze rider quickly appeared. L'tor and M'tal exchanged surprised looks, wondering what the Istan wingleader could do about Benden Hold.

"Didn't you make your wing drill on all the recognition points on Pern when they wouldn't tell you where they'd gone?" C'rion asked J'lantir.

"Well, yes," J'lantir replied. He gave C'rion a strange look. "And, oddly, they seemed pleased."

"I think we know why," C'rion told him. "They're doing nothing now, aren't they?"

"It would be unwise to have them here," J'lantir agreed, pointing to the members of his wing who had arrived *between* times with yet another vital load of fresh fruit from the Southern Continent.

"Can you send them, with our compliments, to Benden, Telgar, Fort, and High Reaches Weyrs to act as guides?"

"I could," J'lantir replied dubiously, "but I'm not sure D'gan would want—"

"Forget Telgar," M'tal said, shaking his head. "D'gan's made it plain that he'll handle this by himself."

"Which means that you're sneaking in food with your wings," C'rion guessed shrewdly.

M'tal smiled. "As is B'ralar from the west."

C'rion shook his head angrily, a bitter look on his face. "What that dragon ever saw in that particular rider . . ."

"He's just as scared as the rest of us," M'tal said. "I can't agree with his actions, but I can understand his reasoning."

"We'll see how things are when it comes time to collect the tithe," C'rion replied, thinking that D'gan's holders would acknowledge his lack of help with a lack of goods in tithe. He turned to J'lantir. "Regardless, get those layabouts of yours into action."

"At once, Weyrleader," J'lantir said with a nod, lack of sleep and *timing* making his step falter.

"He'll be all right," C'rion said in response to M'tal's worried look.

"But will his wing?"

"Well," C'rion said consideringly, "they must be because they're still here." M'tal did a double take and the Istan Weyrleader chuckled. "If they'd had any problems *between* back in time, they wouldn't be here *now*, would they?"

"You mean they wouldn't exist in the present if they'd died in the past, don't you?" M'tal said after a long moment.

"Precisely," C'rion agreed.

"Another reason I don't like *timing* it," M'tal muttered to himself. "It's impossible to explain."

C'rion chuckled sympathetically.

"All the same," M'tal went on, "there *is* a limit on how much fruit we can get from Southern."

"And on how long we can work like this," C'rion agreed as another wing of dragonriders burst from *between* to load up with another cargo of fruit.

"Two days?" M'tal wondered. "Maybe three?"

Beside him, C'rion nodded in glum agreement.

———◆———

Neesa took Druri and Jassi out of Kindan's arms nearly the moment he returned.

"Yanira will look after them," Neesa said. "She's got the whole playroom under control."

Kindan paused, looking around the Great Hall. Something was different. It looked lighter. He saw groups of people moving up and down the lines of cots purposefully.

"I figured out how to juice that fruit," Neesa told him. "We're feeding that to the worst off, dribbling it down their throats." She wrung her hands nervously and grimaced. Then she brightened. "But the others, the ones getting better, we're feeding them a mixture of the juice and the pulp."

She gave Kindan a frank, worried look. "How long do you think the dragonriders can keep bringing us food?"

Kindan shook his head.

"Not that it'll help if we don't get people to tend to the herds soon," Neesa said. "Or check that the grain silos aren't infested."

"We'll think of something," Kindan said.

"Well, *I* think you should get some rest," Neesa told him firmly. "I've said the same thing to the Lord Holder as well." She shook her head grimly. "I know *I'm* exhausted and I've heard that it was only the two of you tending the whole Hold for days on end—you must be beyond beyond."

"There's still work to be done," Kindan replied, clutching the sack against his chest.

"And how do you plan to do that?" Neesa demanded tartly.

"Step by step, moment by moment," Kindan told her, making a silent salutation to Vaxoram's spirit. "Right now, I need a place to read."

"You'd want to go upstairs then, to the Lord Holder's quarters," Neesa told him. "Jelir said they've cleared it out, it's fit to live in. Lord Bemin himself said you're to take the first room on the right." She directed him to the end of the Great Hall and pointed to the stairs as she returned to the kitchen. "You get off your feet while you're reading and don't worry if you fall asleep."

"No time for that," Kindan told her as he began his way up the long winding stairs.

"No time!" Neesa swore, shaking her head as he vanished out of sight. "Just like the Lord Holder."

—◆—

The moment Kindan set foot on the rich carpeting of the corridor leading down the Lord Holder's quarters, he felt an eerie presence. It wasn't just the essence of Lady Sannora, or that of Bannor and Semin; it felt more like he was in the presence of hundreds of Turns of Lord and Lady Holders. Over the Turns how many lives had been lived here, how many laughs laughed, how many tears shed? It was a palpable thing, not quite a weight, certainly not oppressive, but there all the same.

The first door on the right was open, inviting. Kindan stepped through the doorway and stopped dead. It was *her* room.

Decorated in floral pinks and golds, the room showed signs of Lady Sannora's touch, as well as small pebbles and polished stones that were obviously Koriana's. There was a large workdesk. Sheets of paper lay on it, many with barely legible writing—Koriana had been sent to the Harper Hall to improve her writing, among other things.

He pulled back the padded chair, suddenly uncomfortable in his worn and dirty clothing. He looked around and found a small hand towel near a freshly filled washbasin and set it on the padded seat before settling into the chair.

Slowly, carefully, gently, reverently, he set Koriana's papers to one side. With equal care, he opened the sack and retrieved Lenner's notes.

The light in the room was good, reflected cleverly through from the hallway and from the ceiling above. A glowbasket lay near to hand, the glows turned over to preserve their energy, ready to use when night came.

Kindan organized Lenner's notes in chronological order and began to read. At first they were the common everyday notes of a healer working his craft, notes on cuts and prescriptions, decoctions. Then worried references to the various flu decoctions that had worked in the past, and finally the first mention of deaths.

Kindan never knew when he started crying, only that the tears were smearing the ink on the page and he couldn't have that. He wiped his eyes with his hands, and turned back to work only to discover that his eyes wouldn't focus. He tried again, focused, and began once more.

He wasn't aware of falling asleep. He never heard Bemin enter the room and never woke as the Lord Holder changed his clothes and slipped him into the bed.

He dreamed of Koriana, the scent of her hair in his nostrils. He thought that they were once again lying together in the apprentice dormitory at the Harper Hall. He would wake up in a moment—

His eyes opened. It was night. Koriana was not at his side. He was in a bed much larger and softer than he'd ever been in. And then he remembered. Koriana was dead, he was in her room, the scent of her hair must have come from her pillows.

Nervously he shifted, tensed, ready to spring out of the bed. How had he gotten here? What would Lord Bemin say?

"The sheets can be cleaned," Bemin's voice called from the doorway. Kindan saw him illuminated by a dim glow. "Go back to sleep."

"But—"

"It's little and poor hospitality for all you've done," Bemin told him. His voice softened as he added wistfully, "Besides, it reminded me of putting Bannor in bed when he'd been up late." He started to leave, then turned back. "So please humor me."

Kindan nodded and turned over in the bed. It was a long while before he drifted back to sleep but when he did, he dreamed of Koriana laughing and dancing in a summer field.

✦

Koriana's laughter faded and the scent of her hair was replaced by a sharper, more pungent odor that woke Kindan up. *Klah.*

"It's midday," Bemin called from the door, a tray in his hands. "I'd prefer to let you sleep longer, but—" he cut himself off, placed the tray on a bedside table, and dragged up a chair for himself.

"What, my lord?" Kindan asked, sitting up and feeling strange to be in a bed when the Lord Holder had clearly been awake for hours, and also feeling strange that he felt no discomfort lying in Koriana's bed in Bemin's presence. It wasn't just that the Lord Holder had put him there; it was that Kindan felt Bemin *welcomed* him there.

"Drink and eat, while I talk," Bemin said, handing Kindan a mug of *klah.* Kindan took the mug and nodded in thanks. Bemin took a breath before continuing, "Fort Hold was home to more than ten thousand holders before this plague." He gestured toward the grave below. "I figure we've buried over a thousand and there are probably as many bodies we haven't yet discovered." Kindan nodded gravely. "That means that we'll have about six thousand left—"

"My lord? Surely you mean eight. Two from ten leaves eight," Kindan said respectfully.

"There are easily two thousand who will starve or die from illness resulting from the plague," Bemin replied. "We need at least three thousand healthy people to supply our basic needs and we need them every day. More than half the hold is still recovering from this illness—there aren't enough hands to keep things running until the rest recover."

Kindan paled; he hadn't realized the peril that remained. He didn't question Bemin's numbers; *he* had only a vague understanding of the workings of a major Hold, Bemin had Turns of practical experience.

"The fruit?"

"Enough for a few days yet," Bemin agreed. Bleakly he continued, "But not enough to get our coal brought down, get the infested apartments cleaned, set up the kitchen, bring up the stored meats, clear the silos, check on the livestock."

"If not, what will happen?"

Bemin shook his head. "I'm certain that the Hold will survive, I just can't be certain that thousands more won't die before winter's end." He paused before adding, "And this is not just Fort Hold; every Hold on Pern must be in about the same state."

The Lord Holder rose up irritably and started pacing the room. "I'm sorry I told you," he apologized to Kindan. "It's just that, after we've come so far, I felt you had to know."

"I understand, my lord," Kindan replied. "And thank you."

"For what?" Bemin asked, surprised.

"For treating me like a son."

The Lord Holder stopped in his tracks, turned to Kindan, flushed, and nodded mutely. For a moment, they needed no words: Kindan understanding Bemin's trust and faith in him; Bemin knowing that Kindan accepted both the privileges and responsibilities of his offer.

After a moment, Kindan rose from the bed, gently smoothing the covers and looked around for his clothing.

"I've sent it to be washed," Bemin said. "Although you might want to have your clothes destroyed." He glanced at a bundle laid out at the end of the bed. "Bannor was much bigger than you, but Koriana liked to dress man-style whenever she could, so I thought you might fit in her clothes." His mouth twitched. "Only Fort Hold colors, I'm afraid, not harper blue."

Kindan ran his hand reverently over the fabric. "I'd be honored," he told the Lord Holder. He glanced around. "But I would soil the clothes."

"There's a bath beyond there," Bemin told him, waving at a doorway. "The water's only warm, however."

"Warm will be enough," Kindan said cheerfully, carefully picking up the clothes and heading to the bathroom.

It took him longer than he would have liked to get clean and, as the water soon ran colder, he took less time than he would have hoped for the first shower in many sevendays. In the end, however, he was clean and refreshed in a way that only a person who has been so long without bathing could be. He finished his toilet and was pleased to discover that Koriana's old clothes were nearly a good fit on him.

Lord Bemin was still waiting for him when he returned, only now he was seated once more and eating a roll. He invited Kindan to sit with him and they ate and drank in a companionable silence. At last, Bemin gestured to the Records on the table and raised an eyebrow inquiringly.

"I fell asleep before I could finish them," Kindan explained ruefully.

"Do you think there's any point?" Bemin asked politely, although his body language made his own view clear.

"I won't know until I'm done, my lord," Kindan replied.

"Very well," Bemin said with a nod. "Please don't be too long, they're clamoring for you downstairs." He smiled. "It seems most of my Hold believes that I can't operate without your presence."

"A vile lie, I assure you," Kindan answered with a grin of his own.

Bemin surprised him with a hearty guffaw. He rose and strode to the door, turning back to say, "All the same, don't be too long, if you can. All vile lies aside, I appreciate your wisdom and your company."

"I'll be there as soon as I've finished," Kindan promised.

Bemin nodded, serious again, and strode away briskly down the hall. His steps on the great circular staircase died away slowly, leaving Kindan alone with the eerie presence once more.

He returned to the writing desk and bent to his reading, intent on catching every word of the late Masterhealer's writings.

Two hours later he had more questions than answers. He rooted around the table, looking for a scrap of paper and finally, in desperation, turned over one of Koriana's old scratch pieces and began to make notes.

The first symptoms. The first illness. The first death. The second patient. The third patient. He filled in names and dates, brows furrowed as he tried to discern a pattern.

"Must establish incubation period," Lenner had scrawled on one Record.

"Yes, I know that," Kindan murmured. "But what is it?"

He dredged his memory, trying to recall what Lenner had said about diseases. First there was the latent period when there were no symptoms, then the infectious period when the illness could be spread, and finally, the—Kindan couldn't remember what it was called—it was the time after between being infectious and either recovering or dying.

People who were infected and recovered had immunity from the disease, Kindan was certain. But some vague memory from his conversations with Mikal led him to believe that sometimes the same disease could reinfect a recovered person. If that were the case, however, then Kindan would certainly have been infected again. But he could still be in the latent period, not yet infectious himself.

"No, once I know the latent period, I can tell if I might still be infected and not infectious," he said out loud, hoping that hearing the words would help him *remember* them. They certainly sounded like something he'd heard once from either Mikal or Lenner.

First, figure out the latent period, Kindan told himself. He remembered his trip to Benden Weyr. He and the others had been gone nearly a sevenday. When they'd come back everyone was falling ill.

A sevenday. He looked back over his notes. That seemed right. Maybe less, maybe only five days. But a sevenday, not more. Kindan realized with a sense of relief that it had been more than a sevenday since he'd felt ill. He probably hadn't been reinfected. He couldn't be sure, couldn't be certain until he remained free of infection for the life span of the disease: the total of the latent, infectious, and terminal phases.

His instinct told him that the disease lasted no more than three sevendays, that the infectious phase was four to six days, *maybe* a sevenday but no more, and that the final phase was probably about the same, less than seven days before a person was clear of infection.

So if a person showed no symptoms for three sevendays, they were unlikely to be contagious, unlikely to have this killer flu.

He got up from the writing desk, bringing his scrap paper with him, and headed down to the Great Hall.

◆

"Kindan!" Merila called as she saw him. "Great, can you take over? I'm exhausted."

"Yes," Kindan said, seeing in one glance the extent of the midwife's fatigue, her stumbling gait, the dark rings under her eyes, the way she more jittered than moved. "Don't get up until you wake up on your own."

"Morning, then," Merila said. She gestured to a group of cots set off by themselves. "Maybe your friends will feel better by then."

Kindan nodded, but his eyes lingered on the cots in the distance. He headed for them first.

"Kindan," Verilan exclaimed when he caught sight of him, "I thought you were dead."

"I'm not," Kindan told him cheerfully. "It's good to see you, too." He examined the moodpaste dabbed on Verilan's head and was relieved to note that it was nearly green, only a hint of red showing. "Can I get you anything?"

"A bedpan would be nice," Kelsa chimed from the other cot. "Or permission to use the necessary."

"No," Kindan said immediately, waving down one of the holders and signing for a bedpan with his hands. The holder nodded in understanding and sped off. "Wait a bit, we've got one coming."

"I never thought I'd pee again," Kelsa said. "And now I've got to go."

Kindan, who had heard and dealt with much more horrific bodily functions in the past several sevendays, had no reaction to this admission, except to tell her acerbically, "Hold it."

He checked her forehead and wasn't surprised to see that the moodpaste was a comforting green: He had already guessed that Kelsa was well on her way to recovery by the tone of her voice and the directness of her speech.

"Verilan," Kindan began, remembering his notes, "do you know if Lenner had determined the illness's duration?"

"It seemed like forever," Nonala murmured from her cot. "But I guess it wasn't that long."

"We all got fevers within a sevenday of your leaving," Verilan informed him. He made a thoughtful face. "It seemed like the fever lasted a sevenday, maybe less."

"Mmm," Kindan murmured, wishing he had more evidence for

his theory. Not that it mattered much. If he was right, the holders who survived wouldn't spread the illness or get infected again but, according to Bemin, another quarter of them or more would die of starvation before winter's end.

There had to be something he could do. Some way to get more help. But everyone on Pern was too sick—and suddenly Kindan had the answer. All that was required was to risk the dragons and riders of Pern.

"Valla!" he called, sending his thoughts to the bronze fire-lizard. He had images of writing a long note, describing his theories, and then he had a better idea. "Get J'trel, Valla, get the blue rider!"

CHAPTER 16

Step by step
Moment by moment
We live through
Another day.

IGEN WEYR
STAR STONES

A dry, warm wind—warm even in winter—blew across the top of the abandoned Weyr. Drought had ruined Igen Hold and deprived Igen Weyr of tithe. Disaster had finished the Weyr off. The dragonriders were all gone now, having moved north to merge with Telgar Weyr. Once proud and bold, the Igen riders had instilled their values into the hardy Telgar folk, and an Igen rider was now Telgar's Weyrleader.

But the old Weyr remained, colored slightly by wind-borne dust from the desert, deserted but not forgotten, a relic of better days, glories of past Turns.

A bronze dragon burst from *between* over Igen's mighty Star Stones. Shortly thereafter a blue dragon with two riders appeared a short way off. The dragons landed long enough to disembark their passengers, then found perches in the high warm walls of Igen Bowl.

The riders arranged themselves so that the bronze rider was upwind of the blue rider and his passenger, so that the steady winds of Igen kept any possible infection from the bronze rider.

Those same winds made it difficult to talk, so that the downwind portion of the conversation was conducted at just below a yell.

"Kindan, it's good to see you," M'tal began, grinning broadly at the young harper. The lad looked much aged, but M'tal was not surprised; the plague had made old men out of boys well before their time.

"And you," Kindan called back.

"You wanted to speak with me," M'tal said.

"With all the Weyrleaders, actually," Kindan replied. "But I'll settle for you at first."

M'tal could not bear to tell the youngster that none of the other Weyrleaders had agreed to this meeting.

"How are things at Fort?"

"Better," Kindan called back. "But not for long."

M'tal took the news gravely.

"Bemin figures that two thousand died, and another two thousand or more will starve unless help comes."

"What sort of help?" M'tal asked. "We can only keep the fruit supplies going for another day or two at the best."

"Help setting the Holds back up," Kindan told him. "Bemin says that normally three thousand are needed to keep the Hold going."

"Three thousand?" M'tal repeated in surprise. The Weyrs operated with far fewer people than that. Then again, he reflected, the population of Benden Weyr was much smaller than ten thousand.

"They don't have dragons to help," Kindan called back.

The lad had a point, M'tal admitted to himself. "What are you proposing?"

"Station a wing of dragons at every major Hold, get them to help the Holds get going again," Kindan replied.

"But the plague!"

"I think it's over," Kindan said. "If not, it doesn't last more than three weeks. Keep the wings in the Holds for three weeks after the last infection and they should be safe returning to the Weyr. There won't be any infection to bring."

"But a wing is only thirty dragons and riders at best," M'tal replied. "What can they do?"

"They're healthy," Kindan said. "They can help haul coal, set up carts, round up livestock, transport holders quickly from one place to the other."

"And if one wing's not enough, Weyrleader, then we could send two," J'trel chimed in. "I'm proof that dragonriders can survive this illness."

"Weyrleader C'rion said you're too stubborn to die," M'tal answered, grinning to take the sting out of his comments.

"I've got people to live for," J'trel said diffidently. "Some of them are holders."

"We all live for holders and crafters, I believe," M'tal commented drolly. He leaned back and closed his eyes in thought. When he opened them again, he nodded firmly toward Kindan. "Very well, I'll take your suggestion back to the Weyrleaders."

"And you?"

"I've already ordered Gaminth to dispatch wings to Bitra, Lemos, Benden, and all the holds minor," M'tal said. He wagged a finger at Kindan. "For all Pern, you'd better be right."

Kindan nodded, feeling a huge weight in his stomach.

"We'll know in three weeks," J'trel said. Of M'tal, he asked, "Do you think B'ralar will send help?"

"Yes, he will," M'tal said. "It may be the worst mistake we ever make, and the last, but it has torn us apart to sit idly by while the rest of Pern dies."

"Then we must get back," Kindan said. "Bemin will have preparations to make."

"Did you tell him?" M'tal asked in surprise.

"No, he doesn't even know I've gone," Kindan replied.

——✦——

Bemin might not have known that Kindan had gone, but he certainly was aware when Kindan returned.

"Where were you?" the Lord Holder shouted when he spotted Kindan entering the Great Hall. "We've looked everywhere!"

"Is there a problem?" Kindan asked, looking around the Great Hall nervously. Could he have been wrong, could the plague still be infectious?

"No, but Merila woke up and went looking for you and when we couldn't find you, I—" Bemin broke off, his hands clenched into fists at his side.

"I went looking for more fruit," Kindan said, touched by the unspoken depth of Bemin's affection.

"Fruit?" Bemin repeated in surprise. "There's enough of that, it's men we need."

J'trel, who had been watching the exchange with growing amusement from the sidelines, murmured, "He got them, too. A right proper harper, he is."

Kindan looked questioningly at him.

"Can't help but speak in riddles," J'trel explained. He turned as, suddenly, outside there were excited cries.

"What's happening?" Bemin asked, rushing toward the doors.

"More fruit," J'trel said, grinning. He and Kindan reached the courtyard just as the first wing of dragons landed.

"J'lantir!" J'trel called excitedly to the bronze rider in the front. "What are you doing here?"

"Keeping an eye on you," the bronze rider growled. J'trel had the sense to look abashed. J'lantir turned to Bemin and bowed. "My Lord Holder, I present greetings from the Weyrleaders of Ista, Benden, and Fort Weyrs."

"Three?" Kindan said in surprise.

"There was some discussion about the Harper Hall deserving all four," J'lantir said lightly, "but we felt that D'vin would best serve as reserve." He turned back to Bemin. "At your harper's request"— and he nodded at Kindan, who looked thoroughly nonplussed- - "we are pleased to provide you with the better part of three wings of dragons to aid you and the harpers in their recovery." He bowed low. "What do you desire?"

Bemin turned to Kindan, lunged, and grabbed him in a great bear hug.

✦

"It's over now," Kindan said finally, staring hollow-eyed at the dragon-riders. It had been nearly a month since the dragons had landed outside Fort Hold's Great Hall. There had been no new case of the fever in a fortnight.

The days that followed had been no less wearying than the days of the plague, particularly when Kindan succeeded in con-vincing Bemin and J'lantir that it was time to reinhabit the Harper Hall. J'trel and J'lantir had gone there alone the first day and after that had refused to let any of the harpers near the Hall until they had completed all their work, clearing and cleaning up the Harper Hall.

Three large mounds outside the Healer Hall were covered with fresh earth, waiting for spring to cover them with green.

Kindan had been overjoyed to discover that Selora was among the survivors of the Harper Hall. In fact, apart from the younger apprentices, Selora was the only survivor of the Harper Hall—all the journeymen, Masters, and older apprentices had succumbed to the plague. Kindan couldn't imagine how the Harper Hall would ever recover.

"There are harpers and healers in the holds," Selora had assured him. "Some of them will come back."

———◆———

J'lantir's pronouncement that the Harper Hall was once again fit for habitation was met by a combination of jubilation and sorrow.

Kelsa, Nonala, and Verilan were anxious to return to their quarters. Selora had gone ahead, accompanied by Neesa—who'd overridden Bemin's worried protests with a simple, "Oh, Yanira will handle it all, you'll see!"—to prepare a welcoming feast.

Kindan was surprised when, just outside the Harper Hall's archway, a large bronze dragon appeared overhead and settled quickly onto the landing field. When he saw M'tal jump down, his face lit with joy.

"I wanted to be here when you returned to your Hall," M'tal told him. "Salina wanted to come as well, but we decided not to risk that."

"The danger's past," Kindan assured him.

"Not that," M'tal replied with a grin. "The danger of leaving a whole Weyr unsupervised."

Selora and Neesa had laid on a great feast in the Harper Hall's dining room. Bemin was there, as were Jelir and many of the other Fort Holders, and the dragonriders.

Even so, the great dining room was only partly filled with everyone sitting at the apprentice tables. The Masters' table and the journeymen's tables remained empty, and Kindan realized that the Harper Hall would never seem the same to him again, that it had gotten smaller and yet somehow less intimate than before.

He looked at Benden's Weyrleader. "Could you send for Master Zist? He'll be needed here."

M'tal gave him a worried look. "Kindan," he began, but the harper stopped him with an upraised hand.

"I sent Valla this morning," Kindan assured him. "Master Zist is alive. As the senior Master, he becomes the next Masterharper."

"Of course," M'tal agreed. "I'll have him here tomorrow."

Kindan wanted to protest, but contained himself.

"The dragons are tired," M'tal explained. "And so are the riders."

Kindan smiled wanly. "It seems I heard you say those words not so long ago, at High Reaches Weyr."

When at last the feast was over, Kindan, Kelsa, Nonala, and Verilan made their way back to the apprentice dormitory and their old beds.

"So what are we going to do?" Kelsa asked as she turned over the last glow and darkness filled the room.

"I think we should get up early," Kindan replied.

"Why?"

"M'tal will bring Master Zist tomorrow," Kindan told them.

"Master Zist?" Verilan repeated in dread tones. "I've heard stories about him."

"All true," Kindan replied, smiling in the dark.

Sleep came slowly to him; he was unused to the dormitory and also the night noises of the Harper Hall after so long in the Great Hall of Fort Hold. When it did come, he dreamt that Koriana was lying beside him.

When he awoke the next morning, he realized that the lump he'd felt lying by him was Valla, who chirped and chattered cheerfully to him as he got up and headed into the showers.

"You can start on clearing up the Archive Room," Selora told them as they finished breakfast. She spread her gaze to include the rest of the apprentices. "All of you."

"You take charge, Verilan," Kindan said as they entered the large hall that was the Archive Room.

"No one ever sorted through all the damp stuff," Verilan sniffed. "I think the dragonriders must have thrown it all out," he added mournfully. Idly he picked up a Record that had fallen to the floor and reverently set it on one of the reading tables. He glanced at Kindan, as if looking for instruction. Kindan shrugged and looked back at him expectantly.

"Right," Verilan said, hitching up his shoulders and pointing to a group of the youngest apprentices. "Pick up every Record on the floor and pile it here." He pointed to another group. "You lot start checking the stacks nearest where the fire was. I want you to look for fire damage and water damage first. Bring any damaged Records over to that table, there. Sort through the rest of the Records and rearrange them into chronological order."

When the apprentices started discovering damaged Records, Verilan made a third group of trustworthy scribes and set them to work transcribing the damaged Records onto new paper. Kindan noticed that Verilan sent a younger apprentice to retrieve the supplies from Master Resler's old quarters; Kindan couldn't blame him for not wanting to go there himself, he knew that Verilan thought highly of the late Master.

The apprentices threw themselves into the task with relish and were all thoroughly absorbed as midday approached. Kindan was so engrossed himself that at first he didn't notice the sound of a drum.

"Kindan," Kelsa whispered urgently, "the drums."

Report, the message said.

"That's Zist," Kindan told her excitedly.

"But he just said 'report,' " Nonala complained. "He didn't say who."

"You'd better get going," Verilan said to Kindan, looking up from his table. "It's never good to keep a Master waiting."

◆

Verilan was right; Zist was tapping his thigh irritably as Kindan entered the Masterharper's quarters.

"It took you long enough," Zist grumbled irritably, gesturing for Kindan to take a seat. "Where's your report?"

"Master?"

"I knew Murenny better than that," Zist growled, "he'd expect a full report by now." He jerked a thumb toward his workdesk. "There's materials there, get started. And don't leave out any details."

Kindan was surprised at Zist's gruff manner; he'd expected at least a polite hello before being set to writing.

"Mind you that it's legible," Zist warned, fingering the drum that he'd laid on the breakfast table beside him.

That was the last word the Master said for the next several hours as Kindan wrote first a rough draft and then a proper copy. Somewhere along the way—he couldn't quite remember when—Kindan found tears starting in his eyes. He tried blinking them away, but they persisted. He paused for a moment, not wanting to mar his Record. He looked back at the Record; he had just been writing about Vaxoram.

A hand reached over him and grabbed the page from the table.

"You're done with this one, aren't you?" Zist asked in a soft, kind voice. Kindan nodded, he hadn't realized that Master Zist had been reading the pages as soon as he finished them.

He was surprised a moment later when behind him Master Zist snorted and exclaimed, "You've a long ways to go before you're a Master, what do you mean making Vaxoram a journeyman?"

Kindan turned to respond hotly, "Vaxoram earned the right. For all I knew, I was the last harper on Pern." His voice cooled as tears filled his eyes once more. "It was all he wanted."

" 'Want' is not all that makes a journeyman," Zist replied acerbically. In a softer tone, he added, "But *Journeyman* Vaxoram *had* earned the right." He gave Kindan a firm nod. "And so the Records will show."

Kindan gave him a grateful look. Zist sighed, then picked up his drum.

Songmaster report, he rapped out. With a smile to Kindan, he asked, "Who do you think will come?"

"Kelsa," Kindan replied instantly. "If she doesn't die of fright."

"Is she good?"

"She's the best," Kindan told him fervently.

"Are you speaking as a friend or a harper?" Zist asked him, his bushy white eyebrows low over his eyes in a frown.

"First as a harper, second as a friend," Kindan told him honestly.

"Well, we'll see," Zist said as they heard footsteps coming up the stairway. He raised a finger to his lips and motioned with his other hand that Kindan should get back to work. "Listen carefully, and see what you can learn."

When the knock came on the door, Zist drawled out a long, deep "Yes?"

"You sent for me?" Kelsa replied through the door.

"I sent for the Songmaster," Zist replied. "But you may come in."

Kelsa opened the door and peered around hesitantly.

"Come in," Zist ordered, his finger pointing to a spot right in front of him. Kelsa walked nervously to the indicated spot and stood, her fingers moving anxiously at her side. "And you are?"

"Kelsa, Master," she replied with a squeaky voice.

Zist cast an amused glance toward Kindan, but as he was busy writing his Records and had his back to the proceedings, he didn't see it. Valla, who had entered the room when Kindan had started crying and had found a perch on a bookshelf overlooking the worktable, saw the Master's look and chirped amusedly at Kindan.

"I sent for the Songmaster," Zist said. "Why did you come?"

"The Master is dead," Kelsa told him. "I thought I could help."

"You did, did you?" Zist asked. He gave her a thoughtful look. "I need a song."

"Master?"

"I need a song about the events of the plague," Zist told her. "I need a song that is uplifting but honest, a song that tells everyone why the Weyrs stood aloof and how they came to help when they could.

"Can you write that song?"

"I can try," Kelsa temporized.

"I did not ask if you could 'try,'" Zist responded harshly. "This song will be sung by all the harpers on Pern. I need it by this evening." He held up the pages of Kindan's Records. "You can use these," he said, handing her the papers. "Can you do it?"

Kelsa glanced at Kindan's back, straightened her own, and declared with chin held high, "Yes, Master, I can."

"Good," Zist said approvingly. He gestured toward the sleeping quarters. "You'll find instruments and a writing table in there. Get started now. I'll bring you more Records as he"—he nodded toward Kindan—"finishes them."

Zist waited until he could hear Kelsa's tuning in the room next door, then stood up and went over to the desk where Kindan was working.

"Be quick," Zist urged him, taking another completed Record from the table and sitting back down at his table to read it. A moment later he walked it through to Kelsa. Kindan could hear them conferring indistinctly and then Zist said clearly at the doorway, "Yes, yes, that's a good choice. Keep working."

Zist returned to his desk and sat for a while in thoughtful silence. When he moved again, it was to pick up the drum.

Voicemaster, report.

"Who will that be?" he asked.

"Nonala," Kindan replied at once. "She's the best."

"Did she work with you?"

"Not as much as I'd like," Kindan answered honestly. "My voice has been a mess since it cracked."

"Good," Zist replied. "If you'd told me that she had worked with you, I would have sent her packing."

Despite himself, Kindan smiled at the Master's remark.

"Your fire-lizard is still young, is he up to taking a message?" Zist asked from behind him. Kindan glanced up at Valla, then turned to face Master Zist.

"Sometimes," he replied. "He learns quicker than most."

"Well," Zist said, "hard times speed things up." His glance remained on Kindan for a moment longer, unfathomable. "Can you have him take a message to Jofri? I want him to come here as my second and handle defense, dance, and civics."

"He'd be good at that," Kindan said, gesturing for Valla to hop down to him.

"I don't recall asking for an apprentice's opinion," Zist said severely.

"Sorry, Master," Kindan replied, extending a hand for the Master's note. "Where is Master Jofri now?"

"Fort Weyr," Zist replied. In a softer voice he added, "At least he was safe."

"How was it in the mines?" Kindan said, asking the question he'd been dreading for a while.

Zist sighed. "It was bad, but not as bad as here," he said. "Dalor is in charge now."

"Dalor?" Kindan repeated in surprise.

"Master Natalon and his wife did not survive," Zist responded. "Nuella and Zenor are all right, although it was touch and go with her, as is Renna—she's acting as healer for the moment. While this plague affected people of all ages, all the miners between seventeen and twenty-one succumbed, much the same as here." He turned his head toward the stairway as they heard footsteps. "Let's see who showed up," he said to Kindan as someone knocked on the door.

It was Nonala. She entered without permission and stood close to Zist. "You sent for me?"

"Are you the Voicemaster?"

"I'm the best in the Hall," Nonala replied firmly.

"Good," Zist said approvingly. He nodded his head toward the sleeping quarters. "Young Kelsa is composing a song in there. I want it sung tonight at the evening meal."

Nonala's eyes widened for just an instant. Then she glanced at

Kindan's back and nodded firmly. "I'll need my own choice of singers."

"Everyone except him and her," Zist replied, pointing at Kindan and the doorway to the other room.

"He's not very good," Nonala told Zist frankly.

"His voice just cracked," Zist replied, much to Kindan's surprise. He remembered Master Zist as a perfectionist, not given to taking second best.

"It was never all that good to start with," Nonala responded. "Passable at best."

"Ah," Zist said approvingly, "I see that you really *are* a Voicemaster."

Nonala stood a bit taller, elated.

"Very well," Zist concluded, "wait here while Kelsa finishes the song, then get to work."

"Finishes?" Nonala asked, showing her first signs of fear—to take a song, one written by Kelsa and not yet finished, to its first performance in less than a day was more than a bit daunting.

"Not up to the challenge?" Zist asked with a hint of a smile.

"Have you seen the stuff she writes?" Nonala demanded, suddenly all in motion. "It's nearly impossible!"

"If it's nearly impossible, then it's clearly possible," Zist told her, smiling. Nonala started to give him an angry reply, then snorted and smiled back. Zist waved toward a spare chair, but Nonala demurred. "I think I'll go listen in, if I may."

With a nod, Zist waved her off to the far room. He rose again silently, and retrieved another finished Record from Kindan.

"Last one," Zist said enigmatically when he'd finished reading Kindan's writing. He picked up the drum and rapped: *Archivist, report.*

"That'll be Verilan," Kindan predicted confidently. "He should have been made journeyman long ago, but he's too young."

"Age is not my concern," Zist replied. "Experience and maturity are what counts."

This time the steps came earlier, and were rushed; the knock on the door was perfunctory, and the door was thrown open before Zist could speak.

"Verilan reports," the youngster said soberly. One hand was stained with ink, but he did not look at all abashed by it, rather treating it as part of his apparel. "The Archives will be restored by this evening."

"Verilan, is it?" Zist asked, lazily pushing the drum out of his lap and back onto the table. "I sent for the Archivist."

"I am the Archivist," Verilan replied. "Master Resler is dead."

"But you're just an apprentice," Zist said scornfully.

"I'm the Archivist," Verilan persisted staunchly.

"Prove it," Zist said. He turned to Kindan. "Aren't you done yet?"

"Yes, Master," Kindan said, printing out the last line of his Record. He turned with the page in his hand and passed it over to the Master.

"About time," Zist murmured. He glanced at the Record and handed it over to Verilan. "Kelsa is in the other room writing a song using this Record," he told him. "You are to make a copy and then have your scribes make copies for every hold, major and minor.

"When they are done with that," Zist continued, "Kelsa will have a song for you to copy also. You must have both completed by dusk, ready to send."

Verilan nodded curtly and marched into the other room. He was back a moment later, retrieving stylus, ink, and paper from the workdesk, unperturbed by Zist's ominous gaze.

As Verilan retreated to the back room, Zist said to Kindan, "Go tell Selora that we will have a new song tonight."

Kindan desperately wanted to stay with his friends, but he knew Zist too well to argue, so he nodded and left.

"Let me know when your fire-lizard returns!" Zist called at his retreating back.

✦

"A new song, eh?" Selora said, her look inscrutable. "Hmm, well, we'll need help in the kitchens, then, because new songs mean lots of food." She threw an apron to Kindan. "You can get started with the dessert."

Kindan suppressed a groan. Perhaps things were getting back to normal after all.

In fact, Selora was hard-pressed for help and feeding even thirty harpers meant a lot of cooking. Kindan was hot and sweaty by the time the soup was set to simmering, the shepherd's pies were cooking in the oven, the bread was set to cooling, the fires were stoked, and the greens washed.

Selora consulted some internal clock that only cooks seemed to possess and told Kindan consideringly, "You'd best go change, Master Zist would have your hide if you came to dinner looking like that."

Kindan was still wearing Koriana's clothes and was reluctant to part with them. Besides, he wasn't sure if he had any clean clothes left.

Seeing his concern, Selora told him, "Lord Bemin sent you down some clothes. I had someone lay them on your bunk."

Kindan took the time to wash and brush his teeth before returning to his bunk. He was astonished to see not one but three sets of clothes on a hanger—all in harper's blue. He eyed the finish critically; it appeared that the apprentice stripes were merely tacked on. Well, there was nothing for it, he could fix them later.

The fresh clean cloth felt good against his skin. There was just a hint of a special fragrance, the smell that Kindan would always associate with Koriana's hair. He was just ready to leave when Verilan, Nonala, and Kelsa came rushing in.

"He sent us to change!" Kelsa wailed.

"You should gripe, we've only had one practice, and I'm going to

have to sing soprano," Nonala replied, heading toward the rest-
room.

"Hey, who put these clothes here?" Verilan complained as he
approached his bunk. Kindan looked over and saw that Verilan,
too, had a new set of harper's blue.

"Maybe Lord Bemin," Kindan said. "He sent some down for
me."

"For all of us," Kelsa exclaimed, glancing appreciatively at the
finery. "But they must have rushed, the sewing's not all that good."

When he returned to the kitchen, Selora sent him out peremptorily. "You're to go to the Dining Hall!"

Kindan came up to the Dining Hall just as it was filling. Something was bothering him, but he couldn't identify it. From the Masters' table, Master Jofri waved at him and Kindan waved back, his
face splitting into a grin.

Something . . . about the clothes. But before Kindan could figure it out, Verilan, Nonala, and Kelsa came rushing into the hall
along with the rest of the apprentices. Kindan turned to Kelsa,
mouth open, ready to ask a question when Master Zist entered the
room, dressed in a fine new Masterharper's outfit.

He was flanked, Kindan noted with surprise, by Lord Holder
Bemin, Weyrleader B'ralar, and—best of all—M'tal. Behind them
came Jelir, Neesa, Melira, Stennel, and Yanira, carrying baby
Fiona. Behind *them* came the High Reaches Weyrleader, D'vin,
and C'tov! In back of them was a last group—Dalor and Nuella,
Kindan's friends from his youth in the mines. They were dressed in
their finest clothes and the twin brother and sister waved cheerfully at Kindan.

The dignitaries were seated at the journeymen's table which
surprised Kindan greatly, but not nearly as much as it did Verilan,
who looked completely nonplussed.

"Do you know—" Verilan began in an excited whisper, only to
be cut off by Master Zist's resounding voice.

"We are honored tonight by hold, craft, and weyr," Zist told the group.

"Something's up," Kelsa declared, glancing around the room suspiciously.

"I know," Verilan agreed fervently.

"We have all been through many perils and much pain," Zist continued. "Now that they are past, it is time to begin again.

"Tonight marks a new beginning for Pern," he said. "And tonight we celebrate it." He took a deep breath and turned to the apprentices. "You have survived great pain and loss, you have been called upon to meet the sternest of challenges, and you did not fail. Your childhood ended abruptly and far too early." He nodded sorrowfully toward them, then paused for a moment.

"Songmaster Kelsa, please rise," Zist said.

Kelsa rose to her feet, her face white.

At she did, Jofri rose beside Master Zist, and so did all the dignitaries at the journeymen's table.

"You're going to walk the tables, Kelsa!" Nonala declared in sudden comprehension.

"Apprentices, please rise and escort Kelsa to her new table," Zist said, his voice no longer somber, his eyes twinkling.

"I don't think I can move!" Kelsa moaned.

"Of course you can," Kindan declared, pushing her with his hand.

Slowly, steadily, Kelsa walked around the apprentice table and over to the journeymen's table, to be greeted enthusiastically by the Lord Holders, Crafters, and Weyrleaders.

"Congratulations, Journeyman Kelsa," Zist said to her. The hall burst with the noise of clapping hands and stomping feet.

Zist waited until everyone was seated once more. "We're not done yet," he told the apprentices with a wink.

"Oh, no!" Nonala exclaimed.

"Voicemaster Nonala, please rise," Zist said, smiling at her.

"Come on, Nonala," Verilan urged.

"You earned it," Kindan agreed fervently. Kelsa rushed back over to help and together the four walked the tables to deposit a shocked Nonala at the journeymen's table.

"One more," Zist said after the tumult died down. "And then we can eat."

Kindan nodded toward Verilan.

"No, it's you," Verilan said, shaking his head. "After all you've done, it has to be you."

"I was banished, remember?" Kindan told him. "I'm lucky to be here at all."

"But—"

"Archivist Verilan, please rise," Zist's voice boomed out, dispelling any doubt.

Verilan sat, rebellious, until Kindan rose and grabbed him under the elbow.

"You've *earned* this," Kindan told him forcefully. "By all rights you should be Master now."

Reluctantly, Verilan stood. When Nonala and Kelsa came eagerly to him, he couldn't help but smile back at them. He completed his circuit around the tables and sat at the journeymen's table but he continued to look back at Kindan, his expression mirroring the injustice he felt.

The food came out and Kindan ate heartily, glad to realize that he and Selora had made such a great feast for such illustrious company. Still, he couldn't help from time to time glancing wistfully toward his friends, wishing not so much that he were there with them as that he had their company.

The meal was finished and dessert served before Zist rose again.

"It is a rule of the Harper Hall that a person cannot be promoted until they've eaten one meal in their present rank," Zist said. There was a gasp from all the apprentices and journeymen as these words registered amongst them.

Jofri rose beside Zist and they walked over to the journeymen's table.

"Journeyman Verilan," Jofri said soberly, "please rise."

"Me?" Verilan squeaked. "No, it should be Kindan."

"Get up, Verilan," Kelsa commanded him. "Get up, or we'll lift you."

Reluctantly Verilan rose.

"Only once before has an apprentice been elevated to Master in the same day," Zist told the gathering as he and Jofri escorted Verilan over to the Masters' table. "And that was Master Murenny."

"But you are the youngest Master on record," Zist said to Verilan. "As you might well know."

Verilan could only nod mutely.

Kindan roared his approval along with the rest of the room. When the noise died down, Zist rose again, gesturing to Nonala.

"Journeyman Kelsa has written a song to mark the events of these past sad months and Journeyman Nonala has kindly agreed to sing it," Zist said. He nodded to Verilan and addressed the Weyrleaders, Holders, and Crafters. "And Master Verilan will provide copies of the Records for your harpers as well as copies of this song."

Nonala assembled her chorus and with a firm nod prepared them to sing.

"This is called 'Kindan's Song,'" Nonala said, her voice reverberating through the room.

Step by step
Moment by moment
We live through
Another day.

Fever consumes us
Death surrounds us
Still we succeed through
Another day.

Tears trickled down Kindan's face as they did down all the faces in the Harper Hall and he recalled the faces of those who had died, countless, in the plague.

The song was over and there was a silence in the hall before Kindan realized that people were standing behind him. He felt arms on his, urging him upward.

M'tal and Bemin were at his side, lifting him.

"Rise, Kindan," Zist's voice boomed through the hall, filling every corner.

Step by step, moment by moment, Kindan walked the tables.

ЄPILOGUЄ

Harper in your garments blue
Sing a song of tales quite true
Harper with your drum so loud
You make us all feel quite proud.

BENDEN WEYR,
AL 497.1

The sun was setting in the evening sky when the great bronze dragon erupted from *between* over the Star Stones. The watchdragon bugled a query and then a greeting.

Wheeling sharply, Gaminth began a steep descent into the Weyr Bowl.

"Are you ready, Harper?" M'tal called over his shoulder.

"Yes."

AUTHORS' NOTES

According to the *Merck Manual,* Eighteenth Edition, (Copyright 2006 by Merck & Co, Inc.) influenza A epidemics occur in the United States every two to three years. "Pandemics caused by new influenza A serotypes may cause particularly severe disease." Influenza B viruses can cause epidemics in three- to five-year cycles.

The Great Influenza of 1918 was a pandemic of grimmer proportions than either the usual influenza A or B epidemic/pandemic cycles. It was particularly devastating among the eighteen- to twenty-one-year-old population because, sadly, people at those ages had the most well-developed immune systems. In combating the influenza, the matured immune systems would attack the lining of the lungs and, tragically, the victim's lungs would fill with liquid, causing death by drowning (more specifically, Acute Respiratory Disease Syndrome or ARDS—SARS is a variant of this).

For more information on major influenza pandemics, we recommend *The Great Influenza* by John M. Barry, published by Penguin Books, 2005 (with a new afterword).

ACKNOWLEDGMENTS

We would like to thank Shelly Shapiro, our longtime editor at Del Rey, for all her hard work in making this book great. She was aided by Judith Welsh, our editor at Transworld, and we'd like to thank her, too.

Once again, the redoubtable Martha Trachtenburg did a sterling job of copyediting the book, catching many things that we'd missed and making suggestions for the improvement of our verse. Thanks, Martha. We're sorry about all the handkerchiefs.

Georgeanne "Gigi" Kennedy, daughter and sister, respectively, provided her moral support, encouragement, and occasional keen insight as with all other Pern books.

Finally, we'd like to thank our agents, Diana Tyler of MBA Literary Agency, and Donald Maass of the Donald Maass Literary Agency for their support, cheer, and great feedback on the rough draft.

Any mistakes, errors, or omissions are, as always, strictly our own.

ABOUT THE AUTHORS

ANNE MCCAFFREY, the Hugo Award–winning author of the bestselling Dragonriders of Pern® novels, is one of science fiction's most popular authors. With Elizabeth Ann Scarborough, she co-authored *Changelings* and *Maelstrom,* Book One and Book Two of The Twins of Petaybee. McCaffrey lives in a house of her own design, Dragonhold-Underhill, in County Wicklow, Ireland. Visit the author's website at www.annemccaffrey.net.

TODD MCCAFFREY is the bestselling author of the Pern novel *Dragonsblood,* as well as *Dragon's Kin* and *Dragon's Fire,* which he co-wrote with his mother, Anne McCaffrey. A computer engineer, he currently lives in Los Angeles.

Having grown up in Ireland with the epic of the Dragonriders of Pern, he is bursting with ideas for new stories of that world, its people, and its dragons. Visit the author's website at www.toddmccaffrey.org.

ABOUT THE TYPE

This book was set in Fairfield, the first typeface from the
hand of the distinguished American artist and engraver
Rudolph Ruzicka (1883–1978). Ruzicka was born in Bo-
hemia and came to America in 1894. He set up his own
shop, devoted to wood engraving and printing, in New York
in 1913 after a varied career working as a wood engraver, in
photoengraving and banknote printing plants, and as an art
director and freelance artist. He designed and illustrated
many books, and was the creator of a considerable list of individual prints—wood engravings, line engravings on cop-
per, and aquatints.